DILLY CO

RUNAWAY WIDOW

Complete and Unabridged

MAGNA
Leicester

First published in Great Britain in 2022 by
HarperCollins*Publishers*
London

First Ulverscroft Edition
published 2022
by arrangement with
HarperCollins*Publishers*
London

A catalogue record for this book is available
from the British Library.

ISBN 978-0-7505-4912-7

Published by
Ulverscroft Limited
Anstey, Leicestershire

Printed and bound in Great Britain by
TJ Books Ltd., Padstow, Cornwall

This book is printed on acid-free paper

RUNAWAY WIDOW

London, 1859. When Lady Patricia Greystone's husband dies suddenly, she is left with nothing. At twenty-four, she finds herself a penniless widow. Determined not to return to her family cap in hand, she strikes out on her own.

Patricia's voice is her only hope. She makes her living singing at inns and on the streets. But a dangerous figure from her family's past is lurking in the shadows, and before long she finds herself fleeing the city.

Without her family around her, will Patricia lose her way?

For the late Walter Stanley Ellis, my maternal grandfather, who still inspires me every day.

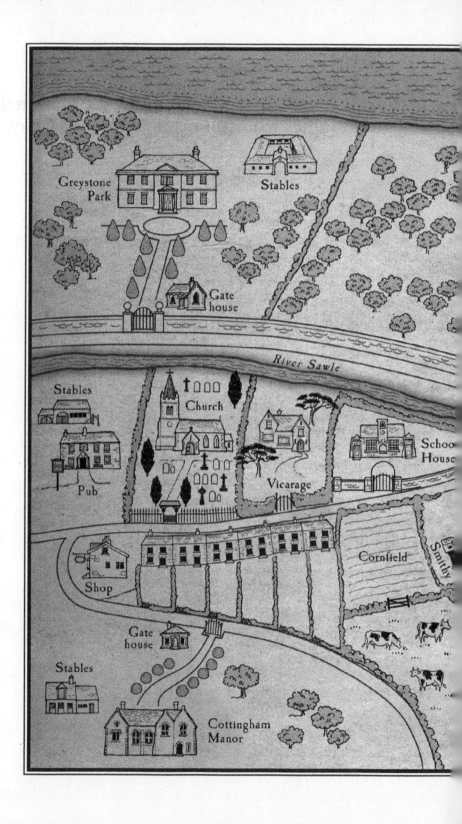

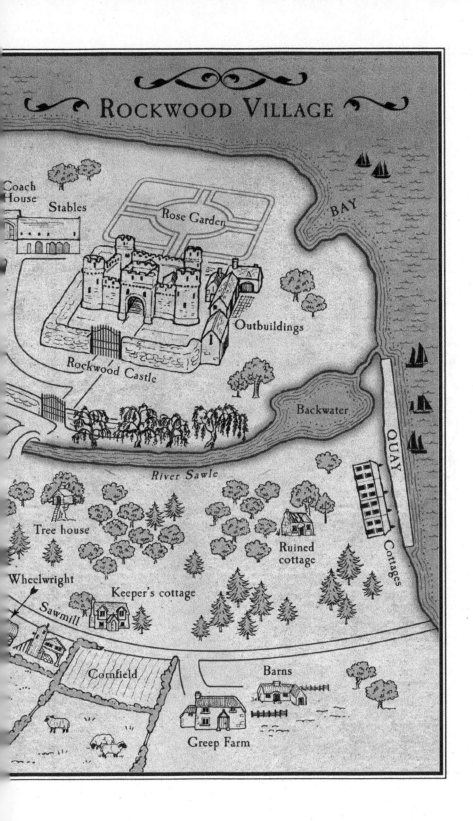

ROCKWOOD VILLAGE

Coach House
Stables
Rose Garden
BAY
Outbuildings
Rockwood Castle
Backwater
QUAY
River Sawle
Tree house
Ruined cottage
Cottages
Wheelwright
Keeper's cottage
Sawmill
Cornfield
Barns
Greep Farm

❧ The Carey Family ❧

Lady Hester Carey m Vice–Admiral Sir Lucius Carey m Lady Prudence Carey
(Neé Dodridge)   (1776–1853)   (deceased)
(b. 1804)

Claude de Marney m Felicia Carey m Wilfred Carey
(b. 1805)   (b. 1806)   (1800–1851)

Captain Alexander m Rosalind (Rosie) —‖— Piers   Walter m Louise   Patricia (Patsy) m Sir Michael
Blanchard   Carey   Blanchard   Carey   Shaw   Carey   Greystone
(b. 1827)   (b. 1830)   (b. 1825)   (b. 1832) (b. 1827)   (b. 1834)   (b. 1806)

Adela (Dolly)
Blanchard
(b. 1854)

Sarah   * Bertram (Bertie)
Farthing   Carey
(1829–1847)   (b. 1827)

Tommy Carey
(b. 1844)

* Unmarried

1

Patricia Greystone stood by one of the tall windows in her elegant London home, gazing out into the nothingness that was a London particular. The thick, greenish-yellow peasouper had blanketed the city from early afternoon with no sign of clearing. The only glimmer of light came from the streetlamp directly in front of the house, but even that was diffused to nothing but a soft glow. Outside there was silence as if the world had come to a sudden end, and the smell of sulphur and soot seeped into the room. A soft rap on the drawing-room door made Patricia turn away from her vigil.

'Enter.'

The door opened to admit the Greystones' long-serving butler, Foster. In his hands was a silver salver on which lay a folded and sealed document. 'A boy brought this for you, my lady.'

Patricia crossed the floor to snatch up the sheet of paper. She recognised her husband's seal and her fingers shook with impatience as she unfolded the brief note written on paper with a House of Commons heading. 'Thank you, Foster, there's no reply. The House is sitting late and Sir Michael will not be home for dinner.'

'Very well, my lady. Will you be dining at home?'

'Yes, I suppose so. That will be all, Foster.'

Patricia sighed and turned away. Yet another evening

1

ruined, although this time it was the fog that made it impossible for her to attend the dinner party at the home of Lord and Lady Stanton, whose lavish entertainments were legendary. Greystone was probably debating something utterly thrilling like the proposed sewage works east of the city, which had become a vital necessity after the Great Stink the previous summer. In July and August the Houses of Parliament had been evacuated because of the pervading smell from human and manufacturing effluent. However, her husband's late night sittings were coming a little too often these days, curtailing their social life to an ever increasing extent. Had it not been for the fog Patricia would have attended the Stantons' soirée on her own, but it was doubtful if anyone would venture out in these adverse conditions.

She went to sit by the fire, watching the glow fairies sparkle and then die away on the sooty fire back, and the orange, red and blue flames licking around the lumps of jet-black coal. Suddenly and unexpectedly she was thinking of her childhood home. Rockwood Castle in Devonshire had not been the most comfortable place to grow up, with its draughty corridors and dampness seeping through the stone walls. There was a time when she and her siblings had been forced to live off the land, but at home there had always been love, laughter and companionship, spiced by squabbles and differences of opinion. She smiled as she recalled her rebellious youth. She must have tried her elder sister's patience to the limit, but Rosalind had always been there to support her when she needed her most. Their relationship had been strained by their mutual involvement with Alexander Blanchard, whom Rosalind had once spurned and Patricia had almost married. Rosalind had eventually married Alexander after a stormy marriage to his cousin Piers, which ended in divorce. But sisterly love had triumphed and now Rosalind and Alexander were proud parents, devoted to each other and their growing family.

A glowing ember bounced onto the hearth but Patricia chose to ignore it. She had a small army of servants to do menial tasks, leaving her with nothing to do other than to change her clothes three times a day with the help of her personal maid. There were always invitations to accept and others to send out, for Patricia's life nowadays was one of socialising, entertaining and being entertained. With a husband many years her senior she was used to being treated as delightful and decorative by his contemporaries, who either patronised her or flirted outrageously, which did not amuse their matronly wives. Patricia had learned as a bride of twenty to parry the gentlemen's advances with a fluttering of her long eyelashes or a sweet smile, whilst inwardly writing them off as pathetic old men.

She stretched her feet towards the comforting blaze, smoothing the satin skirts of her emerald-green dinner gown. She knew this colour suited her and it was Greystone's favourite. The décolleté neckline flattered her youthful figure and brought a sparkle to her husband's eyes. She loved Greystone, but she was not in love with him and never had been. She had married with her eyes open and her sights set on wealth and position, but she had kept her side of the bargain, and her husband had nothing with which to reproach her.

They had agreed from the start that there would be no children from their union. Greystone had two grown-up daughters. Christina was now married to

3

the local squire's son in Rockwood village, and Sylvia, as yet unwed, lived in the family home, Greystone Park, chaperoned by her formidable cousin, Martha Collins, and her timid companion, Miss Moon. Patricia was fond of her stepdaughters, although they had found it difficult to accept their father's decision to marry someone less than half his age, but they had gradually come round. Perhaps, she thought dreamily, she ought to bring Sylvia to London at the start of the Season. Sylvia, at the age of twenty-three, was too old to be a débutante, but there might be some eligible bachelors who would find her naïve charms attractive. Miss Collins and Miss Moon would not be included in the invitation. Patricia had had enough of domineering women, her mother and Hester, their former housekeeper included.

Patricia jumped at the sound of someone knocking on the door. 'Enter.'

Foster appeared in the doorway with his usual impassive expression. 'Begging your pardon, my lady, but there is a gentleman at the door who wishes to see you.' He approached Patricia's chair, once again proffering the silver salver on which sat a deckle-edged visiting card. 'Shall I tell him that you are unavailable?'

'Who on earth would have braved the fog to visit at this time in the evening?' Patricia studied the copperplate writing with a sigh. 'Tell Lord Eldon that I am otherwise engaged.'

The words had barely left her lips when a tall, handsome man with dark auburn hair and a wicked twinkle in his grey eyes strode past Foster. He came to a halt and with an exaggerated gesture he swept off his top hat and bowed.

4

'Forgive the intrusion, Lady Greystone.'

Patricia made a determined effort to look casual as she rose to her feet, but she was always pleased to see Larkin Eldon, despite the fact that he was a notorious flirt with questionable morals. She was fully aware that he had a tendency to gamble recklessly, his actions cushioned by the huge fortune he had inherited from his late father. It was said that he could drink the hardest toper under the table and still present as being reasonably sober, but despite his raffish reputation he was immensely popular with both men and women. He could charm the sternest matron, should the necessity arise, and one look from him would set the débutantes' hearts aflutter. Patricia was not so naïve, but there was something irresistible about Eldon and she genuinely enjoyed his company.

'My husband has not returned from the House, Eldon,' she said primly. 'The sitting has gone on longer than expected.'

'So I believe, my lady.' Eldon handed his top hat, gloves and greatcoat to Foster. 'I trust you won't send me out into the peasouper without allowing me to recover from the exertion of walking here this evening. I had to feel my way along the railings outside the houses to reach your home. The fog is so thick I almost had to crawl on my hands and knees.'

Patricia knew she had lost the first round in the battle of wills, and if she were to be honest with herself she was delighted to see Eldon. She was fully aware that his ardent pursuit of her company was a reaction to her refusal to be one of his many conquests, but Eldon could make her laugh and he was an excellent guest at a dinner party or a soirée. He excelled as a dancing partner and he had introduced her to the

5

excitement of card games such as faro and baccarat, and the thrill of picking the winning numbers in roulette. He had made flirtation an art.

Foster cleared his throat. 'My lady?'

'It's all right, Foster. Lord Eldon is welcome to stay until he feels he can brave the weather again.'

'Will his lordship be dining tonight, my lady?'

Patricia met Eldon's amused look with a shake of her head. 'I don't think so, Foster.'

Foster bowed and left the room, straight-faced as ever but somehow managing to express his disapproval.

'Aren't you going to offer me a brandy? I did come all this way just to see you, Patricia.'

'Eldon, you never do anything unless it is for your own amusement or pleasure. If you want a glass of brandy you know where to find the decanter and a glass.'

He laughed. 'You know me so well, my dear.' He strolled over to a side table to select a decanter and he poured a tot into each of the two glasses. 'You will join me, won't you?' He handed one to her with a persuasive smile. 'Come now, don't frown at me, Patricia. You'll crease that lovely alabaster brow.'

'I might have preferred sherry. You should have given me the option, Eldon.' Patricia accepted the drink anyway.

He took a seat opposite her and raised his glass. 'I know you better than that, Patricia. You say all the correct things, but you enjoy a tot as much as I do, although admittedly not in quite the same quantity.'

'I should hope not.' She sipped the brandy and the warming effect of the alcohol made her relax a little. She sat back in her chair. 'Why are you here, Eldon?

You must have known that the Stantons' dinner party would have been cancelled because of the fog.'

'Of course I did, and I also knew that your husband would be delayed at the House. Surely the fact that I braved the terrors of the London particular to come here this evening must convince you of my utter devotion to your beautiful self?'

Patricia eyed him over the rim of her glass. 'I think you were bored, Eldon. You simply wanted to create mischief by coming here and compromising my good name.'

'You do yourself an injustice, Patricia. I came here because I care about you. Besides which, you are the one woman in London with whom I can be myself. You speak your mind and you are good company, added to the fact that you are extremely beautiful and utterly desirable.'

'And you are a rogue and an arch flatterer, but I must admit I was a trifle bored.'

'I knew it and I've come to rescue you from a long and extremely dull evening. If I had my way we would always be together.'

Patricia downed the last of the brandy. 'Are you telling me you wish to marry me, Eldon?'

He placed his empty glass on a drum table at the side of his chair. 'If you weren't already married to Greystone that is exactly what I would wish.'

Patricia met his earnest gaze and began to giggle. 'You are such a liar, Eldon. If I was unmarried we wouldn't be having this conversation.'

'Do you doubt my feelings for you, my angel?'

'Quite frankly, yes, I do. How old are you, Eldon?'

His eyes widened in surprise. 'I'm thirty-three. I'm in my prime.'

'I think if you had wanted to marry, you would have done it many years ago. After all, you have all the assets that any matchmaking mama would consider requisite.'

'Tell me about them, Patricia.'

'You are quite presentable and you are extremely wealthy. You have a title and a country estate even larger than Greystone Park. Added to which, you have rooms in Albemarle Street.'

He put his head on one side. 'All true, of course, but is that how you chose Greystone? Did you assess his assets in a similar fashion?'

'Of course I did, Eldon. On the other hand I do love my husband. He gives me everything I want and more. We understand each other perfectly.'

'But you remain faithful to him, even though he's a cold fish.'

'Don't call him that. You know nothing about our relationship. I wouldn't disgrace the family name by having affairs, so you will never know me better than you do now, Eldon.'

He clutched his hand to his heart. 'You wound me, my dear. I am not a philanderer; my regard for you is genuine.'

Patricia rose to her feet and tugged at a bell pull. 'You are a roué and lies trip off your tongue without any effort on your part, but you are the most amusing man in London and that is the only reason I tolerate you.'

He pulled a face. 'I'm being dismissed? Or are you inviting me to dine with you?'

'If you're worried about finding your way home in the fog I'll send one of the footmen to guide you with a flaming torch.'

'No, that won't be necessary. I admit defeat tonight, but I won't give up, Patricia. One day I will make you mine, married or not.'

Patricia turned to Foster as he entered the room. 'Lord Eldon is leaving, Foster.'

'Unwillingly, I should add.' Eldon rose to his feet. 'But I will see you at the opera tomorrow evening.' He took Patricia's hand and raised it to his lips, looking her in the eyes with a gaze that left nothing to her imagination.

'Yes, providing the fog lifts.' She snatched her hand free. 'Safe journey, Eldon. I'll give my husband your regards.'

He smiled and blew her a kiss as he allowed Foster to usher him from the room. Patricia sank back onto her chair. Eldon's suggestive glance had made her pulse race, but she was not going to allow him to win. She had made a bargain with Greystone and she intended to keep her word.

'Shall I inform Cook that you will be dining soon, my lady?'

Foster's voice brought her back to the present with a jolt. 'Yes, Foster. I'll be dining on my own.'

When dinner was announced Patricia went to the dining room and sat in state at the head of the table. She picked at her food, although it was delicious and beautifully presented. For the first time in her married life she felt lonely. Perhaps it was the feeling of being isolated by the penetrating blanket of foul-smelling fog that had unsettled her, but she went to her room as soon as she had finished eating. She rang for her maid and within minutes Betsey hurried into Patricia's elegant bedchamber, slightly out of breath.

'I'm going to bed now.'

'Very well, my lady.'

Patricia waited while Betsey undid the tiny fabric-covered buttons at the back of her dinner gown, followed by the laces on her stays. Despite the fire blazing up the chimney the room felt damp and Patricia shivered when Betsey slipped the fine lawn nightgown over her head.

'Has my husband returned from the House, Betsey?'

'Not to my knowledge, my lady. The fog is getting thicker by the minute, if that's possible.'

'Then I hope it's an all-night sitting. It would be madness to attempt to get home in these conditions.'

'Shall I do your hair, my lady?'

Patricia nodded and sat on the dressing table stool. 'I hope the fog's lifted by morning.'

'It generally does, my lady.' Betsey took the pins from Patricia's elaborate coiffure one by one, placing them in a silver pin tray.

Patricia closed her eyes while Betsey brushed her long golden hair in smooth, soothing strokes, but after a while she raised her hand. 'Thank you, Betsey. That will be all.'

'Good night, my lady.' Betsey curtsied and hurried from the room, leaving Patricia alone once again.

The silence in the street below was eerie and, with the servants' quarters far away below stairs, Patricia felt suddenly that she was the last person left on earth. She climbed into bed, pulling the covers over her head. Sir Michael had his own room but tonight she would have willingly shared her bed with her husband. His conjugal visits were infrequent, although fairly regular, and Patricia knew that he kept a mistress hidden away somewhere, but she accepted this as part of life. Most of the married women she knew had husbands who enjoyed the favours of others, and for the most part the wives chose to ignore such peccadillos. Patricia sighed. She had chosen this life with her eyes open and she did not regret her decision. She almost wished that she had invited Eldon to stay for dinner, but she knew in her heart that would have been a mistake. Eldon was too attractive to be safe, and too amusing to be ignored. She huddled down between the sheets and drifted into a dreamless sleep.

★ ★ ★

Next morning Patricia was in the middle of eating her breakfast when Sir Michael strolled into the dining room, bringing with him the smoky smell of the lingering peasouper.

'Good morning, Patricia. I trust you slept well.'

'Yes, thank you, Greystone. You didn't come home last night.' It was a statement rather than a question, and Patricia eyed him warily. She knew that his latest mistress lived in one of the more squalid streets in Westminster, and she wondered if he would make an excuse or if he would tell her the truth.

'It was too dangerous to travel far. The session continued for most of the night and what little sleep I had was in my office.' Sir Michael examined the selection of dishes on the vast mahogany sideboard. 'I'm devilish hungry.' He selected bacon, sausages and a couple of fried eggs before taking his seat at the table. 'What did you do last evening? I assume that the Stantons' dinner party was called off.'

'Yes, it was, and I would have hesitated to go on my own, although Eldon called in with some ridiculous

11

story about feeling his way along the railings to get here.'

'That sounds about right. It was one of the worst peasoupers I've seen for a long time. What with the smoke from the manufactories and domestic chimneys and the terrible stink from the river last summer, we really need to think about cleaning London up before we suffer even further outbreaks of disease.'

'Yes, of course. I suppose a new sewage system in very important. Will you be free to attend the opera this evening?'

'I hope so, but if not I'm sure Eldon will be only too happy to escort you.'

Patricia eyed him curiously. 'Doesn't it worry you that Eldon is a terrible flirt?'

'Not at all. I trust you implicitly, Patricia. We had an understanding when we married and it suits us both to honour it. Don't you agree?'

'Yes, of course I do.'

'Then you won't be too upset when I tell you that I have to go away for a while.'

'Go away? Where?'

'It's a diplomatic mission abroad, but I'm not free to divulge any details, even to you.'

'But you know I wouldn't say anything, Greystone.'

'I do, but there are plenty of people who are very clever at extorting information. It's their job and they do it very well.'

'I see. How long will you be away?'

'I don't know, but I hope the business in hand will be dealt with quite quickly.'

'Am I to stay here in London on my own?'

Sir Michael smiled indulgently. 'You have a houseful of servants to take care of you, my love. But if you

12

feel you would like to spend time in Devonshire, that is quite all right, too.'

'It sounds as if you expect to be away for some time.'

'I have to be prepared for a longer stay than I would wish, but I will keep you informed by letter. I can't tell you any more than that.'

'When do you leave?'

'Tonight. I'm sorry it's such short notice but I had no say in the matter.'

'We are attending the opera at Covent Garden.'

'I will escort you there, but I will leave before the interval. Everything must look normal. I'll make sure that Eldon sees you home safely.'

Patricia stared at her husband in disbelief. 'You put your trust in him?'

'No, my love. I trust you to behave as the wife of a prominent politician should, and I know you won't let me down.'

'So if I understand you, Greystone, I may remain in London and accept invitations to dine or to go to the theatre, and you are quite happy for Eldon to stand in for you.'

'I wouldn't put it like that, but you are very young, my dear. I can't expect you to go into a convent simply because I have been called away on business. Eldon might be a bit of a rake but he is a gentleman and he knows how far he can go. You will be safer in his company than that of some others I could name.'

'Why can't I come with you? I would love to travel abroad, wherever it is.'

'This is a serious diplomatic mission. I have to go on my own, apart from Maynard, of course. He's busy packing my things as we speak. You can always go home to Greystone Park. I'm sure Sylvia would be delighted to have your company. You and she were always chatting and giggling together when you were girls.'

'Is that how you really see me, Greystone? Am I simply a friend of your daughters whom you happen to have a fancy for?'

'What nonsense you talk sometimes, Patricia.' Sir Michael ate the last slice of bacon with obvious enjoyment. 'I will miss my English breakfasts. Let's hope I can complete my duties quickly and efficiently and be home before Easter.'

Patricia rose abruptly to her feet. 'You'll excuse me, Greystone. I have an appointment with my modiste this morning.'

She left the room without waiting for his response. Shocked by his sudden news and annoyed by her husband's casual dismissal of any feelings she might have, Patricia went to her room and put on her outdoor garments. She would have no compunction in spending as much money as she pleased. Her modiste was excellent but not cheap, although a whole new wardrobe would be a little compensation for the disruption to her social life. The gossips would be kept busy when she attended functions without her husband, but they would delight in spreading rumours anyway. Sometimes her mischievous spirit won and she deliberately gave them something to talk about, but Greystone had always been there to act as a buffer against the harsh realities of London society. Patricia had a feeling that things would be very different with her husband out of the country.

2

Patricia entered the opera house in Covent Garden on the arm of her husband. The foyer was crowded with people in evening dress, and out of politeness Patricia and Greystone stopped to speak to some of their many acquaintances. Patricia maintained an outward show of normality, but she was far from happy about Sir Michael's proposed trip to an unnamed destination for an unspecified length of time. How she would explain his sudden departure had been a bone of contention between them and one of their rare differences of opinion. She wanted to tell the truth as far as she knew it, but Sir Michael insisted that his absence should be kept as secret as possible. It was a diplomatic mission and a sensitive issue.

Eldon thrust his way through the crowd, beaming at both of them. 'Good evening. I trust you're both looking forward to the performance.'

Sir Michael smiled and nodded. 'Of course.'

Patricia did not answer. She had spotted the intendant who had given her the opportunity to sing in the chorus several years ago when her mother was the star of the opera. 'Excuse me, Greystone. I've just seen an old friend. I must have a word with him before he disappears backstage.'

Eldon chuckled. 'I'd forgotten you once had a budding theatrical career, Patricia. Maybe he'll offer you a part in his next production.'

Patricia chose to ignore this remark and she edged her way through the throng, smiling and acknowledging friends, but heading relentlessly towards Garson Thorne, the man who had made her mother an operatic star.

He spotted her immediately and raised his hand in greeting. 'Lady Greystone, this is indeed a pleasure.'

Patricia shook his hand, smiling. 'It's good to see you again, Garson. We don't have to be formal. You always called me Patsy when I was a very insignificant member of the chorus.'

'Never insignificant, my dear. Your presence lights up any stage and singles you out from the crowd — just like your dear mama.'

'It's kind of you to say so, but I wish I had her range.'

'You might, given the right training. But you are now above that sort of thing.'

'I'm married to an important man, but that doesn't mean I have lost my identity, Garson. In fact Greystone encourages me to be independent.' Patricia glanced over her shoulder to where her husband was having a conversation with Eldon. She was annoyed to think that they might be discussing how to keep her amused during Greystone's absence. 'If I wished I could return to the theatre.'

'Really?' Garson Thorne's shrewd grey eyes lit up with enthusiasm. 'I challenge you to keep your word on that, Patsy. If you are sincere you should come to the theatre tomorrow morning. We can't discuss business matters here and now.'

His prompt response to her casual remark came as a shock, but Patricia was feeling reckless. 'I'll be there. Shall we say ten o'clock?'

'I thought you society ladies didn't rise until at least midday.'

'You're forgetting that I am the daughter of a

16

professional singer. I know how hard Mama works and I will do just the same.'

'Ten o'clock it is. I look forward to seeing you, Patsy.' Garson turned away as a lady decked in jewels accosted him.

Patricia went to join her husband and Eldon. 'When are you leaving, Greystone? Will you stay until the interval?'

'I've booked a box. I'll wait until the curtain comes up and then I'll slip away.' Greystone eyed her, frowning. 'What did Thorne want?'

'Just to pass the time of day. He's an old friend.'

'Well, I don't want you mixing with his like when I'm away. You might place yourself in a difficult position while I'm not here to protect you. I've asked Eldon to make sure that you are looked after, but on second thought, I think you ought to leave London. Eldon will escort you to Greystone Park first thing in the morning. After all, you have your sister and brothers close by, should you need them.'

'Greystone, I am not a child. I don't need nursemaids.'

'I want you to promise, Patricia. Have I your word that you will go to Devonshire tomorrow?'

'People are staring at us, Greystone.'

'I want you to promise that you will do as I ask.'

'Yes, all right. I promise I will go home. If not tomorrow, because I have engagements to cancel, then I will go the next day. Please let us take our seats or we'll miss the first act.'

'Don't worry, my dear, I'll look after you,' Eldon whispered as they made their way to their box.

'I can take care of myself, thank you, Eldon.'

Patricia sank down on a velvet upholstered chair

in the luxurious loge above the stage. She was immediately drawn into the operatic world and she leaned forward in order to get a better view. She was so entranced that she did not notice her husband get up and leave, and it was not until the end of the act that she realised he had gone.

Eldon sat back in his seat. 'You really were enjoying all that warbling, Patsy. I personally prefer comic opera.'

'You don't like Mozart?'

'I'm sure he's all very well, but one day I'll take you to Wilton's concert hall in Graces Alley. You'll see real life there and probably more genuine music lovers than those who have come here more to be seen than to enjoy the performance.'

'You are such a cynic, Eldon. Anyway, the curtain is going up again, so please be quiet.'

He chuckled. 'Yes, my lady. By the way, I've ordered Champagne for the interval.'

She shot him a sideways glance. 'I'm surprised you didn't order a tankard of ale or a glass of porter.'

'I see I've touched a nerve.' Eldon leaned closer, lowering his voice. 'You're planning something, Patricia. I know that look.'

'You know nothing about me.' Patricia turned her head to gaze at the stage. 'Hush, I want to enjoy this without interruptions from anyone.'

Eldon sighed and sat back in his chair. 'A glass or two of Champagne is definitely called for.'

At the end of the performance, her mood lifted a little after two or three glasses of Champagne, Patricia allowed Eldon to escort her home in a hansom cab. She had been tempted to stress her independence by taking a cab alone, but the press outside the theatre

18

was so great that she was forced to rely on Eldon's ability to catch the eye of a cabby without seeming to try. She suspected that his habit of tipping generously was well known amongst cabbies and it certainly paid off as they were transported back to Duke Street without undue delay.

'Aren't you going to invite me in for a glass of brandy or even a cup of coffee, Patsy?'

'No, Eldon. It's late and I have my reputation to consider.'

'I don't remember that stopping you in the past.' 'It was different when Greystone was at home, but now, as he pointed out, I have to be careful.'

'Oh, well, you know best, my dear. I'll call tomorrow to find out when you wish to travel to Devonshire.'

'You heard me tell my husband that I have things to do before I can think of leaving London. I'll send a message when I'm ready. Besides which, Greystone might only be gone for a few days, or a week at most.'

'He told me that it could be several weeks.' Eldon eyed her suspiciously. 'I will call as I said, if only to assure myself that you are all right. Good night, my dear. I'll wait to see you safely indoors.'

There was no way to escape him other than to enter the house. She did not look back but she knew that Eldon would not climb back into the cab until Foster had closed the door.

'Sir Michael has been called away on an urgent matter, Foster,' she said casually.

'Yes, my lady. Sir Michael informed me of his plan to travel. You can be assured of my discretion at all times. Will you be staying in London or shall I make arrangements to travel to Devonshire?'

'I'll let you know tomorrow, Foster. Send Betsey to me, I'm going to my room. Good night.'

★ ★ ★

Unusually for her, Patricia was nervous when Garson Thorne handed her the libretto of the next work to be performed and asked her to sing. Apart from intoning hymns in church on Sundays she had not used her voice in such a way since she had last appeared on this very stage. She cleared her throat and missed the cue delivered by the pianist.

'I'm sorry, Garson. I'm a little rusty.'

'Don't worry, my dear. Just do your best and remember to put feeling into your words. Think of how your mama tackles a new part and it will all come back to you.'

Patricia took a deep breath and began to sing, putting everything she had ever learned from her mother into the role.

'*Brava,*' Garson said when she came to the end of the aria. 'Well done. That was excellent. It's true you need practice, but you have inherited your dear mama's talent.'

'I'm not sure about that,' Patricia said modestly. 'But I do enjoy singing, and I would love to have a small part in your next production. When does it start?'

'We begin rehearsals in four weeks. Will you be available?'

'You're giving me a part?'

'Of course. Did you imagine for one moment that I would turn down the chance to have Felicia's daughter in the cast of my next production? But will your

20

husband allow you to appear on stage?'

'Oh, yes,' Patricia said with more confidence than she was feeling. She was not sure what she had hoped Garson would offer her, but she had assumed that it would happen during Greystone's absence. 'The only problem is that I have to travel to Devonshire tomorrow.'

'When do you expect to return?'

'As quickly as possible.'

'If you are to be gone for more than a week I can recommend a *répétiteur* to retrain your voice, which will make it much easier for you when rehearsals begin.'

'A *répétiteur*? I don't understand, Garson.'

'A voice coach, my dear. The best one in the business is Signora Valentina Gandolfi. I know she is in London at this moment, and I would be happy to approach her for you.'

'Do you think she could accompany me to Devonshire at such short notice?'

Garson moved closer, tapping the side of his red nose. 'The signora is rather too fond of the grape, if you know what I mean. When she is sober she is a brilliant *répétiteur*, but if she succumbs to temptation she has a problem, which usually leads to being turned out of her lodgings.'

'She doesn't sound very reliable,' Patricia said doubtfully.

'But she is very affordable, if you get my meaning, and just at the moment I'm sure she would love a sabbatical in the country.'

'And you really think that she could help me?'

'Undoubtedly. Would you like me to arrange it? I'm sure she would be ready to leave at very short notice.'

Patricia thought quickly. She could pass Signora

21

Gandolfi off as one of her mother's friends who was in need of respite in the countryside, and no one need discover the real reason for the strange woman's presence. After all, there was only Sylvia to persuade, and Sylvia was unlikely to challenge anything her stepmother said or did.

'I agree, Garson. Tell the signora to meet me at Waterloo Bridge Station at nine o'clock tomorrow morning. I'll purchase a ticket for her, but if she proves too unreliable I'll send her back to London.'

'I'm sure that Valentina will be on her best behaviour. This is a chance too good to be missed.'

Patricia held out her hand. 'I'll say goodbye then, Garson. I'm sure I'll be back in London within the next few weeks, but you can always contact me by sending a letter to Greystone Park, Rockwood.'

Garson raised her hand to his lips. 'We will go far together, Patricia. I put your mama on the road to becoming famous and I can do the same for you.'

Patricia left the theatre feeling smug. She would love to prove that she was as good as her mother when it came to talent, and anyway, if nothing came of it, or if Greystone returned earlier than expected, she would have passed the time enjoyably. She walked to the Strand and hailed a passing cab.

She arrived home to find Eldon pacing the drawing room like an agitated husband.

'What are you doing here? I don't remember inviting you to call on me this morning.' Patricia tossed her reticule onto the sofa, standing arms akimbo.

'You went out unchaperoned, Patricia. What would Greystone say to that?'

'Since he will never know, it won't be a problem.'

'Where did you go?'

22

'Eldon, stop behaving as if you own me. It's none of your business.'

'Greystone asked me to keep an eye on you.'

'I am not a child, and I'm sure that my husband didn't mean you to spy on me.'

Eldon threw up his hands, smiling ruefully. 'All right. I give in, Patricia. But you must allow me to show some concern when your behaviour is rash.'

'I am going to Devonshire tomorrow, Eldon. I will be accompanied by a respectable chaperone and Betsey, my maid.'

'I see.' Eldon eyed her thoughtfully. 'I did promise Greystone that I would see you safely back to your home in Devonshire.'

'There really is no need.'

'At least I can see you onto the train. What time does it depart?'

Patricia thought quickly. 'A quarter to ten,' she said glibly.

'Then I will be at the station to help you with your luggage.'

'Now I have a lot to do, so if you don't mind . . .'

'You want me to leave?'

'Yes, I do.'

'Then you will have to allow me to take you out to dinner this evening? It might be the last time I see you for some weeks if Greystone is away for a long time.'

'I suppose you won't go unless I agree?'

He smiled. 'Precisely.'

'All right. You may call for me at half past seven.'

'As always I am your devoted slave, my dear.' Eldon advanced on her and was about to kiss her on the cheek but she turned away.

'Good day, Eldon.'

'You are a hard-hearted woman, Lady Greystone.' Eldon let himself out of the drawing room, leaving the door to swing closed behind him.

Patricia strolled over to the nearest mirror and patted her blond curls in place. She smiled at her reflection, safe in the knowledge that her pale rose-petal complexion was as smooth and youthful as ever and her eyes had not lost the intense blue of spring violets. She might not be beautiful but she knew that she was pretty and she could get her own way through charm alone. She blew a kiss to the young woman in the mirror, laughing at her own vanity. She would dine with Eldon and tease him mercilessly, but tomorrow she would be a free woman, for a while at least.

★ ★ ★

There was no mistaking Signora Valentina Gandolfi. Patricia and Betsey were already on the platform when the sound of a rich contralto exercising her vocal chords with the tonic sol-fa scales made people stop and stare at the large woman dressed in bright green velvet with a flowing cloak and a fur-trimmed bonnet. Signora Gandolfi rushed through the barriers followed by a porter with a trolley laden with luggage. She came to a sudden halt in front of Patricia.

'My dear Lady Greystone, I would have known you anywhere. You are so like your dear mama. We were once great friends but our lives have taken different paths and I haven't seen Felicia for years.'

'Signora Gandolfi.' Patricia held out her hand. 'How do you do?'

'How do you do, Lady Greystone?' Signora Gandolfi pumped Patricia's hand. 'So good of you to invite

24

me to your country house. I'm sure we will work very well together.'

'Let us hope so, Signora.' Patricia picked up her skirts. 'We'd better board the train now. It will be leaving very soon.'

'Of course, my lady.' Signora Gandolfi turned to the porter, giving him orders in fluent Italian. 'Put the luggage in the guard's van, you stupid fellow,' she added in perfect English. She watched him until he reached the guard's van and then she heaved her ample frame into the carriage and slumped down in the corner opposite Patricia.

The whistle blew and, with a hiss of steam and a roar of the engine, the great iron beast rolled forward. Patricia glanced out of the window to see Eldon racing along the platform waving his top hat. She lifted her hand in acknowledgement and smiled.

'You know that gentleman, my lady?' Signora Gandolfi eyed Patricia curiously. 'It is an affair of the heart, perhaps?'

'No, indeed. He is an acquaintance, that's all.'

'Ah, yes. I understand. Is it far to your country house? I do not like trains — they are dangerous things.'

'It will take a while, I'm afraid.'

'Then we should begin our work now, my lady.' Signora Gandolfi puffed out her chest and hit a note that would have shattered glass had the carriage windows not been so thick.

'Perhaps a few scales and breathing exercises?'

Betsey shrank into the opposite corner, staring at the signora as if she were a madwoman.

'I think not,' Patricia said firmly. 'We don't want to frighten the passengers in the other compartments.

They might think a murder was being committed.'

Signora Gandolfi's bushy black eyebrows drew together over the bridge of her aquiline nose. 'You are saying that my notes are like a scream of agony?'

'No, no, of course not, but I fear that the other travellers are not as sophisticated as we are. I doubt if they have ever heard an operatic voice, let alone a fine soprano like yours.'

'Ah, yes. I see. Well, anyway we should not give them a free concert. You are quite right, my lady. I think I will sleep. Please wake me when we arrive at our destination.'

Signora Gandolfi sat back in her seat and her head dropped, seemingly cushioned by her large bosom, which protruded above tightly laced stays. Seconds later she began to snore loudly.

Patricia exchanged amused glances with Betsey and she stifled a sigh of relief. Signora Gandolfi might be an excellent voice coach but she was going to prove to be a handful. Patricia spent the next hour trying to decide how best to keep the signora occupied when they arrived at Greystone Park.

The problem was solved by Ivy Lugg, who was now the head parlour maid at Greystone Park. She seemed to sense that Signora Gandolfi might prove to be a difficult guest, and she spirited her away to a guest bedchamber that had recently been cleaned and aired.

Sylvia was not so helpful.

'I wasn't expecting you, Patsy. Why have you come here without Papa?'

'Your father is going to be very busy for the next few weeks, so I thought I'd come to Greystone and keep you company for a while.'

26

'I have Cousin Martha and Miss Moon to do that, whether I like it or not.' Sylvia frowned. 'You never normally consider my feelings like this. What has changed?'

'This is my home, too. I felt like getting away from the dreadful peasoupers and the noise and bustle of London. I don't like to think of you living here with just the two older ladies for company. Where are they, by the way?'

'Cousin Martha had to visit her sick aunt and Miss Moon went with her. They'll be back in a few days. Anyway, I do very well on my own, thank you. I am quite happy being mistress of Greystone Park.'

Patricia peeled off her leather gloves and laid them on a side table in the Chinese parlour. 'If you found yourself a rich husband you would have a home of your own.'

'It was Christina who wanted to marry well, and look at her now. Her husband is still a curate and she is in the family way again. They live in a wing of a draughty old vicarage with an aged vicar and his waspish wife. It's not what she dreamed of.'

Patricia walked over to the fireplace to warm her hands. 'Maybe not, but she loves Oscar, and he will inherit Cottingham Manor one day. They won't always be poor.'

'I will only marry for love. I'd rather be an old maid than marry a man twice my age, even if he is enormously wealthy.'

Patricia shot her a sideways glance. 'I know what you think of me, Sylvia, but your papa and I are well suited. I have no complaints and neither has he.'

'Then why are you here on your own, apart from that strange woman who looks as if she has come from

27

a fairground? Why aren't you in London supporting your husband, and why haven't you given him an heir? A son would inherit Greystone Park and keep you safe when Papa dies.'

Patricia chuckled. 'How morbid you are. Not that it's any of your business, but your pa and I agreed that we didn't want children, so you don't have to worry about being ousted from your position here. I think I might amuse myself by trying to find you a suitable husband.'

'Don't patronise me, Patricia. I remember when you ran off with Barnaby Yelland when he was an apprentice blacksmith, even though Lucy Warren was expecting his child. Then you were engaged to marry Alexander Blanchard, but he left you at the altar and finally you managed to lure my father into giving you his name. So you'll excuse me if I don't take advice on affairs of the heart from you.'

'You always had a spiteful tongue, Sylvia. Anyway, you and I have to get along because I'm your step-mother now, in case you've forgotten.'

'How could I forget that? You certainly won't allow it.'

'No, but we can still be friends. We used to have fun — remember how I used to beat you at croquet?'

A wry smile curved Sylvia's lips. 'You always lost. Christina won every time.'

'Well, she won't win now with two small children clinging to her skirts, will she? I doubt if they can afford a nursemaid, and her mother-in-law is hardly the sort of woman who would want to look after them.'

'Glorina dotes on them, as a matter of fact, but Christina is convinced that she would be a bad influence on them. She thinks that gypsies cast spells on

28

small children and turn them into changelings or some such nonsense. Glorina is only allowed to see the babies with someone responsible standing by in case she spirits them off to the woods.'

'Glorina Cottingham might have Romany blood in her veins, but she's been married to the squire for more than twenty-five years. I think she's proved that she is just like the rest of us, only a little more outspoken, and she loves to shock the dull people of Rockwood and Cottingham. I don't see her telling fortunes or studying a crystal ball.'

Sylvia shrugged. 'I know that, but you try telling my sister anything when it comes to her children. She's as protective as a tigress.'

'That I would like to see. Christina was such fun before she became a mother.' Patricia turned her head as the door opened to admit Signora Gandolfi, who had changed out of her green travelling gown and was now wearing a loose-fitting black velvet robe spangled with sequins. On her head she wore a turban adorned with ostrich feathers.

'*Do re mi fa sol la ti do*,' she intoned with outstretched arms. 'I think it's time for our first lesson, Lady Greystone.'

3

'I knew it,' Sylvia said crossly. 'You came here to practise your singing without a thought for me. You are just like your mama, Patsy. Does my father know about this?'

'Who are you, Signorina?' Signora Gandolfi demanded, scowling. 'Don't you know that you are in exalted company? I used to perform at La Scala, Milan and —'

Sylvia held up her hands. 'Oh, please! I've heard all this before. Each time Mrs de Marney visited Rockwood we had to listen to her singing an aria from one boring old opera or another.'

'Signora Gandolfi is here to coach me, Sylvie. I don't want anyone else to know,' Patricia said hastily. 'This has got to be our secret.'

'How are you going to keep it a secret with that woman singing her head off? I heard her trilling away as she went upstairs, but then I simply assumed she was happy to be here. You must be hiding this from Papa or you wouldn't have descended upon us like this.'

'I can explain if you'll let me.' Patricia turned to Signora Gandolfi, who was taking deep breaths as if she were going to launch into an aria or explode. 'My stepdaughter doesn't understand, Signora.'

'Then I suggest you explain matters. I cannot work under pressure, you must appreciate that.' Signora Gandolfi glanced around the room. 'Is it too much to ask for a glass of sherry wine? I am rather hungry, too.

It's a long time since breakfast.'

Sylvia rolled her eyes. 'You arrived without warning.' She walked to the bell pull and tugged at it. 'I'll send a message to the kitchen that we will be three at table for dinner this evening. However, please don't start singing in front of the servants or it will be all round the village in less time than it takes to snap your fingers.'

'I do not apologise for my ferocious amount of talent. Sometimes I open my mouth and the music issues forth unbidden. I am a professional, miss.'

'Sylvia is right,' Patricia said quickly. 'We need to keep this as private a matter as possible, Signora. Perhaps you could allow your talent to issue forth in your own room, or in the music room, which I have chosen for our practice sessions.'

There was a sharp rap on the door and Ivy entered, bobbing a curtsey.

'There will be two extra for dinner this evening, Ivy,' Sylvia said sulkily. 'Inform Cook that we have guests who will be staying for the foreseeable future.'

'A decanter of sherry wine and three glasses, please, Ivy,' Patricia added hastily.

Sylvia sniffed. 'Two glasses, Ivy. I don't imbibe.'

'That's strange. You used to enjoy wine with dinner and I remember you sneaking a glass of port when your papa wasn't looking.' Patricia waved Ivy away. 'Two glasses then, please.'

Sylvia turned to Patricia when the door closed. 'You don't have to say please and thank you to servants. You should know that.'

'They are human beings like the rest of us. I don't think being polite to underlings is a fault. Anyway, I didn't come here to quarrel with you, Sylvie. Let's try

31

to get on as we used to and put our differences aside. I, for one, enjoy a glass of sherry wine and I adore Champagne.'

Signora Gandolfi nodded sagely. 'Champagne is the only wine that leaves a woman beautiful after drinking it — I believe that was said by Madame de Pompadour.'

Sylvia frowned. 'She was a courtesan. I'm not sure you ought to repeat that in company, Signora.'

'My goodness, you have become a little prude,' Patricia said, laughing. 'You have spent too much time on your own, Sylvie. Perhaps I ought to have invited Eldon to stay. He would have taken pleasure in introducing you to polite flirting.'

Sylvia jumped to her feet. 'I will tell Papa that you are trying to lead me astray, Patricia. I don't want to meet your louche London admirers.'

Patricia shrugged. 'It's your loss. Eldon is annoying but he is also very charming and quite harmless, if you know how to handle him.' She held up her hand. 'I hear the clink of glasses. Are you sure you can't be tempted to join us, Sylvie?'

'No, indeed. You may try to turn me into a shameless hussy, but I will resist.' Sylvia tossed her head and left the room, almost colliding with Ivy and her silver tray laden with a decanter and glasses.

'Your stepdaughter needs some lessons in life,' Signora Gandolfi observed drily. 'I will enjoy a glass of sherry wine. It is good for my voice. I introduced your mama to the advantages of imbibing sensibly, Patricia.'

Ivy placed the tray on a small drum table beside Patricia's chair.

'Thank you, Ivy. That will be all for now.'

32

Patricia filled two glasses and handed one to Signora Gandolfi. 'When do we start our lessons?' she asked when the door closed on Ivy.

'I will have a siesta and then I take a walk to refresh my lungs.'

'Perhaps we could fit in an hour after you return from your constitutional?'

'I usually have some sherry wine before dinner, and after that I retire to my bed. We have to nurture our voices and a good night's sleep is important.'

'So we begin tomorrow morning?'

'If I feel it is the right time to start I will say so, but it depends on the weather.'

'The weather?'

'If it is fine and sunny we will work; if it is cold and raining we will study the libretto.'

'It doesn't sound too taxing. In other words I have every afternoon free.'

'Of course, and we do not study on Sundays.'

'You attend church?'

'No, I stay in bed and rest. I will have my meals brought to my room.'

Patricia sipped her sherry thoughtfully. Perhaps she ought to have invited Eldon to stay. At least he would have been good company. On the other hand, Sylvia was obviously in danger of becoming a reclusive killjoy. The lively young girl that Patricia had known for most of her life seemed to have been taken over by a puritanical woman who was afraid of life and in danger of becoming a recluse.

'These are very small glasses,' Signora Gandolfi said, holding hers out for a refill.

* * *

33

By the time dinner was announced that evening Signora Gandolfi was very merry indeed. She had to be helped from her chair by Ivy, who struggled with the signora's considerable weight and retreated hastily. Her place was taken by Henry, a tall footman, who managed to steer the intoxicated guest to the dining room, and having placed her in her chair he stepped away, staring tactfully into space. Patricia waited for Sylvia to make a scathing comment, but she took her place at the foot of the table, saying nothing. However, her sour expression spoke volumes and for once Patricia agreed with her. Signora Gandolfi smiled happily and held up her glass, which Henry dutifully filled with wine.

The food was brought to the table and both Sylvia and Patricia ate sparingly, but Signora Gandolfi devoured everything that was placed before her, washed down with several glasses of Bordeaux. She had barely finished a dish of trifle when her eyelids began to droop and her head dropped to one side.

Sylvia leaped to her feet, throwing down her table napkin. 'Really. This is too much, Patricia. You've brought a drunkard to my home. You must take charge because I don't want to spend the next few days or even weeks in her company.'

Patricia signalled to Henry, who was standing to attention at the foot of the table. 'I'm afraid you will have to carry her to her room. Do you need help?'

'I can lift her, my lady.'

'Ivy, please send Betsey to help the signora to bed.' Patricia rose to her feet. 'We'll have coffee in the drawing room.' She walked to the door without waiting for Sylvia, who hurried after her.

'What are you going to do about that creature? We

can't have this every evening.'

'You're right. She needs someone to keep an eye on her and I know exactly who to ask. That's if Rosie will allow me to borrow Fletcher for the duration.'

Sylvia's eyes opened wide. 'You're going to bring that woman to Greystone? Are you mad?'

'Fletcher can handle matters better than you or I, Sylvie. It would take a brave person to argue with that woman.'

'Can't you simply send the Italian creature back to London?'

'Not very well. Getting a part in Garson's latest production depends upon how my voice improves.'

'I knew you were up to something.' Sylvia threw open the drawing-room door. 'I thought you would want to go back on the stage. You are just like your mama.'

Patricia took a seat in a wingback chair by the fire. 'My mother is world famous, Sylvia. She is the toast of Milan, Vienna and Paris. She's been invited to perform in New York following Jenny Lind's tour of America. You can't get more famous than that.'

'And I suppose you see yourself following in her footsteps. What will Papa say when he finds out? He won't want you cavorting on the stage.'

'Your papa and I have a very good understanding of each other. He won't try to stop me if I can prove my capabilities.'

'You are deluding yourself. Papa won't stand for it and I refuse to have that drunken woman in my home.'

'I'm sorry you feel like that, Sylvie, but you have no choice. I am the mistress of Greystone Park. Fletcher will take the signora in hand. You'll see.'

Patricia arrived at her old home, taking a moment to study the ancient castle with its four crenellated towers and walled bailey. The stonework had mellowed with the passing of time and the approach through the parkland was green and pleasant, even in late winter. Patricia had never been particularly interested in the history of the castle, although she and Aurelia Blanchard had been convinced that it was haunted, and that skeletons remained hidden in an oubliette somewhere deep in the bowels of the dungeons. She smiled as she remembered how young and naïve they had been. Perhaps she ought to invite Aurelia to stay at Greystone to relieve the boredom of dealing with Sylvia's constant grumbling. The carriage waited until the huge iron gates were opened before entering the cobbled bailey, coming to a halt outside the main entrance where Jarvis stood ready to greet her.

'Good morning, Jarvis. It's good to see you looking so well.'

Jarvis inclined his head. 'Thank you, my lady. Welcome home.'

'It's been four years since I left here to marry Greystone, but whenever I return and step inside it feels like yesterday. Nothing changes at Rockwood.'

'Indeed, my lady. May I take your cape?'

Patricia slipped the fur-lined garment off her slender shoulders and handed it to Jarvis. 'Is my sister at home?'

'You'll find her in the morning parlour. Shall I announce you, my lady?'

'No, Jarvis. I'll give her a surprise.' Patricia was about to walk past the rusty suit of armour, which

36

was attributed to Sir Denys Carey, a knight of old, when she stopped and automatically closed the visor. 'Don't gape, Sir Denys. You know me well enough,' she said, smiling.

The years fell away as she trod the familiar well-worn corridor to the morning parlour. She could almost hear the sound of childish laughter and the deeper tones of her elder brother's voice as Bertie called to her to come and see his latest catch, or the brace of pheasants he had shot for their dinner. Now Bertie, a soldier wounded in the Crimean War, was a cripple confined to a Bath chair. Walter, the book-worm, was married to Louise, the vicar's daughter, and he was an up-and-coming writer of poetry and short stories. So much had changed since they were children together. As she paused outside the morning parlour, Patricia smiled to herself. They had grown up with wealth and position; then it had all evapor-ated like morning mist and they had been poor. Their fortunes had revived when Rosalind married Piers Blanchard, only to fall again when he was convicted for illegal trading and sent to the penal colony in Aus-tralia. Rockwood Castle must have witnessed many such ups and downs within the Carey family over the centuries.

Patricia opened the door and walked into the room. Rosalind was seated by the fire cradling her three-month-old baby, Phoebe, while her four-year- old daughter, Dolly, cuddled up at her side. Two-year-old Rory was sitting on the floor playing with a set of colourful wooden bricks. Despite her decision not to have children of her own, Patricia could not help being touched by the domestic scene and the beauty of the golden-haired little ones.

'Patsy, this is a lovely surprise,' Rosalind said, smiling. 'What brings you to Rockwood?'

'I'm not supposed to tell anyone, but you're my sister and I know you can keep a secret.'

Rosalind's eyes lit up with amusement. 'Go on, I'm listening.'

Dolly tugged at her mother's sleeve. 'I can keep a secret, too, Mama.'

'Little pitchers have big ears,' Patricia said warily.

'Of course.' Rosalind nodded. 'Ring for Molly and she'll take the children for their morning walk. Phoebe needs to go down for nap, anyway.'

Patricia rang for Molly Greep, the farmer's daughter who had started work at the castle as a humble kitchen maid and was now the children's nanny. Patricia sighed: it was good to be home. Even though she had longed to get away when she was younger, Rockwood still held a special place in her heart.

'Are you going to stay with us, Aunt Patricia?' Dolly asked eagerly.

'Not exactly, dear. I'm living at Greystone Park at the moment, but I will come and see you often, and your mama will bring you to visit me.'

'I can ride my pony,' Dolly said confidently. 'I am a good rider, am I not, Mama?'

'You are indeed, but perhaps a little too adventurous. Alex takes her out regularly, but it's always a relief when they come home in one piece.'

'I don't fall apart, Mama,' Dolly said severely. 'I am all joined up.'

Patricia laughed and picked her up, giving her a cuddle. 'You are so funny.'

'I'm very serious, Aunt Patricia.' Dolly wriggled until Patricia put her down.

'I can see you have your hands full, Rosie.' Patricia managed to step aside, avoiding a brick hurled by Rory, who giggled as if it was the funniest thing he had ever seen.

'Yes, I know, but I adore my babies. I've never been so happy, Patsy.'

'I can see that and I'm glad. You and Alex were made for each other. Thank goodness he avoided marrying me. It would have been a disaster.'

'But you're happy with Greystone?'

'Yes, of course.' Patricia looked round as the door opened following a brief knock, and Molly entered the room.

'You rang, ma'am?'

'Yes, Molly. It's time for the children's walk, and Phoebe's nap. I'll come up and see them later.'

'Come along, Miss Dolly, and you, Master Rory.' Molly scooped the baby into her capable arms. 'You can have some milk and a biscuit and then we'll go for our walk, as it's sunny and dry.' She herded the small children from the room, closing the door with her free hand.

'Sit down and tell me everything,' Rosalind said, smiling. 'What is so secret that it can't be said in front of a four-year-old?'

Patricia sank down on the sofa. 'Greystone has been sent abroad on a highly confidential diplomatic mission. I have no idea where he's gone or when he'll return, but I assume it won't be soon. It's so secret and sensitive that no one must know.'

'I see . . . Well, that's interesting, but why have you come down to Devonshire on your own?'

'Do you remember Garson Thorne at the Opera House?'

'I recall the name, but I didn't really know him.'

'He has a part for me in his next production. He's assigned a woman, who was a friend of Mama's, to coach me, but she's proving to be quite a handful. I wondered if I could borrow Fletcher for a couple of weeks.'

'What do you want with Fletcher? What can she do?'

'She can take the signora in hand. The woman is impossible, but she's apparently the best coach in the business and I am desperate to get the part.'

'I can't think why. I thought you were so happy with Greystone and the life you lead in London.'

'I am. There's nothing wrong with my marriage, but Greystone might be away for months. I don't know where he is or how to contact him, and frankly I'm bored already.'

'Surely you have friends who will keep you entertained?'

'That's the trouble. I have acquaintances and but no one I can really talk to.'

'What about Lord Eldon? I seem to remember that you were very friendly with him.'

'Larkin Eldon is an amusing libertine and I enjoy his company, but I have to be careful. The gossips would love to link our names together and I owe it to Greystone to keep away from scandal.'

'You have changed, Patsy. At one time you would have relished it. But do you think that appearing on the operatic stage will solve anything?'

'It will be something that I've done for myself. I feel sometimes as if I have no substance at all — that I'm a shadow of my husband with no thought or feelings of my own. Can you understand that?'

'I think so, although that's not how it is between Alex and me. We are partners in every sense of the word.'

'How is Alex? How are you managing without an income from the clay mine in Cornwall?'

'Now there's an odd quirk of fate, if you like. Aurelia's husband had a chance to purchase shares in the mine. Martin has made a real success of the business, much, I should think, to the annoyance of Lady Pentelow who said he would never amount to anything.'

'I've lost touch with Aurelia since she married Martin Gibbs. I've been so wrapped up in my own affairs that I've neglected friends and family.'

'You lead a very busy life. We all understand.'

'I have wondered how Aurelia would get on living in a cottage after being brought up in such a grand style of comfort at Trevenor.'

'Well, they did live in the village to start with. Then the manager's house became vacant when Pedrick left, and they moved in there. I haven't seen it, but apparently it's quite commodious. Anyway, Martin had a chance to buy the business outright, and Alex bought shares in the mine. It's proved to be very profitable.'

'I'm glad to hear it.'

'And Alex manages the estate for Bertie with the help of Wolfe, who collects the rents. No one argues with him.'

'You seem to collect strange strays, Rosie. But I am happy to see you looking so well and happy. You know I would always help you if you needed money. Greystone is very generous.'

'Thank you, I know you would, but we bought the old sawmill on the edge of the village and Ben Causley runs it. You remember Ben — his father owns the

Black Dog in the village.'

'Of course. It's so good to know that everything is running smoothly.'

'The fortunes of Rockwood Castle are well and truly on the rise, and it's all legal this time, thanks to Alex.'

'I'm amazed that he's managed to settle down to life out of the army.'

'It hasn't always been easy for him, but he's very determined and he's a devoted father.'

'Do you ever hear from Piers? I don't know if convicts are allowed to send letters home.'

'No, nothing, and I don't expect to. Piers gave me my freedom and for that I'll always be grateful to him. We were happy at first, but he couldn't resist the temptation to make easy money. Anyway, let's not talk about sad things. How long do you think you might stay at Greystone Park?'

'I really don't know, but I have a feeling I'll be glad to escape from the signora's clutches, so you will definitely see more of me.'

'Come for luncheon tomorrow and I'll make sure that everyone is here. Walter and Louise have a suite of rooms in the east wing, although they will be moving into the old gamekeeper's cottage soon, and Bertie occupies Grandpapa's quarters. Wolfe and Fletcher look after him, although Bertie is very independent now he has the Bath chair.'

'What about Tommy? Is he here?'

'Tommy and Nancy are both away at school. Louise taught them until a year or so ago, but she decided they would both benefit from attending academies that would broaden their horizons. Although Nancy is fifteen, so she will be coming home for good at the end of term.'

'I really should know all these things about my family. London isn't so very far away but it must be two years since I was last here.'

'Patsy, you have your own life to lead. Greystone is an important man and your first duty must always be to help him in his career.'

'I wonder if he will feel the same if I happen to do well on the stage.'

'I don't know, but you'll find out soon enough if you go through with it.'

'You are a wonder, Rosie. I don't know how you can cope with motherhood, let alone sharing your home with almost the whole family, as well as a few strays that have wandered in over the years.'

'It's easy, and I enjoy having everyone round me. Maybe if you had children . . .'

Patricia held up her hands. 'Don't start all that again, Rosie. I am happy as I am, or at least I will be when I get the part in Garson's new production. That's why I need to keep the signora happy and under control. May I have Fletcher, or is she indispensable?'

'I think you should ask her yourself. She's out walking the grounds with Bertie at the moment, but if you stay for a while you can speak to her when they return. I know that Bertie will want to see you before tomorrow anyway.'

Patricia put her head on one side. 'I know I'm part of this family, but I feel like a visitor. I wonder if that's how Mama felt every time she returned after a tour.'

'I think our mother is so wrapped up in her career that she has no thoughts for anyone or anything else, except perhaps dear old Claude. She is lucky to have him.'

'You don't think I'm like her, do you, Rosie? You would tell me if I had developed Mama's selfish attitude, wouldn't you?'

'The very fact that it worries you means that you are nothing like Mama. As far as she is concerned the world revolves around her and her voice. I don't blame you for wanting to try and emulate her on stage, but you are not like her in any other way, Patsy.'

Patricia pulled a face. 'Our parents had a lot to answer for, didn't they? Papa was always off on one of his plant-finding trips, which killed him in the end, and Mama was never here. She left Hester to bring us up — where is Hester, anyway?'

'She'll be in her parlour, or she might be in the linen room or the butler's pantry. Hester might be Lady Carey now but she still manages the household.'

'I must see her before I speak to Fletcher. I don't want her to feel left out.'

'That thought wouldn't have occurred to you before you married Greystone. You've changed, Patsy.'

'I suppose I've grown up, at least a little. Perhaps I was rather spoilt as a child.'

'Yes, you were, not to put too fine a point on it, but everyone loved you all the same.' Rosalind rose to her feet, shaking out her crumpled skirts. 'You look so elegant in that lovely silk gown, Patsy. I feel like a drab.'

'That's nonsense, but your clothes are rather outdated. Perhaps you ought to come to London and spend a few days with me. I could take you to my modiste.'

'Meggie Brewer still makes my clothes and I'm quite happy with that, but thank you for the offer. Anyway, let's go and find Hester. You're quite right, she will want to be the first to see you again. By that time Bertie should be back from his outing with Fletcher.'

'Yes, I remember Fletcher vaguely — she was like a man in a dress.'

'Don't let her hear you say so, but you're right, and she's strong enough to lift Bertie from his chair to his bed if Wolfe isn't there to do it for her.'

'I can't wait for her to meet Signora Gandolfi,' Patricia said, chuckling.

4

Hester greeted Patricia with a wry smile. 'So you've turned up again. I thought you were too grand for us country folk now.'

Patricia kissed Hester's wrinkled cheek. 'There's no need to remind me that I've neglected my family, Hester. I know it's an age since I last visited Rockwood.'

'It's nearly two years, madam. You've been too busy with your flashy London crowd to bother with us.'

Rosalind frowned. 'Don't be too hard on her, Hester. Patsy has plenty to do as a politician's wife. She has to be a perfect hostess to Sir Michael's friends and colleagues.'

'It doesn't sound like hard work to me,' Hester said, sniffing. 'You always took the easy way with everything, Patricia. But I'm glad to see you, nonetheless.'

'Thank you, Hester. I'm pleased to see you, too.' Patricia bowed her head. She knew she would never get the better of Hester, no matter how hard she tried, but Hester did not look impressed by this outward show of humility. She stood, arms akimbo, giving Patricia a searching look.

'So why have you graced us with your company, my lady?'

'I wanted to see you all, of course, and I need to borrow Fletcher for a few days.'

'Ah!' Hester said triumphantly. 'I knew there would be a hidden motive. I raised you, Patricia Carey — I know you better than you know yourself.'

46

'You won't make me feel guilty, no matter how hard you try, Hester. I've told Rosie everything and she understands why I need someone like Fletcher.'

'And your brother doesn't, I suppose. Bertie is a cripple, Patricia. I don't know why you think Fletcher can help you, but Bertie is in greater need.'

Patricia tossed her head. 'You haven't changed. You're still treating us as if we were five-year-olds.'

'Now, now, don't argue,' Rosie said hastily. 'I think the matter is out of our hands, Hester. Patsy can put her case to Fletcher and Bertie, and it will be up to them to decide.'

Hester sniffed. 'Patricia, much as I love you, you have always caused trouble. I hope you mean to behave yourself while you're here.'

'Of course I do. I'm not the spoilt child I was when I lived at home. All I want is a little assistance with a rather difficult person who is staying with me at Greystone Park.'

Rosalind rose to her feet and reached for her shawl. 'Bertie should be home very soon. Shall we go out and meet him? It will be a lovely surprise.' 'I have things to do,' Hester said stiffly. 'No doubt we'll see you again before you rush back to London, Patricia.'

'You most certainly will. I want to see as much of my family as I can. Come along then, Rosie. Let's go and find Bertie and Fletcher.'

Hester shrugged and stalked out of the room, leaving Patricia and Rosalind to subside into giggles as if they were still children.

'Hush, Patsy,' Rosalind said breathlessly. 'She'll hear you.'

'I don't care. We are equals now, Hester and I. She has no authority over me and that doesn't please her.'

'Never mind, Hester. She's a good soul and I love her, but she can be a bit strict sometimes. I can't wait to see Bertie's face when he sees you. He was always fondest of you.'

'Nonsense. Bertie loves us both equally. I want to see Walter, too, before I return to Greystone Park.'

'Well, you know where you're most likely to find him.'

'The library!'

'Of course. He's had two books of poems published and he's halfway through a novel. I can't wait to read it.'

'Everyone in the family is clever in their own way, except for me. I have yet to prove myself.'

Rosalind linked her hand through the crook of her sister's arm as she opened the drawing-room door. 'How can you say that, Patsy? What have I done that is remarkable?'

'You've created a home and you have given birth to three beautiful children. I call that truly amazing.'

Rosalind laughed. 'When you are a famous operatic star I will come to the theatre and applaud you. I'll tell everyone present that you are my sister.'

'You would do that, wouldn't you?' Patricia said slowly. 'You really would.'

'Of course. Now let's go and find Bertie and Fletcher, and then you must see Walter before you go home, although I hope you'll stay for luncheon.'

'I would love to.'

* * *

Fletcher was pushing the Bath chair over the cobblestones in the bailey when Patricia and Rosalind

48

emerged into the winter sunshine. Bertie's eyes lit up and a wide grin spread across his handsome features.

'Patsy! I didn't expect to see you today.'

She rushed to meet them and gave her brother a hug. 'How are you, Bertie? I must say, you're looking well.'

'I am as fit as a fiddle, as they say. Apart from the fact that my legs don't work. The doctors were hoping that I might regain some control over them, but it doesn't seem likely now.'

Patricia shot a sideways glance at Fletcher. 'Good morning, Cora.'

Fletcher bridled. 'I prefer Fletcher, if it's all the same to you, my lady.'

'Don't be churlish, Fletcher,' Bertie said sharply. 'We've had this conversation before.'

'Sorry, guv. I forget meself occasionally.'

'No harm done, Fletcher.' Patricia managed a bright smile, although she was slightly in awe of the large woman, whose muscular arms would not have looked out of place on a bare-knuckle fighter.

'Come inside.' Rosalind adjusted the blanket that covered Bertie's legs. 'It's getting colder. Patsy's come for a prolonged visit this time, Bertie. Isn't that lovely?'

'Where's Greystone? Is he here too?'

'I came on my own,' Patricia said casually. 'Greystone has business abroad so he won't be home for a while yet.' She moved swiftly out of the way as Fletcher gave the Bath chair a mighty shove towards the open door.

'I'd better get the master indoors.'

'It's good to see you, Patsy. But what are you doing here?' Bertie clutched the arms of the chair as Fletcher picked up speed with the determination of a rider whose horse was approaching a fence.

'Patsy has something she needs to ask you and Fletcher,' Rosalind said hastily.

'With your permission, ma'am, I'll get the master settled by the fire before you question him further.' Fletcher's words were respectful, but there was no doubting her intention whether or not anyone agreed with her. She forged ahead, pushing the chair and bumping it up the steps to the front entrance.

Patricia looked on helplessly,but she knew better than to argue with Fletcher, who had obviously done this many times before. Eventually they reached the drawing room and Fletcher lifted Bertie effortlessly, placing him on the sofa. She tucked the blanket around him as tenderly as if he were a small child and then she stood back.

'Thanks, Fletcher,' Bertie said gruffly. 'Go and get a cup of tea. I'll ring if I need you.'

'I need to ask you both something first.' Patricia barred Fletcher's way. 'It concerns you as much as it does my brother.'

'I can't see what you might want with me.' Fletcher eyed her warily. 'Do you want me to brain someone? I don't do that sort of thing nowadays.'

Patricia shook her head. 'I don't know what that means, but it sounds violent. I just need your help to keep someone in control.'

'A madman, perhaps?'

'No, not a man at all.'

'Surely you can stand up to any woman you know?'

'What's this all about, Patsy?' Bertie demanded. 'Why all the mystery?'

Patricia sank down onto the nearest seat. 'Greystone will be away for a while and I am bored on my

50

own in London. I have the offer of a part in an opera. It's just a small role but I know I have a good voice, just like Mama.'

'What's stopping you then, Patsy?'

'Nothing really, it's just that the intendant sent a voice coach to further my training, and I can't handle her on my own. She has a drinking problem and she does exactly as she pleases. Heaven knows, I'm used to running two households, but I have never met any-one like Signora Gandolfi in my whole life.'

Bertie chuckled. 'I never thought I'd live long enough to hear you say something like that, Patsy. This creature must be quite extraordinary. What do you say Fletcher?'

'I say send her back to Italy where she came from.'

'I wish I could,' Patricia said, sighing. 'The truth is that if I don't study with her I won't get the part, but it's impossible to pin her down. She always has an excuse or else she's so tipsy that she has to go to bed.'

'What do you want me to do about it?' Fletcher eyed her sceptically.

'I don't know. I thought you might have some way of making people do as they are told.'

'It seems to me it's your problem, missis. I'm needed here to look after Sir Bertram.'

'What do you say, Bertie?' Rosalind asked anxiously. 'Your health and wellbeing are very important.'

He looked from one questioning face to another. 'I think I could manage for half a day at a time, pro-viding Fletcher was here to help put me to bed. It's bad enough being reduced to a helpless child without having to ask for assistance all the time, but I could cope for a few hours.'

'What do you think of that, Fletcher?' Patricia

waited while Fletcher considered the proposal. It was impossible to gauge the large woman's intentions by her expression.

'Give me an hour and I'll fix the foreign woman,' Fletcher said at length. 'She won't gainsay you when I'm done with her.'

'Are you certain you're all right with this, Bertie?' Patricia leaned towards her brother. 'I'm not so selfish that I would deprive you of your support.'

He chuckled. 'Patsy, you are so like Mama. Once you've made your mind up about something nothing will stop you, but if Fletcher is willing to help you then it's all right with me. When she comes home she can tell me all about it.'

'When do you want me, missis?' Fletcher sniffed. 'I don't do anything for nothing, so to speak.'

'You can name your price,' Patricia said eagerly. 'If you can make the signora behave as she should I will pay you what you ask.'

'Let me meet this character first.' Fletcher walked to the door. 'It all depends on how difficult she really is and how much effort I have to use.' She flexed her fingers. 'If you get my meaning.' She let herself out of the room, leaving everyone in stunned silence.

Rosalind was the first to recover. 'She didn't mean what she said, did she, Bertie?'

'You were the one who brought her here, Rosie. What do you think?'

'I think you had better watch her carefully, Patsy,' Rosalind said thoughtfully. 'Fletcher is capable of anything if roused, but she's not stupid. She won't risk her position here by going too far with the Italian woman.'

'I agree.' Bertie yawned. 'I was up early this

morning. Would you two mind if I had a nap before luncheon? All this excitement has made me sleepy.'

'Of course not.' Patricia rose hastily to her feet. 'I want to see Walter anyway, and Louise, too.'

'And I need to go to the nursery and make sure the children are behaving well.'

Bertie leaned back against the cushions. 'When is Tommy coming home again? I want Patsy to see how he's grown and what a fine boy he is now.'

'He'll be home for the Easter holidays. Let's hope you are still here, Patsy.'

'I can't make any promises, but it seems likely that I will be here for a while.'

'Alex should be home soon,' Rosalind said tentatively. 'You won't pick a fight with him, will you, Patsy?'

'Of course not. Whatever happened between us in the past is over and done with. He's made you happy and that's all that matters to me, Rosie.'

★ ★ ★

Mealtimes at home had always proved to be a battle for attention when Patricia was growing up. As the youngest of four siblings she had tried to overcome this by talking over the others and speaking out whether she knew what she was talking about or not. This had proved to be very risky behaviour and as a young girl she had often been sent away from the table to think about her misdeeds. Today, however, she found herself the centre of attention with everyone hanging on her every word. It was a unique and pleasurable experience. Even Hester, usually her strictest critic, made no adverse comments and appeared to listen intently when Patricia talked about her life in political circles. Walter's wife, Louise, whom Patricia had once pitied as being the vicar's plain spinster daughter, had blossomed since her marriage, and Walter did not hide the fact that he adored her. They were expecting their first child later in the year and Walter seemed to be taking the prospect of fatherhood very seriously. Patricia had felt inclined to tease him, but even she could see that his wife and unborn child were very important to him, and it would be unkind to make fun of him now. She managed to hold her tongue and turned the subject to Signora Gandolfi, mimicking the temperamental former opera star, which made everyone laugh.

After one such impersonation Bertie wiped his eyes on his table napkin. 'Perhaps you ought to consider appearing in comic opera, Patsy.'

'I agree,' Louise said, laughing. 'You've brightened our day, Patricia. I would love to see you on the stage.'

'Maybe you and your mama will appear in the same production one day,' Alexander said, chuckling. 'I would definitely pay to see that performance.'

Rosalind shook her head. 'You don't like opera, Alex.'

'I'd make an exception, should the occasion arise.' Alexander laid his hand on his wife's as it rested on the table top and they exchanged fond smiles.

'Two of them in the family would be too much to bear.' Hester rose from her seat. 'But you have talent, Patricia. Anyway, if you'll excuse me, I have lists to write and I need to speak to Mrs Jackson about menus for the coming week. No doubt I'll see you again soon, Patricia.'

'Of course. I intend to make the most of the time with my family.' Patricia smiled sweetly, but to her surprise she realised she meant what she said, and it was with great reluctance that she left Rockwood Castle an hour later, accompanied by Fletcher.

* * *

For the first time since she married Sir Michael, Patricia realised that she found Greystone Park too large and too empty to be comfortable. Perhaps it was the contrast between her old home, which was filled with love and laughter, and the silent but elegant, luxurious and rather sterile atmosphere of Greystone Park. She was beginning to understand why Sylvia was so miserable living in isolation above stairs, and it was not simply due to the increasing bouts of ill health that had beset her recently. She might be waited upon hand and foot, but despite having Martha Collins and Miss Moon living with her, Sylvia was lacking in companionship. Patricia knew that she must miss Christina, in spite of their sisterly squabbles, but Sylvia barely mentioned her sister.

When Patricia arrived home with Fletcher she found Sylvia arranging hothouse flowers in the entrance hall.

'What is she doing here, Patsy?' Sylvia demanded, glaring at Fletcher.

'Fletcher has come to do me a favour, Sylvia, so mind your manners.' Patricia had spoken more sharply than she intended and she tempered her words with a smile. 'Fletcher is going to help with the Italian problem. Where is she?'

'She's in the drawing room, singing her head off. I had to come down here to get away from her. Either she goes or I do, Patsy.'

'We must allow Fletcher to do what she thinks is

best.' Patricia turned to Fletcher, who was gazing around the large, marble-tiled entrance hall in apparent awe.

'How did they get them plaster angels on the ceiling?' Fletcher demanded, frowning. 'They must be thirty foot off the ground and that's only a guess. I never seen nothing like it in me life.'

'I haven't given it much thought,' Patricia said tactfully. 'Would you like to meet the signora now? The sooner you can deal with the problem the sooner we can get you home to look after my brother.'

'Lead on, although I think I could follow that sound without a guide.'

'I'd better take you,' Patricia said hastily. 'I'll introduce you to the signora and the rest is up to you.'

'She's been at the sherry wine again,' Sylvia said gloomily. 'I had to send Johnson to the cellar to fetch more bottles. I do wish you'd brought Foster back from London with you. It's so difficult living here without a butler.'

Fletcher curled her lip and seemed about to make a remark but Patricia forestalled her. 'If I'm to extend my stay here I'll send for Foster, but at the moment it's only going to be for a month at the most. Come with me, Fletcher. Let's see what you can do with our drunken opera star.' Patricia led the way up the wide, curving staircase to the first landing. The drawing room overlooked the deer park at the back of the building and was lit by four tall windows that reached from just below the ceiling to the floor. Standing the middle of the room with a glass in one hand and a decanter in the other, Signora Gandolfi was in the middle of an aria and she continued singing, even when Patricia and Fletcher entered the room.

Patricia held up her hand. 'Signora Gandolfi. Please stop for a moment.'

The signora hit a high note and held it with her whole body shaking and the cut-glass chandeliers tinkling wildly.

Fletcher strode up to her and snatched the decanter and the glass. 'That's enough of that, lady.' Signora Gandolfi wavered on the high note and her voice faded away. She stood, staring open-mouthed at Fletcher.

'This is Fletcher, Signora,' Patricia said firmly. 'She has come to give you some much-needed advice.'

'I've never been so insulted,' Signora Gandolfi gasped, clutching her hands to her bosom. 'That person attacked me.'

'If you think that's violence you want to see what I can do if I puts me mind to it.' Fletcher placed the decanter and glass on the nearest side table. 'Now you can stand or you can sit, but either way you are going to listen to me, lady. Do you understand?'

Signora Gandolfi's plump cheeks paled and she sank down on the sofa. 'Do you know who I am, you peasant?'

'Yes, I know very well who you are, lady. You can drop the foreign accent for a start.'

'What are you saying, Fletcher?' Patricia demanded nervously. 'I told you that this is Signora Gandolfi.'

'She's no signora and she ain't no Gandolfi. This here person is Maud Grubb from Plaistow, although she's taken on so many false identities that she probably don't remember her real name.'

Patricia sat down suddenly. 'You must be mistaken, Fletcher.'

'Not me. She used to sing in the Grecian Saloon at the back of the Eagle pub in the City Road. Then she got in with an Italian magsman who I suspect taught her everything she knows.'

'But she is well known to the intendant at the Royal Opera House — it can't be the same woman.'

'Oy! Don't I have a say in this?' Signora Gandolfi demanded angrily. 'That person is making it up. I am a world-famous operatic star.'

Fletcher advanced on her, hands fisted. 'Are you calling me a liar, Maudie?'

'You are a liar, Cora Fletcher. You are the criminal, not I.'

Fletcher came to a halt, pointing gleefully at the signora. 'See! She knows me name. How would she know that if she weren't as low as what I am? We was up before the beak together a couple of years ago. I got time but she got let off — I dunno why, the old cow.'

Patricia shook her head. 'All right, Fletcher. Thank you, but this leaves me with an even bigger problem. You, Signora Gandolfi or Maud Grubb, whatever your real name is, are too fond of drink to be any real use to me. On the other hand I believe you are a good singer and probably a reasonable coach, providing you stay sober.'

Maud cowered, averting her gaze. 'I will, my lady. I promise to give up the demon drink while I'm here with you.'

'Better lock up the silver if she stays, missis,' Fletcher said gloomily. 'But if I hear that you've broken your promise, Maudie, I won't be best pleased. I think you know what that means.'

'You don't have to worry about that, Cora. I know when I'm beaten.'

Patricia stood up, frowning. 'I hope you do, Maud.

From now on you can be yourself and we will have a lesson every morning after breakfast, but if you so much as take a nip of sherry wine that's the end of our arrangement and you'll return to London on the next train.'

'I understand, my lady.' Maud raised her head, clasping her hands tightly in front of her.

'Very well. You have a second chance, but there won't be a third. Now sober up, and we'll speak later.'

'Just keep an eye on her, missis,' Fletcher said in a low voice as Patricia ushered her out of the room. 'She's a drunkard and light fingered. She's likely to forget everything if she drinks too much, but if she gets out of hand just send for me.' Fletcher cracked her knuckles. 'I'll deal with her.'

'I most certainly will.' Patricia took a full purse from her pocket and offered it to Fletcher. 'Accept this with my thanks.'

'No, missis. I done nothing other than recognise another hustler. I'm reformed but she ain't, so don't trust her too far. Having said that, she's got a voice like a nightingale when she's singing. You could do worse for a teacher.'

'Thank you again, Fletcher. But I said I'd pay you.'

'I don't need it. I got my job looking after the master and a better home than I could ever have hoped for. I don't need money, but ta for the offer.' Fletcher saluted and strode off towards the staircase, looping her long skirt over her arm to expose skinny legs ending in men's heavy-duty boots.

Patricia followed her more slowly, wondering whether to tell Sylvia the truth. They might laugh about all this one day, but the road to success on the stage was proving to be a rocky one.

A routine developed during the next two weeks. Patricia practised every morning with Maud there to help her improve her technique. Sometimes they ate luncheon together and at other times Patricia drove herself to Rockwood Castle. She left the pony and trap in the care of Hudson, who was now head groom, Gurney having given up the hard physical work in the stables to become the coachman. During these visits Patricia spent much of her time with Bertie, and her admiration for her older brother was boundless. His bravery in living with such a terrible disability was impressive and his sense of humour was undimmed by suffering. He might have displayed bravery on the battlefield, but it took even more courage to face living with the loss of his independence.

Patricia reacquainted herself with Walter, who had always been the introvert, and she found a friend in Louise. Quite often she took Sylvia with her on these visits and Sylvia seemed to enjoy being with the family. She even laughed at Bertie's jokes and chatted amicably with Rosalind. If Sylvia went missing she was always to be found in the nursery, entertaining Dolly and Rory, or cuddling baby Phoebe. Maud was never included in these outings, but she seemed content to stay behind at Greystone Park and if she managed to snatch a glass or two of sherry, she kept her drinking under control and was always on time for lessons.

On a chilly day at the beginning of March with wild winds blowing off the sea and the bare branches of the trees bent almost double, the trap swayed from side to side on the return journey. Patricia was afraid they might overturn, but the sturdy, sure-footed pony kept going and soon they were in the shelter of the high brick wall that surrounded Greystone Park. Patricia drew the trap to a halt outside the stables and was surprised to see a carriage drive past them. It appeared to be empty and it looked like one of the carriages that plied their trade outside the railway station in Exeter. Her heart leaped, leaving her breathless. Had Greystone returned sooner than expected? She had not realised how much she missed him until this moment. She leaned over to speak to the head groom as he hurried out to take the horse's bridle.

'Jones, did you see who was in that carriage? Was it Sir Michael?'

5

'I'm sorry, my lady.' Jones held out is hand to help her alight outside the colonnaded portico of the elegant Georgian house. 'I'm afraid I didn't see who was in the carriage.'

Patricia handed him the reins. 'It seems we have a mystery visitor.' She spoke lightly but her heart was racing as she walked purposefully to the front entrance. The door was open and Johnson, the head footman, seemed to be having difficulty in persuading the well-dressed gentleman to leave.

Patricia did not need him to turn round. She would recognise the tall, elegant figure of Lord Eldon anywhere. She quickened her pace. 'Eldon, what are you doing here?'

'You see, my man, as I said, I am a friend of the family.' Eldon turned to Patricia with a disarming smile. 'I missed your company, my dear Lady Greystone, but your man seems to think I am an interloper.'

'You are an interloper, Eldon. You have no business here, but I suppose you had better come in.' Patricia nodded to Johnson. 'It's all right, I know this gentleman.' She handed the footman her cape and gloves. 'Is Miss Sylvia at home?'

'Yes, my lady. I believe she's in the orangery.'

'Thank you, Johnson. We'll have tea and cake, or would you like something stronger, Eldon?'

'I'm not averse to a cup of tea and a slice of seed cake, my dear. I can be quite genteel when the situation arises.'

'Tea and cake in the orangery then, please, Johnson.' Patricia walked on ahead without waiting to see if Eldon was following. She led the way to the rear of the building where a glass conservatory ran almost the whole length of the mansion. Sylvia was seated on a chaise longue between two orange trees and a host of smaller potted exotics and ferns. She looked pale, and the cough that had been troubling her for some time seemed to drain all her energy. However, on seeing Eldon she sat up, swinging her feet to the marble-tiled floor.

'Patricia, you startled me.'

'I'm sorry, Sylvie. We have a visitor. I wanted to introduce you to Lord Eldon. I don't think you've met previously. Eldon, may I present my stepdaughter, Sylvia Greystone?'

Sylvia's hand flew automatically to smooth her hair back from her forehead. 'How do you do, my lord?'

Eldon approached the chaise longue, stopped and bowed from the waist. 'How do you do, Miss Greystone? It's a pleasure to meet you.'

'If you've come to see my father I'm afraid he is not here,' Sylvia said pointedly.

'Lord Eldon called to make sure that we are coping well without your papa.' Patricia shot a sideways glance at Eldon. 'Your father asked him to keep an eye on us, Sylvie, although I did tell Lord Eldon that we are quite capable of looking after ourselves.'

'It's just a courtesy call, Miss Greystone,' Eldon said with a disarming smile. 'I've always wanted an excuse to visit this beautiful house. I believe you have one of the finest deer parks in the country.'

Sylvia's cheeks flushed prettily. 'Yes, indeed, my lord. We are very proud of our estate, although it isn't at its best at this time of the year.'

'Nevertheless I was very impressed with what I saw from the carriage window, Miss Greystone. I would love to see more.'

'I told Johnson to have tea and cake brought here, Sylvie,' Patricia said conversationally. 'Where are you staying, Eldon? The Black Dog in the village takes in travellers.'

'I stopped there on my way but they are fully booked. I will return to London this evening.'

'You must stay here, must he not, Patsy?' Sylvia's cheeks reddened and her eyes sparkled as she turned to her stepmother. 'Papa would have wanted that, surely?'

'Of course,' Patricia said reluctantly. 'We have plenty of rooms. I'll have one made ready for you, Eldon.'

'Thank you, Patricia,' Eldon said smugly. 'I left my portmanteau with your footman.'

'You obviously came prepared to stay.' Patricia resigned herself to the inevitable. Eldon could be very entertaining and his presence might be just the tonic that Sylvia needed, although Patricia would have preferred him to remain in London.

'Greystone Park is famous for its hospitality.' Sylvia jumped to her feet. 'Shall I ring for a servant to take Lord Eldon's luggage to his room, Patsy?'

'I think I hear the sound of cups rattling on their saucers. There's no need to do anything, Sylvie. I'll instruct Ivy to do what is required.'

Sylvia sank back onto the chaise longue. 'Yes, of course. I keep forgetting that you are mistress here now, Patsy. I've grown used to issuing orders in your absence.'

Patricia was saved from answering by the appearance of Ivy with a tray of tea and cake. Patricia waited until the tray was placed on a small wicker table. 'Lord Eldon will be staying for a day or two, Ivy. I think the Magenta Room will suit him best. Please send Johnson up with Lord Eldon's portmanteau and tell Cook there will be a fourth person at dinner tonight.'

Ivy bobbed a curtsey, giving Eldon a sideways glance as she went on her way.

Eldon took a seat in a rattan chair. 'A fourth for dinner? Has Greystone returned unexpectedly?'

'No, he hasn't, Eldon. The fourth person is my voice coach. If you remember, it was a condition for my joining the operatic company that I underwent private lessons from an experienced teacher.' Patricia chose her words carefully. She had not told Sylvia of the signora's deception and she had decided to go along with the fiction that Maud Grubb was a retired opera singer.

'Do I know this person?' Eldon accepted the cup of tea that Patricia handed him.

'Not unless you've had singing lessons,' Patricia said sharply.

'Isn't it rather odd to invite such a person to dine at the family table?' Eldon raised an eyebrow.

'Signora Gandolfi knows my mama,' Patricia said defensively. 'We have treated her like any guest to Greystone Park and we work every morning. Perhaps Sylvia would like to show you round the estate tomorrow.'

'I would love to,' Sylvia said eagerly.

'Then I look forward to it.' Eldon sipped his tea. 'How do you entertain yourself in the afternoons,

65

Patricia? I imagine life is very quiet in the country.'

'I think you will find it very boring.' Patricia cut a slice of cake and laid it on a plate. 'You said you liked cake. I don't think I've ever seen you eat anything other than oysters and caviar.'

He held out his hand to take the plate. 'I am a man of simple tastes beneath the veneer of sophistication. Tea and cake are my favourites.'

'You are such a liar, Eldon.' Patricia laughed. 'I would lay bets that you haven't eaten cake since you were in the nursery, and tea is the last beverage you would choose.'

Sylvia replaced her teacup and saucer on the tray. 'I think you are being very unfair to Lord Eldon, Patsy.'

'You don't know this man, Sylvie. On further acquaintance you will begin to see through him.' Patricia rose to her feet. 'I must leave you both to entertain each other. Eldon, I trust you not to shock my stepdaughter with your risqué stories.'

'Stop patronising me, Patricia,' Sylvia said crossly. 'You are only a few months my senior. You might have married my father but that doesn't give you the right to patronise me.'

'Sylvia and I will deal very well together, Patricia.' Eldon put his plate down with the cake untouched. 'She will show me the delights of Greystone Park while you do whatever it is that cannot wait.'

Patricia knew that he was laughing at her but did not respond. She left the orangery and went to her own room where she could be certain of remaining undisturbed.

★ ★ ★

Patricia managed to avoid Eldon until that evening when she found Sylvia entertaining him in the drawing room before dinner. Eldon was sipping sherry as if he enjoyed it, which made Patricia smile, as his preferred drink was brandy. However, she did not comment and she poured a glass for herself.

'I'm sorry to have neglected you, Eldon, but I had a letter to finish.'

'I thought you didn't know where your husband had been sent, my dear?'

'I didn't say I was writing to Greystone. I do have other people with whom I correspond.'

Sylvia put her glass down on a side table. 'Are you writing to Aurelia? I seem to have lost touch with her since she married that common fellow.'

'I was writing to Nancy,' Patricia said quickly. 'The poor child must be quite homesick in boarding school.'

'I didn't know you were fond of Nancy?' Sylvia eyed her suspiciously.

'Does it matter to whom I was writing? Why are you asking all these questions?'

'I'm sorry,' Sylvia said hastily. 'I've never known you to be a letter writer in the past.'

'Well, sometimes I do sit down and correspond with friends or family. Anyway, how have you two spent your afternoon?'

'We went for a lovely long walk,' Sylvia said dreamily. 'The sun came out and I was able to show Lord Eldon around the walled garden and the croquet lawn where you and I used to play with Christina. That seems so long ago now.'

'It was very stimulating.' Eldon drained his drink, holding the glass up to the light as if admiring the cut crystal.

67

'Would you like another sherry, Lord Eldon?' Sylvia asked eagerly.

'Perhaps his lordship would like something stronger? A cognac, perhaps?' Patricia met his amused gaze with an innocent smile.

'Sherry would be delightful, Miss Sylvia.' Eldon handed the glass to her with a charming smile.

Sylvia snatched it from him as if afraid that Patricia might rob her of her chance to do something for their handsome guest. Eldon had dressed in style in readiness for dinner, and Patricia had to bite her lip to prevent herself from remarking on his fore- thought in bringing his evening clothes to the country when he intended to stay at the village inn. However, she thought better of it. There was no point in entering a verbal sparring match with Eldon, even though she would be certain to win. He was obviously out to charm Sylvia, but she would soon put a stop to that. If Eldon wanted to marry an heiress he had better look elsewhere. She would not want her childhood friend to marry a rake who would make her life a misery. It was obvious that Sylvia had already fallen prey to his charms, which made things rather complicated.

It was a relief when Ivy entered the room to announce that dinner was served. Eldon proffered his arm to Patricia, and she allowed him to lead her to the dining room even though it seemed to upset Sylvia. It was, Patricia thought grimly, time to put Eldon in the picture. Sylvia would inherit a reasonable sum of money in the event of her father's death, but she was not the heiress he needed to boost his dwindling income.

With all this going on, Patricia had completely forgotten about the signora and it was a surprise to find her already seated at the dining table.

'Eldon, may I introduce Signora Gandolfi —'
Patricia began formally, but a roar of laughter from
Eldon silenced her.

'Maudie Grubb. I don't believe it. What are you
doing here?'

Maud leaped to her feet, clutching her hands to her
bosom. 'Larkin Eldon!'

Patricia looked from one to the other. 'You know
each other?'

'Who is Maudie Grubb?' Sylvia demanded in a
dazed voice.

Eldon took a seat beside Maud. 'Maudie and I are
old friends. She used to sing in the Grecian Saloon
at the back of the Eagle pub. When I was in my salad
days my friends and I used to go east to drink in the
local public houses. That's how I met Maudie, who
used to entertain us royally.'

Sylvia sank down on her seat. 'I'm confused, Patsy.
What is going on?'

'Nothing for you to worry about, Sylvia.' Patricia
made an effort to sound calm. 'It's just a coincidence.
Stage people get around, you know. It doesn't make
any difference to the fact that Maud — or the signora,
as we've come to know her — is an excellent voice
coach.'

'I don't think Papa would approve of all this,' Sylvia
said primly. 'I wish that Christina was still living at
home. She would know what to do.'

'Be quiet, you silly girl,' Maud said angrily. 'I've had
to put up with your miserable countenance ever since
I arrived here, *and* I've been bullied by that dreadful creature who looks like a man in skirts. I wish I'd
stayed in the East End where at least you know who's
who and what to expect.'

Eldon snatched a bottle of wine from the sideboard and filled Maud's glass. 'Now, now, Maudie. No need to get in a state, old girl. Drink this and enjoy your meal. I have a feeling it's going to be your last one in this house.'

'I don't know why you would assume that, Eldon,' Patricia said coldly. 'Maud and I have come to an arrangement and it precludes her drinking more than one glass of claret at dinner. She can stay as long as she remains sober. Otherwise I will have to summon Fletcher to convince her of the error of her ways. I cannot afford to miss my daily lessons.'

Eldon gave her a searching look. 'You really are determined to make a success of your new career, aren't you, Patricia?'

'Yes, Eldon. I am, and nothing is going to get in my way.'

'What will you do when your husband returns and you find he objects to his wife appearing on stage?'

'Greystone and I trust each other. You wouldn't understand.'

'You mean that Papa allows you to do as you please,' Sylvia said bitterly. 'You were always spoilt, Patricia. Everyone at Rockwood went out of their way to please you.'

'I could say the same of you, Sylvia.' Patricia took her seat at the head of the table. 'But that's enough of family squabbles. Eldon, why don't you regale us with some of your less risqué stories? I'm sure we could do with a little light entertainment.'

'I could tell you some tales about his exploits, my lady.' Maud chuckled and raised her glass to Eldon. 'Him and his rich friends used to carouse and cause havoc in the City Road. They was turned out of the

Eagle in the end and banned from most of the local pubs.'

'Thank you, Maud,' Eldon said with a wry grimace. 'I don't think the ladies want to hear about my youthful misdeeds.'

Patricia smiled sweetly. 'But we do, Eldon. Please go on, Maud. This is going to be very amusing. Tell us the worst.'

Needless to say, Maud drank far more than one glass of claret. Eldon kept topping up her drink.

Patricia knew that it amused him to see Maud drunk and incapable, but the signora was a seasoned toper and the more she drank the more outrageous her stories became.

Sylvia's eyes widened and her cheeks went from a sickly pallor to blush red as she listened to Eldon's exploits, as told by a very intoxicated Maud. At one point Patricia feared that her naïve stepdaughter was going to faint away from shock, but somehow Sylvia managed to listen, even though she was clearly appalled by Maud's revelations. However, she managed to last until the end of the meal before claiming to be exhausted and in need of a good night's rest. By this time Maud had fallen asleep and was in danger of falling off her chair.

Patricia rang the bell and Ivy appeared so quickly that she might have been standing outside the door.

'The signora is indisposed,' Patricia said firmly. 'Send for Johnson. He will have to carry her to her room. You had better accompany them to put the signora to bed, Ivy. You may clear the table later.'

'Yes, my lady.' Ivy hurried from the room.

Patricia pushed back her chair and stood up. 'I hope you're pleased with yourself, Eldon. I won't get

71

any sense out of Maud tomorrow.'

'I was hoping to have a whole day with you, my dear.' Eldon rose to his feet. 'I doubt if Sylvia will want anything to do with me after this evening's revelations.'

'You only have yourself to blame for that. You must have known that Maud would drink herself stupid.'

'I thought it would be amusing, but it backfired on me.' Eldon moved swiftly to hold the door open. 'I suppose you are shocked, too.'

'I'd heard most of those tales before,' Patricia said casually. 'Your reputation goes before you, Eldon.'

He followed her from the room. 'You never fail to surprise me, Patricia. How may I entertain you now? A game of backgammon or loo, perhaps?'

She shot him a sideways glance. 'It's a fine starlit night. I really fancy a walk in the grounds.'

'My dear, it's freezing. I could see frost on the ground when I looked out of my bedroom window.'

'All the better. If you don't want to brave the chill I'll go on my own.'

'I'll come with you, of course, but do you often go out in the dark unaccompanied?'

'Not in London, but I used to creep out at night when I was young and lived at Rockwood. Aurelia and I went searching for ghosts one night when she was staying with us.'

'Did you meet any?'

Patricia laughed. 'I don't think so. But on another occasion we did hear strange noises deep down in the cellars.' She beckoned to a small maidservant who was scurrying towards the dining room. 'Before you clear the table I want you to find my maid. Tell Betsey to fetch my fur-lined cloak and gloves.'

72

'Yes, my lady.' The maid scuttled off in the direction from which she had just come.

'You really do intend to go out for a walk, don't you?' Eldon stared at her with a mixture of amusement and astonishment in his dark eyes.

'I never say things I don't mean. You ought to know that by now. I suggest you fetch your overcoat, unless you want to freeze.'

★ ★ ★

Muffled in fur, with the hood protecting her from the sharp sea breeze, Patricia led Eldon into the deer park with her gloved hand tucked in the crook of his arm. A full moon lit their way, accompanied by dazzling starlight, which reflected off the frosty spikes of grass and the silvery surface of the lake. Patricia inhaled the cold air with eyes closed, filling her lungs with ice. She exhaled and opened her eyes. 'Isn't this beautiful? Doesn't it make you feel more alive, Eldon?'

'I suppose it does. I've never stopped to take in the beauties of nature or the wonders of the universe. My night revels have always been conducted in public houses or gaming clubs.'

'So I've heard. You don't know what you've been missing.'

He smiled down at her. 'I'm beginning to think you're right. You look like a fairy-tale princess in the moonlight.'

'Now that's just flattery. But there is a sense of unreality that you get at this time of night when everyone else is tucked up in bed or huddled round a log fire. It's like living in a dream where you are the only person on earth.'

Eldon chuckled. 'Do I have a place in this dream?'

'You're here, but not here.' Patricia laid her hand over her heart. 'I know you don't have romantic thoughts about me, Eldon, but I want you to know that I value you as a friend, nothing more.'

'You do not know what I think, my dear. If you did, it might surprise you.'

'Or shock me. I enjoy your company, but if you are to remain here for a while, I need you to be gentle with Sylvia. She is obviously smitten by your dubious charms, and I don't want to see her hurt.'

'Has it occurred to you that I might find her innocence charming?'

'It's obvious that you do, but I know you well enough to realise that it amuses and flatters you.' Patricia came to a halt at the edge of the lake. 'Promise me you won't lead her on.'

'Is that the whole reason for this moonlit walk?'

'No, not really. Like you I am very selfish. I do what I want, when I want. But I am not hard-hearted, and I'm fond of Sylvie. We were childhood friends and she deserves better than you.'

'One thing I've always admired about you is your honesty, Patricia. You haven't fallen into the trap that people in political circles tumble into, of saying one thing and meaning another.'

'I should hope not.'

He patted her hand as it rested on the thick sleeve of his overcoat. 'Be assured that I will handle Sylvia with care, but now I think it's time for us to return to the warmth. Even in this flattering light I can see that the tip of your pretty nose is very pink.'

'You say the most unflattering things but manage to make it sound like a compliment,' Patricia said, laughing. 'I agree. I can't feel my toes or the tips of my fingers. I suggest we go indoors and enjoy a hot cup of coffee and a glass of cognac. Greystone keeps a good cellar.'

★ ★ ★

Next morning at breakfast it was obvious that Maud was not feeling very well. Dark circles beneath her eyes and a yellow pallor to her skin made it clear that she was suffering the after effects of too much wine the previous evening.

'Why don't you go back to bed, Signora?' Patricia said sharply. 'I know that Eldon plied you with claret, but you could have refused to drink it.'

Maud held her hand to her head. 'I will go and lie down, if you don't mind.'

'Not at all. You are no use to me in that state.'

'I think my time here is over anyway,' Maud said quietly. 'I don't think I can teach you anything more.'

'Really?' Patricia stared at her in surprise. 'I thought I had to have lessons for the whole month.'

'As I said, there's very little I can teach you now. You need to practise every day as I've shown you, and don't allow Eldon to throw you off course. That man is a devil.'

'I'll allow that he enjoys making mischief of sorts, but a devil he is not.'

'Then you don't know him as I do. Take advice from an older woman, dearie. Send him packing.'

'You are obviously out of sorts. We'll talk about this later.'

'It won't alter my mind, my lady. I'd leave today

if I didn't feel like death, but I will return to London tomorrow.' Maud rose unsteadily to her feet and tottered from the dining room, passing Eldon in the doorway. She shot him a malevolent glance before slamming the door behind her.

'I take it that Maudie is feeling a little under the weather,' Eldon said, chuckling.

'She is, and it's all your fault. In fact she's leaving for London tomorrow because she doesn't want to stay here with you.'

Eldon went to the sideboard and helped himself to bacon, fried eggs and three sausages. 'She must think that you're good enough to sing for Garson Thorne. I know Maudie and her pride wouldn't allow her to walk out if it reflected badly on her.'

'She seems to think that you are the devil incarnate.'

'I'm flattered. However, you know that's not true.'

Patricia sipped her coffee. 'Do I? Why did you come here in the first place, Eldon? Don't say it was for my sake because I won't believe you.'

'A temporary lack of funds made it necessary for me to leave my creditors back in London, but don't worry, my annual allowance should be in the bank within days, and then it's safe for me to return to my rooms in Albemarle Street.'

'I might have guessed that it was necessity that drove you here, Eldon. I suggest you pack your bag and leave tomorrow with Maud.'

'But I'm enjoying my stay in the country, my love. I value your company, you know that.'

'I think you do, but I don't like being taken advantage of.'

'As if I would do such a thing. Don't forget that

76

Greystone asked me to keep an eye on you in his absence.'

'My husband obviously has more faith in you than I do. Anyway, sit down and eat your food before it gets cold. We'll discuss this later.'

Eldon took his seat and began to eat. Patricia finished her coffee in silence, leaving her slice of toast uneaten on her plate. She found it hard to believe that her course of tuition was at an end, and she blamed Eldon for scaring off Maud. For all her faults she was an excellent voice coach.

'Why are you frowning, Patricia?' Eldon asked abruptly. 'If it's because I allowed Maudie to drink too much I'll apologise to you and to her, if it makes you happy.'

'I think it would take more than an apology,' Patricia said ruefully. 'Maud wishes to return to London and my lessons are at an end. I don't know where that leaves me with regard to the part in Garson's next production.'

'Perhaps Greystone will be home sooner than either of you anticipated. Surely you wouldn't want to be involved with the opera company if your husband returned?'

'I don't know, and that's the truth. I wanted to prove myself, Eldon. I don't suppose you can understand that. I wanted to be good at something in my own right.'

A smile lit his grey eyes and his lips curved into a sympathetic smile. 'You are, Patricia. You bring beauty and light into people's lives. Isn't that enough for you?'

'Now you are simply flattering me, and it won't work. I know how people think of me, and to others

77

I'm shallow, and I married Greystone for money and position.'

'Isn't that the basis of most marriages, my dear?'

'There you are: you are just as cynical as the rest of the world.'

'But you told me that you didn't marry for love.'

'I didn't, of course, but I care for Greystone. I like and respect him, and he's good company, when he has time for me.'

'Ah, that's the nub, isn't it? You feel neglected. Allow me to give you all the attention you need.' Eldon bit into a slice of sausage, exposing a set of even, white teeth.

'You are the big bad wolf,' Patricia said, laughing. 'But you are amusing.' She looked up at the sound of a knock on the door. 'Come in.'

Johnson entered carrying a salver, which he presented to Patricia. 'A messenger brought this, my lady. He didn't wait for an answer.'

'It looks official,' Patricia said worriedly. Her hand shook as she broke the seal and unfolded the letter, which was written on parchment with the House of Commons heading.

'You've gone very pale, Patricia.' Eldon dropped his knife and fork on his plate. 'For God's sake, what does it say?'

6

Patricia passed the document to him. 'There must be a mistake. It can't be true.'

Eldon scanned the lines of copper plate writing, his brow creased in a frown. 'My dear girl, I am so sorry.'

'Greystone can't be dead. He was on a diplomatic mission. Surely he wouldn't have been travelling by train? I mean, he's an important man. They would have sent him in a private carriage.'

'It says clearly that he was involved in a fatal railway accident in France. I am genuinely sorry, my dear. What can I do to help, Patricia? Just say and I'll do anything.'

She shook her head. 'No, it must be an error. Greystone was very much alive when he left. He can't have died in a stupid accident.'

The door burst open and Sylvia rushed into the room. 'Johnson says there was an urgent letter sent to you, Patsy. I can tell by your face that it's bad news.'

Patricia shook her head. 'No, it's not real, Sylvie. This letter is a hoax, or else it's a terrible mistake.' Eldon rose to his feet and guided Sylvia to the nearest chair. 'Sit down, Sylvia. I'm afraid, you're right. Patricia has received a very distressing communication.'

'Is it Papa? What's happened? You have to tell me.'

'He's dead,' Patricia said with a break in her voice. 'That's what the letter says. But I don't believe it. This happened before, only it was Papa who died abroad. It can't be happening again.'

'But how? When? I don't understand.' Sylvia turned

to Eldon, her face ashen and her eyes brimming with tears.

Eldon showed her the letter. 'This is all we know, Sylvia. I am truly sorry.'

Sylvia tossed the document onto the floor. 'I won't believe it. Not my papa. I want Chrissie. She will sort this out. Send for my sister, please, Patsy.'

'Of course we will,' Patricia said dazedly. 'Like you, Sylvie, I can't accept the fact that Greystone is never coming home. It's such a terrible shock.'

Eldon laid his hand on Patricia's shoulder. 'Perhaps we should return to London. Maybe the Home Office could give us more details. I'm sure there must have been some sort of investigation.'

'Yes, you're right. We'll travel to London today.' Patricia rose slowly to her feet, taking a deep breath. 'I'll ring for Betsey to pack my things and I'll send Johnson to Cottingham Manor to fetch Christina. Miss Martha and Miss Moon will be home soon. You won't be left here on your own, Sylvie.'

'You'll abandon me to the mercies of the singing creature, will you?'

'No, of course not. The signora is also leaving.' Patricia walked to the mantelshelf and tugged at the bell pull. 'Will you go to the stables, Eldon? Tell Jones to have the carriage ready to take us to the railway station in Exeter.'

Eldon nodded. 'Yes, of course. We'll leave as soon as you are ready.'

★ ★ ★

After a tedious journey Patricia entered her elegant London home with a feeling of relief. She had parted with Maud at the railway station and she had said goodbye to Eldon on the doorstep. Perhaps she should have invited him in, but she was exhausted both mentally and physically. The shock of learning of her husband's death by letter had started to wear off and was replaced by a nagging feeling of unreality. Greystone had managed everything during their four years of marriage. It was only now that Patricia realised that she knew nothing about their finances or the running of two large establishments. She had made a pretence of examining the quarterly accounts, but she relied on two very competent housekeepers to do the necessary work.

Foster and all the London servants had read the sad news of their master's death in *The Times*, and the clocks had been stopped, the mirrors covered up and the blinds lowered. Patricia immediately ordered the blinds to be lifted. It was bad enough suffering a loss, without living in a cave of semi-darkness. She thanked Foster for his sympathy and although she hated having to show her ignorance, she asked him if he knew the name of Sir Michael's solicitor. Foster, who seemed to know everything, told her that it was Gilbert Selly, who had chambers in Lincoln's Inn. Patricia sent one of the lower footmen with an urgent request for Mr Selly to call on her next day.

In the meantime she found a rapidly increasing pile of condolence letters, which she took to Greystone's study and placed on his desk. She had barely ventured into this room while her husband was alive, and now she could smell his favourite cologne and she could feel his presence as strongly as if he were in his usual seat. Like Greystone himself, the desk was neatly organised, with nothing out of place. The books on the floor-to-ceiling shelves were set out according to size, and no doubt in alphabetical order. The oil paintings that hung on the oak-panelled walls were landscapes in muted colours, with a black and white etching of Greystone Park itself in pride of place. The only personal item on view was a gold half-hunter watch, which rested in a stand shaped like a clock tower. Patricia had seen Greystone wear the watch when they were out and about, and it seemed strange that he had not taken it with him on his travels. She picked up the half-hunter and clasped it in her hand. The engraved gold warmed instantly to her body temperature and she held the watch to her cheek. She would miss Greystone more than she had thought possible.

She placed the watch in her skirt pocket and let herself out of the study, closing the door behind her. She would face the condolence letters tomorrow, but now she needed to sit and think quietly. She walked slowly upstairs to the drawing room on the first floor and went to sit by the fire, taking the watch from her pocket and holding her hand. Somehow it made her feel closer to the man she had married with so little thought to the future of their relationship. All she knew was that she would miss him, and the prospect of dealing with everything on her own was daunting. She had resigned herself to a lonely supper seated at the vast dining table in the room where they had entertained the prime minister and other dignitaries, when Foster announced Lord Eldon.

'Show him in, Foster, but if anyone else calls I am not receiving visitors.'

'Of course, my lady.' Foster bowed out of the room. Moments later the door opened to admit Eldon. 'I know you wanted to be left in peace, Patricia, but I thought it would be a mistake for you to be all alone in this big house on your first evening at home.'

She nodded. 'Thank you, Eldon. I was feeling a little overwhelmed.'

He strolled over to the fireplace to warm his hands in front of the blaze. 'I see you've found Greystone's pocket watch. It's a fine example. I've often admired it.'

'He left it in his study. I can't imagine why he didn't take it with him.'

'Who knows . . .'

Patricia eyed him curiously. He looked extremely dapper in his evening suit. Allowing for the fact that he was something of a peacock, it was hardly the sort of outfit anyone would choose for a quiet evening by the fire. 'Where are you going? I don't want to hold you up.'

He smiled. 'I am going to take you out to dinner. I've booked a table at Rules. We'll go there early. The *maître d'hôtel* knows me, so we'll have a quiet nook and no one will notice us.'

'I don't know, Eldon. It doesn't seem right, somehow. I mean, my husband has been killed in a terrible accident, and yet I'm seen out with a notorious rake like you.'

'That's hardly flattering, but probably quite fair. However, you can't enter a nunnery and you have to eat. What do you say? Or perhaps you would rather mope here and eat what the servants have made for themselves, given the short notice they had of your return.'

'You are very persuasive, and I suppose you are right. I have to face the world some time.'

83

'Then I suggest you go to your boudoir and put on something a little more suitable. We'll go as soon as you're ready and I'll have you back here at a respectable hour so that not even your butler will disapprove.'

Patricia hesitated. She knew that it was not the type of behaviour expected of a newly widowed woman, but the thought of spending a solitary evening in a house that was haunted by the memory of her time with Greystone was too much to bear. She rose to her feet and placed the watch on the mantelshelf.

'Very well, although I hope no one recognises us.'

★ ★ ★

As Eldon had promised, the *maître d'hôtel* had placed them at a table that was all but hidden from general view, and the waiters hovered around attentively. Patricia had found the thought of food nauseating, but she had not eaten since breakfast and she realised that her appetite had returned. Eldon knew exactly what she liked to eat and he ordered for both of them. After a glass or two of wine Patricia began to relax and the horrors of the train crash receded like the fading memory of a bad dream.

Eldon watched her while she ate a delicious bombe of hazelnut praline ice cream. 'What will you do now, Patricia? Do you intend to stay in London?'

She looked up with the spoon poised, ready to eat another tasty morsel. 'I don't know. I haven't given it much thought.'

'Your ambition to sing in the opera, perhaps at the new Opera House, is that still an option?'

'I can't think about that now, Eldon. I feel as though my mind is a peasouper. Perhaps it will be easier when

84

I've spoken to Mr Selly in the morning.'

'Would you like me to be there for you?'

She met his intense gaze and realised that he was serious. 'Thank you, but I can cope with Selly. I can't imagine that there will be any difficulties. After all, I am Greystone's widow. I assume that everything will come to me.'

'You know where I live, my dear. You only have to send for me and I'll come post-haste.'

* * *

Patricia had not expected to sleep much that night, but whether it was due to sheer exhaustion or the good food and wine she had enjoyed at Rules, she slept peacefully until morning when Betsey brought her a cup of chocolate.

'What time is it?' Patricia asked sleepily.

'It's eight o'clock, my lady.'

Patricia snapped into a sitting position. 'I should get up now, Betsey. Mr Selly, the solicitor, is coming at ten o'clock.'

'Very well, my lady. I've laid out your grey silk gown.'

'I suppose I should be wearing black, but I have nothing suitable for a grieving widow.'

'There are mourning warehouses in town, my lady. Jay's in Regent Street and Peter Robinson specialise in suitable clothing.'

'We'll pay them a visit after the solicitor has been. I really can't get used to the idea that I'm a widow. Does that seem terrible?'

'It's been a dreadful shock to us all, my lady. The servants are very upset. Sir Michael was a good master.'

'I'll drink my chocolate and then get dressed. I'll have an early breakfast, and then I'll wait for Mr Selly in the drawing room.'

'I'll fetch some hot water so that you can have a wash, my lady.'

★ ★ ★

Two hours later, having eaten a good breakfast and drunk several cups of coffee, Patricia was in the drawing room waiting for the solicitor to arrive. On the dot of ten o'clock Foster entered the room to announce Mr Selly.

'Show him in, Foster.' Patricia rose from her seat by the fire, holding out her hand to the small, bewhiskered man who hurried into the room carrying a leather document case.

He bowed over her hand. 'Good morning,my lady. Please accept my condolences.'

'Thank you, Mr Selly. It is a very sad day for me. Won't you take a seat?'

He swished his coattails aside as he took a seat on an upright chair. 'I have Sir Michael's will in my case. Would you like me to tell you the details or would you prefer to have the family present?'

Patricia eyed him in surprise. 'Surely everything comes to me, as Sir Michael's wife?'

'I'm afraid it isn't as simple as that, my lady.' Selly stroked his beard, eyeing her worriedly. 'If you are happy to have me go over the details now, that is quite all right.'

Patricia sensed that she was not going to like what she was about to hear and she crossed the floor to gaze out of the window. In the street below a moving column of umbrellas made her think suddenly of mushrooms on the march and she stifled a nervous giggle. 'Please go ahead, Mr Selly.'

He opened his case and took out a document tied with red tape, which he unfastened with irritating slowness. 'You may read it for yourself, but the gist of the will is that the property named as Greystone Park is left in its entirety to Sir Michael's daughters, Mrs Christina Cottingham and Miss Sylvia Greystone.'

Patricia turned to stare at him in amazement. 'Surely that can't be right. Greystone Park should belong to me. Sir Michael only had daughters; there is no son and heir.'

'Sir Michael made the decision, my lady.'

'But the income from the estate must come to me, or at least a part of it?'

'The estate is encumbered. Apparently Sir Michael borrowed money to further his career in politics using the estate as collateral. Any monies made from rents are to be used to repay the loan, and the same applies to this house, unfortunately. There is a substantial mortgage, which you will be unable to honour unless you have private means.'

Patricia sank down on a spindly legged chair. 'I have no money of my own, Mr Selly. Will I have to sell the property?'

'In that case I fear so, my lady. Although if you cannot keep up the repayments in the meantime the lender is entitled to reclaim the property.'

'But there is money in the bank. We've always been wealthy. Surely I have enough to live off?'

'Sir Michael had a large overdraft, which will need to be paid off from the sale of the property, assuming that a good price can be negotiated.'

'So I am left with nothing?' Patricia stared at him dazedly.

'I am so very sorry, my lady. I wish I had been the bringer of better news.'

'Will Greystone Park have to be sold, too? Surely I have some stake in that property?'

'Sir Michael's daughters will be able to manage if they have a good bailiff, but you have no claim on the estate. They might very well wish that you had inherited the problem, if that's any consolation.'

'It isn't. I feel humiliated. Why would my husband treat me like this?' Patricia cried angrily. 'Greystone was supposed to love me and take care of me.'

'Sir Michael dealt with me when he revised his will a year or so ago. He was certain that he could turn his fortunes around with the business ventures he had begun. Unfortunately the shares tumbled on the stock market and he lost all his investments. You were supposed to have the interest, had there been any, to look after you for the rest of your life. However, it seems that Sir Michael had been badly advised.'

'This is terrible.' Patricia rose unsteadily to her feet. 'What will I do?'

'Your stepdaughters might take you in. I believe that Miss Sylvia lives in the mansion largely on her own, apart from the servants. She might be glad of your company.'

Patricia shook her head. 'The girls were my friends when we were younger, but they resented the fact that their father married me.'

'You have a family estate in Devonshire, I believe. If I were to give you advice I would suggest that you go home to Rockwood Castle until all the details of Sir Michael's estate have been settled.'

'Do I have a choice, Mr Selly?'

'Perhaps you have friends in London who would be pleased to accommodate you until all matters pertaining to the estate are settled?'

Patricia thought of Eldon and laughed. 'I think this is the time when I discover who my real friends are, Mr Selly.'

'I am sorry to be the bearer of yet more bad news, my lady.' Selly tucked the document into his leather case. 'With your permission I will undertake to supervise the registering of the will for probate.'

'Yes,' Patricia said dully. 'Of course.'

Selly rose to his feet. 'If I might give you a word of advice, my lady. I'd suggest you put this property up for sale immediately. It might serve you well to leave matters in my hands so that you can return to Devonshire and be with your family.'

'Is there no way I can remain here, Mr Selly? I was hoping to begin a new career in opera.'

'That may well happen, ma'am, but you would have to repay the mortgage as well as meet the servants' wages. Perhaps furnished rooms closer to the theatre might be a more practical option.'

'I hadn't thought that far, Mr Selly.'

'Of course not, my lady. This must be a very difficult time for you. I'll take my leave now, but if you need any help or advice please do not hesitate to call on me.'

'Thank you, I will.' Patricia watched him walk out of the door with a feeling of unease. No doubt his advice had been sound, but she was shaken by the sudden turn of events and unsure which way to go. She was still sitting in the same position when Eldon arrived a little later.

'How are you today, my dear? Did Selly have any good news for you?'

'I am all but bankrupt, Eldon. Apparently Greystone left more or less everything to his daughters, although there was precious little. He seems to have gambled on the stock market and lost heavily.'

Eldon sat down on the sofa. 'There must be some mistake. Surely as his wife you are entitled to something?'

'Mr Selly says I would have this house if I can afford the mortgage repayments. Greystone was in debt but he never spoke about monetary matters. I'm not a rich widow, Eldon. I'm not much of a catch.'

'I never look at you in that light, Patricia. I may be a libertine but I'm not a cad.'

'I'm sorry, Eldon. I didn't mean to offend you, but I'm temporarily at a loss to know what to do next.'

Eldon leaned forward to lay his hand on hers. 'What did Selly suggest? He has more experience in matters like this than I do.'

'He said either I should find furnished rooms nearer to the theatre, or I should go home to Rockwood Castle. Unless, of course, I wanted to throw myself on the mercy of my stepdaughters and ask them if I can live with Sylvia at Greystone Park.'

'What do you want to do, Patricia? That is the most important question.'

She shook her head. 'I don't know. I can't believe this is happening to me.'

'I find it hard to believe that Greystone would have abandoned you to your fate,' Eldon said slowly. 'If I had the money I would purchase this house for you, but, as you know, my funds are low at the moment. I'm afraid my weakness is the card table and both my properties are mortgaged to the hilt.' He hesitated, adding with a wry smile, 'I could marry Sylvia and insist that you came to live with us. How about that?'

A reluctant laugh escaped Patricia's lips. 'I believe you would do so, if I asked.'

'She will have suitors queuing up at the door when the news of her inheritance gets out. Say the word and I'll do it, but it will be for you and not for myself.'

'I think the gentlemen will run away when they discover that the estate is encumbered.'

'Even so, I would turn myself into a businessman if it would help you through this difficult time.'

'You are a rogue, Eldon, and I don't believe you for a moment. You are just saying these things to take my mind off my problems.'

'Perhaps, but I hate to see you sad. You are always such a ray of sunshine in a dreary world.'

'Now you are flattering me, but it does make me feel better.' Patricia tugged at the bell pull. 'Life has to go on even when problems seem insurmountable. I really need to go to Oxford Street or Regent Street to purchase some more suitable garments. I hate black, but society insists that widows dress like crows for two years. It's like a double punishment.'

'I agree. We men are used to wearing sombre garments, but I do dislike to see women swathed in bombazine and crepe. I suggest you go to Jay's funeral warehouse and I insist that you choose parramatta silk. It's the least of the evils.'

'But first,' Patricia said firmly, 'I am going to Covent Garden to see Garson Thorne. He should have had a report from the signora by now and I'll find out if I have a part in his new production.'

'Would you like me to accompany you? I am free

all day.'

'Yes, I think I would, Eldon. For once you are being really helpful.'

He pulled a face. 'I'm not sure how to take that, Patricia. But being an optimist I will hope it is a compliment.'

★ ★ ★

Garson Thorne was standing outside the orchestra pit arguing fiercely with a man who looked as though he had come straight from the City. Patricia held back until the well-dressed gentleman had stalked out of the auditorium. She approached Garson with a bright smile.

'Good morning, Garson. How are you today?'

He stared at her uncomprehending and then a slow smile banished the angry lines on his face. 'Good morning, my lady. As you probably noticed I was having trouble with one of our backers. These City investors are a strange lot. They want facts and figures that I simply do not have.' He cast a curious glance in Eldon's direction.

'I'm sorry, I should have introduced my friend Lord Eldon. Eldon, this is Garson Thorne, the most talented opera director in the country.'

'You flatter me,' Garson said, extending his hand to Eldon. 'How do you do, my lord?'

'Eldon, please. I dispense with my title except when dealing with tradesmen. I find it helps to get credit if they think they are dealing with the aristocracy.'

'I wanted to know if the signora had been to see you, Garson,' Patricia said casually. 'We had a very profitable few weeks in Devonshire. I'm eager to know if I have the part in your production.'

'I did see Maud briefly this morning,'Garson said, frowning. 'She told me that you are recently bereaved. Please accept my condolences.'

Patricia lowered her gaze modestly. 'Thank you, Garson. I appreciate that.'

'But surely you will be in strict mourning? You won't wish to appear in public for a year or even more.'

'Not at all. I am all the more eager to have a career of my own. Greystone left me well provided for, of course, but I have always wanted to follow in my mother's footsteps.'

'Well, Maud said you have the potential for a fine voice, but you definitely need to develop it before I can give you a leading role.'

'Naturally. I understand that perfectly.' Patricia reached for Eldon's hand and held it in a firm grasp.

'Are you sure you want to continue with this, my lady? Perhaps you have not fully realised the scale of bereavement you will suffer?'

'Greystone and I had a good marriage, but he would want me to be happy. I am prepared to accept a small part if that's what you think I can handle at this stage.'

'Very well. You have the part of Clorinda, a serving maid. My assistant will give you the libretto so that you can take it away and learn the words. We start rehearsals after Easter.' Garson turned away at the sound of someone on stage calling his name. 'You'll excuse me, my lady. I have much to do.' He strode off, stopping to speak to a young man, who nodded and came hurrying towards Patricia and Eldon.

'I am the assistant stage manager. If you'll come to the office with me I'll give you a copy of the libretto.'

'Thank you.' Patricia followed him with Eldon at

her side.

When they reached the tiny, cramped office, littered with papers and bundles of flyers, empty coffee cups and an array of colourful costumes hanging from hooks on the wall, Patricia cleared her throat. 'I need to know how much I will be paid. I have to find rooms nearby and . . .'

The young man eyed her curiously. 'I can't say exactly, ma'am. It will be up to Mr Thorne eventually, but if you take my advice you'll find someone to share the costs. Unless you reach the top you'll find that the salaries are quite low.'

'Thank you, again.' Patricia grasped the sheet of papers. 'I'll bear that in mind.' They left the theatre and walked slowly down Southampton Street towards the Strand.

'I had no idea it would be so hard,' Patricia said worriedly. 'I suppose the low pay is why Mama used to come home and stay until the next production was about to start. How on earth will I manage on my own, Eldon?'

7

The house in Duke Street was up for sale and the servants had been given notice, with the exception of Foster, who was to return to Greystone Park. Patricia had studied the part of Clorinda and realised that Garson had been serious when he said it was a minor role. She had learned the words in an hour or two, but without the music to accompany them she was unable to rehearse.

She found herself very much alone in London. There were plenty of letters of condolence and half-hearted offers of help, but no invitations to dine out or to the theatre. It was becoming obvious that a young, attractive widow was not the most welcome guest. The only person to call on her was Eldon, which he did every day, and he insisted on taking her riding in Rotten Row when the weather permitted. They had tea and cake at Gunter's and he escorted her to the National Gallery, all perfectly respectable outings, but even he was unable to break through the social chains that bound her to her home.

At the beginning of April, Patricia found herself on the train heading for Exeter. Eldon had wanted to accompany her, but she refused his offer, telling him that she would have to stand on her own two feet in the future. Foster was returning to Greystone Park and she decided to travel with him. Always reliable, Foster handled the purchase of tickets and with an imperious motion of his hand he summoned porters to take everything to the luggage compartment.

Patricia could only stand back and watch with a feeling of relief. Although she had insisted that she did not need help, she realised now just how much her late husband had protected her from the realities of the world, and she missed him. She was not heartbroken, but she was heart sore, and at times she felt like a lost child. Going home to Rockwood seemed like the only option at present.

When they arrived at Exeter railway station Foster took charge once again. He retrieved their luggage, although his things were packed into one small valise, and he hired a cab to take them to Rockwood Castle, with a carter to take the mountain of trunks and hat boxes. Despite Patrcia's request for him to sit inside the carriage, Foster insisted on travelling on the box with the cabby, and they set off for home.

When Patricia parted with her former butler at the castle she knew for certain that she was saying goodbye to her old life. She was still Lady Greystone, but Sylvia and Christina had both made it clear that they did not want her to live at Greystone Park. Patricia had been too proud to argue. She watched the cab drive off with Foster now seated comfortably inside and the carter unloaded the luggage, aided by Jarvis, the butler, and James, the footman.

'Patsy, come inside. Don't stand there in the wind and rain.' Rosalind stood in the doorway, beckoning enthusiastically.

'I didn't realise it was raining,' Patricia said dully. She stepped over the threshold into her sister's warm embrace.

'Patsy, I am so sorry for your loss. If it hadn't been for the little ones I would have travelled up to London to be with you.'

'I know you would, Rosie. Thank you for inviting me to live here with you, but it will only be a temporary arrangement.'

'Take off your mantle, Patsy. Jennet will look after it for you.' Rosalind turned to the housemaid, who stepped forward, holding out her hand to help Patricia take off her outer garment.

'You're shivering. Come and sit by the fire.' Rosalind slipped her arm around her sister's shoulders. 'Jennet, we'll have tea in the drawing room.'

Patricia walked past the ancient suit of armour without bothering to close the visor, even though it gaped stupidly as if its former owner was staring at her in astonishment. Sir Denys Carey's spirit would have to roam the castle walls, for all she cared. The feeling of regression to childhood and helplessness almost overcame her.

'How did this happen, Rosie?' Patricia said sadly. 'A few weeks ago I had two homes, servants and a carriage of my own. Now I have nothing.'

'You have us, Patsy. You have a family who love you, and this will always be your home. You're exhausted; come and sit down and tell me everything. The children are with Molly, and Bertie is having a nap. Hester is in her parlour and Alex is out somewhere with Wolfe, so we won't be disturbed.'

Half an hour later, revived by tea and two slices of Mrs Jackson's excellent shortbread, Patricia began to relax. 'I really appreciate this, Rosie. I've told you everything about me, so what's been happening here?'

Rosalind stretched out her feet, warming them on the hearth. 'Life goes on as usual. Tommy and Nancy will be home from school in a couple of days. Bertie is looking forward to seeing his son, and they are so alike it's unbelievable. Nancy will have finished her education and it will be lovely to have her here. She's wonderful with the children.'

'Is she part of the family or will you take her on as a servant?'

Rosalind's eyes widened in horror. 'She's very much one of us, Patsy. Don't forget that for a moment. She's bright and intelligent and full of fun. In fact she's a delight to have around.'

'I'm sorry. I'm just out of touch with the goings-on here. I was so immersed in Greystone's political career that I neglected everyone else. No wonder Sylvia doesn't want to know me now.'

'You could say the same of any of us. I'm totally involved with my babies and Alex. We run the estate together and we might not be wealthy landowners but at least our tenants are happy and loyal. Our land is productive and we aren't in debt. What more could you ask?'

'I'm not like you, Rosie. I wish I was, but I think I'm more like Mama. I can't wait to start a career on the stage. When I appeared previously I loved everything about the excitement of performing. I can't just sit around dressed in black, dwindling into a pathetic widow.'

Rosalind laughed. 'You will never be pathetic, and I doubt if you will remain a widow for long.'

'I have to face facts. I'm twenty-four and I'm virtually bankrupt unless the house in Duke Street sells for a great deal more than is expected. I need to work, and there is nothing else I can do other than sing, even if my voice isn't as good as Mama's.'

'Just give yourself time to get over the shock of everything that's happened. You need to rest and stop worrying about the future. We've been through bleak times before and we've come through everything so far.' Rosalind looked up as the door opened to admit Hester.

'So you've turned up again, Patricia. Welcome home.'

'Thank you, Hester. You almost sound as if you mean it.'

Hester's lined faced crinkled into a smile. 'You know I do. You have a chance to begin again, poppet. You might feel low at the moment but you'll bounce back. I've lived through four generations of Careys, if you count little Miss Dolly as being a chip off the old block, as they say in common parlance. You are not going to sink beneath your present problems, Patsy. Careys swim with the tide — they don't go under.'

Patricia had never heard Hester make such a long and heartening speech. She exchanged surprised glances with Rosalind.

'That's very true, Hester,' Rosalind said hastily. 'Well said.'

'Thank you.' Patricia wiped a tear from her cheek. 'But I'll feel more normal when you start scolding me again, Hester. I never could do anything right, as far as you were concerned.'

'Someone had to keep you in order, poppet. You were spoiled by everyone, even your mama, and she only thought of herself for the most part. We're not going to let that happen to little Dolly, are we, Rosie?'

Rosalind smiled. 'You say that now, Hester, but I've seen you sneaking sugar plums to her and little cakes. Dolly has you wound around her little finger.'

'Maybe, but she is a little angel, most of the time. Now let's be practical. How long do you intend to stay here, Patricia?'

'Just until rehearsals begin after Easter. I have to find myself somewhere to live in London.'

Hester clicked her tongue against her teeth, shaking her head. 'What a state of affairs. I thought better of Sir Michael. I don't know what he was thinking of when he made his will. He should have taken care of you.'

'He made the will before we married,' Patricia said quickly. 'His solicitor told me that Greystone did alter it fairly recently, when he believed that he was going to make a fortune on the stock market.'

'That's no excuse, and as to those two girls of his,' Hester rolled her eyes, 'they are a couple of spiteful cats, that's all I can say.'

'Don't dwell on it now, Patsy,' Rosalind said sympathetically. 'I'm sure we can work something out. After you've rested and had a cup of tea I'll help you unpack your luggage. James will have taken it to your room by now.'

'What happened to your maid?' Hester demanded, bristling. 'Did she desert you, too?'

'I hired Betsey in London and she didn't want to come to the country. Anyway, I think she had her eye on one of the under footmen. I won't be able to afford a maidservant of my own, at least not for a while. Perhaps when I start to get bigger parts I'll be able to set up my own establishment.'

Hester and Rosalind exchanged worried glances, but Patricia was too tired after her long journey and the emotional trauma of leaving her old life behind to care what the others might think.

'You'll be perfectly fine,' Rosalind said hastily. 'Don't worry about anything, Patsy. You're welcome to stay here for as long as you like. I'll enjoy having my sister at home again.'

★ ★ ★

Patricia had not given the move back to Rockwood Castle much thought, but as the days wore on she was beginning to realise how hard it was not to be the mistress of her own home. In the four years she had been married to Sir Michael she has been used to giving orders and having them obeyed instantly. Money had been no object and the hardest decisions she had had to make each day were what gowns she would wear. Now when she awakened in the morning she had nothing to think about in particular. She did her best to be a good companion to Rosalind, but she found her sister's domestic life utterly boring, although she would have died rather than say so. Fletcher openly disapproved of her and Wolfe eyed her warily as if she were a danger to all men.

If she were to be honest, she missed Eldon. She knew that he was not someone to be taken seriously, but that was part of his attraction.

Life at Rockwood Castle was slow but crowded. If she wished to be alone she had to retire to her bedchamber or go for a long walk in the grounds. She had known the servants, both indoors and out of doors, since she was a child and although they were suitably deferential she knew that they remembered everything she had ever done, and most of it was not to her credit. She found herself wishing that Mama and Claude would arrive out of the blue, as was their wont. At least Mama was full of amusing anecdotes about her appearances on the world's stages, and she knew all the latest gossip and scandals.

Try as she might to fit in, Patricia was uncomfortably aware that she had no real place in the household. Rosalind was unfailingly kind and supportive, but Walter always had his head stuck in a book. Bertie was kept busy running the estate from his Bath chair or the study, with Wolfe at his side like a big shaggy guard dog. Louise was fully occupied with her pregnancy, having lost two babies previously in the early stages, and with the best will in the world, Rosalind was kept busy with household matters and three small children, whom she obviously adored. If Patricia had worried about her relationship with Alex, her fears were soon put at rest. Alexander was too good-natured to remind her that they had once been engaged to be married, and he clearly adored Rosalind and the children. However, he too was fully occupied with business matters and no longer the fun-loving army captain who had once captured her imagination and made her heart beat faster.

It was lovely to have young Tommy at home from school, but it was Nancy who caught Patricia's attention. Nancy, at the age of fifteen, was no longer a gawky child, all spindly arms and legs, and she showed promise of becoming a beauty when she was fully mature. She was very reserved in company and although Rosalind treated her like one of the family, Patricia sensed that Nancy did not feel totally involved. This struck a chord with Patricia and she felt a certain kinship to the orphan whom Rosalind had plucked from a life of servitude. No one knew who Nancy's parents were or how she came to be in the orphanage, but it was obvious to Patricia that Nancy was not a child of the streets. There was a refinement in her looks and manner that set her apart, and a sadness in her eyes that went straight to Patricia's heart. She began to take an interest in Nancy and, as the weather improved, she often invited the girl to walk with her to the village or to watch the fishermen landing their catch on the quay. On a blustery but sunny day just before Easter, Patricia had decided that the atmosphere in the castle was too stifling and as she could not find Nancy she set off for a walk to the top of the cliffs. She loved to look out for ships sailing away to foreign lands, wishing that she was a passenger on one of them, heading for excitement and adventure. She clutched her cloak more tightly around her body as the wind whipped playfully at her garments and tugged at her bonnet strings. She was standing on the top of the cliff, looking out to sea, when her attention was caught by a figure seated on the rocks below. Realising that it was Nancy and she was all alone, Patricia made her way carefully down the stony path to the beach.

'I used to come here often when I was your age,' Patricia said breathlessly. 'May I join you, Nancy?'

'Yes, of course. I'm sorry, I was supposed to be helping Hester with some mending, but I hate sewing.'

'So do I. Not that I ever did much, although Hester did try to make me work a sampler when I was seven or eight. I kept getting the thread into knots and in the end she gave up. Some of us were never meant to do that sort of thing.'

'Rosie said you are an opera singer,' Nancy said shyly. 'Will you be leaving us soon?'

'Yes, in a few days. I have to return to London to rehearse my part, although it's a very small one. I doubt if anyone will notice me.' Patricia perched on a rock, having made sure first that it was dry. 'I'm just starting my career on the stage.'

'You'll be like Mrs de Marney,' Nancy said, smiling. 'She doesn't come often but she's always nice to me when she's here. Mr de Marney is very kind, too.'

'Of course they're good toy ou, Nancy. You're one of the family.'

'I know I'm not related to any of you. I remember being in the orphanage and then working for the vicar and his nasty wife. If it hadn't been for Louise I would have run away.'

'That was all a long time ago. We love you and you're one of us now.'

'I don't think anyone loves me,' Nancy said seriously. 'Everyone is very kind to me, but they love Dolly and the others. It's different.'

'I'm so sorry you feel that way. I do understand.'

'How can you?' Nancy's pansy-brown eyes filled with tears. 'You are part of the family by birth. I came here more or less by accident.'

'I was the youngest and when I was your age I felt very much alone. Rosie was so much more grown up than I, and my brothers teased me endlessly. Hester says I was spoilt — and I was in a fashion — but in another way I was left very much to my own devices. I was often lonely and I suspect that is how you feel now.'

Nancy looked away. 'I don't wish to sound ungrateful. I've been given a chance in life I would never have had before, but the truth is I don't belong anywhere. I'm not a Carey and they didn't even know who my parents were at the orphanage, which is why they called me Nancy Sunday.'

Patricia wrapped her cloak more tightly around her as the breeze freshened. 'But that gives you the opportunity to forge your own path in life, Nancy. You've had a good education and you're very pretty, with a nice manner. You have the chance to shine in your own right, not from something you inherited.'

'You make it sound so easy, Patricia.'

'I know it isn't, but I think one day you'll go far, Nancy Sunday.' Patricia rose to her feet. 'I'm getting cold. Shall we go for a walk along the beach before we go home?'

'Would you take me to London with you when you leave Rockwood, Patricia?'

'Good heavens, why would you want to leave home, Nancy?'

Nancy rose to her feet and fell into step beside Patricia. 'Because you understand how I feel, and you haven't got a maid. I overheard the servants talking about it. They said it wasn't right that a lady like you didn't have her own maid.'

'You want to be a lady's maid?'

'I don't think I'm fitted for anything else.'

'That's not true. You ought to aim higher. You're better off here, Nancy. I can't afford to pay you and I haven't even got a place to live.'

'I don't care. I want to see London and I could look after your clothes and make sure you had proper meals. Hester was very particular that I had to learn the basics of housekeeping, and Mrs Jackson has taught me how to cook in the school holidays. At least, I know my way around a kitchen.'

'I don't know. It's not something I can decide on my own. I'll have to talk it over with my sister. She's the one who's responsible for you.'

'But you haven't any objections?' Nancy asked eagerly. 'You will take me with you if Rosie agrees?'

105

'I can't promise anything, but I will speak to Rosie. I'll be guided by her. Does that satisfy you, Nancy?'

'Yes,' Nancy said doubtfully. 'I think so, but I'm afraid Rosie won't allow me to go.'

'We'll see about that. I can be very persuasive when I put my mind to it.'

★ ★ ★

Rosalind was not keen on the idea and neither was Hester. Both of them tried to dissuade Patricia, but that made her all the more determined to rescue the lonely girl from a home where she felt out of place. However, that did not solve the problem of where they might live in London, and for once in her life Patricia was unsure of herself. She had a small income from shares that Sir Michael had not sold off, but she suspected that this would end when the estate was finally settled. It seemed that her clever husband had not been a brilliant businessman, or else he had been badly advised. With no help from her family Patricia decided on a course that she knew would meet with their total disapproval, so she kept her plans to herself.

On Good Friday when everyone else had gone to church, Patricia had excused herself saying she had a really bad headache. She dressed in her riding habit and waited until everyone had left for the village before hurrying to the stables to instruct Hudson to saddle a horse. He did so reluctantly and she could see that he was dying to know where she was going alone and unattended by a maid, but she was not going to give him the satisfaction. She headed off in the direction of Cottingham Manor where she expected to find the squire's wife at home on her own. Glorina was not an ardent churchgoer, but the squire kept up the tradition and he would have taken most of the household with him.

It was a fine day with bright sunshine and a welcome haze of fresh green leaves on the trees with golden daffodils waving their trumpets in the breeze like a beautiful orchestra playing a silent melody. Clumps of yellow primroses made bursts of colour beneath the hedgerows, and birds were busy feeding their young nestlings. Patricia was not someone who delighted in the beauties of nature, but even she felt more cheerful and positive on such a lovely day.

As she had hoped, Glorina was at home and she seemed pleased to have a visitor. The squire's wife, who played ruthlessly on her Romany background in order to rebel against the mores of society, was an attractive middle-aged woman with flaming red hair and eyes the greenish-brown colour of oak leaf. She rose to her feet when Patricia was shown into the room.

'Patricia, I was waiting for you to come and see me.'

'Good morning, Mrs Cottingham,' Patricia said nervously. 'How did you know I would visit you?'

'My dear, I am half gypsy. You know that, of course. I have second sight and people come to me when they need my help. What can I do for you? Do sit down and tell me.'

'Well, if you know so much you must have an idea why I've come here.'

'*Touché*, my dear. However, it only needs one to listen to the local gossips to learn that your husband has left you virtually penniless. Especially as my dear daughter-in-law is one of the beneficiaries of his lack of forethought and his inability to handle his finances.'

'I suppose so. Anyway, Christina didn't want me to marry her father. Neither of the girls was happy having me as her stepmother.'

'Can you blame them, Patricia? In their place I might have acted in precisely the same way.'

'Yes, I know, but that doesn't help me now. I have a chance to follow my mother in a career on the stage.'

'So I heard. I believe you dabbled in opera before you married Greystone?'

'Yes, and I've been offered a part in the production at the new Opera House in Covent Garden.'

'So what is the problem?'

'Money, of course. I have nowhere to live because the house in Duke Street is encumbered and up for sale. I don't know whether to risk going to London with very little money or if I should stay at Rockwood until all matters are settled and maybe I will have at least a pittance from the sale.'

'But you will lose your part in the opera, even if it is a small one.'

'Yes, that's true. I wonder if you would read my palm, or whatever it is you do. I need advice from someone who is not related to me.'

Glorina laughed. 'I understand perfectly. Families always think they know best. I know mine did. They told me not to marry Cottingham, but I did and I haven't regretted it. He might wish I could be a little more the lady of the manor, but he is resigned to my foibles. Hold out your hand, Patricia. I'll do my best.'

Patricia peeled off her glove and proffered her hand. Glorina took it and held it, staring intently at the lines on Patricia's palm. She took so long that Patricia was beginning to feel nervous.

'What can you see?'

'There is a man. A tall, dark man who is dangerous, but conversely he might be your saviour. I don't quite understand the message. He is very handsome and charming, but he is not the man for you. I see glory and I see trouble. I see poverty and I see strife. I can't tell you anything more.'

Patricia snatched her hand away. 'That's not very helpful, Glorina. I wanted to know whether or not I should return to London. Will I succeed in my career?'

'That, I think, is up to you.'

'Who is this man? Is it Lord Eldon?'

'I don't know that person and I can only see this man in outline, but he is well dressed and very charming. Be very careful, Patricia. You could have some success, but there is failure and heartache in the future as well. If I were your mother I would tell you to stay at Rockwood.'

'But you are not my mother,' Patricia said warily.

'My Romany blood tells me that you need to follow your heart and your ambition. Don't be afraid, Patricia. You will overcome all the obstacles put in your way, but it won't be easy. The path to happiness is stony and you could easily slip and fall.'

Patricia sighed. 'That's all talk, Glorina. I need funds and I am desperate for somewhere to live. Does your second sight see an address for me in London?'

Glorina closed her eyes. 'I see another man, but he is not of your class. I smell the sea and also sawdust. I don't know what it means.'

'Is there anything you can see that is actually helpful?' Patricia demanded impatiently.

'My sister, Starlina, lives in Bleeding Heart Yard. She will help you if you are in desperate need, but don't go to her unless it's absolutely necessary. She doesn't suffer fools gladly.'

'Thank you,' Patricia said, rising to her feet. 'I don't think somehow that I will venture into a place of that name.'

Glorina shrugged. 'As you please, but I will say that you are going to tread a difficult path, Patricia. You might be glad of help one day.'

'Perhaps, but until then I'll keep well away from Bleeding Heart Yard. Thank you for your help, such as it was.' Patricia tossed her head and stalked out of the drawing room, almost bumping into the Cottinghams' butler, who seemed to have been waiting outside the door.

'I'll show you out, Lady Greystone.'

'Thank you, but I can find my own way.'

'If you would care to wait in the entrance hall I'll send for your horse, my lady.'

'Oh, very well. Thank you.' Patricia glanced round at the dark wainscoting and the equally dingy ancestral portraits, and she shuddered. Suddenly Cottingham Manor seemed to have taken on a sinister and mysterious atmosphere. She wondered if she had done the right thing by telling Glorina what she thought of her advice. Perhaps she had been rude, but it had been borne of frustration. It was probably bad luck to cross a gypsy, especially when she had given her a warning. Patricia paced the floor, waiting anxiously for the butler to send for her horse. She could not wait to leave the somewhat macabre atmosphere of the manor house.

★ ★ ★

110

When she reached home, just before the family arrived back from church, Patricia had come to a decision. She would leave Rockwood as soon possible and Nancy could accompany her if Rosalind could be persuaded to agree. It did not matter that she had nowhere to go. Garson Thorne would be able to find them temporary accommodation and she would look for somewhere more suitable before rehearsals began. It would be an adventure, she kept telling herself.

8

Patricia remembered her mother's former lodgings well. Garson had been very helpful and had taken them to the modest four-storey house in Maiden Street, close to Covent Garden itself. He had introduced them to the landlady, Mrs Humphries, who remembered Felicia Carey before she had married her manager, Claude de Marney. Both Patricia and Rosalind had stayed there for a few days when they had come to London to beg their mother for help. In those days Rockwood Castle had been in a sad state of dilapidation and money had been short. Felicia had been unhelpful when it came to financial aid, but it was during this visit to London in the year of the Great Exhibition that Rosalind became involved with Piers Blanchard. He was both hand- some and charming, and their somewhat turbulent relationship had culminated in a marriage that was to be brief and ended in divorce when Piers was sent to the penal colony in Australia. Recalling this as she stood on the threshold, Patricia wondered if this was what Glorina had seen. Perhaps it was hindsight and it was Rosalind's history that had shown itself to the squire's gypsy wife.

Mrs Humphries showed Patricia and Nancy to their room on the top floor. 'This is my least expensive accommodation, ladies,' she said breathlessly. 'I remember your mama and Mr de Marney. They still stay here on the odd occasion, but now they are too grand to remain for long.'

'I don't know about that,' Patricia said irritably.

'Perhaps they can afford a better hotel.'

Mrs Humphries bridled visibly. 'You won't find more comfortable or cleaner rooms anywhere in this area. My breakfasts and suppers are famous,but they cost extra. You'll be eating here, I suppose, Miss Carey?'

Nancy stared at Patricia in surprise. 'But you're not — '

'I'm not intending to eat in the dining room,' Patricia said hastily, casting a warning look at Nancy. She had forgotten to warn her that she had reverted to her maiden name. 'Thank you, but we will make our own arrangements for meals.'

'I don't allow food to be brought into the rooms. It encourages rats.'

'We'll eat at the theatre.' Patricia glanced round the room with a tiny window in the sloping ceiling. A pigeon stared back at her, tapping its beak on the grimy glass pane. 'There's only one bed, Mrs Humphries.'

'It's a double, Miss Carey. Can you pay for two singles?'

'I can sleep anywhere.' Nancy set their luggage down on the bare boards. The only hint of comfort in the dingy room was a rag rug and an old armchair that was so well worn the horsehair stuffing poked through the upholstery.

'Well, are you going to take it or not? Believe me I have people queuing up to take my rooms. I'm only giving you the option as a favour to Garson, who is a personal friend.'

'It will be dark soon,' Nancy said in a low voice.

Patricia opened her reticule and took out a leather purse. 'How much is it for a week, Mrs Humphries?'

'For the two of you shall we say seven and six?'

'Seven shillings and six pence, for this garret?' Patricia stared at her in horror.

'As the young lady said, it's getting dark outside. London is a very unfriendly place after nightfall if you haven't got a roof over your head.' Mrs Humphries folded her arms, smirking at Patricia.

'Very well, we'll stay for a week.'

'And another seven and six deposit, refundable when you leave, if I am satisfied that you have left the room as you found it.'

Patricia opened her mouth to protest but Nancy snatched the purse from her and counted out fifteen silver shillings, which she placed in Mrs Humphries' hand. 'There you are, and I think we should get clean linen and towels thrown in for that price.'

Mrs Humphries retracted her neck into her starched collar reminding Patricia of a grumpy tortoise. 'Very well, but there's a charge for laundry.'

'I would never have guessed,' Patricia said acidly. 'Take the money, ma'am. No doubt you'll send up some water for the washstand.'

'What washstand? Look round, miss. There isn't one, but there's a pump in the back yard next to the privy.'

Patricia took a deep breath. It was true that life had not been luxurious at Rockwood Castle in the days when money was short, but she had never had to resort to such humiliation as using a common privy or fetching water to fill her wash basin. She took a deep breath; now was not the time to falter in her quest for independence. 'One week, Mrs Humphries, and then we will find somewhere more suitable.'

Mrs Humphries laughed, exposing a row of

114

blackened and broken teeth. 'You say that now, miss, but just you wait and see.' She left the room, still cackling with laughter.

'Why didn't you tell her that you're Lady Greystone?' Nancy demanded crossly. 'She would have found us better accommodation.'

'I don't think so. I imagine she would have charged us double for this pigsty. Tomorrow I will visit my bank and withdraw funds. Don't worry, Nancy. This is just temporary. We will not be here for long, I can assure you of that.'

★   ★   ★

After a largely sleepless and extremely uncomfortable night, Patricia was relieved to open her eyes and see a beam of light filtering through the crust of grime on the window above her. She rose from the bed to find Nancy sleeping peacefully on the floor, curled up like a kitten. It was then that the full horror of their new surroundings hit her. Last evening she had been too tired to argue with the landlady, but it was cold in the room beneath the eaves and there was no fireplace, so not even the offer of extra payment would bring them the much-needed comfort of a fire. All her life Patricia had been used to someone, even if it was her sister, bringing her a cup of hot chocolate before she rose from her bed, and she had taken for granted the pitchers of hot water the maids dragged up flights of stairs to her washstand. Now the harsh reality of existence outside the comfort of home was beginning to dawn upon her, and it was not pleasant. She nudged Nancy gently with her foot.

'Wake up, please. I need to go downstairs to the

115

back yard and I don't want to go on my own.'

Nancy stretched and yawned. She opened her eyes and gazed blearily up at Patricia. 'What's the matter?'

'It's time to get up. I want you to come downstairs with me. I don't like this place and who knows what is outside in the yard?'

Nancy scrambled to her feet. 'Better get dressed first. There'll be rats and all sorts out there. You need to have your boots on.'

Patricia stood there shivering. It might be spring but the chill of winter seemed to be living on in the garret. 'Help me to dress, please, Nancy.'

'I will help you,' Nancy said slowly. 'But if you're going to be like ordinary folk you'll need to learn to dress yourself.'

'I've never done that. We've nearly always had servants to wait on us and I've had a personal maid for the past four years. I don't know how to fasten stays or tie the laces on my boots.' Patricia's voice broke on a suppressed sob. She had always felt so confident in herself and now, for the first time in her life, she was doubting her own ability to manage the world around her.

'It's all right. I'm used to doing things for myself. We weren't waited on in the orphanage or at school, and the vicar's wife was very strict when I worked for her. I am so grateful to Rosie for saving me.'

'You aren't my servant, Nancy. I need to be like everyone else, but it's not going to be easy and I'll need your help.'

'Of course. Anything I can do, just ask.'

Patricia eyed her thoughtfully. 'I think it will be better if we tell everyone you are my younger sister. I think of you as part of the family, anyway.'

116

Nancy grinned. 'I'm quite happy to be your maid, if necessary.'

'We are equals, Nancy. Don't you forget that.' Patricia stepped out of her nightgown and reached for her chemise. 'But I will need help with my stays, and I really do need to go to the privy soon. We have to be at the rehearsal rooms at nine o'clock. I would still be in bed if I were back in Duke Street or at Greystone Park.'

'But you said you were going to the bank.' Nancy picked up Patricia's stays and wrapped them around her.

'I'm sure that Garson will allow me time to sort out my affairs,' Patricia said airily.

★ ★ ★

Garson shook his head, frowning. 'I'm sorry, Patricia, but you are in rehearsal now. I hope you are going to take your part seriously. It might be small but you are very fortunate to have been given a solo. If your mama was not such a dear friend I doubt if I would be giving you this chance.'

Patricia bit back a sharp response. 'I need to get some money, Garson. What am I supposed to do?'

'We have a break at midday to allow everyone to rest and take some light refreshments and then we work until I'm satisfied that we are making progress.'

'I'll go to the bank at midday.' Patricia went to sit with the rest of the cast while Garson ran through the scene he wanted to start with. She had nothing to do until the second act and she was tempted to sneak out anyway, but one look at Garson's determined jawline was enough to make her change her

117

mind. She remained seated and studied the libretto until she knew all her words and most of the other parts, too. She found to her surprise that she had a very retentive memory, especially if she was familiar with the melody. Nancy seemed to be at home with the performers as well as the stage hands, and she made herself known to the wardrobe mistress by admiring the costumes, which were being fitted and altered where necessary. Patricia had introduced her as Nancy Carey, her younger sister, and everyone accepted the relationship without question. By the time Patricia was called to wardrobe to be measured for her costume Nancy had charmed the wardrobe mistress, who was eager to do everything possible to please the newest member of the cast. Patricia realised with something of a shock that Nancy was far more astute than she had imagined.

It was Nancy who brought her a cup of coffee, which was strong and black but it revived Patricia's flagging spirits as the morning wore on, and it was Nancy who found a pie seller in Covent Garden so that they could snatch a late breakfast before going to the bank at midday.

Patricia sailed into the manager's office very much in her Lady Greystone persona, but the manager did not seem impressed. If anything he looked slightly embarrassed and his thin cheeks flushed uncomfortably as he gave her the bad news.

'I'm afraid I cannot give you a single penny, my lady. Your late husband's will has gone to probate and his assets, which are very few, are frozen.'

'But I have an allowance from Sir Michael,' Patricia protested. 'I've always been able to draw on it for anything I wanted.'

'Unavailable at the moment, I'm afraid.' He cleared his throat, eyeing her over the rim of his spectacles. 'In fact, it's highly unlikely that there will be anything in the fund that your husband set up to give you the allowance. Sir Michael's finances were in a shocking state. I'm only telling you this so that you aren't disappointed when probate is granted.'

'But there must be something, sir. My husband was a very wealthy man.'

'Yes, he was, but poor investments and ill luck, combined with a reckless disregard to the future, have seen everything melt away. Had Sir Michael lived he might have been able to salvage something, but alas it's unlikely that there will be anything left after the creditors are paid off. I am so sorry, my lady. I know how hard this must be for you.'

'You have no idea,' Patricia said angrily. 'Absolutely, no idea, sir.' She stormed out of his office and out of the bank, with Nancy following on her heels.

'It didn't go well?' Nancy eyed her curiously. 'Wouldn't they give you any money?'

'No, and I don't know what I can do about it. I've lost my allowance from Greystone, so we will have to survive on my wage from the opera company, which is a mere pittance.'

Nancy quickened her pace in an attempt to keep up with Patricia. 'You could always return to Rockwood. Your family would welcome you home.'

'I won't give them the satisfaction of knowing I've failed yet again. My marriage will look like a sham if my husband hasn't provided for me, and I was genuinely fond of Greystone. I think I loved him as much as I'm capable of loving anyone.'

Nancy frowned. 'I don't believe that. You've always

been very kind to me. And I know that Rosie loves you, as do your brothers.'

'If I return home now it will look as if I have given up or, even worse, that I have no talent and have been dismissed.'

'Then we'll manage. Perhaps I can take in sewing. The wardrobe mistress seems to need help and I'm quite good with a needle.'

Patricia came to a sudden halt and peeled off the kid glove on her left hand. 'I can sell my wedding ring. I have no use for it now, anyway. And there's my husband's half-hunter watch. That must be worth quite a lot.'

'Surely there must be another way. How much money do we have to last us until you get paid?'

'Not enough if we're to eat three times a day, and I don't mean sitting in the dining room at Mrs Humphries' establishment with the miserable lodgers I've seen going in and out.'

'We can eat cheaply, and if you get desperate I'm sure some of your old friends will ask you out to dinner.'

Patricia cast her a sideways glance. 'Are you laughing at me, Nancy?'

'No, not really,' Nancy said, giggling. 'We can buy pea soup from the street sellers and baked potatoes, or I can buy food in the market. We'll smuggle it up to our room, and if we're very careful Mother Humphries won't find out.'

'I'm so hungry, let's get something to eat now and we'll take it back to the theatre.'

'We've been a long time. Don't you think we ought to go there now? I can always slip out and buy something.'

Patricia nodded reluctantly. 'I suppose so. I'm not used to keeping to a strict time.'

'You are lucky. At boarding school we had to do everything to a strict timetable. Our lives were run by the clock.'

'I never stopped to think about it,' Patricia said slowly. 'I just took everything for granted.'

'Of course you did.' Nancy smiled, shaking her head. 'I've experienced life below stairs when I worked for Mrs Shaw. I know what it can be like.'

'If I ever have my own home again I will try to be a better employer.'

'Come on, Patsy. Best foot forward or we'll be late.'

★ ★ ★

Garson greeted Patricia with a scowl. 'What time do you call this? You are not a prima donna like your mama, Patricia. You have a small part and you were not here when I wanted to hear you sing. I would be within my rights to sack you on the spot.'

Patricia recoiled as if he had slapped her. She was not used to being spoken to in this tone of voice and she was uncomfortably aware that the rest of the cast were looking on, and some of them were openly smirking.

'I — I'm so sorry, Garson. It was unintentional, but I had to visit the bank and I had to wait to see the manager . . .'

He held up his hand. 'I don't want to listen to lame excuses. You are either committed to working with me or you are not, in which case you can leave now.'

'I am,' Patricia insisted. 'I am determined to do my best and make my mark in the world of opera.'

121

'My dear girl, you have everything to learn, and the first lesson is to be at rehearsals on time. If I have to reprimand you once more you will have to leave. Do you understand?'

Patricia swallowed hard. 'Yes, Garson,' she said in a small voice.

'And from now on you will call me Mr Thorne, like everyone else.'

'Yes, Mr Thorne.' Patricia took her position on stage, trying hard to ignore the sniggers from the members of the chorus, who were seated around the room, waiting for their turn on stage.

The rehearsal did not go well. Patricia was still breathless from hurrying and her stomach rumbled with hunger, again causing much amusement to those who were close enough to hear. Garson made her go over and over her lines even before she put them to music, and finally he dismissed her with a wave of his hand that only added to her humiliation.

The leading lady's understudy smiled maliciously when Patricia returned to her seat.

'You think you're so special because your mama is a prima donna, don't you?'

Patricia shot her a sideways glance. 'No, I don't.'

'You haven't got her talent, so you might as well give up now, love.'

'Who are you, anyway?' Patricia demanded angrily. 'I don't recall asking for your opinion.'

'I'm Lavinia Smith, and one day I'll have the leading role, while you're relegated to the chorus, that's if Garson keeps you on.'

'I wouldn't be so sure of that if I were you,' Patricia countered with a toss of her head. 'Please be quiet, I want to listen and learn all I can.'

'Hoity-toity,' Lavinia said crossly, but she refrained from making any comments after that.

The rehearsal went on for so long that Patricia was half asleep when Garson finally announced that they had finished for the day. She found Nancy with the wardrobe mistress and they left the theatre, making their way through the empty marketplace, although as Patricia knew to her cost the porters and carters would arrive very early next morning and disturb her sleep even more than the uncomfortable bed. Nancy hurried on ahead and managed to purchase the last two baked potatoes from a handcart, as well as two hard-boiled eggs and a rather droopy bunch of watercress.

'I've got our supper,' Nancy said gleefully. 'There's a coffee stall further along the road. We'll get a hot drink there.'

'We'll have to be careful about taking food to our room. You remember what Mrs Humphries said.'

'What she doesn't know won't hurt her.' Nancy winked and hid the food under her cape. 'We have to drink the coffee at the stall anyway, so cheer up. You'll feel better when you've eaten.'

'Rehearsal was a disaster,' Patricia said sadly. 'Perhaps I was wrong and I haven't inherited any of Mama's talent. Garson doesn't seem to think so.'

'I saw that person speaking to you.' Nancy shook her head. 'Lavinia Smith is known to be a spiteful cat. No one likes her. Mrs Lake, the wardrobe mistress warned me about Lavinia. She's only jealous because you were given a part and she's just an understudy.'

'That's nice of you, Nancy, but I'm worried she may be right.'

They stopped at the next stall and Nancy paid for

two mugs of steaming hot coffee, which they drank standing side by side on the pavement. Patricia glanced round warily, hoping that no one could see her. Hester would have a fit if she knew that one of her fledglings was eating or drinking on the street, but Hester was safely tucked away in Rockwood Castle. Patricia felt the warmth running through her veins, soothing an empty stomach. Perhaps she had been allowing herself to take spiteful comments to heart. She finished the coffee and returned the mug to the stallholder, who was busy packing up for the night.

'Thank you, that was most welcome.'

'Ta, lady. You looked as though you needed that.'

'Indeed I did, sir.' Patricia gave him a cheery smile. 'Come on, Nancy. Let's see if we can get indoors without being spotted by Mrs Humphries.'

Nancy put her mug down and followed Patricia the short distance to the lodging house. 'You go in first and I'll follow. You can keep her talking if she's on the prowl.'

Luckily for them there was no sign of their land-lady and they made it to their room, giggling like a couple of children. Patricia threw off her cloak and sat down on the bed to eat her food, with Nancy sitting cross-legged on the floor. When they had finished eating the only thing left was the broken egg shells, which Nancy wrapped in newspaper. 'I'll dispose of this when I go downstairs to the back yard,' she said, smiling. 'That was good. I feel better with a full belly.'

'So do I, but I need to find a way to earn more money if we're to survive in London.'

'If I could sing I would help, but it's not one of my talents. Mrs Lake said there's money to be made

124

singing in public houses.'

Patricia shook her head. 'I'd have to be really desperate to do something like that.'

* * *

Next morning and every day for the rest of the week, Patricia and Nancy arrived at the theatre early. Patricia practised her scales and her breathing exercises in the comparative privacy of the empty rehearsal room, and Garson seemed reasonably pleased with her progress. He was, as Patricia began to realise, not one to hand out compliments easily, and she worked hard to win his approval. During rehearsals she sat in awe watching the leading members of the cast bringing the story alive through the power of their highly trained voices, and she was filled with admiration. She was a realist and she knew now that she would never achieve the dizzy heights of a leading role. However, she was not going to give up easily. Despite the discomfort of living in the lodging house, and the diet of pea soup, baked potatoes and the occasional boiled egg, she was determined to continue and to carve out a future for herself on the operatic stage. Despite pawning Sir Michael's half-hunter and her wedding ring, Patricia realised that it was going to be more difficult to survive on her meagre pay than she had previously thought. By the time Mrs Humphries had been paid and money set aside for their one meal a day, there were only pennies left to live on until the following Friday.

Rehearsals continued all day Saturday and Patricia had just left the theatre with Nancy when a man stepped out of the shadows, blocking their way.

125

Patricia stifled a scream and Nancy prepared to run.

'Patsy, my darling. It is I, your most ardent admirer.'

Patricia slapped him on the arm. 'Larkin Eldon, you startled us.'

He took her gloved hand and raised it to his lips. 'A thousand apologies. It was my intention to surprise you, not to scare you to death.'

'What are you doing here, Eldon?'

He held his hand to his heart, his eyes twinkling with amusement. 'You've missed me. I'm so touched.'

'No, I haven't missed you. I've been too busy surviving on next to nothing. My allowance from Greystone ceased when his will went to probate.' Even in the flickering light of the gas-lamps she could see that his expression had changed, and a look of genuine concern creased his handsome features. 'I didn't know that you were so badly done by, my love. I went to Rockwood Castle only to discover that you had run away to London.'

'I didn't run away, as you put it. I left to further my career on stage.' Patricia shivered as a sudden shower fell from a pewter sky. 'Do we have to stand here making small talk in the pouring rain?'

He proffered his arm. 'Of course not. You ladies must allow me to take you to dinner. Rules is only a few steps away.'

Patricia would have liked to refuse, but the thought of a decent meal and a glass of good wine was enough to make her pocket her pride. She felt Nancy flinch at the mention of food, and she managed a smile.

'As a matter of fact that would be quite welcome.'

'Then that's settled. Come with me, ladies.' Eldon led them into the restaurant and was greeted by the *maître d'hôtel* with evident pleasure.

When they were comfortably seated Patricia studied the menu. Her mouth was watering but she tried to appear nonchalant, as if she and Nancy ate here every evening.

'So how have you been managing?' Eldon asked conversationally.

'I have a small part in the opera. Everything is working out very well, and Garson is very pleased with my progress. Anyway, let's talk about you, Eldon. What have you been up to recently?'

'My creditors were becoming a nuisance and I had a gambling debt to repay. I have a rich aunt who lives in Yorkshire so I thought it was time to visit her. She, of course, was delighted to see me and she bestowed a rather meagre sum of money on me. However, it was enough to enable me to call in at Rockwood Castle before returning to London. It's amazing how quickly one can travel around the country these days on the railway. Now, ladies, what will you eat?'

'Have whatever you want, Nancy,' Patricia said firmly. 'Lord Eldon is paying so you need not worry about the cost.'

Eldon eyed her suspiciously. 'Things haven't been going so well, have they, Patsy? I know you and you're a really bad liar.'

'I don't know what makes you doubt me, Eldon.' Patricia sipped the wine that the waiter had just poured into her glass. 'We are very comfortable in our lodgings, aren't we, Nancy?'

Nancy nodded, murmuring something unintelligible.

'I still don't believe you.' Eldon leaned back in his chair. 'I know a hungry woman when I see one, and both you ladies have already consumed a basket of bread rolls while you wait for your hors d'oeuvres.'

'I have been working long hours with little time to eat,' Patricia said casually.

'Then we must remedy that.' Eldon smiled and signalled to the waiter and ordered another basket of rolls and more butter. 'It seems I've come along at the right moment. Now tell me all about your part in the opera, Patsy. Maybe I could sit in on some of the rehearsals.'

'Absolutely not,' Patricia said firmly. 'Garson doesn't encourage visitors while rehearsals are in progress. I can assure you I'm doing very well, so stop worrying. Anyway, never mind me, Eldon. Tell me more about why you had to run away to Yorkshire. Have you been at the gaming tables again?'

'It's nothing for you to worry about, Patsy. I've paid off my debt of honour and the rest of my creditors will wait patiently, as always.' Eldon sat back in his chair as the waiters descended upon them, serving the food they had ordered.

'I hope you don't expect me to pay for the meal,' Patricia said when the last waiter had hurried away.

'But you are doing so well, my dear. You told me so yourself.'

Nancy choked on a morsel of beef, covering it up with a stifled cough.

Patricia shot her a warning glance. 'It's all relative, Eldon. We don't eat like this every night.'

'I wouldn't dream of allowing a lady to pay for her dinner,' Eldon said smoothly. 'You ladies are my guests and I have the pleasure of your company.' He raised his glass to Patricia and then to Nancy, who blushed and giggled.

Patricia leaned towards him, lowering her voice.

'Now tell me the real reason for seeking me out. I'm no longer any use to you socially, and I have no fortune to tempt you, so why did you go to all the trouble of finding me?'

'I have a proposition to put to you, Patricia. But that can wait. Let's enjoy the excellent meal. We'll talk later.'

9

They dined royally and, warmed by good food and wine, Patricia allowed Eldon to escort them back to their lodgings. At any other time she would have been embarrassed to admit that she was living in such humble accommodation, but she was feeling happy and slightly reckless. Nancy wandered on ahead, slightly tipsy, having been allowed to have a glass of wine. They came to a halt outside the lodging house.

'I'll go up to our room,' Nancy said, yawning. 'It's been a long day.'

'I'll follow you in a minute.' Patricia withdrew her hand from Eldon's arm. 'You wanted a word with me in private?'

'So this is where you've been lodging?' Eldon said casually. 'It's hardly the most salubrious area or the most impressive hotel.'

'All right, Eldon. There's no need to gloat. Now say what you have to say. I'm very grateful for the delightful dinner, but I am very tired.'

'I genuinely don't like to think of you living in a cheap boarding house, Patsy.'

'It's only temporary.'

'Nevertheless, I am still residing in my comparatively luxurious rooms just a stone's throw from Duke Street. To put it in a nutshell, my dear, I'm offering you a home and my protection. The girl can come, too. You'll need a maidservant.'

Patricia gazed at him in surprise. 'You are asking me to live with you, Eldon?'

'Yes, that's right. You will be safe and well cared for. What do you say?'

'Are you mad?'

'No, I pride myself on being quite sane, if a little impulsive at times, but this is a serious offer.'

'You want me to live with you as your mistress? Is that what you're saying?'

'That would be a delightful arrangement, but I have two bedrooms. If you insisted you could have a room of your own. I might have a certain reputation when it comes to affairs of the heart, but I am a gentleman by birth.'

'But my reputation would be in tatters. How could you even suggest such a thing?'

'Who cares what others might say or think?'

'I would be ostracised by everyone, Eldon. I would be a common kept woman, and my career in the theatre would be ruined before I've even begun.'

'It might be enhanced by a little scandal, my love. I really care for you, Patsy. I always have, but I had no chance while you were married to Greystone. I can't offer marriage because my aunt would cut me off without a penny. She has an heiress lined up for me, an offer I might have to take up eventually, but that wouldn't affect my feelings for you.'

Patricia raised her hand and caught him a smart blow on his left cheek. 'You are a despicable cad, Eldon.'

He rubbed his cheek with a rueful smile. 'Yes, I know, but my intention is to take care of you, Patricia. Do you really want to live in a cheap lodging house for the rest of your life?'

'Go to hell, Larkin Eldon. That's surely where you will end up.' Patricia turned on her heel and marched into the building, slamming the door behind her. She hurried upstairs to their tiny room beneath the eaves and let herself in to find Nancy sitting on the bed, brushing her hair.

'What a lovely gentleman,' Nancy said dreamily. 'He's so handsome and charming. I think he is in love with you.'

Patricia was trembling as she closed the door. She was upset and, more than that, she was furious that Eldon had even considered making such a proposition. 'The only person Eldon loves is himself, Nancy,' she said bitterly. 'Don't be taken in by his charm and good looks.' She threw her cloak down on the only chair in the room. 'I'm going to bed, and I suggest you do the same.'

'Oh, sorry.' Nancy leaped to her feet. 'I wasn't thinking.'

Patricia sighed. 'No, dear, I'm sorry, I didn't mean to be sharp with you. One day we'll have a better room than this and you'll have a proper bed all to yourself.'

'I don't mind sleeping on the floor,' Nancy said, chuckling. 'We had a lovely meal. What wouldn't I give to dine like that every evening?' She sank down onto the straw-filled palliasse that Mrs Humphries had begrudgingly supplied, and continued applying brush strokes to her long hair.

Patricia stripped off her outer garments and slipped on her nightgown before climbing into bed. The mattress was hard and lumpy and there was a stale smell that lingered in the rough ticking. As she laid her head on the pillow she thought longingly of her home in Duke Street, and for a few moments she was almost tempted to take Eldon up on his offer. But no, that was never going to happen. She had seen the last of

132

Lord Eldon. From now on she would concentrate on forging a career on stage whereby she could be independent and never have to rely on any man again. None of them was to be trusted, she decided wearily. Her husband had left her financially embarrassed and virtually homeless, and Eldon had treated her like a courtesan. She closed her eyes and sank into a deep sleep of pure exhaustion.

★　★　★

No matter how hard Patricia worked at her very small part in the opera she could not seem to please Garson, and after another two weeks of rehearsals she was beginning to think that she had made a terrible mistake. She received little encouragement from the rest of the cast, as most of them seemed to think that she had been given the part because her mother was a famous singer and Garson's friend. Added to all this, the meagre wages she received barely lasted the week. Mrs Humphries had to be paid first and after that Patricia had to eke out what was left for food. On Thursdays she and Nancy existed on pea soup from one of the street vendors and it was hard to function on an empty stomach. Nancy became a scavenger, going round the market after close of business to search for scraps of fruit or vegetables that were edible, and the occasional bunch of watercress. But there was always competition from the homeless, who lived on what they could find, or to steal when they were desperate. The flower-sellers fought over broken blooms that they made into nosegays and sold to passers-by. It was a brave person who took on these women, who fought like tigers to protect their livelihood. Patricia found herself existing in an alien world, hovering between those who enjoyed well-fed, comfortable lives, like Garson Thorne and his established cast members, and the destitute who endured half-lives in the shadows of Covent Garden and Seven Dials.

Matters improved very little after the new production opened in May. The opera was a huge success but Patricia's small part went unnoticed by the critics. Garson congratulated the whole cast but he did not single her out for particular notice, and there was no question of an increase in her wages. As the season wore on and she had to learn different roles, most of which were very small, there were expenses that were unavoidable. Nancy was in desperate need of new boots, and even a pair from the second-hand shop was out of the question. Patricia needed more stage make up and she was desperate for something as simple as a cake of sweet- smelling soap. Washing in cold water every day had made her skin rough and sore, and it was an absolute necessity to visit the public bath house once a week to bathe themselves and wash their clothes. Patricia tried not to think about the hip bath that the servants had filled with hot water in her bedroom at Duke Street, and the delightful scent of lavender soap, or the clean flannel and warm towels handed to her by Betsey. All that was gone now, and it seemed as though she had dreamed of the luxuries she had once taken for granted.

After a particularly gruelling week of performances and also rehearsals for the next production, Patricia was desperate for a bath and clean clothes. Both she and Nancy were at the limit of what they could accomplish with so little food and poor sleep. It was then that Patricia remembered Glorina's predictions. What she had said about a man who could not be trusted must apply to Eldon, who had been conspicuous by his absence for more than three weeks. Then Patricia remembered the name of Glorina's sister. Starlina Beaney lived in Bleeding Heart Yard, Holborn, and if she could foretell the future she might be able to help. It was there that Patricia and Nancy went on a Sunday morning, their only day off in the week.

It was a day more typical of April than May, with lusty showers followed by intervals of bright sunshine. Patricia and Nancy walked briskly, dodging the quick bursts of rain by standing in doorways until the clouds had passed over. They reached Bleeding Heart Yard from Greville Street and found it to be as dark, shady and depressing as the name implied. A public house stood next to a row of dilapidated buildings and semi-derelict warehouses. Men stood in groups around braziers filled with burning coals, while women carried water from the pump in Greville Street with small children clinging to their filthy skirts. The residents eyed Patricia and Nancy suspiciously, and one woman took a clay pipe from her mouth and spat at their feet as they approached her.

Patricia eyed her warily. 'Good morning, ma'am. I'm looking for Starlina Beaney. Can you tell me where she lives?'

'We don't want strangers here.' The old woman spat again, this time aiming for Patricia's boots.

Nancy collared a small ragged boy. 'Do you know Starlina Beaney?'

'What's it to you?' the boy demanded, raising a filthy face to glare at Nancy.

She took a farthing from her purse and held it above his head. 'This is for you if you show us where she lives.'

The boy squinted up at her, wiping his runny nose on his sleeve. 'A halfpenny would do, miss.'

'A farthing now and another farthing if we find Mrs Beaney.'

'She's a witch,' the old woman said gloomily. 'She's a Romany witch and she'll cast a spell on you, or a curse.'

'Nonsense.' Patricia motioned the boy to walk on. 'Take us to her and you will have the other farthing.'

He led them to a doorway in the corner of the cobbled yard. The narrow building, squashed between the pub and a near derelict warehouse, looked as though the life was being squeezed out of the dirty red bricks. The door was battered and broken, barely filling the gap. The boy hammered on the splintered wood.

'Hey there, old Romany woman. You've got visitors.' The boy stood back, holding out his hand.

Nancy held the coin above his head. 'Only if she proves to live here.'

'Come on, you old besom.' The boy backed away as footsteps echoed through the interior of the house. 'She's coming.' He jumped up, snatched the coin from Nancy's fingers and ran off with several other small boys chasing after him.

The door opened just a crack and a beady eye peered out at them. 'What d'you want?'

Patricia stepped forward. 'I'm looking for Glorina Cottingham's sister, Starlina Beaney.'

'Why did she send you here?'

'I don't really know, but I'm hoping you can help.'

'You got money?'

136

Patricia clutched her reticule even tighter than before. She had what was left from her wages after paying the rent to Mrs Humphries. 'Yes, I have.'

The door opened and a waft of foul-smelling air greeted them as Starlina moved aside to let them in. 'Come in and shut the door.' She hobbled off towards the back of the building, leaving Patricia and Nancy little option but to follow her. She led them into a room where a desultory fire gave out minimal heat and a sudden shower beat against the broken windowpanes sending spots of rain onto the bare boards. 'I got nothing, as you can see. I'm a poor woman.'

'She's a liar.' A high-pitched voice from the corner of the room made both Patricia and Nancy turn with a start.

A large African grey parrot was chained to a perch and it stepped up and down, moving from side to side. 'Liar,' he repeated loudly. 'Liar.'

'Shut up, Chiriko,' Starlina said crossly. 'Don't take no notice of that stupid bird.'

'She's got money,' the bird said, cackling with laughter like the old woman.

'What can I do for you, lady?' Starlina eased herself down onto a saggy armchair by the fire. 'Why did my sister send you here?'

'I don't really know why Glorina said you could help. I need money.'

'Don't we all?' Starlina laughed, sounding very much like her parrot. It joined in, cackling hysterically.

'No, I mean I am prepared to earn it, but I need to find extra work and a decent place to live. I can't afford to stay where I am at present.'

Starlina sat back in her chair and closed her eyes.

137

'I see a fat woman and a dingy lodging house. She's cheating you both. You are paying too much for your attic room in Covent Garden.'

Patricia and Nancy exchanged startled glances. 'How did you know where we live?'

Starlina opened one eye and her thin lips curved in a grin. 'Second sight. I know that you are a singer, and not a very good one.'

'That's not true,' Patricia said hotly. 'I am learning to be a better performer.'

'Then you need to practise where the real folk are, not your stuck-up opera-goers. You need to start at the bottom, my love. You will find your talent, but it don't lie in that sphere.'

'How am I to find my real talent then?'

Starlina filled her clay pipe with tobacco and lit it with a spill from the fire. She sat there, staring at Patricia and puffing out smoke, her thin cheeks working like a pair of old leather bellows. 'The Goat and Compasses,' she said at last. 'Puddle Dock.'

'I don't know what you mean. What is the Goat and Compasses?'

'I think it's a public house,' Nancy whispered. 'I don't know where Puddle Dock is.'

'Don't you girls know nothing?' Starlina exhaled smoke into the cold air. 'It's close to Blackfriars Bridge, St Andrew's Hill. Don't you know nothing about London?'

'Not that part, to be sure.' Patricia forced herself to be patient with the old woman. How this person was related to glamorous Glorina was a mystery, but she seemed to have some of her talents and Patricia could not afford to upset her. 'Please continue, Starlina.'

'Go to the Goat and Compasses and speak to Leo

Wilder, he's the landlord. He knows me and he owes me a favour. He might need someone to entertain his customers. I can't promise nothing, but I do see him in your future, although you might not want him there.'

'But you think he can give me work? And what about accommodation?'

'Look, lady, I ain't your nanny. You got to sort out your own future. I'm just giving you a tip to get you on the right road, or the wrong road, whichever it might turn out to be. But fate decrees that you will meet with Leo Wilder at some time in the near future, so it's up to you.'

Patricia could see that she was not going to get any further help from Starlina Beaney and she opened her reticule. 'How much do you want for your invaluable assistance?'

'A florin will do.'

'Two shillings?'

'That's what I said.'

'It's too much,' Nancy said in a low voice. 'Give her a shilling.'

'A curse. A curse.' The parrot squawked, jumping up and down on his perch. 'Ha, ha, Mother give a curse.'

'Be silent, Chiriko.' Starlina shook her fist at him. 'I could put a curse on you if I felt so inclined. A florin or a curse. Take your pick.'

Patricia handed her a silver coin. 'There you are. Thank you, Starlina. I'll go to Puddle Dock and speak to Mr Wilder.'

'Get out the grog,' the bird called loudly as Patricia left the room.

She could not get out of the dark, dingy dwelling

139

place quickly enough, and Nancy almost barged into her when she had to stop to open the front door. The atmosphere outside was little fresher than that within, but Patricia took deep breaths of the smoke-laden air and hurried past the groups of idle men, closing her ears to their lewd comments and catcalls.

It was a long walk through reasonably quiet Sunday streets and the only crowds they saw were the congregations of the various churches spilling out onto the pavements. By the time they reached the pub, which overlooked Puddle Dock, both Patricia and Nancy were footsore and very thirsty. Despite the fact that it was Sunday, the public bar was packed with men, most of whom seemed to work on the wharfs or were seamen enjoying some time ashore. They stared openly at Patricia and Nancy as they made their way to the bar. A potman was serving and he eyed them suspiciously.

'Women aren't allowed in here on their own, missis.'

'I'm not a customer. I want to see Mr Wilder.'

'He might not want to see you.' The potman winked at the men who were leaning on the polished mahogany counter and they laughed.

'Tell him that Starlina Beaney sent me.'

The potman's smile was wiped away by a startled look. He handed a pint of ale to one customer and took the money. 'Wait there, missis.' He disappeared through a door at the back of the bar, returning moments later and beckoned to them.

Ignoring the sly remarks from the drinkers, Patricia held her head high as she threaded her way between the tables to enter the back room with Nancy following close on her heels.

The parlour was surprisingly bright and cheerful with a coal fire roaring up the chimney and a comfortable-looking sofa upholstered in deep crimson velvet, contrasting with the two shabby wing-back chairs that faced each other on either side of the hearth. A man was seated at an oak table with a plate of food, barely touched. He rose to his feet and Patricia was struck by his imposing presence. It was not simply the fact that he was tall and well built, but he had the confident manner of a man used to command, tempered by his slightly raffish appearance. Perhaps it was the single gold earring he wore in his left ear, or the tan leather waistcoat over an open-neck shirt that made him look like a corsair from a romantic novel. His dark hair waved back from a high forehead and his blue eyes twinkled with a hint of humour. 'What can I do for you, ladies?'

Patricia dropped her gaze. It was rude to stare and yet she found it almost impossible not to look at the man who was so different from anyone she had ever met. She took a deep breath. 'My name is Patricia Carey and I've just been to see Starlina Beaney. She thought you might give me a job.'

He motioned them to take a seat. 'Well, now. I'm acquainted with Starlina, but we are not exactly on the best of terms. I can't think why she would have sent you here. This isn't the sort of place for someone like you.'

'Miss Carey is an opera singer,' Nancy blurted out.

'Thank you, Nancy, I can speak for myself.' Patricia clasped her hands tightly behind her back. 'I will be frank with you, Mr Wilder. I am finding it difficult to exist on the pittance paid by the opera company. Starlina thought you might allow me to entertain your customers, by singing,' she added hastily.

Leo Wilder's generous lips parted in a smile. 'I didn't imagine anything less, Miss Carey. But this is not the sort of place that would suit a lady like you and your young friend.'

'I am serious, Mr Wilder.'

'You both look tired and thirsty. Might I offer you a drink?' Wilder glanced at Nancy, who was staring hungrily at his plate of food. 'Perhaps something to eat? Have you walked far?'

'Yes, quite a long way. A glass of water would be most welcome.'

He laughed. 'You're in a public house, Miss Carey. I don't trust our local pump water since the last outbreak of cholera. Perhaps a glass of ale would be safer?'

'Or coffee?' Patricia was not fond of ale, although she might have opted for a glass of cider, but she needed to keep a clear head and they had a long walk back to Maiden Street.

'Coffee it is, then.' Wilder opened a door that appeared to lead into a kitchen, judging by the gust of steam and the tempting aroma of roasting meat. 'Two cups of coffee for my guests.' He closed the door again. 'Well, now, Miss Carey. Tell me why you think my patrons would enjoy hearing you sing?'

'I have a good voice and I enjoy performing. Perhaps opera isn't for me, but to be honest I need the money and I have to find somewhere better for Nancy and myself to live.'

Wilder sat down and rested his feet on the rungs of the next chair. 'I may be a humble publican, Miss Carey, but I can tell you are a lady. Why are you in a position like this? I am very good at sensing if a person is not telling me the truth, so perhaps you would

142

like to convince me why I should take you seriously.'

'You're right, Mr Wilder. I was brought up to be a lady, but I am recently widowed, and my husband left me with nothing but debts.'

'You are very young to be a widow. Have you no family to support you?'

Patricia struggled with the desire to tell him to mind his own business, but she could not face yet another week of near starvation, hard work and an uncomfortable bed. 'I have family in Devonshire, but I have my pride, as I think you will understand. I don't want to be beholden to them or anyone. Nancy and I have managed thus far and we will continue whether you decide to help us or not.'

Wilder folded his arms. 'So, let me get this straight. You come from a good family but you are too proud to ask their help. Your late husband left you high and dry and you have decided that opera is not for you.'

'Not exactly. I plan to continue with the opera company if they have a part for me in the next production,' Patricia said hastily. She could see Nancy edging closer to the rapidly cooling plate of roast beef and glistening roast potatoes doused in rich gravy. 'Mr Wilder, if you don't want that food my young friend is close to starving. Might she finish it up for you?'

He glanced at Nancy and laughed. 'Certainly not. Go into the kitchen, young lady. Tell them that Leo says he wants two more plates of roast beef right away. You both look as though you could do with a good meal. Keep me company while I enjoy my food and then we'll talk business. Do sit down and relax, Miss Carey, or may I call you Patsy?'

Patricia was not going to risk the chance of a good meal and the possibility of paid work by allowing him to see that she was annoyed by his familiar way of addressing her. She managed a smile. 'Yes, of course.' She sat down in the chair that he pulled up for her. 'Something to eat would be very welcome.'

He sat down opposite her. 'So what do you have in mind? Do you propose to sing for your supper, so to speak?'

She had not thought that far ahead and his keen look was unnerving. 'I don't know. I assume you would tell me what was required of me.'

At that moment Nancy returned carrying two plates piled high with roast meat, potatoes and carrots, and a generous helping of gravy. She placed them on the table and sat down, tucking in without waiting to be asked.

'Your friend is very hungry,' Wilder observed, chuckling. 'Let's eat and we'll talk later.'

'Thank you.' Patricia tried not to bolt her meal but the food was good and she was extremely hungry. She realised suddenly that her host had finished eating and was sitting back watching her intently. 'I'm sorry,' she murmured, swallowing a mouthful of hot roast potato. 'We haven't eaten like this for a while.'

'Except for the dinner that Lord Eldon treated us to at Rules,' Nancy said seriously. 'That was topping.'

'You are acquainted with Larkin Eldon?' Wilder raised an eyebrow.

'Do you know him?'

'I asked first, Miss Carey.'

'Yes, I know Lord Eldon, but the least said about that the better.'

'He is very popular with the ladies.'

Patricia replaced her knife and fork, leaving a large potato and some carrots untouched. 'How can you possibly know that?'

'Larkin used to be a frequent customer here. He and his wealthy friends enjoyed coming east to see how the poor live and to gamble away from the prying eyes of the police.'

'You say that Lord Eldon *used* to come here. Does that mean he no longer visits your premises?'

'I haven't seen him for a while, but customers come and go. He could turn up this evening, or he and his friends might have found somewhere more to their liking.'

'You intimated that they came here to gamble illegally.'

'I wouldn't say it was against the law exactly. We do have games behind closed doors occasionally, but this is a respectable tavern. However, our clients are mainly seafarers from all over the world as well as dock workers. Perhaps it's not the right place for an opera singer.'

'I know some popular songs,' Patricia assured him. 'I'll entertain your customers but that's all. I won't mingle with the crowd.'

Wilder was silent for a moment. 'I can't imagine why Starlina sent you here, Patricia Carey. A lady like you simply doesn't fit in with the sort of men who frequent my pub. You'll hear language that will shock you and see things that no young lady should see. This is a rough area and I can't act as your chaperone.'

'I'm not asking for favours.' Patricia met his amused gaze with a steady look. 'I am desperate for honest work. Both Nancy and I need somewhere to stay where we won't be fleeced by a greedy landlady. I assume you have accommodation we could rent cheaply.'

'I suppose Starlina told you that. As it happens there are two small rooms under the eaves that might suit you, but you would need to take a look before you commit yourself, and,' he added firmly, 'I would want to hear you sing before I make up my mind.'

'Of course,' Patricia said confidently. 'When you've finished your meal, Nancy, we'll inspect the rooms that Mr Wilder has to let.'

He shook his head. 'Oh, no, Patsy. I will hear you sing first.'

'Have you someone who could accompany me on the piano? I saw one in the bar as we came through.'

'I thought you would be able to play and sing.'

'Well, I can't. I've always had someone to do that for me.'

'I can play the piano,' Nancy said boldly.

Patricia turned her head to stare at her young friend in surprise. 'You never told me that.'

'I learned at boarding school. I love music and I find I can pick up a tune quite easily.'

'There you are then,' Wilder said complacently. 'What will you sing for us?'

Patricia thought quickly. ''Home, Sweet Home' and 'Come into the Garden, Maud'.'

'I thought we might have a burst of grand opera,' Wilder said with a wry smile. 'Can you play those songs, Nancy?'

'Yes, of course I can, and many more.'

'Very well then.' Wilder rose from his seat. 'Come into the bar and I'll introduce you to my customers. If they're not too drunk I'm sure they'll appreciate the music.'

Suddenly nervous, Patricia could do nothing other than to follow him into the taproom. He led them to the piano and called for silence. It took a while for the chattering to cease, but when Nancy sat down and played the introductory bars of 'Home, Sweet Home', there was complete silence.

Patricia stood by the piano, clasped her hands to her bosom and began to sing. She had not expected such a polyglot audience to sit and listen, but to her surprise there were even some stifled sniffs when she finished the sentimental song. The silence that followed was unnerving and for a moment she was prepared to escape out into the street, but then one man began to clap, followed by the rest of the customers and the potman. There were cries of 'More', and Wilder gave her a nod of approval.

'Thank you,' Patricia said breathlessly. 'I will now sing 'Come into the Garden, Maud'.' She finished again to tumultuous applause, cheers and clapping.

'That's all for now, gentlemen,' Wilder said firmly as he escorted Patricia and Nancy into the back parlour. 'We'd better talk business, Patsy.'

'I agree, but first I'd like to see the rooms you have in mind for us.' Patricia met his gaze with toss of her head. 'We won't be fobbed off this time. Now you can see that I'll bring in customers.'

10

The rooms were beneath the eaves as Wilder had said, and they were not large, but they were clean and each one was furnished with a cast-iron bedstead, a chest of drawers, a wash stand with china bowl and jug, and a wooden chair. Rosalind prodded the mattress and was satisfied that it would be reasonably comfortable. The sheets smelled fresh and there were a couple of fluffy woollen blankets and a patch-work quilt. Rag rugs made pools of colour on the bare floor boards, which had obviously been swept recently. Patricia's room overlooked the wharf and the river beyond, and Nancy's window had a view of the houses at the bottom of St Andrew's Hill.

'How much rent will you charge us?' Patricia asked warily.

Wilder leaned against the doorpost, eyeing her speculatively. 'I don't expect payment, but I won't be paying you a wage. You'll work for tips from the customers, but I'll include your food and drink, providing you don't turn out to be topers. I think we'll all benefit from such an arrangement.'

'Why won't you pay us for our efforts?'

'You could earn more in tips on a good night than you're earning at the theatre, of that I'm certain. You'll need to build up your repertoire, but generally speaking the men aren't too fussy. They like a pretty woman with a sweet voice, and you have a young girl playing the piano to touch the hearts of the toughest old salt.'

'I don't know,' Patricia said slowly. 'What happens if we don't get any tips?'

'You'll have to try a different song. I'd leave that to you. That's my offer. You'd better talk it over. But now I have work to do. Let me know when you've made up your minds.'

He left the room and Patricia could hear his firm-booted steps on the stair treads as he made his way back to the taproom. She turned to Nancy, who had leaped onto the bed and was testing its softness.

'This will be heaven after sleeping on the floor at Ma Humphries' place.'

'What do you think then?' Patricia would not normally have asked a fifteen-year-old's opinion on such an important decision, but she had come to respect Nancy's sharp intelligence.

'It's up to you, Patsy. I mean, I'll only be playing the piano but you'll be entertaining all those workmen and sailors. It will get rough sometimes and you're a lady born and bred. Do you think you could stand all the drunks and the bad language?'

Patricia slumped down on the bed. 'Oh my!' she said, sighing. 'This is much more comfortable than the bed I'm paying such a lot of money for. Free food and drink, Nancy. We wouldn't need to earn a great deal and anything we did get would be ours to keep.'

'You mean you'd share it with me?'

'Of course I would. I can't sing unless you accompany me, and we'll both have to learn to put up with whatever comes. I say yes.'

'I say so, too. But what about your career in the opera?'

'I won't give up easily, although I know I haven't

inherited my mother's gifts. I was foolish to think that I could follow in her footsteps, but I can sing, especially when it comes to popular songs. Let's go downstairs and tell Mr Wilder that we'll be moving in tonight.'

'Tonight?'

Patricia laughed. 'Why not? The beds are made up and I notice we have a fireplace in each of the rooms, so when it's chilly we can keep warm. There's even a little trivet in my room so I can make a pot of tea or heat some soup. This will be luxury compared to living in Ma Humphries' horrible hotel.'

★ ★ ★

Mrs Humphries did not take the news well. 'I should have a week's notice that you are leaving?'

'Well, I'm sure you won't have any difficulty in letting the room,' Patricia replied smoothly. 'You're always telling us that you have a waiting list of prospective tenants.'

'I will have to withhold the money deposit you paid.'

'That's not fair.' Nancy took a step towards her but was restrained by Patricia.

'The rent is up to date, Mrs Humphries,' Patricia said coldly. 'We've left the room in the same condition in which we found it. What right have you to withhold my money?'

'It's in my bank, Miss Carey. I'm the only one who can withdraw it, and I'm keeping it to cover the inconvenience.'

'You are a cheat, Mrs Humphries. You take advantage of people in need of relatively cheap accommodation,' Patricia said angrily. 'We could rent a whole house for

150

what you're charging us.'

'You won't find anywhere cheaper in this district, although if you want to live in Seven Dials or Clare Market you'll find yourselves sharing a room with complete strangers.'

Patricia tossed her head. 'Keep the money. We're leaving and glad to be away from here.' She picked up her valise and motioned Nancy to follow her and she marched out of the building.

'You told her,' Nancy crowed. 'But she should have refunded the deposit.'

'I don't care. I'm just glad to be out of there. Don't say anything to anyone at the opera house about our move to the pub. I know that Garson wouldn't approve, and I'm not entirely sure I'm doing the right thing myself.'

'I thought you wanted to move.'

'I do, but I'm having second thoughts. On one hand, we'll have warm beds and good food, but on the other, it is a rough area, and then there's that outside chance that Lord Eldon might decide to walk into the bar.'

'He did treat us to a nice meal.'

'And he insulted me with his proposition.'

Nancy giggled mischievously. 'But if you'd accepted we would be living in style and you wouldn't have to entertain the customers at Mr Wilder's pub.'

'I know,' Patricia said, pulling a face. 'That makes it even more difficult. But the prospect of comfortable beds and decent food is too tempting. We'll see how it goes, Nancy.'

★ ★ ★

Next evening Patricia left the theatre before the last act, in which she had no part. Wilder had not mentioned a specific time for her to entertain his customers, but she had not considered how difficult it might be to get from the theatre to Puddle Dock or how long it might take. She had been impulsive all her life, although until now she had had someone to curb her caprices. After a considerable wait she managed to attract the attention of a passing cabby. She bundled Nancy into the hansom cab and climbed in after her.

'I'm afraid this is going to be expensive,' Patricia said gloomily as the cabby flicked his whip over the horse's ears and the vehicle moved away from the kerb. 'I was so pleased to be offered work and accommodation that I ignored the difficulties.'

'It's safer to take a cab.' Nancy settled down, clutching the door that protected them from the mud and rubbish being thrown up by the wheels. 'We'll make it up with the tips we get.'

'Yes, of course,' Patricia said with more conviction than she was feeling. She could hear Hester's voice telling her to think before she acted, and Rosie had echoed that advice. The only person who had never criticised her had been her late husband and she found herself missing him more than she would have thought possible. Greystone had his faults but he had made her feel safe and secure, even if it had been an illusion.

They travelled on in silence until the cab drew up outside the pub, where they alighted and Patricia paid the cabby. She was beginning to realise the cost of the luxuries that she had previously taken for granted.

Nancy hesitated outside the pub door. 'It sounds very noisy inside. Is there another way in?'

152

'There must be.' Patricia stood aside as the door opened to eject a drunken seaman, who staggered and fell into the gutter. He lay there for a few seconds before scrambling to his feet, swearing volubly. Patricia grabbed Nancy by the arm and led her down a side passage and through a gate into the back yard of the pub. It was very dark and they stumbled over kegs and empty bottles but eventually managed to reach the door to the scullery. A waft of hot air laced with tobacco smoke, stale beer and hot fat wafted out to greet them. The scullery maid cried out in surprise as they burst into the room where she was standing at the stone sink, up to her elbows in greasy water.

'I'm sorry if we startled you,' Patricia murmured as she backed into the corridor.

There was a maze of dark passages to negotiate and several times they opened doors that led into cupboards or storerooms piled high with bottles, jars and sacks of flour, but eventually they reached the parlour behind the taproom.

'We'd better take off our cloaks and go straight into the bar,' Patricia said hastily. 'I should have asked Wilder what time he expected us to arrive.'

'I knew you would be late.' Wilder appeared in the doorway. 'You need not look so worried. I doubted if you would get here any earlier than this, so you will just have to prove that you can deal with drunken customers, and I expect you to entertain them until we close at midnight.'

'Yes, of course,' Patricia said hastily. 'I'm sorry we are so late.'

'You'll have to sing for your supper and work hard for your tips.' Wilder shrugged and opened the door to the bar. 'After you, ladies.'

153

Patricia entered the smoky den followed by Nancy and they stood for a moment, unsure how to begin, but Wilder strode past them clapping his hands for silence.

'Gentlemen, as I promised you, we have the Puddle Dock songbird, Miss Patricia Carey, to entertain you, accompanied by young Nancy. Watch your language and no spitting.' Wilder pushed through the assembled drinkers, making way for Patricia and Nancy to reach the piano.

Trying to convince herself that this was simply another performance, Patricia announced the title of her song and Nancy began to play the introduction to a sea shanty, 'The Arethusa', followed by 'The Jolly Young Waterman'. Patricia had learned the words to a few of these lively songs at school, and she hoped that they might be popular with the locals as well as the seamen. She came to the end of the second song and there was unnerving silence — then someone began to clap and the rest of the drinkers joined in, stamping and cheering to show their appreciation. It was flattering to have such a good audience although they were very demanding, and if Patricia stopped to take a breather there were shouts of encouragement, urging her to sing again. The smoke made her throat and eyes sore and the constant demands of the rowdy customers exhausted her. She was aware that some of the younger men were ogling Nancy, who blushed rosily and kept her head down as she concentrated on pounding the piano keys. If the remarks became too personal or suggestive Wilder was there in a moment to reprimand the transgressor, or to throw out a persistent drunk. Patricia found herself admiring his strength and his ability to deal with aggressive

154

behaviour. By the time Wilder rang the bell to call time Patricia was losing her voice.

'You did well,' Wilder said as he locked the door behind the last straggler. 'You've earned your supper tonight, ladies.'

Nancy swayed on her feet. 'I don't think I can eat. I'm too tired. Would you mind if I went straight to bed, Patricia?'

'Of course not, but you should eat something.'

Wilder raked over the coals to make the fire safe for the night. 'There's food laid out in the parlour. I suggest you have something before you go upstairs. Cook makes a very decent cup of cocoa.'

'Thank you,' Patricia said tiredly. 'We will have something.' She guided Nancy into the parlour where the table was laid with bread, cheese, cold beef and pickles. As Wilder had said, there was a steaming jug of cocoa.

Nancy collapsed onto the wooden settle and toyed with a slice of bread and butter while Patricia filled a mug with cocoa and passed it to her.

'I dare say we'll get used to this way of life,' Patricia said hopefully. 'I haven't counted the tips, but we seem to have amassed a tidy sum.'

Wilder entered the parlour, closing the door to the taproom and locking it. 'Drunken sailors tend to be generous. I don't know if you will stand it here, but at least you're willing to try.'

Patricia drew up a chair and sat down. She filled a plate with cold meat, cheese and pickles. 'I'm starving.'

'It's easy to see that you've had people to take care of your needs,' Wilder said with a wry smile. 'I doubt if you'll stay here for long. You'll soon get tired of the hours and the trials of dealing with drunkards.'

'I haven't got much choice.' Patricia spoke more sharply than she had intended. 'I mean I need the money and somewhere to live. I've yet to try out the bed, but it felt reasonably comfortable. After living in Mother Humphries' lodging house anything would seem luxurious.'

Nancy rose to her feet, covering her mouth to suppress a yawn. 'I'm going up now, Patricia. I'll say good night.'

'Sleep well, Nancy. I'll be following you very soon.' Patricia picked up her knife and fork and began to eat. She knew that Wilder was watching her but she chose to ignore him. The food was plain but excellent and she could look forward to a good night's sleep.

'I know you aren't interested in my opinion,' Wilder said slowly, 'but I think you ought to go home to your family in Devonshire. They are obviously people of means and you are a lady. You aren't cut out for this sort of life.'

Patricia swallowed a mouthful of roast beef. 'I think that's up to me. I did well tonight, didn't I?'

'Yes, I'm not denying that, but I had to keep an eye on you.'

'I'm not a child,' Patricia said angrily. 'I can look after myself.'

Wilder laughed. 'I must be mad taking on you and the young girl, but you're good for trade, and I'm always up for a challenge.'

Patricia pushed her plate away and stood up. 'So am I, Wilder. I'll say good night and I'll see you in the morning before I go to the theatre.'

'Just a minute, Patricia. Before you walk off in high dudgeon, we need to get one thing straight.'

She turned her head to glare at him. 'And that is?'

'Neither you nor Nancy must walkout alone. This is a rough area even in broad daylight. I've assigned someone to see you safely to the theatre each day, and to bring you home after the performance.'

'You can't do that.'

'I can and I will. As far as I'm concerned you might prove to be a good investment if tonight's performance was anything to go by. I am protecting my own interests by keeping you both safe.'

'Who is this person?'

'You will meet him in the morning. Good night, my songbird.'

Patricia was too tired to argue. She left the room with all the dignity she could muster and made her way upstairs. She would prove Wilder wrong about her ability to be independent, just as she would show Mama and all the family that she, Patricia Greystone, was a woman to be reckoned with.

Sounds of snoring emanating from Nancy's room convinced Patricia that she was asleep. Nancy had really outdone herself with her piano accompaniment, and she needed a good night's rest. Patricia went to her room, undressed and climbed into the bed. She sank down into the feather mattress and closed her eyes. It was sheer bliss and she drifted into a dreamless sleep.

★　★　★

Next morning Patricia was awakened by the sound of cranes clanking, barrels rolling and dock workers shouting to each other. Ships' horns tooted and steamers chugged up and down the river, sounding so close that they might have been in the street below. She raised herself and washed in cold water before getting dressed. Satisfied that it was a reasonable time to go downstairs for breakfast, she left her room and knocked on Nancy's door.

'Who is it?' Nancy demanded nervously.

'It's only me,' Patricia said, smiling to herself.

'Don't worry, Nancy. I'm going down to breakfast. Are you ready?'

The door opened and Nancy stood there in her nightgown. 'Almost. Give me a minute and I'll be with you. Don't go downstairs without me.'

Patricia waited in the doorway. 'There's no need to be nervous. Wilder won't allow any of his staff to bother us. He's been a perfect gentleman, even if he is arrogant and conceited, and clearly thinks that women are all stupid and helpless.'

Nancy slipped her plain linsey-woolsey gown over her head and sat down to put on her boots before coming to the door. 'You don't like him, do you?'

'He's given us a roof over our heads and the chance to earn a little extra money, but I don't have to like him to work here. We have to do our job and keep out of his way. I certainly wouldn't like to get on his wrong side.'

'I thought he was quite nice,' Nancy said as she followed Patricia down the narrow flight of stairs. 'He looked after us last evening.'

'That's part of the problem. He thinks we are incapable of taking care of ourselves. I know this is a rough area and I'm not going to wander around the docks on my own, but there's no need for him to hire a bodyguard for us.'

'Really? Is that what he's going to do?'

158

'So he said last night. I can't wait to see who is going to be our shadow for the foreseeable future. Unless, of course, I find more suitable employment elsewhere.'

'My bed was so comfortable,' Nancy said wistfully. 'And the food here is very good.'

'I haven't said we're leaving, not yet anyway. Come along, let's have breakfast before we have to meet the person who is going to escort us to the opera house. Although I've a good mind to refuse his services. You and I are quite capable of looking after ourselves.'

They entered the parlour to find that Wilder was just finishing his breakfast. He rose from his seat and motioned them to join him at the table.

'Good morning, ladies. I trust you slept well.'

'I did, thank you,' Patricia said warily. 'You seem to be in a very good mood.'

'I am always cheerful, unless of course someone annoys me and then you will see a different side of me.' Wilder turned to Nancy with a smile. 'I suggest you go into the kitchen and tell Cook what you would like to eat. He has a soft spot for you already, Nancy, but don't worry. Gardner has six children of his own, the eldest a girl your age, so you are quite safe with him.'

Patricia took a seat opposite Wilder. 'Do you see danger in everyone and everything?'

He nodded. 'You would, too, had you been raised in this area of London. It's quite different from your smart houses in Mayfair and the wealthy squares.'

'I realise that.' Patricia took a warm bread roll from the basket and broke it into small pieces. 'We will have to leave very soon. I daren't be late for rehearsals.'

'Don't worry. I have your escort ready to drive

you to the theatre. He will pick you up at a time you request.'

'Do I have to pay for his services?'

'No, that's taken care of. Blease owes me a favour or two.'

'Blease?' Patricia stared at him, frowning. 'That's an unusual name.'

'Maybe you know him. I believe he comes from your part of the country.' Wilder rose from his chair. He went to open the taproom door. 'Blease, there you are. On time, as ever. Come and meet the lady you will be protecting.'

Wilder held the door open and a well-dressed man strolled into the parlour. Patricia recognised him instantly.

'Miss Carey, might I introduce my friend Blease Ewart.' He turned to the man. 'Blease, this lady is Miss Patricia Carey, an opera singer and entertainer here.'

Ewart came to a halt. 'We've met, Wilder. It was several years ago, but I know Miss Carey and her family.'

Patricia rose swiftly to her feet. 'I do know you, but your name was Ewart Blaise.'

He shrugged and twisted his lips into as mile. 'Those were the days, my dear Miss Patricia. I was the owner of Rockwood Castle, for a while at least.'

'You were not,' Patricia said angrily. 'You pretended to be Piers' elder brother but it was all a lie. Your father was a shepherd and your mother a servant girl. What are you doing here?'

'Come, come, Patsy,' Wilder said smoothly. 'Blease is here to be of service to you and Nancy. I didn't realise you had met, but that is all in the past.'

'I would rather take my chances with the ruffians

160

who frequent the worse rookeries than to be beholden to you, Ewart Blaise, or Blease Ewart, whatever your name is. Don't come near me or my young friend. We don't need your services.'

11

Ewart shrugged. 'Surely what is past can be consigned to history. I am a changed man.'

'So you say, but we all thought that Piers had turned over a new leaf and it appears that he was still a criminal at heart, like you.'

'I'm not responsible for Piers Blanchard. I heard that he'd been transported to the colonies, but that had nothing to do with me.'

Wilder cleared his throat. 'This is all very interesting, but a waste of time. You are free to leave here on your own, Patricia — I am not your keeper — but if you have any sense you'll accept Blease's offer.'

Patricia turned on him angrily. 'Don't speak to me like that, Wilder. What gives you the right to meddle in my affairs? I didn't ask you to provide me with an escort and I certainly wouldn't trust this man.'

'Perhaps we'd better go,' Nancy said nervously. 'We don't want to be late.'

'Suit yourself, Patricia.' Ewart took a seat by the fire and spread his hand out before the blaze. 'I have better things to do.'

'I have no doubt of that,' Patricia said acidly. 'Whatever it is I don't wish to know.' She snatched up her cloak and reticule and walked into the taproom, ignoring the early morning customers with her head held high. She did not stop until she was a good way from the building.

'What was that all about?' Nancy demanded breathlessly. 'Who is that man and why were you so angry with him?'

'I'll tell you later. It's too complicated to go into now and we have to hurry. Garson won't forgive me if we're late again.'

★ ★ ★

Garson was waiting for them in the auditorium when they finally arrived at the opera house. He did not look pleased.

'What sort of time do you call this, Patricia?'

'I am truly sorry, Garson. But we've found rooms that are better, although further away. I promise you it won't happen again.'

He stood with his arms folded, glaring at her. 'No, it's not good enough. I've given you so many chances because of my friendship with your dear mama, but this is not going to continue.'

'I will try harder, I promise.'

'You promised before and look what happened. No, Patricia. I am sorry. You have some ability but you will never have a voice or a stage presence like Felicia. You will not be in my next production, although you may keep your part until we finish the run at the end of the week.'

Patricia gazed at him in despair. She was too proud to beg and in her heart she knew that what he said was true. She did have a good voice but she had neither the power nor the range that her mother possessed. She bowed her head.

'All right, Garson. I understand.'

He sighed. 'You are a disappointment to me, Patricia.' He hurried away, leaving Patricia and Nancy standing at the back of the auditorium.

'Perhaps I can get work in wardrobe,' Nancy suggested tentatively. 'It doesn't pay very well but it would help.'

'I need some fresh air.' Patricia clutched her hand to her forehead. 'I'm going outside. I can't breathe.'

Nancy hurried after her. 'Are you all right? What about the rehearsal?'

'You heard Garson. I'm no longer with the company. I don't care what happens.' Patricia burst out through the stage door, standing on the pavement to take deep breaths of the none-too-clean air.

'But he said you can continue until the end of the week.'

'He can give the part to someone else. There's always an understudy lurking in the wings awaiting their chance. I've had enough of Mr Garson Thorne's rules and regulations. We're free, Nancy. I've finished with the theatre for ever.'

A slow clapping sound made the both turn with a start. Blease Ewart was leaning against a lamp post, applauding Patricia's impassioned speech and grinning.

He straightened up and strolled over to them. 'You are an actress indeed, Patricia Carey. You always were, if I remember correctly, although I had very little to do with you when I was involved with your family.'

'What do you want, Ewart?' Patricia demanded crossly. 'How did you come to know Wilder, and why did you offer to be our escort?'

'Why indeed? I'm wondering that myself since you've proved to be nothing but rude and ungrateful.'

'That doesn't answer my question. Do you hope to get to my family through me?'

'My dealings with the Careys ended years ago,

164

leading to my enforced exile to France. I returned a few months ago and I ended up at the Goat and Compasses with just a few shillings in my pocket. Wilder helped me to get back on my feet.'

'If you expect me to feel sorry for your plight, you will be disappointed. You were prepared to take Rockwood Castle from my family, and you would have done so, had Alex not seen through your deception.'

Ewart eyed her with a calculating expression in his steel-grey eyes. 'You did not marry him, then? I saw the way things were and he had eyes only for your sister. What a pity.'

'You are a nasty man,' Patricia snapped. 'As a matter of fact, I married Sir Michael Greystone, but, sadly, he died not long ago. I chose to revert to my maiden name for professional reasons, but I am actually Lady Greystone.'

'Do you expect me to bow to you, my lady?' Ewart's eyes gleamed maliciously. 'If you married so well why are you singing in a dockside pub?'

'Her husband died, you half-wit,' Nancy cried angrily. 'Go away and leave us alone.'

'Yes, I don't know why you followed us here,' Patricia added. 'I have nothing further to say to you.'

'So be it. Go on your way, lady. I wash my hands of you.' Ewart turned his back on them, but he did not seem eager to move on.

Patricia grabbed Nancy by the hand. 'Come with me.'

'Where are we going?' Nancy asked anxiously. 'Perhaps we ought to return to Rockwood?'

'I refuse to give them the satisfaction of knowing that I cannot support myself. Everyone at home thinks I'm less than capable of looking after myself, so I'm going to prove them wrong.'

'If you say so.' Nancy fell into step beside her. She glanced over her shoulder. 'I think that man is following us.'

'Let him. I don't care what he does. I want nothing to do with Blease Ewart, or whatever he calls himself now.'

Patricia marched on but she was not concentrating on the route they took and before she realised what was happening they were in the middle of Clare Market. All around them was the now familiar hustle and bustle amongst dilapidated buildings and rookeries. Bare-footed children dressed in rags slunk along in the shadows like feral dogs, and the stench of overflowing privies and animal excrement was overpowering. Patricia quickened her pace, but in doing so she attracted a group of grimy urchins, who surrounded her, demanding money.

She clutched her reticule to her bosom. 'Go away. I won't give you anything if you continue to behave like guttersnipes.'

Before she knew what was happening the tallest youth sprang at her and snatched the reticule from her hands. He waved it over his head, laughing loudly, and the others in his gang joined in. They cavorted in circles around Patricia and Nancy, snatching at their clothes and jeering. A ragged girl appeared from seemingly nowhere and she tugged at Nancy's bonnet strings, dragging the one and only straw bonnet that Nancy possessed off her head. She donned it, dancing around, laughing and calling Patricia names that in ordinary circumstances would have made her blush.

'Stop this at once,' Patricia said in a low voice. She

could not quite control the tremor in the tone, and that seemed to amuse her tormentors even more.

'She's told us to stop.' The leader of the gang jingled the coins in Patricia's reticule. 'We'll eat today, mates.'

'No, you won't.' Blease Ewart snatched the bag from the surprised boy and clouted him round the ear for good measure. 'That will teach you not to steal a lady's purse.' He turned to the girl who was wearing Nancy's bonnet. 'Give that back or I'll call the constable.'

'I can get a few coppers for this, mister,' the girl said, poking out her tongue.

'You will have time to think about that when you're behind bars, my girl. Now give the lady her hat.'

'You got to catch me first.' The girl started to run but Nancy was too quick for her and she stuck out her foot, tripping the bonnet thief up so that she fell flat on her face in the filth. Nancy retrieved the hat and put it on her head, tying the ribbon tightly under her chin. The girl, who was covered in mud and dung, scrambled to her feet. Tears rolled down her cheeks, leaving white tracks.

'You wouldn't laugh if you hadn't eaten for two days,' she mumbled.

'Wait.' Patricia opened her reticule and took out a couple of pennies. She pressed them into the girl's dirty hand. 'Get some food. There must be some other way than stealing from others.'

The girl wiped her nose on the back of her hand.

'You don't know nothing, miss.' She ran away, pursued by the other street Arabs.

'That wasn't a good idea,' Ewart said, looking round at the gathering crowd, none of whom looked too friendly. 'Walk on quickly. Don't stop for anything.' He pushed ahead, clearing the way for Patricia and Nancy. The crowd dispersed but only because a fight had broken out over a piece of meat that someone had attempted to steal from a nearby stall. Patricia and Nancy seized the opportunity to get away as quickly as they could and they did not stop running until they were within the relatively safe confines of Lincoln's Inn Fields.

'You see, you do need me,' Ewart said, bending over to catch his breath. 'You don't know these streets like I do. You would have lost everything, had I not followed you.'

'They are so poor.' Patricia came to a halt, shaking her head. 'I've never seen poverty like that.'

'You were brought up in a castle, Miss Carey,' Ewart said stonily. 'How could you know how others less fortunate have to survive?'

'I didn't realise how things were. I thought I was poor, but I know now that was just an illusion. Compared to those people I had riches beyond belief.'

Nancy patted Patricia's shoulder. 'You're not to blame. We're all born to different stations in life. The trouble is I don't know where I belong. Maybe I should be out there picking pockets with the rest of them.'

'Or you could be a rich man's child,' Patricia countered. 'Your mama might have been a servant girl who caught her employer's eye. One thing is certain: you are not a common girl, Nancy. Never let anyone tell you differently.'

'This is all very charming,' Ewart said, curling his lip. 'We'd best head back to Puddle Dock. You can decide what you want to do when we get there.'

'I don't suppose I have much choice.' Patricia took Nancy by the hand. 'Come on. At least we have a roof over our heads, which is more than can be said for some of those poor people we've seen today.'

'Hurry up, ladies,' Ewart said crisply. 'I have business to attend. I wasn't planning to spend the day with you.' He marched on ahead, sweeping innocent passers-by out of the way.

Patricia and Nancy exchanged weary glances.

'I don't know who is worse,' Patricia sighed. 'Street Arabs or Blease Ewart. He seems to do exactly as he pleases.'

★ ★ ★

Wilder was behind the bar when they entered the tap-room.

'I see you caught up with them, Blease. Although I wasn't expecting you back so soon.'

'I'm just doing my job. I owe you, Wilder.' Ewart stood in the doorway. 'I'll be off then. The young ladies have no need of me for the rest of the day, but I'll be in for a drink this evening.'

Wilder acknowledged him with a nod before turning his attention to Patricia. 'That was a very short day's work.'

'I left the opera company. I decided it wasn't for me.' Patricia stripped off her gloves and tucked them into her reticule. 'I almost lost this to a thief. Ewart made them return it to me.'

'You see, I told you the streets aren't safe for someone like you, Patricia. You should not be here at all.' Wilder eyed her keenly. 'I think you need a cup of coffee with a dash of brandy in it. You're very pale.'

'It was frightening,' Nancy said boldly. 'I thought we were going to be set upon. Your man saved us.'

Wilder turned to the potman, who was busy polishing tankards. 'Take over, Jonas. I'll be in the parlour if anyone needs me.' He ushered Patricia and Nancy into the back room. 'Sit down and I'll tell Cook to make a pot of fresh coffee.'

Patricia found that her knees were suddenly weak and she sank down on the settle next to Nancy. 'Thank you, but there's no need to fuss.'

'Allow me to do something to help you, woman. You are far too independent for your own good.' Wilder strolled into the kitchen, returning moments later with a pot of coffee. 'It seems that my man in the kitchen has sixth sense. He'd made coffee for me, so we'll share it.' He placed the pot and mugs on the table and reached for a bottle of brandy from the dresser. 'Now then, if you want my opinion I think you should return to Devonshire, as I said before, but I suspect that you have other plans.'

Patricia accepted a mug of steaming hot coffee to which Wilder had added a generous tot of brandy. She sipped it tentatively. 'Yes, you're right. I was shocked by what I witnessed today. Ewart tells me that the area we wandered into by mistake is called Clare Market.'

'You want to steer clear of places like that.'

'The children who accosted us were very young and extremely poor. They were barefoot and filthy.'

'They live by their wits. It's a way of life.'

'But that's awful,' Patricia protested angrily. 'Why should they live in poverty?'

'There are the workhouses for those who are really destitute.'

'I'm talking about young children. They don't

deserve to go into such places.'

Wilder swallowed a mouthful of coffee. 'There's no point you fretting about it, Patricia. There's little or nothing you could do to alleviate their misery. They are too many.'

'I suppose so.' Patricia sipped the hot drink. 'Are there no charities that help these people?'

'Plenty, I am sure, but the rest of us have to earn our living in any way we can.'

Nancy rose to her feet. 'Is there anything I can do to help, Mr Wilder? I have nothing else to do today.'

'Yes, you have.' Fired with enthusiasm and warmed by the hot coffee and brandy, Patricia stood up. 'I don't believe that nothing can be done, Wilder.'

He stared at her, eyebrows raised. 'You're not going to do anything rash, are you?'

'I don't know what you mean. I've led a pampered existence until recently, but even now I am so much better off than the people I saw today, and particularly the children.'

'What do you intend to do?' Nancy asked excitedly.

'I'm not sure yet.' Patricia picked up her discarded cape and gloves. 'Where is the nearest pawnbroker, Wilder?'

'Now, Patricia, if you're thinking of selling anything of yours in order to feed a few urchins, allow me to give you some advice.'

She tossed her head. 'Thank you, Wilder. But I know what I must do.'

'All right then, but don't go to old Hawkes, he's a robber. There's a better place in Old Fish Street. You'll find it easily enough, but . . .'

'Thank you, Wilder.' Patricia did not wait to hear the rest of the sentence. 'Wait for me here, Nancy. I have something to collect from my room.' She hurried upstairs to her bedchamber and opened her valise. In a secret compartment at the base she kept a velvet bag containing the few pieces of jewellery, which Greystone had given her during their marriage. She selected a pair of gold earrings and put them in her purse. Having replaced the case, she went downstairs to join Nancy, who was waiting for her in the parlour. Of Wilder there was no sign.

★ ★ ★

The pawnbroker gave Patricia only a fraction of the earrings' worth, but she was not in a position to argue, and she accepted the money as well as the ticket that would redeem the pledge for an agreed sum.

'They were so pretty,' Nancy said sadly as she and Patricia walked away. 'I remember you wearing them when you visited us at Rockwood Castle.'

'Full stomachs are worth more than gold earrings. I'm going to buy as much food as I can with the money and we'll take it to those children in Clare Market.'

'They were very fierce. Maybe we ought to go somewhere less dangerous.'

'Nonsense, Nancy. Why would they harm anyone who meant them well? I just want to show them that there are people who care about them.'

'I haven't had anything to eat today; neither have you. We didn't have time for breakfast.'

'Don't worry. We'll stop at one of the food stalls and get some pea soup or a baked potato with lots of butter. You'll like that, won't you?'

Nancy nodded wordlessly.

Patricia walked on purposefully, stopping once to

purchase a large wicker basket from a second-hand shop, and again to buy them food from a stall on Ludgate Hill. Refreshed and revitalised, Patricia went on to fill the basket with bread rolls, cheese and apples, before making her way to Clare Market. However, once there she was beginning to doubt the wisdom of returning to such a terrifying rookery. The groups of men standing round, smoking clay pipes or chewing tobacco and spitting streams of liquid onto the cobblestones, appeared even more menacing. She was suddenly aware that although she had worn her plainest linsey-woolsey skirt and pin-tucked cotton blouse, with a shawl draped around her shoulders, both she and Nancy stood out amongst the ragged, unwashed people who frequented the streets and crowded into the tumbledown lodging houses.

On their way home that morning, Ewart had told her that it was possible to escape the law using series of passages linking the buildings in the rookery through the attics. She wondered how he had come by such information, but it confirmed her suspicions that he was still a criminal. They would not be seeing much of Blease Ewart from now on, of that she was certain. She dragged her thoughts back to the present as Nancy tugged at her sleeve.

'I don't like the look of those young ones,' Nancy said urgently.

Patricia glanced over her shoulder and saw a group of street Arabs trailing them. She came to a halt and turned to face them.

'I haven't got anything worth stealing,' Patricia said loudly. 'But I've brought you some food. You're welcome to it.' She placed the basket on the ground and stood back. As if from nowhere, children large

173

and small appeared and fell on the food. There was a frantic scrum for the contents of the basket and in seconds it was emptied. Unfortunately it was the oldest and strongest who took the food, leaving the younger, frailer children sobbing and hungry. Patricia realised her mistake and she felt hot tears burning the backs of her eyes.

'Look round,' Nancy whispered.

Patricia turned her head to see the groups of men and women had broken up and they were advancing on them with menacing expressions.

'I suppose you think that's clever.' A tall, muscular man wearing a bandana tied around his head, gypsy-fashion, stood before her. He wore a tattered cotton shirt, open to the waist and his coarse fustian trousers were secured by a wide leather belt. 'Tormenting nippers what are starving with your meaningless charity. Look what you done, you stupid bitch. You made the little 'uns cry when their bellies are aching for food.'

'I'm so sorry,' Patricia said slowly. 'I meant well. I didn't want that to happen.'

'Because you're a stupid, nose in the air, do-good. Well, that shawl of yours will fetch a tidy sum in Rosemary Lane, and that will feed a few nippers.' He turned to the crowd who were closing in on them. 'What say we strip these rich ladies and sell their duds to buy vittles?'

'Or gin?' A woman in the crowd suggested, laughing hoarsely.

'Do something,' Nancy urged in a frantic whisper. 'They're not joking.'

Patricia clasped her hands in front of her, closed her eyes and started to sing. Her voice rang out loud and clear, echoing off the tall buildings. The sentimental words of 'The Hazel Dell', mourning the death of poor Nelly, seemed to stop the mob in its tracks. The roar of the crowd subsided and there was a stunned silence as everyone listened to the sad tale, sung in Patricia's clear soprano. She forgot everything other than the drama of the words and the emotion of the musical score, but it was only when she came to the end of the song that she realised how much it had affected those listening.

Nancy nudged her in the ribs. 'Sing something else.'

Without stopping to think Patricia launched into 'Ben Bolt', another heart-rending song about sweet Alice who lay beneath a grey granite stone in the grave-yard. It was hardly a cheerful air, but it seemed to go down equally well. When she came to the tear-jerking end there was stillness and then someone started clapping, followed by another and another until the whole market was alive with thunderous applause and calls for her to 'sing again'.

'I'm sorry, but I have to go now.' Patricia had to raise her voice to a shout in an attempt to make herself heard.

'Let's leave while they're happy,' Nancy whispered, tugging once again at Patricia's sleeve.

Waving her hand and smiling, Patricia edged her way through the crowd. Hands reached out to pat her on the back or simply to touch her skirt as she quickened her pace, but the burly man who had threatened her at the beginning appeared in front of her, causing her to come to a halt.

'I am truly sorry about the food,' Patricia said lamely.

He held up his hand. 'You got the voice of an angel, miss. Sing to us again tomorrow and we'll forget about before.'

'You want me to come here and sing for you?' Patricia gazed at him in amazement.

'That's what I said. Us poor folk can't afford to go to them fancy theatres, but it don't mean we're heathens.'

'Of course not,' Patricia said hastily. 'Very well, if you think people would like to hear me sing again I will come, and I will bring food for the little ones.'

'Then I'll make sure them as needs it most gets it, miss. If I ain't around just ask for Jedidiah Wilkins, butcher.'

'Thank you,' Patricia said dazedly. 'I will.'

'You promise to come, miss?' Jedidiah gave her a stony stare. 'Us don't take kindly to people who don't honour their word.'

'I will come tomorrow at the same time.'

'Let the ladies pass.' Jedidiah flexed his muscles and the crowd parted respectfully. He led Patricia and Nancy to the relative safety of Sardinia Street and then backed away without a word.

'Well, now!' Patricia watched him as he headed off in the direction of Clare Market. 'Who would have believed that?'

'I'm just as surprised as you.' Nancy clutched Patricia's arm. 'Look who's coming.'

'I don't believe it.' Patricia turned her head and gasped. 'Are you still following us, Ewart?'

Blease Ewart strolled up to them with an ingratiating smile. 'That would be my pleasure, Patricia, but it's pure coincidence. I said I had business to attend to and I've just come from my solicitor's chambers. Why are you here?'

'You won't believe this,' Nancy began, ending with

176

a sharp yelp as Patricia stepped on her foot.

'I'm sorry, Nancy. How clumsy of me,' Patricia said, smiling. 'We went to the theatre to collect some of our things, but I don't have to explain my movements to you, do I?'

'Of course not. May I escort you back to Puddle Dock? You remember what Wilder said about protecting your safety, I trust?'

'Yes, of course, but we are not your responsibility.' Patricia was about to walk on but Ewart barred her way.

'And yet I do feel somewhat responsible, Patricia. I grew close to your family during the time that Piers and I were at loggerheads. I haven't been idle during these past years.'

Patricia looked up as the first drops of rain splattered on the pavement in front of them. 'I think we should find shelter.'

Ewart hurried them into a doorway. 'It's only a shower. It will pass in a few minutes.'

'I don't mind getting wet,' Nancy said pointedly.

'It's a long walk back to Puddle Dock.' Patricia placed herself between Nancy and Ewart. She knew how much Nancy disliked him, and although she felt the same, she felt as protective about Nancy as if she were her younger sister. However, the shower was brief and it stopped almost immediately, enabling them to walk on.

'I hope you will allow me to buy you luncheon in one of the chop houses.' Ewart treated Patricia to an engaging smile. 'The Cock in Fleet Street is very good, or Ye Olde Cheshire Cheese in Wine Office Court.'

'There's no need, really.' Patricia quickened her pace, but Ewart took longer strides in order to keep up with her.

'I behaved badly in the past, Patricia. I want to make it up to you and your family.'

She stopped and turned to face him. 'I'm sorry, Ewart, but I don't believe you and what's more I don't trust you. I remember only too well how you tried to cheat us out of our inheritance, so please go about your business and leave us alone.'

'You'll be sorry you treated me like this, Patricia. I'm an easy-going man but I never forget a slur on my good name.' He stormed off, leaving her staring after him.

'I have a nasty feeling that isn't the last we'll see of Blease Ewart,' Patricia said slowly.

However, Ewart did not come to the pub that evening, and Patricia decided not to tell Wilder about their narrow escape from the mob or the loss of her job at the theatre. She performed again for the customers at the Goat and Compasses and the tips were generous. The applause she received from the men in the bar was just as enthusiastic as that of the operagoers, if not more so. Perhaps she had been too ambitious as regards her operatic career. Mama had always told her that she alone had the talent in the family. But then Patricia remembered the reaction of the ordinary people to her singing, and she went to sleep that night with sounds of applause ringing in her ears.

12

Next morning, armed with two baskets filled with loaves of bread, slabs of butter wrapped in cabbage leaves and several meat pies, Patricia and Nancy set off for Clare Market. Patricia was nervous as they entered the notorious rookery, the stench from the butchers' shops and the tripe house mingling with the rancid odour of rendered fat and excrement. How people managed to exist in a place like this was a mystery, but Patricia was not one to give up easily and she pressed on, looking round for a familiar face. Within minutes they were surrounded by feral children and ragged women. The word had got round about the food that the lady in the straw bonnet had brought them, and eager hands tore at Patricia's skirts. Nancy gave a cry of fright as a young boy snatched a pie from her basket and ran off, pursued by a gang of smaller children.

'Where is Jedidiah Wilkins?' Patricia had to raise her voice to a shout in order to be heard above the babble of voices and shouts from the costermongers. She tried again. 'Jedidiah Wilkins.'

'Who wants me?' Jedidiah's deep voice boomed out from across the narrow lane, and he stepped out of his shop, wiping his hands on his bloodied apron.

Patricia waved to him, holding her basket out of reach from grasping hands. 'Mr Wilkins, we've come as promised.'

He strode through the crowd, which parted respectfully. 'Give me the food and I'll make sure it goes to the most needy.'

Hungry people milled around him, snatching at anything they could as he distributed the contents of the baskets, taking care to give to the youngest and weakest before allowing others to have a share. Patricia looked on, wishing that she had been able to purchase double the amount, although she had spent the last halfpenny of the money from the pledge on her gold earrings. However, it was a small price to pay when she saw a child munching a slice of bread and butter and another running off with an apple clutched in his dirty hand.

Jedidiah placed the empty baskets at their feet. 'All gone — that's the trouble with charity. Once it's gone that's the end of it, and tomorrow they will be just as hungry.'

'I would bring more if I could afford it,' Patricia said sadly. 'I had no idea that people suffered such dreadful deprivation or lived in such disgusting conditions.'

Jedidiah let out a bark of laughter. 'Spoken like a rich woman. Run away back to your big house, miss. You've done your bit for mankind.'

'Mr Wilkins, that's not fair.' Patricia grabbed his shirtsleeve as he was about to walk away. 'I turned my back on my past, or rather my past turned its back on me. However, I am almost as poor as these people nowadays. I live in an attic room at the Goat and Compasses, Puddle Dock, and I sing for my supper.'

He hesitated, looking down at her with grey-green eyes narrowed. 'I think you should sing to the people here. They're getting angry now the food has gone. Do what you did yesterday.'

'Yes, Patsy,' Nancy urged. 'Please do something.

They look very unhappy.'

Before she had a chance to protest, Jedidiah picked Patricia up and lifted her onto an upturned cart as if she weighed less than a feather. 'Sing for us again.'

Patricia's heart was pounding as she looked down into a sea of thin, scarred and dirty faces, but she knew what she must do. Slowly the grumbling and mumbling died away and there was silence while the people gathered to listen to Patricia singing 'Come into the Garden, Maud'. It seemed to go down well and she followed it with a cheerful sea shanty that had proved very popular with the clientele in the pub. She finished to a round of rapturous applause and requests for more.

'Lift me down, Mr Wilkins, if you please.'

'It's Jed to my friends.' He took her by the waist and swung her to the ground. 'You have the voice of an angel. You should sing to a bigger audience than this.'

'My career on the stage is at an end. I wasn't good enough to continue.'

'Maybe not as an opera singer, but you still have a lovely voice. You are young and pretty, and you have a way with you. Look around. This is a tough area and these people are not easily pleased. It takes something special to make them forget the lice and fleas that infest their bodies, let alone the gnawing pangs of hunger they suffer all the time.'

'You sell them meat. You could price it more cheaply. I can't feed them all.'

'I do what I can, but I have to live.'

'I've done what you asked,' Patricia said, glancing round uneasily. The good humour of the mob could change in a split second and she was nervous. 'Let me

181

go now, please.'

'All right, but you won't be able to forget what you've seen here, or the effect you've had on ordinary people who simply love a good song.'

'I must go now. Thank you for helping me, Jed.' Patricia snatched up the empty baskets and handed one to Nancy. 'If I can raise more money I will come again and bring food for the little ones.' She hurried off without waiting for him to respond.

'Come and sing for us again, love.' An old woman, sitting in a doorway, grabbed the hem of Patricia's skirt. 'I was asleep and I woke up to hear you singing. I thought I'd died and gone to heaven and it was an angel calling to me.'

'Thank you.' Patricia gazed at the wrinkled countenance. The woman could have been any age from fifty to seventy, but her eyes, beneath hooded lids, were a startling blue. 'I will try to come again and sing for you, ma'am. Do you have any family to take care of you?'

'Not so you'd notice, love. I had five children but four of them didn't live longer than a twelve month. The one who survived was wild and always in trouble. My Benny ran away to sea when he was eleven and that were nigh on twenty years ago. I ain't seen him for more years than I care to remember. He might be drownded for all I knows.'

'I am so sorry.' Patricia pressed a penny into the old woman's hand.

'Best move on quickly, miss. Them round here soon forgets their goodwill, especially if they think you've got money.'

Patricia glanced over her shoulder at a group of youths who were eyeing Nancy. 'We're going, ma'am,'

Patricia said hastily. 'Good luck and I hope your son comes home soon.'

'Come on. Let's go.' Nancy headed off towards the Strand, leaving Patricia little choice other than to follow her.

★ ★ ★

It was midday when they arrived back at the pub. Patricia opened the door with a feeling that all was not well, and as she stepped inside she came face to face with Lord Eldon and Blease Ewart.

'Patricia, my dear.' Eldon strode towards her, holding out his hands. 'Blease told me that you were living here.'

'You know that man?'

'Don't look so surprised. Blease and I belong to the same London clubs.'

'Really? That doesn't explain why you've come here. I told you before that I wanted nothing to do with you, Eldon.'

He laughed. 'My dear girl, I've been coming here for years. Wilder is kind enough to allow us to use his parlour for our card games.'

'Illegal gaming,' Patricia said acidly.

'Whatever you like to call it. I didn't think you were such a prude, Patricia. You were always one to cock a snook at rules and regulations.'

'Maybe, but I am not a law breaker. Anyway, how you choose to spend your time has nothing to do with me.'

Eldon put his head on one side. 'My dear, can we not have a truce? I did not mean to offend you when I offered you somewhere to live. I would have respected your privacy.'

'And ruined my already shaky reputation. I don't think we have anything to say to each other, Eldon.'

Ewart walked over to join them. 'I see you have been handing out alms again, Patricia.'

'Mind your own business, Mr Ewart.' Nancy stepped in between them. 'Miss Carey doesn't want anything to do with you either.'

'Go back to the schoolroom, Nancy. This is a conversation for adults, not children.'

Patricia could see that a heated argument was brewing and she glanced towards the bar where Wilder was watching them closely. He met her anxious gaze with a brief nod and strolled over to tap Eldon on the shoulder.

'My Lord, the parlour is free if you and Mr Ewart would like to eat now.'

'We will if Lady Greystone will join us, and her maid, too.' Eldon treated Patricia to his most charming smile.

'You know very well that I'm Miss Carey now, Eldon,' Patricia said angrily. 'And Nancy is not my maid. If anything, you might call her my accompanist. We earn our living by entertaining the customers every evening. I'm sure you wouldn't want to share your food with common entertainers.'

Ewart threw back his head and laughed. 'Let's see you answer that one, Eldon. Patricia has got your measure, my friend.'

'My dear, whatever you might be, you are not commonplace,' Eldon said smoothly. 'Do join us, and your young protégée. We will delight in your company, won't we, Blease?'

'Of course, we will. Wilder, set up two more places

184

and tell your cook we have two more at table. And open a couple of bottles of claret.'

Wilder turned to Patricia, raising an eyebrow in a silent question.

She hesitated. It would be wise to refuse, but she was very hungry and she could see that Nancy was pale with fatigue. They were both in need of a good meal and Wilder's hospitality did not stretch to luncheon each day. 'All right,' Patricia said reluctantly. 'But only because we haven't eaten today. We will accept your invitation, but first we need to take off our outdoor garments.' Patricia headed for the door with Wilder close behind her.

'I can send them packing if they annoy you, Patricia.'

'Thank you, but I've known Eldon for years. I can handle him.'

Wilder opened the parlour door and ushered her inside. 'All right, but if I sense that they are overstepping the mark I will take pleasure in throwing them out.'

'There really is no need. Lord Eldon might be a rogue but at heart he's a gentleman.'

'I don't call it gentlemanly to make offensive remarks to a lady.'

'You really are quite prim and proper at heart, Wilder,' Patricia said lightly. 'I am impressed.'

'I have standards that I like to keep and I expect others to respect them. Eldon is a libertine and a gambler. You are well shot of him, Patricia.'

'He was never anything but a friend and occasional escort when my husband's political work prevented him from accompanying me to social events. Ignore Eldon, I do.'

'If you say so. But I'm keeping my eye on both of them nonetheless.' Wilder went into the kitchen, closing the door behind him.

A gust of heat laced with the tempting aroma of roast meat tantalised Patricia's taste buds and she realised how hungry she was. Nancy burst into the parlour.

'That man Ewart keeps pinching me. I'll slap his silly face if he touches me again.'

'I'll have a word with him, Nancy. Let's enjoy a good meal first and then we'll leave them to their own devices. I don't know about you, but I'm starving.'

★ ★ ★

Eldon was on his best behaviour at luncheon, and Ewart followed his lead. They kept Patricia and Nancy entertained with amusing anecdotes, none of which was in any way offensive or embarrassing. Patricia was reminded why she had found Eldon good company in the past. She settled down to enjoy the food and a glass of wine, although she shook her head when Ewart tried to persuade Nancy to drink claret. She had seen the way he looked at the young girl and Nancy was obviously intimidated by him. A sharp word in Ewart's ear was called for and Patricia waited for a chance to get him on his own. It came at the end of the meal when Eldon went into the kitchen to order coffee and Nancy asked to be excused.

Patricia waited until Nancy had left the room. She leaned across the table, fixing Ewart with a hard stare. 'I know what you're trying to do, Ewart. Leave Nancy alone or you'll be sorry.'

He laughed. 'What will you do about it, Patricia?

186

The girl is plainly attracted to me. I can always tell.'

'So seducing young girls is part of your charm, is it, Ewart? Nancy can't stand the sight of you, and if you continue to harass her I will tell Wilder and have you thrown out of the pub.'

Ewart sat back in his chair, his cheeks flushed from drinking almost a whole bottle of claret and his eyes glittering with malice. 'You Careys are an arrogant bunch. You think you rule the world but your family are living in the past.'

Patricia leaped to her feet. 'Don't insult my family, Ewart. You are no one. If anything, you should be in prison for the crimes you committed.'

'What's going on?' Eldon closed the kitchen door behind him. 'Why are you arguing?'

'Ewart has his eye on Nancy and I told him to leave her alone. She's still a child.'

'A child's mind, maybe,' Ewart said, winking. 'A woman's body, definitely.'

'You are disgusting, Ewart. Keep away from Nancy and me. I don't want anything more to do with you.' Patricia turned on Eldon. 'You are just as bad as he is.'

Eldon threw up his hands. 'I said nothing. We were friends, Patricia. Nothing has changed.'

'This is a public house and I have no say in who comes through the door, but that doesn't mean I have to put up with your arrogance. I want nothing to do with either of you.'

Patricia marched out of the parlour, holding her head high, but she was more upset than she would have wished to admit. Eldon was her last contact with the life she had led as Lady Greystone. She was tempted to rush upstairs, pack her bags and return to

Rockwood Castle and her family. Perhaps she ought to go back to her solicitor and fight for the right to live at Greystone Park, but that would take more money than she could raise on the few valuables she had left. The alternative was to return to Rockwood and live the life of a widowed younger sister, subservient to everyone, even young Tommy, who was Bertie's heir. It would be almost as bad as being a spinster, who was tolerated but had no real place in the family hierarchy.

By the time she reached the top floor Patricia had come to a decision. She knocked on Nancy's door.

'Is that you, Patricia?'

Patricia opened the door. 'May I come in?'

'Of course.' Nancy wiped her eyes on her hanky. 'I'm sorry I walked out, but that man is hateful.'

'I agree entirely.' Patricia perched on the edge of the bed. 'I've told him what I think of him. In fact I told both of them that we don't want anything to do with them.'

Nancy's eyes widened. 'Were they angry?'

'I don't know and I don't care. I am furious with Ewart for making improper advances to you, and Eldon is little better. He thought it amusing until I put him right.'

'What will we do now? We can't stop them from coming into the pub.'

'We are going to continue exactly as we have been doing, with one exception.'

Nancy's eyes lit up with interest. 'Tell me, please.'

'I am going to sing in public as I did in Clare Market. I'll pick busy places and you can go round with a collection box. We'll use the money we make to buy food for the poor.'

'You mean we're going to work hard and give all the money away?'

'Being rich doesn't necessarily make you happy. When Greystone was alive I could have anything I wanted.'

'And you were happy. You've often told me so.'

'Yes, but it was all so false. I married my husband because I thought that wealth and status were all that mattered. I was fond of him and I wasn't unhappy, but it was all so superficial.'

'You didn't have to sing to drunks in a smoky public bar to earn your board and keep.'

Patricia laughed. 'That is so true, but I feel more alive now than I ever did when I was Lady Greystone, the perfect wife and hostess. Now I look back on those days it was like playing a part in the opera.'

'I'm trying to understand,' Nancy said sadly. 'But you still have Rosie and Alexander and the children. Wouldn't you like to go home and be with them?'

'Maybe, but I want to prove myself first. Nancy, if you would like to return to Rockwood I'll give you the train fare and take you to the station tomorrow. You do not owe me anything. I love your company but I would not be your friend if I forced you to stay when you really wanted to go home.'

'No, I want to be with you, Patricia. I don't know where I really belong, because I don't know who I am. I'll never know who my parents were or where I came from.'

'You're part of our family now, that's all that matters.'

'You've be so kind to me, and I'm really fond of everyone at Rockwood, although maybe not so much of Hester. I know she has a kind heart beneath the stern exterior, but I will always be the odd one out. She thinks my place is in the servants' hall.'

'No, that's not true, Nancy. Don't let Ewart or Eldon or anyone make you feel inferior. I want you to stay because I value your company and your good sense. I love you like a little sister.'

'I will stay and I'll help you to raise money to feed the poor, but it won't be easy. We were almost mobbed the first time we went to Clare Market.'

'We know what to expect now, Nancy. We'll show everyone what we can do.' Patricia gave her a hug. 'I'm so glad you want to stay with me.'

★ ★ ★

After a great deal of discussion about what might be the most financially rewarding place to entertain the crowds, Patricia and Nancy decided to head for Regent Circus South next morning. It was a busy thoroughfare with business people, affluent shoppers, housewives followed by their bustling maidservants, and gentlemen of leisure crowding the pavements. Crossings sweepers worked hard all day to keep the road clear of dung and detritus, and flower girls plied their trade, urging people to buy bunches of violets or sprigs of dried lavender. Watercress sellers vied with costermongers selling fruit and vegetables and it was in this busy place that Patricia climbed on top of an apple crate she had purchased for a couple of pennies in Covent Garden, and began to sing. She was extremely nervous and her hands were damp with perspiration as she clasped them to her bosom, but her voice was loud and clear and perfectly in tune as she intoned with words of 'Home, Sweet Home'.

No one seemed to notice her at first, and she was beginning to fear that the competition from the traffic and the cries of the costermongers would drown her attempts to be heard. Nancy clasped a straw bonnet in her hands, holding it out to passers-by although most of them walked on, barely noticing her.

After several hours Patricia had almost exhausted her repertoire and her voice was growing hoarse. She was in the middle of 'Ben Bolt' when a sudden shower sent people running for shelter.

'How much have we made?' Patricia asked, shivering as the rain soaked through the thin cotton of her print gown.

Nancy did a quick calculation. 'One shilling and tuppence. I think it's too busy here, Patricia. Everybody rushes about without seeing anyone else, let alone listening to your lovely voice.'

'I thought people might be more generous in the West End, but it seems it wasn't worth the long walk.'

'What we need is a pony and trap,' Nancy said, shivering and brushing rainwater from her eyes. 'That would make it easier to travel and you would have a ready-made stage.'

'You might as well wish for a chariot, Nancy. We haven't got that sort of money. Anyway, I think we're done here for the day. Let's make our way back to the Goat and Compasses. Tomorrow we'll do better.'

'At least we're one and tuppence better off now.' Nancy wrapped her shawl around her shoulders. 'My feet are so sore.'

'Mine, too. We'll learn from this. I refuse to admit defeat.'

It took them almost an hour to walk back to Puddle Dock. Wilder looked up as they entered the taproom, which was empty of customers except for two old men who sat in a corner, smoking their clay pipes and drinking ale.

'You look exhausted,' Wilder said casually. 'Where have you been all day?'

'It was a long walk. I could do with a nice hot cup of tea.' Patricia placed the apple crate on the floor and rubbed her sore fingers. She could feel painful splinters in her hand and her feet ached.

'Are you going to tell me what you've been doing? I have a vested interest in my songbird and her accompanist.'

'It was Patricia's idea.' Nancy slumped down on the nearest chair. 'We've been taking food to the poor in Clare Market but first we had to earn money.'

'You've been giving away food?' Wilder looked from one to the other in amazement.

'Nothing from your kitchen, Wilder,' Patricia said tiredly. 'I pawned my earrings and bought food for the children, mainly.'

'The crowd turned nasty when the food ran out yesterday, so Patricia started to sing,' Nancy added eagerly. 'They loved her, Mr Wilder. We had a job to get away. Anyway, today we tried the West End, but they were all too busy rushing about to pay much attention.'

'So you've become a street singer?' Wilder came from behind the bar, pulled up a chair and sat down. 'You never fail to surprise me, Miss Carey, or Lady Greystone, as I believe you should be called.'

'Eldon has been talking.' Patricia sighed. 'That man is a gossipmonger.'

'What are you doing, Patricia?' Wilder demanded angrily. 'Are you trying to get yourself killed by an

192

angry mob? What is a lady like you doing in a place like this, anyway?'

Patricia turned to Nancy with a tired smile. 'Would you mind asking Cook if we might have some tea? I'm sure you could do with some refreshment.'

'Of course.' Nancy hurried into the kitchen, allowing the door to swing shut behind her.

'Now then, are you going to tell me the whole story? You've given me snippets of the truth, now I want to know who I am dealing with.'

'What did Eldon tell you?'

'Nothing more than I already knew from the little you told me, apart from the fact that you have a title. What on earth is Lady Greystone doing here in Puddle Dock? Are you running away from something, Patricia?'

She smiled ruefully. 'I wanted to prove to my family that I am not the flighty young girl I once was. I needed to convince myself that I could run my life without someone telling me what to do and what to wear. I didn't choose to be poor, it just came about because my late husband failed to make a new will.'

'It doesn't sound as if he cared much what might happen to you.'

'I don't imagine he expected to die so suddenly. He was in his prime.'

'But he died all the same.'

Patricia nodded. 'I didn't know that he had lost all his money or that the estate was encumbered. His daughters inherited Greystone Park and the debts, which they will struggle to pay off. They were my friends when we were growing up, but they didn't want me to marry their father.'

'So you decided to become an opera singer.'

'Mama is well known in operatic circles. I thought I could emulate her success, but I was mistaken.'

'And yet you have a lovely voice. My customers would agree to that.'

'Why did you take me on, Wilder?'

He stood up to open the door for Nancy, who came in from the kitchen carrying two mugs filled with tea.

'I'll take mine upstairs, if you don't mind,' Nancy said, yawning. 'I think I'll take a nap before we have to perform this evening.' She placed a brimming mug on the table in front of Patricia.

'Of course. I think I might do the same when I've had my tea. I'll see you later, Nancy.' Patricia waited until Nancy had left before turning to Wilder. 'You didn't answer my question.'

'You came here recommended by Starlina. That woman knows things that are a mystery to others. I knew there must be a reason for helping you and the young girl.'

Patricia sipped the tea. 'Why do you think she sent us to you?'

'I'm still trying to work it out, but she was right about one thing — you are good for trade. But you are also a problem, because you don't listen to me when I tell you that you shouldn't walk the streets on your own. Fortunately you went to a decent area today, but you had to walk through rough streets to get there. I thought Ewart was genuine when he offered to escort you, but I think now he had an ulterior motive. What am I going to do with you, Lady Greystone?'

'I am not your responsibility, Wilder.'

'You put yourself into my hands when you agreed to live under my roof. You could simply stay here and entertain my customers, but you had this sudden urge to do good.'

'You make it sound like a bad thing.'

'It will be if you get mobbed and set upon by starving guttersnipes or dragged into a dark alley and assaulted by drunks. Do you understand what I'm saying, Patricia?'

'Are you telling me I should give up my attempts to raise money for such a good cause?'

'There are charities that handle those things. Leave it to them. I can't help you if you don't admit that what you're doing is too dangerous for someone like yourself.'

The potman put his head round the door. 'Sorry to interrupt, boss. There's a big fellow in the bar who's demanding to see Miss Carey. He looks and smells like a butcher. Shall I send him packing?'

13

'It sounds like Jed Wilkins.' Patricia jumped to her feet, spilling some of her tea on the table top. 'He's the man who helped us in Clare Market.'

'Find out what he wants, Jonas.'

'He asked for me,' Patricia protested. 'Stop fighting my battles for me, Wilder. I can deal with this.'

Jonas held the door open for her. 'I'll be right behind you, miss.'

'Thank you, but I know Mr Wilkins.' Patricia entered the taproom, which was empty apart from Jed Wilkins, whose large presence seemed to take up more space than several ordinary men. 'What can I do for you, Jed?'

He wiped his hands on his trousers, glancing warily at Wilder who had followed Patricia into the bar. 'They've been asking for you, miss. Those who heard you sing want to know when you're coming back.'

'I've been trying to raise money, but I didn't do too well today. I haven't any food for them, but I'll go out tomorrow . . .'

Jed held up his large hand. 'It ain't just the vittles. Well, in part I suppose it is, but mainly they want to hear them songs you sang.' Jed put his hand in his pocket and took out a collection of farthings and halfpennies. 'They took a hat round and raised this. I know it ain't much compared to what you must have been paid in the opera house, but it's all they could afford.' He stepped forward and pressed the money into Patricia's hand.

196

'I don't know what to say.' She stared at the coins, her eyes filling with tears. 'They are so poor. This should have been spent on food for the children and old people.'

'It's what they wanted, miss. Could you see your way to giving us a song or two?'

'Of course I will.' Patricia dashed a tear from her cheek. 'I'm very touched, but you must give this money back.'

He shook his head. 'They may be poor, miss, but they're proud. They don't want nothing for nothing. You keep the money. Just come and perform like you done yesterday.'

'Miss Carey isn't a street performer, Wilkins.' Wilder faced up to him and even though he was a tall, broad-shouldered man, he was dwarfed by the giant butcher.

'I can speak for myself, Wilder.' Patricia moved to stand between them. 'Of course I'll come, but I'll need you to stand with me. Not all of them are friendly.'

'That I'll do with pleasure, miss.'

'Wait a minute.' Wilder held up his hand. 'You know what the streets round here are like, Wilkins. I've been telling Miss Carey not to venture out on her own, especially to places like Clare Market.'

Wilkins nodded. 'Yes, boss. I agree.'

'You're talking about me as if I wasn't here,' Patricia protested. 'I am not afraid to go out alone in daytime.'

'Perhaps you should be, miss. I've got use of a pony and trap that I use to cart the carcasses from the abattoir to my shop. I'll come for you tomorrow morning at ten o'clock, if that's all right with you?'

'If it's not too much trouble that would suit me very well. Thank you Mr Wilkins.'

'Ten o'clock it is, miss.' Wilkins backed towards the doorway and let himself out into the street.

'Are you sure about this, Patricia?' Wilder folded his arms, glaring at her in disbelief.

'I've led such a selfish life, Wilder. I've never done anything for anyone in the past and now I'm trying to atone. The poverty I saw was truly shocking and if I can do something to help others it might make up a little for how I behaved in the past.'

'If you want my opinion, Patricia, I think you're wasting your time and your talent. Of course the people want to hear you sing — but going round the streets isn't for someone like you.'

She turned on him furiously. 'What do you know about it? I'm trying to make enough money to buy food for those who are close to starvation.'

'Don't you think you could do more by using your influence with the people in charge of governing the country to provide help for the needy?'

'I don't know what you mean.'

Wilder leaned against the doorpost, his expression serious, for once. 'There's only so much one person can do. Governments make the big decisions. You were married to a politician, weren't you?'

'I was, but after Greystone died I found myself very much alone. I was never really accepted by his political colleagues and their wives. They thought I had married him for money and position.'

'And were they correct?'

Patricia smiled wearily. 'Well, yes, in a way, although I was fond of Greystone. But I can't go back, Wilder. Even if I wanted to I have no London home now, and I'm not welcome at Greystone Park. I've told you all this before.'

'I will probably regret saying this again, but I really think you should return to your family.' He held up his hand as she opened her mouth to protest. 'You can do very little for the people who inhabit the rookeries of Clare Market and beyond. If you stay here for too long you'll waste your youth and beauty, not to mention your talent, and you'll be old before your time.'

'If I return to Rockwood I'll have failed to prove that I can look after myself.'

'Then don't go there. Join your mother wherever she is performing now. You can't save the world, so save yourself, Patricia.'

She met his concerned gaze and she knew that he was speaking from the heart. There was a guarded expression in his eyes, but she knew that Wilder was not the sort of man to show emotion. She had tried to ignore the fact that she was attracted to him from the start, and it was getting more difficult to remain aloof. It was also clear that the feeling was mutual. They were on dangerous ground, and if she weakened now she might be on the brink of making yet another big mistake. Wilder had been right about one thing: this was not the sort of life she had been born into and trained for. It would be so easy to give in to temptation, but it would be almost certain to end in heartbreak.

'My mother and her husband are in Milan at the moment,' Patricia said hastily. 'I learned that from Garson Thorne at the opera house.'

'Then go to Italy. Maybe you'll find what you're looking for there.' He turned away and went behind the bar.

'I'll think about it,' Patricia said doubtfully.

'If you need money for the passage . . . '

'No, thank you. I have a few things I can pawn to

pay the fare. I haven't made my mind up yet, but I will consider it seriously.'

'But you still intend to go to Clare Market tomorrow.'

'I promised I would and I can't let them down.'

★ ★ ★

Wilkins arrived at Puddle Dock next morning driving a dilapidated cart drawn by an equally aged and sad-looking horse. Patricia felt desperately sorry for the animal, and she could not help comparing it with the sleek thoroughbred chestnut mare that Greystone had purchased for her. However, all the things that she had taken for granted were fading to a distant memory, as if they had belonged to someone else. She pushed such thoughts to the back of her mind as she clambered up to sit beside Jed. Nancy sat on the floor of the cart, complaining bitterly that it smelled of animal fat and blood.

If Patricia had expected a rapturous welcome she was disappointed. The stalls were crowded with people trying to shout each other down as they vied to get the best bargains, and the stench was growing unbearable as the sun beat down and the temperature rose. Hardly anyone took notice when Jed called for silence. Patricia felt suddenly nervous and she wished she had spent the money on food for the children, who eyed her expectantly and then melted away, having lost interest. She started to sing, but it was almost impossible to make herself heard above the noise in the narrow street. Then, as if from nowhere, something hit her on the forehead and she was momentarily blinded by a trickle of juice from a rotten tomato. It was followed by a barrage of equally squashy vegetable matter, and even a roar from Jed Wilkins did nothing to stop the crowd gathering and enjoying the spectacle.

'Sit down. I can't do anything to stop this,' Jed said angrily as he flicked the whip over the horse's head.

The startled animal lunged forward, causing Patricia to collapse onto the seat, very nearly losing her balance. She would have fallen off if Jed had not caught her with one large hand and pulled her to safety. The cart rattled over the cobblestones and they left Clare Market in a hail of stones and clods of horse dung. Nancy curled up in a ball, sobbing with fright, but Patricia was furious and she shook her fist at the youth who hurled the last clod of muck at the cart.

'Why?' she demanded as she clutched the side of the vehicle. 'What went wrong, Jed?'

He shook his head. 'I dunno. There was a different crowd there this morning. I should have seen trouble brewing before it happened.'

'You couldn't have known,' Patricia said reluctantly. 'They took a collection yesterday and today they were throwing things at me. I don't understand.'

Jed shot her a sideways glance. 'I'm sorry, miss. I never thought it would end like that.'

'I meant no harm. I only wanted to do something to help the poor.'

'There's some folk you can't help. Those who wanted you there was shouted down, and they'll be sorry, but they can't do nothing about it. That's the way of the world.'

Patricia lapsed into silence. She was conscious of her dishevelled appearance and she was bruised and sore. The stains on her blouse and skirt would be hard, if not impossible to remove. Her bold venture had ended in disaster. She looked over her shoulder and saw Nancy still curled up, sobbing as if her heart would break.

'Don't cry, Nancy. Don't take it personally. It was a mistake to go back there. We won't do that again.'

Jed drew the cart to a halt outside the pub. 'I'm sorry, miss. Truly sorry.'

'It wasn't your fault,' Patricia said as she climbed down stiffly. 'I won't be coming again.'

'You're right. You keep to what you know.' Jed waited until Nancy has alighted and then drove off, his shoulders hunched and his head bowed.

Patricia placed her arm around Nancy's shoulders. 'Are you all right?'

'Sorry to be such a baby, but I was scared. I thought they were going to kill us.'

'They behaved like animals. We won't go there ever again. I think Wilder was right, Nancy. We should go back to where we came from.'

'To Rockwood Castle?'

'Eventually, but I think I'd like to go to Italy to find my mother. I haven't seen her for two years. Maybe she could find me a small part in the opera.'

'I thought you'd had enough of that sort of singing.'

Patricia opened the pub door. 'Not necessarily. I know I have a good voice, I just need help to get started. Maybe my future lies in Milan.'

'Good God, what happened to you?' Wilder stopped what he was doing to stare at them, and his lips twitched. 'It doesn't look as if your open-air concert went well.'

Jonas sniggered and a group of seamen stared open-mouthed.

'Yes, it's very funny,' Patricia said crossly. 'And you

202

were right, Wilder. It was a terrible mistake to go back there. We were pelted with rotten fruit and vegetables and even worse.'

'I think a trip to the public baths is called for.' Wilder turned away, his shoulders shaking. 'I won't say I told you so, but please go and change. You ladies smell like a farmyard.'

Patricia tossed her head. She marched through the taproom, dragging Nancy by the hand. 'If you say anything else, Wilder, I will never speak to you again.' She marched upstairs to her room, parting with Nancy at the door. 'Wilder was right. We need to go to the wash house.'

★ ★ ★

After a couple of hours spent in the public baths and wash house, Patricia and Nancy returned to the Goat and Compasses. As they entered the taproom Patricia was aware of a gaudily dressed woman standing with her back to her. There was something very familiar about her and she was chatting to none other than Lord Eldon.

'Nancy, will you take our things upstairs, please?' Patricia pressed the bundle of almost dry clothes into Nancy's hands. 'I'll be up in a moment.'

Nancy took one look at Eldon and hurried into the parlour, closing the door firmly behind her.

'Patricia, my dear, you look radiant. What has brought such colour to your cheeks?' Eldon beckoned to her. 'Come and join us. You know the signora, of course.'

Maud Grubb turned and gave Patricia an ingratiating smile. 'Larkin told me you was here, Patsy. I've

203

missed you, love.'

Patricia took a deep breath. 'Still drinking, Maud?'

'Just a little tipple to set me to rights, dear. Won't you join us?'

Patricia saw Jonas giving her an inquisitive look and she shook her head. 'No, thank you, Maud. I have things to do.'

'Nothing that can't wait, I'm sure.' Eldon pushed past a group of dockers and made his way to a table in the corner. 'Come and sit down, ladies.'

Maud was there almost before the words were out of his mouth. She pulled up a chair and sat down, patting the empty seat next to her. 'Come on, Patsy. I want to hear what you've been doing since we parted.'

Patricia hesitated. She wanted to refuse, but there must be a reason for Eldon to bring Maud to Puddle Dock and she was frankly curious. She sat down beside her.

'I left the opera company and I work here, Maud. Does that satisfy you?'

'You ain't so proud now, are you, dearie? You was a lady when we last saw each other, and now you're the same as Maud Grubb — a street singer and public house entertainer. Ain't that ironic?'

'Now, now, Maudie. Don't be naughty,' Eldon said jovially. 'We all know that Patricia has had some bad luck, and both you and I have had plenty of that, haven't we?'

'We certainly have.' Maud tossed back a glass of port in one mouthful. 'How about a refill, Larkin, love?'

'In a minute, Maudie. Don't be greedy.'

'Why are you here, Eldon?' Patricia demanded. 'You haven't come simply to pass the time of day with me.'

He sat back in his seat, eyeing her with an amused smile. 'That's the Patsy I know and love. Straight to the point and no nonsense.'

'Stop shilly-shallying about, Eldon.' Maud leaned towards Patricia, lowering her voice. 'Starlina told me that you were thinking of joining your mama in Italy.'

Patricia stared at her in amazement. 'How could Starlina have known that? I have only just come to that conclusion myself.'

'Starlina has second sight, dearie. You know that. Anyway, is it true?'

'If Starlina says so, then I suppose it must be right.'

Eldon sighed. 'Don't be angry, Patsy. To tell you the truth both Maud and I need to get away from London for a while. In fact, it would be better if we left the country for a considerable period of time.'

'What have you done, Eldon? And how do you fit in, Maud?'

'Need we go into that now?' Eldon glanced round apprehensively. 'Walls have ears, you know.'

'I'm not discussing this with either of you.' Patricia rose to her feet. 'You have got yourselves in a mess, and I don't know what part you've played, Maud, but don't look to me to help you.'

'It might be to your advantage, dearie.' Maud put her head on one side. 'I could well get transported if my case comes to court. A trip abroad would save my soul.'

'What did you do? I'm not going to listen to either of you until I know.'

'Another glass of port would help me remember, Larkin?' Maud held her glass out to him.

He rose to his feet. 'Are you sure you wouldn't like

a tot of brandy or rum, Patsy? It might help you to relax a little.'

'No, Eldon. Just get what Maud wants. I'll give you five minutes and then I'm going to my room.'

Maud cleared her throat. 'Well, I got a bit swipey and the copper who arrested me said I'd stolen money from the woman I worked for. I took me wages, that's all, but she lied and went to the police.'

'Surely you could prove that she owed you the money.'

'There was the question of a gold necklace and a pair of ruby earrings, too. They said I pawned them but the pawnbroker lied as well. It weren't me. Would Signora Gandolfi stoop to such a low thing?'

'I don't know, but I suspect you might do anything if you were drunk enough.'

'Well, the beak won't believe me, dearie. I've been up before him too many times. I was going to pay the old besom back, but she never gave me the chance.'

Eldon approached the table, handing a glass of port to Maud. 'Sip that, Maudie. You won't get another.'

Patricia eyed him curiously. 'I've heard what Maud has to say, so what about you, Eldon? Why have you got to flee the country?'

'Debtors, my love. My aunt refuses to give me another penny unless I propose to a cross-eyed heiress with as much charm as a plank of wood. I'm afraid it's the old story of gaming debts, coupled with bets on horses that had three legs instead of four. What can I say?'

'What is it you expect me to do exactly?'

'You are respectable, Lady Greystone. If you was to travel abroad with your servants no one would question you. You could get a passport easily, with us

206

just acknowledged briefly. The authorities would trust you.' Maud took a dainty sip of her drink.

'And I would be there to protect you, Patsy,' Eldon said firmly. 'If you were thinking of travelling on your own with the child, you would find yourself in a very difficult position.'

Patricia was silent for a moment. There was something in what Eldon said. Her experience in Clare Market was still fresh in her mind, and she had to admit that women going abroad on their own were likely to find themselves in a compromising situation. When she and Nancy reached Milan safely she could send Eldon and Maud on their way.

'Let me think about it, Eldon,' Patricia said slowly. 'And if I did agree, you, Maud, would have to promise to cut down your drinking. You would give yourself away far too easily.'

Eldon held out his hand. 'You know it's the only way you could travel so far in safety, Patsy, my love.'

She brushed his hand away. 'I would want you to promise not to annoy or molest Nancy or myself. If, and I say *if*, I were to agree to such a mad plan, you would have to behave like a real gentleman, not the rogue you undoubtedly are.'

'My dear, I understand. But please think quickly. I still have my carriage, which we could use to get to Dover, and all I need is a coachman. I had to let mine go, or rather he left because I couldn't pay him.'

'Are you suggesting that we should travel as a family?' Patricia eyed him warily.

'I would be your brother and Maudie would be your aunt, until we reach the coast, of course. Nancy will act as your maid. I have it all thought out.'

Patricia rose to her feet. 'I'm not promising anything. Come back here tonight and I'll give you my answer. I need to discuss things with Nancy first.' She hesitated, turning to give each of them a searching look. 'Just tell me how Starlina knew my plans.'

Maud shrugged. 'Jonas is her brother. He tells her everything.'

Patricia shot an accusing look at the potman, but he avoided meeting her angry gaze.

'Wilder ought to be told about this,' she said firmly.

'I think he knows, dearie.' Maud licked her empty glass. 'That's a good drop of port. I don't suppose you'd care to change your mind and buy me another, Larkin, love?'

Patricia did not wait to hear Eldon's answer. She left them and went straight to the parlour where she found Wilder seated at the table, frowning over an open ledger. He looked up and smiled.

'You look a lot fresher now. I hope you're feeling better.'

'Yes, thank you.' Patricia met his gaze with an unflinching stare. 'Did you know that Jonas is Starlina's brother?'

'Yes, of course.'

'And he passes on anything he hears in the pub to his sister. No wonder she knows other people's secrets.'

'Is there a point to this, Patricia? I'm sorry, but I'm trying to balance the books and it's not easy.'

'Did Eldon tell you that he's in trouble and thinking of going abroad?'

Wilder put down his quill pen and closed the ledger. 'Yes, he told me.'

'And did he also tell you that he and Maud Grubb want me to travel with them so that they can escape the country?'

'Not in so many words, but I guessed as much.'

'You didn't think to warn me?'

'You keep telling me that you want to run your own life and to mind my own business. Would you have believed me, anyway?'

'Maybe not. It all sounds quite preposterous.'

'Are you going to take them up on their offer?'

'They are trying to escape the law, Wilder. If I go with them I put myself and Nancy in danger of being arrested as accomplices.'

He shrugged. 'On the other hand, perhaps it's better to associate with the devil you know. Eldon is a gambler with a certain reputation as far as women are concerned, but I believe he is sincere in his regard for you. As to Maudie Grubb, I've known her for years. She's too fond of the bottle and she's light-fingered, but she's a survivor. Real life isn't neat and tidy, Patricia. People are good and bad in equal quantities, but as I see it, neither of them has done anything to physically harm another person.'

'So you think I should accept their offer to accompany me?'

'That's entirely up to you.' Wilder opened the ledger and picked up his pen.

Patricia uttered an exasperated sigh as she walked out of the room and headed for the staircase. Perhaps she could get more sense out of Nancy.

*　*　*

That evening when Patricia and Nancy went down to the taproom to entertain the customers, they were still undecided. Nancy did not like the idea of travelling with Lord Eldon, and Patricia had her doubts about the wisdom of throwing their lot in with two people who were on the run from the law. She had worried that Eldon might still be in the bar, waiting for her answer, but to her relief there was no sign of him or Maud. She moved to the piano amid murmurs of encouragement from the regulars, and Nancy took her seat at the keyboard. Patricia had just started to sing when the pub doors burst open to admit a police sergeant and two constables. There was a shocked silence as the sergeant marched up to the bar.

'Leo Wilder, I'm arresting you in the name of the law.'

Patricia pushed through the crowd to face the sergeant. 'What has he done, officer? Why are you arresting him?'

'It's nothing to do with you, miss. I would keep out of this if I were you.'

Wilder came round from behind the bar. 'It's all right, Patricia. I'll sort this out.' He turned to Jonas. 'You will have to lock up, but I'll be back soon.'

Patricia watched helplessly as Wilder was escorted from the building. She made her way to the bar. 'What has he done, Jonas? Why have they arrested him?'

Jonas rolled his eyes. 'They can make up charges if they want to. It's easy to fall foul of the law in a place like this.'

'But they must have some good reason to suspect that something illegal has been going on.'

'I should keep out of it, like the copper said, miss.' Jonas tapped the side of his nose. 'Least said the better.'

'Never mind the guv, miss. Give us a song.'

Patricia turned to the man who had spoken with an

attempt at a smile. 'I'm sorry. I don't really feel like singing now. Nancy, come with me.' She hurried from the bar to the sound of boos and hisses.

'What happens now?' Nancy asked breathlessly.

'Heaven knows,' Patricia closed the parlour door. 'If Wilder doesn't return tonight I'll go to the police station to find out what's happening.'

'What do we do in the meantime?'

'I'm going into the kitchen to make a pot of tea. There's nothing we can do but wait.'

'If Wilder goes to prison we'll be in trouble,' Nancy said tearfully. 'We'll have to find somewhere else to live, and other work, too.'

'We're leaving one way or another. But if Wilder doesn't return I think we might have to go sooner.'

★ ★ ★

Nancy had gone to bed and Patricia was about to follow her when she heard the front door rattle. Jonas had gone home and for a moment Patricia thought the police might have returned, but as she peered into the taproom she saw Wilder enter, locking the door after him. She hurried over to him.

'You're back. What happened? Why did they arrest you?'

'I was allowed bail but I'll have to attend the magistrates' court on Monday.'

'What did they accuse you of, Wilder?'

'It doesn't matter. They want me out of here and in all probability I'll lose my licence.'

'I don't understand. What have you done?'

'The police accuse me of harbouring criminals and allowing illegal gambling to take place on the premises.'

211

'I know a good solicitor. You must fight this.'

His face was hidden in the shadows but she sensed that he was smiling.

'I don't stand a chance if this comes to court, Patricia. Eldon told me he needed a coachman. I'm very good at handling the reins.'

14

Patricia gave Wilder a searching look. 'Do you mean that you'd leave your home and your business to travel with us, even though you might lose everything you've worked for?'

'If it's a choice between a few years in prison or the relative freedom of the Continent, then it's not a difficult decision, even if I have to put up with Eldon and Maud for a while.'

'But you are innocent, Wilder.'

'Do you really believe that?'

'Yes. I mean, I think you are. I've never seen anything illegal taking place here. You don't associate with known criminals, do you?'

'I have allowed some gambling to take place, but not on a large scale. As to the association with the underclass, well, that's a matter of opinion. Half the people who live in this area are involved in some kind of unlawful activity or other, and I haven't always been an upright citizen. I'm no better and no worse than any of them, but I stand to lose everything including my freedom if I'm convicted, even on a trivial charge.'

'Then come to Italy with Nancy and me. We don't need Eldon and Maud.'

Wilder reached out to take hold of her hand. 'Patricia, listen to what I have to say. For your own sake, go back to your castle in Devonshire. Forget travelling anywhere with me or with Eldon. We are no good for you.'

She snatched her hand free and backed away. 'You

213

know nothing of what I want or how I feel.'

'Think it over,' Wilder said firmly. 'But I'll be leaving tomorrow night, after we close. You have until then to come to a decision. Either way you can't stay on here. If I go this will become the sort of place that the police say it is now. Neither you nor Nancy would be safe.'

Patricia left the bar without saying another word. She went to her room and slumped down on the bed, too dazed and dispirited to get undressed. The Goat and Compasses might not be the ideal home for herself and Nancy, but she realised now that she had felt safe under Wilder's protection. It was obvious that she would have to find somewhere else to live, but she was not ready to admit defeat and return to Rockwood Castle. The appeal of travelling to Italy to be reunited with her mother was getting stronger by the minute.

Eventually, exhaustion forced her to undress and go to bed but she slept little, waking several times in the night from bad dreams.

★ ★ ★

Next morning Patricia was up early and was the first customer to enter the pawnshop when it opened. The old man behind the counter examined the remainder of her jewellery through an eyeglass. He shook his head, eyeing her with a sly smile as he offered her what was an almost insultingly low price. She bargained fiercely and in the end accepted a sum that was far below their worth, but should be enough to get her and Nancy as far as Milan.

She had thought over Wilder's advice to return

home, but that was not an option. There must be a better life waiting for her somewhere and she was determined to find it. She returned to the pub and went to find Nancy, who was just getting dressed.

'You've been out already?'

'Nancy, I need to talk to you very seriously.' Patricia sat on the edge of the bed. 'Don't give me an answer until you've had time to think through my proposition.'

'Is it about Lord Eldon and Maud Grubb? You know I dislike him intensely, Patsy. I don't want to travel with them.'

'I don't trust them either. Just hear me out before you make up your mind.'

Finally, when Patricia had been through everything, including the disadvantages of travelling with Eldon or Wilder, she sat back and waited for Nancy's answer.

'It's all happened so quickly,' Nancy said ruefully. 'One minute we seem to be doing well and then it all goes topsy-turvy.'

'I know, and you don't have to accompany me, Nancy. You could return to Rockwood. I know that Rosie would welcome you with open arms.'

'But you need me. I can't allow you to go abroad on your own with Wilder or Eldon.'

Patricia pulled a face. 'I'd have Signora Gandolfi to chaperone me.'

'That's exactly what I mean. That woman is worse than useless. I want to see you safe with your mama and Mr de Marney in Milan, but I haven't got a passport.'

'You are named on my passport. When Greystone was sent abroad I thought I would have to join him

215

sooner or later, and I had my maid's name certified on my passport so that she could travel with me.'

'But it won't be my name.'

'I doubt if the foreign authorities are going to be thorough enough to check all the names of servants who travel with their employers.'

'I suppose not.'

'Does that mean you're coming with me?'

Nancy threw her arms around Patricia, giving her a hug. 'It will be an adventure. I don't want to go home to Rockwood without you.'

'That settles it. I'll go and find Wilder now and tell him that we'll accompany him. Eldon and Maud will have to find their own way to escape the country.' Patricia rose to her feet and went to her room. She tossed her bonnet and shawl onto the bed before making her way downstairs to find Wilder.

He had just emerged from the cellar when she entered the taproom. 'I saw you go out earlier, Patricia. Does that mean what I think it means?'

'Yes, I went to the pawnshop and pledged the last of the jewellery that Greystone gave me. I have enough money to get Nancy and me to Milan — or I think I have, anyway. If we run out I suppose I can sing for our suppers.'

Wilder laughed. 'It won't come to that. I'm not wealthy but I have enough to pay expenses. I'll see you safely to Milan and then I'll go wherever the wind takes me.'

'You aren't planning to stay with us, then?'

'I doubt if your mama and her husband would approve of that.'

'They will be very grateful to you for helping us to get away from a difficult situation.'

216

'We'll meet that problem when it arises. In the meantime, pack your things but we're going to travel light. I have three horses in the stable that we can use to get us to Dover. We will travel by train to Paris and then on to Marseilles.'

'What shall I tell Eldon?'

'Say nothing. Don't give him an answer either way. We need to do this on our own, unless you want to be saddled with Larkin Eldon and Maud Grubb for the rest of your life.'

★ ★ ★

Despite it being late May, it was a chilly night. Patricia's breath curled around her head in clouds as she led her horse from the stable to the bottom of St Andrew's Hill. Wilder had already lifted Nancy onto her horse, and he picked Patricia up before she had a chance to protest, settling her comfortably on the saddle.

'Just follow me and don't talk until we're away from here. We don't want to draw attention to ourselves and alert the authorities.' Wilder mounted his steed and rode off without another word, leaving Patricia with little alternative but to follow him. Everything she possessed was packed in two saddlebags. All the grand clothes she had worn in London had been auctioned with the house, and were probably being worn by some worthy merchant's wife. Lady Greystone, her maid and Wilder, her groom, were about to start on a great adventure, or a complete disaster. She wished in a way that she had accepted Eldon's offer of a seat in his carriage, but she had decided to throw in her lot with Wilder and there was no turning back.

They rode through the quiet streets until they were clear of the city boundaries. Eventually, just as Patricia was afraid she might fall asleep in the saddle, Wilder pointed to an inn at the side of the road.

'We'll stop here to give the horses a rest and we'll sleep for an hour or two before travelling on.'

Patricia cast an anxious glance in Nancy's direction. 'We need food as well as rest. Nancy looks as if she's about to collapse.'

'You've both done well. We're not in a desperate hurry, but we do need to get to Dover before word goes round that I'm missing.' Wilder drew his horse to a halt and an ostler raced out of the inn to take the reins.

Patricia dismounted, but Nancy slid off the saddle and would have fallen if Wilder hasn't caught her.

'I'll book a room. A good meal and a rest and you'll be fine.'

Nancy nodded tiredly. 'Yes, I'm sorry, Wilder. I'm not used to long rides, especially at night.'

Patricia slipped her arm around Nancy's shoulders. 'Come on. We'll have something to eat first and then a couple of hours' sleep.'

Wilder strode on ahead and the ostlers took the horses to the stables. Patricia led Nancy into the warmth of the inn where a maidservant was cleaning out the grate in a huge inglenook fireplace. The young girl appeared flustered by the early arrivals but she lit the fire and asked them to sit there while she went to the kitchen and roused the cook.

The long ride and the sharp morning air had given Patricia an appetite and she enjoyed a large breakfast before going to the room that Wilder had booked for herself and Nancy. They lay side by side, fully clothed on the bed and Patricia fell asleep almost instantly.

She was awakened by the sound of loud voices and a scuffle. She sat up trying to hear what the shouting was about, but the voices were indistinct and she swung her legs over the side of the bed. She stood and went to the window. Outside she could see a police constable guarding the door to the inn and another seated on the driving seat of a police wagon. Fear cramped her heart and she knew instinctively that someone had informed on Wilder. Whatever his crimes had been she was certain he did not deserve to be treated like a dangerous felon, but she had to find out what was happening. It was not in her nature to sit back and wait for someone to come and find them, and she made her way out of the room without waking Nancy. She went out onto the landing and leaned over the balustrade.

Down below in the main saloon she saw Wilder with his hands tied, being led from the building by burly constable and a police sergeant. She was tempted to run downstairs and demand to know why they had arrested him, but at that moment Wilder looked up and met her desperate gaze with a wink and a hint of a smile. She knew then that this had not come as a surprise to him, and there was nothing she could do other than continue on the journey they had planned. Slowly she made her way back to the bedroom and sat on the window seat, watching as Wilder climbed into the wagon.

It seemed so final, but for a moment she thought she saw a hand wave from the tiny back window. Patricia rose to her feet and went over to the bed.

'Wake up, Nancy,' she said, giving her a gentle shake. 'We have to leave now.'

Nancy opened her eyes, gazing dazedly up at her. 'What's the matter?'

'Wilder has been arrested and taken away by the police. Someone must have told them that he was leaving the country.'

'What do we do now?' Nancy clutched Patricia's hand.

'We go on as planned. It's what Wilder wanted. I saw the police leading him out of the inn. He looked up and smiled, and I know that he meant us to continue with our journey. There's nothing we can do for him.'

'He was good to us, Patsy. I wish we could help him.'

'It's time to help ourselves. Get up and put on your mantle. We've got a long ride ahead of us.'

* * *

It took them two more days to reach Dover. The second night they slept in a barn in an attempt to save money, and on the third night they stayed at an inn. Patricia paid extra for a bath tub filled with hot water and a meal in their room, which they ate by the fire. Much refreshed, they set off again next morning and arrived in Dover mid-afternoon. Patricia booked them into a small hotel near the harbour and she left Nancy there while she went to the shipping office to purchase tickets on the next boat to Calais. When she returned to the hotel she found Nancy in the lounge taking tea with Eldon and Maud as if it was the most natural thing in the world.

Eldon looked up and smiled as he rose from his seat. 'Isn't this a fortunate coincidence, Patricia? Who would have thought that we would arrive at the same hotel on the same day?'

Patricia ignored his outstretched hand. 'Did you have anything to do with turning Wilder in to the police, Eldon?'

'My dear, how can you think so little of me? Wilder is a good chap. We have much in common so why would I do anything as heinous as that?'

'I don't know, Eldon, but someone did. He was arrested just outside London and taken away by the police.'

Maud took a silver hip flask from her pocket and added a tot to her cup of tea. 'I would say that Jonas Beaney is the one you should suspect. I never trusted him from the start.'

'Why would he do such a thing?' Nancy demanded before Patricia had a chance to speak.

'Maybe Starlina told him to do so.' Maud took a sip of her tea and smiled. 'A little addition makes such a difference to a dull cup of tea. I suppose we'll have to settle for coffee when we're abroad, Eldon.'

'Undoubtedly, my dear.' Eldon pulled up a chair for Patricia. 'Do join us, Patsy. It looks as if we're going to be travelling companions after all.'

She sat down reluctantly. 'Are you sure you didn't tell the police that Wilder was leaving the country, Eldon? I wouldn't put it past you.'

He sat down, reaching for the teapot. 'You misjudge me, my love. I am many things but I do not turn on my friends, and Leo was my friend until you came on the scene. Now he thinks of me as a rival for your affections.'

'Stop talking nonsense, Eldon. I will have a cup of tea, but perhaps it would be better if we found another hotel.'

He filled a cup and passed it to her. 'Come now, Patsy. We have one night in the same establishment. That can't mean anything to anyone, and tomorrow we board the packet to France together, but all that signifies is that we are fellow travellers.' He looked up as a waiter hovered behind him. 'Yes, my man. Did you want something?'

'Your rooms are ready, Lord Greystone. Please ring the bell if you require anything.' The waiter backed away as if in the presence of royalty.

'Lord Greystone?' Patricia was so angry that the words almost choked her. 'You have stolen my late husband's title?'

'Just borrowed it, my dear. I guessed that you and darling Nancy would end up here, and it made sense to follow our original plan. It was much easier than I thought to get a forged passport bearing Greystone's name. It does help to mix with the criminal underworld.'

'How dare you use my husband's name, Eldon?'

'I will revert to my own identity when we are safely on the Continent, Patricia.' Eldon sat back in his chair. 'Come now, let's enjoy this evening. We'll dine together in style.'

Maud raised her teacup in a toast. 'I second that, Patricia. Fate has flung us together so let us make the most of it.'

'I think we'll dine in our room.' Patricia looked to Nancy for confirmation but Nancy was asleep in her chair. 'You can see that my young companion is exhausted. We've been travelling for the best part of three days now.'

'Of course, you must do what you wish.' Eldon rose

from his seat. 'Would you like me to carry Nancy up to your room?'

'I would not.' Patricia slammed down her cup onto its saucer and stood up. 'Let's get one thing clear, Eldon. We might be travelling companions, as you put it, but that's all. If you lay one finger on Nancy, or me for that matter, I will denounce you for an escaped criminal and have you arrested whether it is in England, France or Italy. Do you understand?'

He sank back onto his seat. 'Perfectly, but that's a trifle hard, Patricia. You used to be such a fun-loving young woman. You were ready to take on anyone. Now you are a turning into a prim and proper matron. I doubt if Greystone would recognise you.'

Patricia shook Nancy and helped her to her feet. 'We'll travel on the same ship because we have no alternative, but once we are on French soil that's the last you'll see of us, Eldon. That goes for you too, Maud.'

'What's the matter?' Nancy asked sleepily. 'Have I done something wrong?'

Patricia guided her from the room and headed for the stairs. 'No, dear. I'm cross with Eldon, not you. Anyway, I have the tickets and we set sail on the tide tomorrow morning. I'm really sorry that Wilder won't be accompanying us, but perhaps I can do something for him when I've spoken to my stepfather.'

'I hope so. I like Wilder. He's been kind to us and he never makes me feel uncomfortable like Lord Eldon does.'

'Maybe the police will arrest Lord Eldon before he has a chance to board ship. That would be amusing, wouldn't it, Nancy?'

'Oh, yes. I'd like that,' Nancy said, giggling. 'I'll

have so much to tell Tommy when we eventually get home to Rockwood.'

Patricia used the key that the concierge had given her to unlock the door to their room. 'Yes, you're right, Nancy. Rockwood Castle is home — I'm beginning to realise that more and more.' She ushered Nancy inside and closed the door. 'If you want to go there tomorrow I won't stop you. I'll pay your fare and you can leave first thing in the morning.'

Nancy slumped down on the bed. 'I'm going to Italy with you, Patricia. There's no question about it.' She lay down and closed her eyes.

★ ★ ★

When they landed in Calais late next afternoon Eldon insisted on handling their passports and he seemed to revel in his new identity as Lord Greystone. He handed the documents back to Patricia with a satisfied smile.

'There you are, my love. We are now officially Lord and Lady Greystone, at least in the eyes of the French.'

'Don't be ridiculous, Eldon.' Patricia folded the single sheet of paper and tucked it into her reticule.

'I have the train tickets here. We'll be in Paris before you know it. I can't wait to do some sight-seeing.'

Patricia turned away. Let Eldon enjoy his fantasies. He and Maud could do what they pleased but she, Patricia Greystone, would be on the first train to Marseilles next morning with Nancy. However, when they finally arrived at the Paris hotel that Eldon said was central and relatively inexpensive, Patricia was pleasantly surprised. Quite what she had expected she did not know, but the room allocated to herself and Nancy

224

was clean and reasonably comfortable, and the delicious aromas of cooking emanating from the kitchens below ground were teasing to her appetite. At dinner they shared a table and Eldon was on top form, showing off his knowledge of French and his taste in fine wines. Patricia hoped that he was not expecting her to pay for the expensive meal but she was too hungry to argue when the food was set before her. If the waiters thought it odd that her ladyship's maidservant dined with the family they were seemingly too accustomed to the eccentricities of their English visitors to raise an eyebrow.

After dinner Maud and Eldon retired to the hotel lounge to take coffee and share a bottle of brandy, but Nancy was ready for bed and Patricia did not relish the idea of spending even more time with the already inebriated pair. She made her excuses and followed Nancy from the lounge, but found herself in the middle of a crowd of theatregoers, who were waiting to be seated in the dining room. She could not understand their rapid French, but she did catch her mother's name, together with nods of approval and smiles of delight.

She caught Nancy by the sleeve as she was about to mount the stairs. 'You studied French at school, didn't you?'

'Yes, but I wasn't very good at it.'

'Nor I, but I heard a woman mention my mother's name. It sounds as if they've seen her recently. Can you tell me what they're saying?'

Nancy stood very still, pretending to read a poster advertising a theatrical performance. She turned to Patricia with a wide grin. 'They are talking about your mama. She's performing at the Opera here in Paris.

We don't have to travel very far for you to see her.'

'I can't believe it. Why does Mama never let us know where she is?' Patricia edged her way back through the queue, making her way to the concierge's desk. In halting French she asked for a leaflet from the Paris Opera. Clutching it tightly in her hand, she joined Nancy on the staircase. 'Let's go to our room and I'll study this. I do hope that tonight wasn't her last performance or something silly like that.'

In the quiet of their room Patricia sat on the bed with Nancy at her side and together they translated the programme word for word. Patricia sat back and breathed a sigh of relief. 'Their season is nearly over, so thank goodness we arrived now and not in a week's time. It's wonderful to think that Mama is here in Paris and we don't have to travel all the way to Italy to find her. I'll sleep like a baby tonight, but I'll be up early.'

'You're going to the theatre?'

'Yes, I need to find out where Mama and Claude are staying. I'm sure they'll tell me when I say I'm her daughter.'

'Can I come too?'

Patricia ruffled Nancy's hair. 'Of course. This is our adventure. We won't tell Eldon or Maud. Anyway, I dare say they will stay in bed until noon and wake up with very bad headaches if they drink the whole bottle of brandy.'

★ ★ ★

Patricia awakened early and was eager to be off to the theatre, but she knew she must curb her patience and wait until the box office opened its doors. She toyed

226

with a croissant at breakfast and sipped a cup of coffee, although Nancy devoured her food with obvious enjoyment. Patricia could not wait to set off and as soon as they left the dining room she sent Nancy to fetch their outdoor garments while she went to ask the concierge the quickest route to the theatre where her mother was appearing.

The Paris streets were thronged with people walking purposefully or strolling along as if they had not a care in the world. Patricia tried to be patient but she and Nancy often had to step into the road in order to pass a loitering couple, and had to suffer the shouts and gesticulations of the drivers of the fiacres and business traffic as she stepped in their path. Eventually, after taking a couple of wrong turns and having to retrace their steps, they came to the theatre where Felicia de Marney's portrait smiled down at them from gaudy posters. Patricia tried the main doors but they were locked, and the doorkeeper would not allow them to enter. After several attempts to make him understand their plight, Patricia was getting desperate. She was wondering what to do next when a fiacre drew to a halt in the side street and a well-dressed middle-aged man stepped down onto the pavement. His cashmere coat with a velvet collar was complemented by expensive leather gloves and a beaver top hat. Although she could not see his face, there was something very familiar about him that made her look again.

He paid the driver and was about to enter the theatre when Patricia called out to him. 'Excuse me, sir.'

He stopped and turned to look at her. 'Patricia?'

15

'Claude. Thank goodness!' Patricia enveloped him in a hug. 'I'm so glad to see you.'

Claude de Marney's waxed moustache quivered and his eyes widened in surprise. 'What are you doing here, Patricia?'

'We were on our way to Italy. I thought Mama was performing in Milan.'

'We finished the season there and came on to Paris.' Claude glanced over her shoulder. 'That can't be Nancy.'

Patricia laughed. 'It's two years or more since you were at Rockwood, Claude. Come and join us, Nancy.'

'You were a little girl when I last saw you, Nancy, but I see you're a young lady now,' Claude said, smiling. 'But this is so unexpected. Why were you on the way to Italy, Patricia? Is everything all right?'

'Not exactly, but it's a long story, Claude.' Patricia shivered as a cool breeze rustled the leaves on the trees that lined the street. 'The doorman wouldn't allow us into the theatre. May we go inside and I'll tell you everything?'

'Of course. What am I thinking of keeping you two standing on a street corner?' Claude surged forward. He marched past the doorman waving a silver-headed cane as he spoke in rapid French.

The doorman retreated and Patricia nodded to him as she walked past. It would not do to appear smug as she might need to enter the building at a time when Claude was not there to help her. Claude led her and

Nancy through a maze of narrow corridors to an office, which was small and smelled strongly of French tobacco smoke, stage makeup and stale perfume. He motioned them to sit down on the two high-backed chairs and he perched on the edge of a desk, folding his arms.

'Well now, this is a most pleasant surprise, but what made you travel all this way to find us, Patricia?'

'You know that my husband died in an accident, I suppose?'

Claude nodded gravely. 'Yes, your mama and I were very sad to hear the news. Unfortunately we could not get away without breaking your mama's contract.'

'I understand,' Patricia said solemnly. 'It was very sudden, and of course it was a terrible shock. He was buried abroad so there was no funeral at home.'

'It must have been awful for you, Patsy. But you are well provided for, I'm sure.'

'That's the problem, Claude. Unfortunately Greystone had omitted to revise his will when we married. He left Greystone Park to his daughters and neither of them want anything to do with me. I only recently discovered that my late husband had made some bad investments, which had eaten away all his capital. My home in London was sold to repay some of his debts, and I found myself having to earn my own living.'

'But surely you went home to Rockwood, Patricia? Rosalind would look after you, as she always did when you were younger.'

'I know, but I want to be independent, Claude. I don't want to rely on my family to keep me.'

'I suppose you've taken legal advice?'

'Yes, of course, and there's really nothing I can do. Sylvia and Christina didn't want me to marry their father. The property is theirs and I have no say in the matter.'

'I am so sorry, Patsy my dear. How have you been managing?'

'I went to see Garson Thorne at the opera house and he gave me a small part in his latest production.'

'So you are still determined to follow in your mother's footsteps.'

'I suppose so, but the wages at the opera house were appalling. It was costing me everything I earned simply to keep myself and Nancy in a dreadful lodging house.'

'You seem to have suffered a cruel reversal of fortune, my dear. I am so sorry.'

'Thank you, Claude. I left the opera company because I could see no future there for me, and I was hoping that Mama might be able to offer me some help and advice.'

'Of course she will be delighted to see you, but our time here is almost over. In fact tomorrow night is the last performance. Felicia and I will be leaving next day, heading south for the summer. You are more than welcome to come with us. I know I speak for my dear wife as well.'

Patricia and Nancy exchanged anxious glances. 'When you say you're going to the south, what does that mean exactly?'

'Your mama needs to keep away from the damp climate of England so we purchased a villa on the hills above a small village on the south coast.'

Patricia frowned thoughtfully. 'That doesn't sound like the sort of place for me, Claude. I have to find work or return to Rockwood as an object of pity. I started singing in the streets, although at the time it was to raise money for the poor.'

'Yes, that's right,' Nancy said, speaking up for the first time. 'The people loved her, Mr de Marney. It wasn't until we went back to Clare Market a second time that things turned nasty.'

'Your mama would be horrified to learn that you had to sink to such a level.' Claude shook his head. 'What else haven't you told me, Patricia? Why did you feel it necessary to leave London? Couldn't you have waited until you'd made arrangements to join us? It's only a matter of luck that I arrived outside the theatre this morning.'

'I was never one to take the easy way, Claude,' Patricia said with a rueful smile.

'Your mama always said that you were a rebel, but you might have gone all the way to Italy and found that we had left. You were taking an enormous risk.'

'I'm not afraid to face a challenge.'

'I can see that, Patricia.' Claude eyed her warily. 'What do you think your mama can do for you?'

'I was hoping that she might introduce me to some of her influential friends, Claude. I am desperate for work and I have inherited a little of Mama's talent, or so I think.'

He smiled reluctantly. 'It would not be wise to tell her that you are a rival.'

'I would like to see her, Claude. Although I don't think we will accompany you to the country. I've grown accustomed to living in the city. I love Rockwood Castle, of course, but I can't imagine spending the rest of my days there.'

Claude straightened up, becoming business-like. 'Well, I suggest you both come with me now. I'll take you to your mother, Patricia. I think this is something that you and she need to talk about.'

Patricia rose to her feet. 'That's what I wanted in the first place. Come along, Nancy.'

★ ★ ★

Felicia was still in her robe with her face covered in a mask of white cream. The scent of attar of roses filled the hotel room when Patricia walked in and saw her mother seated by the fire.

'Mama, we've come to surprise you.'

Felicia clutched her hands to her bosom, her mouth dropping open in surprise. 'Patricia?'

'Yes, Mama, and Nancy, too.'

'Claude, fetch me a clean towel.' Felicia held out her hand and Claude hurried into the adjoining room, reappearing moments later with a white towel, which he handed to his wife.

Felicia wiped the cream from her face, leaving her skin pink and shining.

Patricia eyed her mother critically. Even at the age of fifty-two Felicia was still a handsome woman who showed little sign of ageing. Her golden hair was piled high on her head, with curls escaping to frame her perfect oval face.

'You look wonderful, Mama,' Patricia said truthfully. 'You look younger than ever.'

Felicia blushed and smiled. 'You are flattering me, Patsy. Sit down and tell me how you came to be here, and how did you find Claude? Or did you bump into each other in the street?'

'Almost.' Patricia turned to Claude with a persuasive smile. 'Do you think we might have some coffee? If it isn't too much trouble. Or perhaps Nancy would

232

prefer lemonade.'

'I like coffee.' Nancy flopped down on a chair by the window. 'I like the French coffee, anyway.'

'Of course.' Claude opened the door. 'I'll go and find a waiter. If I ring the bell we'll be waiting for hours. Tell your mama what you told me, Patricia. I'll be back in a minute.'

Patricia seized the chance to enlarge on the privations and humiliations she had suffered since the death of her husband. She left nothing out as she described the life that she and Nancy had led in London and their time spent at the Goat and Compasses, although she kept any mention of Wilder to a minimum. There was no need to let her mother know that they had been living in a den of iniquity. Felicia listened open-mouthed and was unusually silent. Patricia had just reached the part when she had seen Claude alight from the fiacre, and at that moment he returned carrying a tray of coffee.

'They are short-staffed at the moment.' He placed it on a low table beside his wife's chair. 'Shall I pour, my dear?'

'Leave it, Claude. You'll be sure to spill coffee everywhere.' Felicia picked up the silver pot and filled four cups. 'Help yourselves.' She sipped her drink, looking from one to the other. 'You seem to have suffered some bad luck, Patricia. I suppose you'd better come to the South of France with us. Unless you have any better ideas.'

'As a matter of fact, as I said to Claude earlier, I really don't think living in the country would suit me. I want to be able to earn my own living.'

'And how do you propose to do that?'

'Like you, Mama. I know I haven't your talent, but

I can sing, and people seem to enjoy listening to me. I was hoping that you might be able to introduce me to a theatre producer who would find work for me.'

Felicia stared into her coffee cup. 'I only know people in my own sphere, Patricia. You would not survive on your own in Paris.'

'I might if I had work and somewhere to live. I don't want to be a burden to you and Claude.'

'You are still my daughter and I think you should accompany us to our villa. It's very pretty and there are several other properties owned by titled English people. It's quite a select area with plenty of soirées and dinner parties.'

'That's not how I want to live, Mama,' Patricia said wearily. 'I could go back to Rockwood Castle and take up my position as the poor widowed sister, but I am worth more than that.'

Felicia replaced her coffee cup and saucer on the tray with an exasperated sigh. 'Really, Patricia, why do you always have to be so awkward? You always have to make everything into such a drama.'

'No, I don't, Mama.'

'I haven't forgotten the fuss you made when Claude and I were married.'

'That was because you took over the wedding ceremony and the celebration afterwards that I was supposed to have, Mama.'

Felicia rolled her eyes. 'You're forgetting that Alexander was absent at the time, Patricia. The wedding would have been cancelled otherwise and the guests would have had to go home.'

'Alex was in a French hospital, Mama. You showed no sign of pity for him or any sympathy for me. People thought I had been jilted.'

'Well, you didn't marry him when he returned home, did you? I seem to remember hearing that it was you who broke off the engagement, and Alexander married your sister. Maybe he had a lucky escape.'

Patricia took a deep breath. 'I didn't come here today to have the past raked over, Mama. All that is consigned to history, and the fact is that I want to earn my own living. I don't wish to be beholden to anyone.'

Claude had been standing by the fireplace, listening quietly. He cleared his throat. 'Ahem, I know this isn't entirely up to me, but I think you have a simple choice, Patricia. Either do as your mama suggests, or else you must find your own way. We would be willing to pay your fare back to England, if that's what you want.'

Patricia's hand shook with suppressed anger as she placed her coffee cup and saucer on the tray. 'I can see that I will get no help from either of you.'

'We have offered you a home, Patricia,' Felicia said angrily. 'What more do you expect us to do?'

Patricia rose to her feet. 'Nothing, Mama. Come, Nancy, we'd better return to the hotel and pack our things. It seems we've had a wasted journey.'

'Yes, Patricia.' Nancy put her cup down reluctantly and stood up.

'I won't bother you again, Mama,' Patricia said dramatically. 'But when I am a famous singer you will be sorry you did not do more to further my career.'

'Perhaps you should be looking for another husband, Patricia,' Felicia said acidly. 'Maybe that is where your future lies and then you will stop bothering me. You haven't inherited my talent so there's an end to it.'

'No, Mama,' Patricia said firmly. 'This is just the beginning.' She marched out of the room with Nancy following her.

Once outside in the cool spring air, Patricia's confidence ebbed suddenly. 'Mama brings out the worst in me, Nancy.'

'She doesn't seem to care much what happens to you.' Nancy hailed a passing fiacre. 'Let's get back to the hotel. We can't do anything standing here.'

'Yes, you're right. I need to have time to think.' Patricia gave the driver the name of the hotel and they climbed inside the cab.

'I wonder what happened to Leo,' Nancy said thoughtfully. 'I really liked him, Patsy. I wish he could have come with us.'

Patricia stared out of the window. Paris seemed so different from London. A wave of homesickness washed over her. 'I'm sure that Leo Wilder can look after himself,' she said without much conviction.

When the fiacre drew up outside their hotel Patricia climbed out and paid the driver. She used some of the French coinage that Eldon had had the forethought to get in exchange for English money, although she had no idea how much she had given the man. However, judging by his grin she had overpaid by quite a lot and he drove off chuckling. Life abroad was more complicated than she had imagined.

She marched into the hotel foyer and was met by Eldon and Maud.

'Where have you been?' Eldon asked suspiciously. 'I thought we were in this together, Patricia. You should have told me you were going out. You don't know your way around Paris.'

'And I suppose you do?' Patricia said irritably.

'Yes, as a matter of fact I've been here quite often in the past. Where have you been?'

'It's really none of your business, but I went to the theatre to find Mama.'

Eldon put his head on one side. 'Did you succeed?'

'As a matter of fact I did.' Patricia was about to walk past him to collect the key to her room but Eldon barred her way.

'And how is the beautiful and talented Mrs de Marney?'

'Eldon, you don't know my mother, so please stop quizzing me.'

'I have met her on a couple of occasions.'

'Mrs de Marney invited us to accompany them to the South of France,' Nancy said importantly. 'She has a villa there.'

'Interesting.' Eldon eyed Patricia speculatively. 'Are you going to accept? Maybe we could join you there. I have a fancy for summer in the south and the blue waters of the Mediterranean.'

'I haven't decided yet,' Patricia said evasively.

Maud wrapped her arm around Patricia's shoulders. 'Don't take any notice of him, dearie. You and I could go for a walk and look in the shop windows. Not that I have any money to spend, but I have something in mind that might interest you.'

'Another time, maybe, Maud,' Patricia said hastily. 'I have things to do myself. I'll see you two later, perhaps.'

'We'll dine together, my dear Lady Greystone.' Eldon tucked Maud's hand into the crook of his arm. 'I'll go for a walk with you, Maudie. Maybe we can find a nice little bar and have a drink or two.'

'Maybe people will think I'm Lady Greystone,'

Maud said, giggling.

'I doubt it, my love. They may be foreigners, but they are not stupid.' Eldon led the protesting Maud from the building.

Nancy shook her head. 'They are a very odd couple. Why do you think he brought her here, Patsy?'

'Heaven knows. Eldon does the strangest things, but I'm beginning to think we've made a terrible mistake by coming here. Nothing has turned out as I thought it might.' Patricia collected their key from the concierge and led the way to their room on the first floor. She walked over to the window and stood looking down at the busy street. 'I'm sorry, Nancy. I've brought you nothing but trouble. If you'd stayed at home with Rosie and the family you would have been much better off.'

'I don't agree,' Nancy said firmly. 'I would have missed all this excitement, and I'd never have got to visit Paris. Why don't we go out and see some of the sights?'

'I have just about enough money to pay the hotel bill and our passage home. It's the last thing I wanted to do but I'm afraid we'll have to return to Rockwood.'

'Are you certain about that, Patsy? Please don't do this just for my sake.'

'I have little choice. Without a sponsor I'm not likely to get very far in the operatic world. If we stay here with Eldon and Maud Grubb we'll be bankrupt before we know it.'

'Let's go for a walk. That won't cost anything. We can find out the time of trains to Calais and make plans to return to England, if that's what you want.'

'You're right, of course. Moping around in this dreary room won't help. We'll do as you suggest. You

238

really are very sensible, Nancy.'

Nancy's cheeks flushed and she smiled shyly. 'Thank you. Although being sensible all the time is very dull. I wish I was more impulsive like you.'

Patricia rose to her feet. 'Stay the same as you are, Nancy. You don't want to be like me. I lurch from one disaster to another. Come on, we'll see as much of the city as we can before we head for home tomorrow.'

★ ★ ★

After a few hours of walking the city streets Patricia and Nancy returned to the hotel tired but satisfied that they had seen as many of the famous landmarks as was possible on foot. They were seated in the almost deserted lounge, drinking coffee, when Eldon and Maud breezed in.

Maud sat down on the sofa beside Patricia. Her breath reeked of wine and her eyes were suspiciously bright.

'Well, how did it go today, my dears?'

Eldon pulled up a chair. 'I don't think you need to ask, Maudie. They look a little downhearted to me.'

'We had a pleasant walk around Paris,' Patricia said hastily. 'But we're going home tomorrow. Coming here was a mistake.'

'You aren't tempted by your mama's offer of a life of luxury in the south?' Eldon eyed her intently.

'No, Eldon.'

Eldon and Maud exchanged meaningful glances.

'Then maybe you will be interested in what Maud has to say,' Eldon said casually.

Maud leaned forward, lowering her voice. 'How would you like to join me in performing at Lady

Oakley's ball in a few days?'

'You have an engagement?' Patricia stared at her in astonishment. 'How did this come about?'

'Oh, I happen to know a few people in Paris,' Maud said. 'Of course I will be performing under my stage name of Signora Gandolfi.'

'And you want me to sing with you?'

'That's what I said, dearie. I was going solo, but you and I had plenty of practice when I was coaching you for Garson.'

'But you must have arranged this some time ago, Maud. These things don't happen by accident.' Patricia turned to Eldon without giving Maud a chance to respond. 'What is your part in this?'

He shrugged. 'Maud made the arrangements. I am merely the escort to and from the Oakleys' Paris mansion.'

'Patricia is right,' Nancy said stoutly. 'We've only been here since yesterday evening. It doesn't make sense.'

'I think it does.' Patricia shifted her position on the sofa so that she could look Maud in the eye. 'This was all arranged long before we left London. Tell the truth, Maud.'

'I might have had contact with Lady Oakley. We are old friends.'

'So neither you nor Eldon had any intention of travelling on to Milan. Why did you encourage us to accompany you?'

'It was all arranged on the spur of the moment,' Eldon said, smiling. 'You know me, Patsy. I have connections everywhere, and particularly here in Paris.'

'Even if that were true, why would you make up this elaborate plan to lure me here? You are keeping something from me, Eldon.'

Maud shifted uncomfortably on her seat. 'We'll have to tell her, Larkin. There's too much at stake for us to fail now, at the last moment.'

Eldon glanced over his shoulder but the other guests were seated in the far corner of the room, playing cards. He turned back to give Patricia a long look.

'I know I can trust you, my love. Which is why Maud and I decided to go ahead with this rather risky plan.'

'Whatever it is, I am not interested, Eldon. You've tricked me and I don't like it.'

'Just listen to him, dearie,' Maud said in a low voice. 'You'll change your mind when you learn just what our plan entails.'

'Colette Segal was a notorious courtesan in Paris before she met and married Sir James Oakley, the richest man in the whole of England, who made his fortune out of bird droppings. She has jewels worth a fortune and insists on showing them off at every opportunity.' Maud pulled a face. 'I knew her when she was poor and living in an atelier over a barber's shop. The fact is, I saved her from being arrested on several occasions, and I intend to collect my dues. You don't need to know any more than that.'

'It sounds very suspicious.' Patricia frowned.

'Not at all, dear. Colette invited me to entertain her guests at this most important ball and, to be entertained by myself and Lady Greystone is part of her plan to impress the guests. There are many people here who look down on her because of her humble beginnings. She wishes to woo them with the magnificence of her home and her generosity, and to dazzle them with a display of her husband's wealth.'

'Why does she live in Paris when she's married to

241

an Englishman?' Nancy asked eagerly.

'English aristocracy are even more snobbish than the French.' Eldon signalled to a passing waiter. *'Cognac, s'il vous plaît.'*

'Not for me.' Patricia shook her head. 'I simply want to know what you two are planning. Surely you aren't thinking of anything illegal, Eldon?'

'Have you ever known me to turn down an invitation to wine and dine royally, Patricia?'

'No, but you obviously planned to be in Paris for this occasion, which makes me wonder why you lied to me in the first place.'

'I did intend to see you safely to Milan after the ball. We will have a few days in Paris for you and Maud to rehearse, and who could resist the chance to see this enchanting city?'

'All right. Even if I take that as being true, why do you want me to sing with you, Maud? You are a seasoned performer in your own right. You don't need me.'

'As I said, your title is going to make all the difference. Besides which, I'm thinking of you, dearie. Colette is paying me handsomely and I know you are short of the readies, so I thought I'd include you as a favour. But if you're not interested I can go solo with no trouble.' Maud's eyes lit up as the waiter reappeared carrying a tray of brandy and three glasses. 'Let's drink a toast to our exciting venture. We can rehearse until we're pitch perfect. Just remember everything I taught you.'

'That's all it is, Patsy, my dear,' Eldon said smoothly. 'What do you say?'

16

During the next few days Patricia often wondered if she had done the right thing by agreeing to Maud and Eldon's plan. She suspected that there was more to it than they were prepared to admit, but the promise of payment for her performance, and the possibility that she might come to the notice of an influential impresario, were too tempting to refuse. She had not seen her mother again or received any communication from her. Patricia was hurt although hardly surprised by her mother's casual treatment, and she could only assume that Mama and Claude had travelled to their new home in the South of France without giving her a second thought.

This left Patricia with little alternative but to go along with the plan, but as soon as she received her share of the money she was determined to leave Maud and Eldon to their own devices. In preparation for their plan, Eldon hired a rehearsal room near to the hotel. Patricia and Maud practised their duets, accompanied by Nancy at the piano. They worked for hours each day until Maud was satisfied that they had reached the required standard. She was a demanding teacher and Patricia had a sneaking admiration for Maud's professionalism. However, there was no denying the fact that Maud was less than honest. She had clawed her way up from the poverty-stricken slums of East London and was now mixing with the rich and fashionable Parisians. Patricia could only imagine the struggles that Maud had encountered in her life, but there were many questions lurking in the depths of Patricia's mind. She was still suspicious of Eldon's motives, but she put all worries aside to make sure her performance on the night would be perfect in every way.

Maud, it seemed had thought of everything, and when Patricia raised the question of what she would wear to such a grand occasion, Maud whisked her off to a theatrical costumiers. They were both fitted out with beautiful silk and satin gowns, trimmed with Valenciennes lace and elaborate tassels glittering with bugle beads. A less flamboyant costume was hired for Nancy, who entered into the spirit of the occasion with great enthusiasm. Eldon was not to be outdone, and he chose an evening suit that flattered his fine figure and made him look incredibly dashing. Maud was lavish in her praise, but Patricia held back, thinking he was conceited enough already.

After so much preparation it was a relief when the time came to get into the hired cab and set off for the Oakleys' mansion in one of the most fashionable quarters of Paris. Patricia was suddenly nervous. Snippets of conversation she had caught between Maud and Eldon unsettled her even more. However, it was too late to pull out now and she sat back in the carriage, clutching her fan tightly in her gloved hand. The corsets she wore beneath the hired gown were laced so tightly that she could hardly breathe, and in the close confines of the cab she was aware of a slightly musty smell emanating from the hired garment. She had a sudden vision of who might have worn it previously and she wrinkled her nose in distaste. Maud had sprayed her with cheap cologne but that had made matters worse. Patricia could only hope that in the crowded ballroom no one would notice.

'Smile, Patsy,' Eldon commanded as he helped Patricia to alight from the carriage. 'You look terrified. That is not the way to behave.'

'I'm perfectly all right. You do your part and I'll do mine.' Patricia held her head high as she followed Maud into the building. After the darkness outside the light in the huge entrance hall was dazzling. Hundreds of candles sent off the aroma of hot beeswax, and the light reflected off the crystal chandeliers, flickering and bouncing off the jewels worn by the ladies. Diamond tiaras, necklaces and earrings flashed like fire against slender throats and ears. Sapphires, emeralds, rubies and strings of pearls adorned old and young women alike, and taffeta petticoats rustled with every movement. The scent of expensive perfume and gentlemen's pomade mingled with a hint of cigar smoke and the heady aroma of oriental lilies displayed in silver urns and porcelain vases. Musicians played in the background, the sounds floating above the guests' heads as if the plaster angels on the architrave were welcoming them with heavenly melodies.

Patricia had been to many smart functions in London, but this was something different and slightly theatrical. She felt like a minor character in an unfolding drama. Only Eldon seemed quite at home and he tucked her hand in the crook of his arm as they moved forward to be greeted by Lady Oakley and Sir James. Lady Oakley's diamond necklace created a ring of fire around her throat, outdone only by the emerald and diamond tiara that adorned her ornate coiffure, with earrings to match. When Lady Oakley extended her hand it seemed weighed down by an array of rings and an emerald bracelet completed the set. It was an impressive, if slightly vulgar, show of wealth.

Sir James was polite but Patricia thought he seemed rather reserved, unlike his wife, who oozed charm and delight as she welcomed each and every guest. When it came to Maud's turn, Lady Oakley embraced her like a long-lost sister, and Patricia was quick to notice a look of disapproval flash across Sir James's pudgy features.

'You look stunning, Colette,' Maud said loudly.

'You are too kind,' Lady Oakley beamed at her. 'I am so looking forward to hearing Lady Greystone sing with you, Maudie.' She lowered her voice. 'It's not often that English aristocracy stoop so low as to attend my soirées.'

'Shall we move on, my dear,' Sir James said testily.

'Be quiet, Jimmy. I'm talking to my friend.' Lady Oakley sent her husband a warning look.

'We mustn't take up any more of your time, ma'am,' Eldon said smoothly. 'There will be a chance to converse later, I'm sure.'

'Such a perfect gentleman.' Lady Oakley fluttered her eyelashes. 'I will look forward to that, Monsieur.' When the last guests had been greeted it was time for the dancing to begin. Sir James led his wife onto the floor, and Eldon, never one to be shy, proffered his hand to Patricia. She hesitated for a moment, not wanting to steal the limelight from their hosts, but all eyes were upon them and she accepted his offer. They twirled into the waltz, followed quickly by a polka, and soon the polished boards of the dance floor were crowded with couples. Eldon was an expert when it came to partnering and Patricia had danced with him on numerous occasions. Greystone had taken her to balls but he preferred to mix with the gentlemen, no doubt discussing politics or business matters, and he had been quite happy for Eldon to partner his wife. Patricia had accepted this with good grace, and anyway it was not fashionable for couples to be seen to be too affectionate. She was now on familiar ground and she began to relax.

'That's better,' Eldon said, smiling. 'You look as if you are enjoying yourself, which is what we want. No one must suspect anything is amiss.'

Patricia stiffened. 'What do you mean, Eldon?'

'Just do exactly as we planned, Patsy, my love. Maud and I have everything worked out to the last tiny detail.'

'I don't understand.'

'Nor were you meant to. You would give the game away immediately. Smile, Patricia. We are the centre of attention.'

Patricia could do little other than to obey Eldon's instructions, although she was now deeply concerned. She was about to question him further as they left the floor but she was claimed immediately by a tall, not very handsome, but quite charming Frenchman, and after him there was a succession of would-be partners. She could see Eldon partnering Lady Oakley and they seemed to be on intimate terms already. Eldon was oozing charm and Lady Oakley appeared to be enjoying his undivided attention. Patricia danced with several more gentlemen, some of whom held her too tightly, and others breathed brandy fumes in her face. It was a relief when there was an interval to allow people to rest and sample the magnificent cold supper laid out in an adjoining salon.

Patricia's respite was cut short by Maud, who came to tell her that it was their turn to entertain the guests.

247

For a terrifying moment Patricia felt her throat constrict and she could not remember the words. She was tempted to run away, but Maud had her by the hand and Patricia felt her bones being crushed in a tight grip. The orchestra played the introduction and Maud began to sing. The pressure on Patricia's fingers relaxed and she found herself joining in just as if they were in the rehearsal room. The applause when they came to the end of the duet was deafening and cries of 'Encore' filled the ballroom. Maud had foreseen this and she signalled to the conductor to play the second piece, but just as they had begun, a loud scream from Lady Oakley brought an end to the recital.

There was a moment of panic when everyone crowded around their hostess and Sir James called for all the doors to be locked. Patricia found herself thrust aside as Maud pushed her way to Lady Oakley's side.

'Oh, my love. What happened?'

'My necklace and bracelet have been stolen.' Lady Oakey threw herself into Maud's arms in a swoon.

'Give my wife air! Fetch brandy.' Sir James fended the guests off. 'Everyone will be searched. No one leaves.'

Maud beckoned to Patricia. 'She needs water, not brandy.'

Patricia found a carafe of iced water on a nearby table and filled a glass. She handed it to Maud, who was kneeling on the floor, fanning Lady Oakley vigorously. 'There, there, my duck. Sip the water and you'll feel better.'

'My jewels,' Lady Oakley moaned. 'Who has taken them?'

'Maybe they slipped off, dear,' Maud suggested.

248

'It's very hot in here and you are perspiring heavily.' Patricia looked round for Eldon and saw him helping the butler and footmen to search the gentlemen present. Quite how Eldon managed to set himself above everyone else was a mystery, but all Patricia wanted at this moment was to escape from the stuffy, overcrowded room. She was beginning to feel faint herself when she saw Nancy weaving her way through the throng of guests.

'I have your cape and gloves,' Nancy said in a whisper. 'And Maud's too. The cab is outside.'

'You knew this was going to happen?'

Nancy winked and grinned. 'Not exactly, but Lord Eldon told me what to do in an emergency. Isn't it exciting?'

'That's not what I'd call it.'

'Let's get Lady Oakley to somewhere quieter,' Maud said, rising to her feet.

Patricia helped Maud to raise plump, tightly corseted Lady Oakley to a standing position and they guided her out of the ballroom to a small anteroom. Eldon appeared in the doorway.

'I'm afraid we have to leave you, my lady. I hope your jewels are returned to your safekeeping before the thief gets away.'

'You're too kind, Lord Eldon,' Lady Oakley said faintly. 'I hope we will see more of you before you return to England.'

'Most assuredly, my lady. Nothing could keep me away.' Eldon fixed Patricia with a meaningful look. 'Come, my dear, the carriage awaits.'

Maud patted Lady Oakley on the cheek. 'We'll come tomorrow, my duck. You must try to get some rest. I'm sure your jewels will turn up.'

Eldon ushered Maud and Patricia from the room. Nancy was waiting for them by the main entrance with their wraps and gloves. She handed Eldon his top hat and he put it on at an angle. 'Let's go before the police get here.'

'What have you done, Eldon?' Patricia demanded when they were settled inside the carriage and on their way back to the hotel.

'My dear, I was searched along with the rest of the guests.'

'Well done, Larkin my duck,' Maud said gleefully.

'Will one of you tell me what's going on?' Patricia demanded angrily. 'I know you're up to something but I can't work out what it is.'

'Wait until we get back to the hotel.' Eldon leaned back and closed his eyes. 'A successful evening, I think.'

* * *

Patricia had to curb her impatience until they were in the deserted hotel lounge. A sleepy waiter had gone off to the kitchen to order coffee and some hot chocolate for Nancy.

'We'll get a good night's sleep and tomorrow we'll decide what to do,' Eldon said, yawning.

'What do you mean?' Patricia demanded. 'What happened tonight and how are you two involved? I knew you were planning something, but I hope it had nothing to do with the theft of Lady Oakley's jewels.'

'Don't pretend to be so naïve, Patricia,' Maud said impatiently. 'You are far from stupid.'

'I haven't had a straight answer from either of you and I want the truth.' Patricia looked from one to the other. 'If you don't tell me everything I'm going back to London and you can take your chances.'

'Well, you see, it's like this.' Eldon undid the buttons on his frock coat to reveal two pockets low down in the lining. He put his hand in one and pulled out a diamond necklace and from the other he produced an emerald and diamond bracelet. 'You are party to a jewel robbery, Lady Greystone. I don't think you'll be travelling anywhere without us to keep an eye on you.'

Patricia stared at the jewels in horror. 'How did you do that, Eldon? You were searched.'

'I am Lord Greystone, which counts for something, even here in Paris.' He laughed. 'I simply pulled out my pockets. They were empty, of course, and the servants didn't dare to insult an English lord by going further.'

'But the jacket pockets . . . I don't understand.'

'It's a conjuror's coat, my love. I hired it from the same place you found your ball gowns.'

'So this is what you've been planning all along?'

'Yes,' Maud said gleefully. 'Clever, ain't it?'

'You won't be laughing if the French police turn up here demanding to search our rooms.'

'Why would they suspect us?' Eldon said calmly. 'We are friends of the Oakleys and we're English aristocracy. They wouldn't dare accuse us of such a thing.'

'You committed the robbery with Maud's help. I had nothing to do with it. I want my money for the performance and that's all. Nancy and I are going back to Rockwood.'

'Where you'll be arrested,' Eldon said casually. 'You are involved in this as much as any of us.'

'I'll tell the police it was you.'

Eldon laughed. 'No, my love. As far as the French

251

are concerned it will be your husband, Lord Greystone, who committed the crime. But he is dead. Signora Gandolfi never existed, which leaves Maud and myself to travel freely to somewhere safe. If you return to England you will have to explain the deception, so you will *have* to come with us because you have no alternative.'

'You tried to persuade me to live with you once before, Eldon. It didn't work then and I won't give in now.'

'What alternative do you have, my love? Think about it, Patsy. You'll come to your senses eventually.'

Nancy fingered the jewels. 'Are they very valuable?'

'Worth a king's ransom, my pet.' Eldon tucked the necklace and bracelet away in his concealed pockets.

'You won't get away with it, Eldon,' Patricia said angrily. 'I'll never forgive you for tricking me into aiding and abetting such a crime.'

'Don't be so dramatic, Patricia.' Eldon took a silver case from his pocket. He extracted a cigarillo and lit it with a spill from the fire. 'You are a clever woman beneath all the frills and furbelows. You knew something was amiss.'

'Don't be foolish, Patricia.' Maud glowered at her. 'You are as guilty as we are. We will stay here for a few days and then I'll take the items to a fence I happen to know. We will live simply until then and after that you can do what you like, dearie. But if you peach on us you'll find that we ain't as nice and genteel as everyone thinks.'

'Are you threatening me, Maud?' Patricia faced up to her. 'I don't have to do anything I don't want to.'

'Take it any way you wish, dearie. But tomorrow I will pay a visit to my dear friend Colette and I'll commiserate with her, even though I know she still owns a fortune in jewels. Colette has known poverty, so who am I to criticise her for enjoying the wealth she has come into?'

'You are no friend of hers,' Patricia said bitterly. 'And you are certainly no friend of mine.'

'The waiter is coming.' Eldon motioned them to sit down. 'We'll get through this but only if we stick together. When it blows over you will have enough money to go home and start again, Patsy.' He took a seat. 'Coffee — just what I need — and hot chocolate for you, young Nancy. I hope you've learned something this evening.'

Nancy went to sit beside Patricia on one of the sofas. 'Yes, I'll never trust another man as long as I live.'

★ ★ ★

That night Patricia was exhausted mentally and physically, but she could not sleep. She knew that Eldon was right, and that made things worse. She had wondered why he had stolen her husband's identity and now she knew. He had used her and her family name, and now she had little choice but to go along with his cleverly laid plans. Her wish to return home seemed out of the question, if what Eldon had said was true, and that left her in a difficult position. If she remained with Maud and Eldon she would be condoning a criminal act, but if the French police discovered the truth she would be implicated in the robbery simply by association, and the fact that Eldon had stolen her late husband's identity.

As the night wore on and Patricia lay in bed listening to Nancy's soft breathing, a plan began to form in her mind. She dozed a little and awakened early, intent on extricating herself and Nancy from the web of lies and deceit that Eldon had contrived to weave around them.

She rose from her bed, washed and dressed, and made her way downstairs to the dining room where Maud was at a table on her own.

'Where is Eldon?' Patricia sat down and filled a cup with coffee.

'He heard that there was a card game in progress and he couldn't wait to join them,' Maud said with a sigh. 'I dare say he was up all night.'

'That sounds like Eldon.' Patricia crumbled a croissant and picked delicately at the rich pastry. 'Do you still intend to visit Lady Oakley this morning?'

'Of course. She is an old friend, so who better than I to console her?'

'Then I'm coming with you,' Patricia said firmly.

Maud gave her a searching look. 'What?'

'I'm coming with you, Maud. Don't look so surprised. You and Eldon dragged me into this and I want to keep an eye on you, in case you see anything else you fancy at the Oakley mansion.'

'Are you accusing me of being a common thief?'

'That's precisely what you are. You stole from your employers in London and you worked out this plot with Eldon to defraud a woman you say is your friend.'

Nancy entered the dining room and hurried to their table. 'What's happening today? Is anything exciting planned?'

'Keep your voice down,' Maud said, frowning. 'This isn't a game, young lady.'

'We're going to call on Lady Oakley and offer our condolences.' Patricia met Nancy's eager gaze with a warning look.

'I'm coming, too.' Nancy reached for the coffee pot.

'I don't want you to be involved, Nancy,' Patricia said hastily.

'But I was there last evening, so I am involved whatever you say.'

'All right. I suppose it does look more convincing if I have my maid with me. Although the Greystone name has been disgraced already so matters can't get much worse.'

'I suppose you can accompany me,' Maud said reluctantly. 'But don't mention it to Larkin. I think it might look better if we three go together and we leave him here. His flirtatious behaviour when dealing with women like Colette will get him into trouble, and I don't want Sir James to get suspicious.'

'Quite right.' Patricia finished her croissant and rose to her feet. 'We'll be ready when you are, Maud.'

★ ★ ★

Lady Oakley was prostrate on the day bed in her boudoir. Her maid fussed around her with a glass bottle filled with smelling salts and cold compresses for her lady's forehead.

'My dear Colette, how are you today?' Maud rushed over to kneel by the bed. 'I have been so worried about you.'

'As have I,' Patricia added firmly. 'I hardly slept for thinking about the dreadful occurrence at your wonderful ball.'

Lady Oakley's eyelids fluttered and she opened her eyes to stare at Patricia. 'I do remember meeting you last evening. You are welcome here, Madame.'

'Thank you, my lady. We were all very concerned for your wellbeing.'

Maud shot Patricia a warning look. 'You are one of my oldest friends, Colette. How can I not feel for you? Is there anything I can do?'

Lady Oakley raised herself on her elbow. 'Your company has lifted my spirits, Maud. I think I will get up.' She beckoned to her maid, who rushed forward holding up a silk robe. 'I will get dressed and go downstairs. I am not ill and I intend to show the world a brave face, even in such adversity.'

'Truly courageous,' Maud said approvingly. 'We were toughened by our youthful experiences, Colette. Others might crumble, but we are truly courageous.'

'Thank you, Maud. I've always appreciated your support. However, I must get dressed. My maid will take you to the drawing room and make sure you have refreshments. I will join you directly.'

Maud rose to her feet. 'In memory of the old days, Colette, why don't I help you to dress and your maid can look after my friend? We can chat about our former conquests without anyone listening.'

Colette's eyes lit up and she smiled. 'How delightful. Of course you may stay.' She turned to her maid and uttered a string of instructions in rapid French.

Patricia and Nancy had no alternative other than follow the servant to the drawing room. It was opulent to the point of vulgarity, with heavy crimson velvet curtains and a pink, crimson and blue carpet that Patricia's feet sunk into with each step. The upholstery on the Louis Quinze furniture was gold brocade and every available surface in the huge room was covered with ornaments in delicate porcelain embellished with flowers and chubby cherubs. The hand-painted wallpaper boasted a dazzling display of colourful birds, flowers and cherry blossoms and the heady scent of roses and oriental lilies filled the air.

Patricia sank down amongst satin cushions on one of the two large sofas set facing each other on opposite sides of the ornate Carrara marble fireplace.

'What shall I do?' Nancy asked nervously.

'Sit down until you hear someone coming and then just stand behind me. We'll leave as soon as we can without appearing rude.'

A moment later the door opened to admit a parlour maid carrying a tray of coffee and small cakes, which she placed on a table close to Patricia. Nancy stepped forward and dutifully filled a cup, which she passed to Patricia.

'I don't suppose I could have some,' Nancy said wistfully.

'Drink mine. I really don't want it.'

'Thank you. May I have a cake as well? I'm starving.'

Patricia laughed. 'Help yourself, but if anyone comes you know what to do.'

Nancy perched on stool and sampled the coffee and cakes with evident enjoyment. 'You should try one of the cakes, Patsy. They are delicious.'

'I just want to get out of here,' Patricia said wearily. 'I don't know what Maud is doing but she seems to be enjoying the drama of it all. If it was up to me we'd leave Paris as soon as possible.'

'We didn't do anything. None of this was your fault or mine.'

'Lord Eldon has made sure that I, at least, am implicated, although I don't think anyone would blame you, Nancy. It's up to me to get us out of this and I will, if it's the last thing I ever do.' The words were barely out of Patricia's mouth when Colette swept into the room followed by Maud.

Nancy moved quickly to replace the cup and saucer on the tray and took up her position behind the sofa, folding her hands primly in front of her.

'We've had such a delightful chat,' Colette said happily. 'We talked about the old days, didn't we, Maud? We were so much younger then.'

'That we did, my duck. We were always in demand. We had gentlemen queuing at the stage door simply to catch sight of us.'

Colette sat on the sofa opposite Patricia and arranged her voluminous skirts so that she seemed to be rising from a pool of emerald-green silk like some exotic flower. 'Ring the bell for a servant, Maud. We'll have a glass of Champagne to celebrate the renewal of our friendship.'

'I like that sound of that, Colette.' Maud tugged at the bell pull. 'You have such a beautiful home, dearie. I could drown myself in all this luxury.'

'I know,' Colette said smugly. 'I chose everything myself. Sir James leaves it entirely to me because I have such excellent taste.'

'Well, it is quite exquisite.' Maud fingered a china figurine. 'Beautiful.'

'I am having a soirée this evening despite the events of last night. You would be most welcome to come, including your husband, Lady Greystone. Such a charming man.'

Patricia opened her mouth to make an excuse but Maud spoke first. 'Thank you, Colette. We would love to accept. Too kind.' She met Patricia's imploring look with a scowl. 'Of course we will all come. We wouldn't

miss one of your entertainments for anything in the
world. Would we, Patricia?'

17

Eldon was waiting for them in the hotel lounge when Patricia, Maud and Nancy returned. He greeted them with a frown. 'Where have you been? I thought I told you to stay in the hotel, Maud?'

She tossed her head. 'Since when do I have to kow-tow to you, Larkin? We've been to see my dear friend Colette.'

'What?' Eldon's brow furrowed into deeper lines. 'Are you mad? I told you to lie low.'

'That would be suspicious behaviour considering that Colette and I were such good friends. We visited her to offer commiserations on her losses.'

Eldon gave her a searching look. 'Maud Grubb, tell me that you did not take anything else?'

Maud slipped her hand into her reticule and took out a ruby and diamond brooch. 'This happened to slip into my purse.'

'You really are mad,' Patricia said angrily. 'If I'd known what you intended I wouldn't have gone with you.'

'You provided just the diversion I needed, my duck.' Maud smiled as she tucked the brooch back in her reticule. 'I saw this tossed carelessly into her jewel case and I couldn't resist the temptation. She won't even know it's gone. Her dressing table was like a treasure trove.'

'Maud, this must stop now.' Eldon took her by the shoulders and propelled her to an armchair, pressing her down on the seat. 'Do you understand? Any more

260

pilfering and we will lose everything and end up in a French prison. Besides which, I have bigger plans.'

'What do you mean by that?' Patricia demanded. 'This is getting totally out of hand, Eldon.'

'There's nothing for you to worry about, but all will be lost of Maud can't control the urge to pinch anything that catches her eye.'

'I'm far too clever to be caught, Larkin. In fact we're all invited to a soirée at the Oakley mansion this evening.'

'Now I know you've lost your mind,' Eldon said angrily. 'Sir James invited me to a card game. You will only confuse matters.'

'You may gamble your money away, but Patricia and I are bound to attend or it will look very bad, and Colette might become suspicious.'

'I don't want to go, but I think Maud is right,' Patricia said reluctantly. 'She seems to have a good relationship with Lady Oakley and if we don't attend this evening it will look very odd, especially if the brooch happens to be missed.'

'Colette has so many jewels she won't notice.' Maud peeled off her gloves. 'I could do with a glass of sherry, Larkin. Ring the bell for a waiter.'

'You'll stay sober, Maud. This wasn't what we agreed and I want your promise that you will keep to our original plan.'

Maud rose to her feet, waving her gloves in Eldon's face. 'I haven't forgotten, but you are not in a position to tell me what I may or may not do. Now I'm going to my room to rest and I don't want to be disturbed.' She marched out of the salon, leaving them staring after her.

'Well!' Nancy said, breaking the ensuing silence.

'She's got brass, I must say. If I'd just robbed a friend I wouldn't return to her home and act as if nothing had happened — twice.'

'She certainly has a cheek,' Patricia agreed with a reluctant smile. 'But I think she's right. We have to attend the soirée this evening to avert suspicion. You should join us, Eldon. You know how to charm ladies like Colette.'

'I don't trust Maud. I thought she had reformed but I see now I was wrong. We're in a very delicate situation here, Patsy. I'm relying on you to help me keep Maud in check.'

'You chose to work with her, Eldon. I had nothing to do with any of this. I am returning to England at the first opportunity. You can do what you like.'

'You're forgetting that you are as much involved as we are. I'd advise you to think hard before you do anything rash.'

'You don't frighten me. I will attend the soirée this evening, but after that you and Maud must manage without me.'

'My dear girl, you are deluding yourself.' Eldon glanced over Patricia's shoulder. 'And here is someone who will convince you far better than I that you are part of this scheme.'

Patricia spun round, following his gaze, and Nancy covered her mouth with her hands, her eyes round with fear.

'Good afternoon, Patricia.' Blease Ewart strolled into the salon. 'How nice to see you again.'

'What is he doing here?' Patricia turned back to Eldon, frowning. 'How is Ewart involved?'

'My dear Patricia. I am what you might call the brains behind the scheme. Do you really think that

262

Larkin Eldon is capable of planning a robbery?' Ewart moved towards her with a smile that did not reach his eyes. 'I want you to be involved, my dear. As I told you before, I have a score to settle with your family and therefore with you also.'

'Nancy, go to our room and stay there until I come for you.' Patricia shooed Nancy out of the salon. 'Now then, you can both tell me exactly what is going on? How does any of this concern you, Blease Ewart?'

'Do sit down, Patricia. Let us talk this over like civilised human beings.'

'I don't want to talk to you, but it seems I must if I am to make any sense of all this.'

Eldon pulled up a chair. 'Sit down, Patsy. Blease will explain.'

'I prefer to stand. Speak up then, Ewart.'

'As you know I lived in France for several years, mainly because your family treated me so badly. I had to flee from England although I was innocent of any crime. During my time here I've become fluent in French and own a house in a very pleasant town called Grasse. That is where we will be travelling tomorrow, together with the rest of Lady Oakley's jewels.'

Patricia sank down on the chair. 'Tell me this is a joke. Surely you don't imagine you could get away with a further theft?'

'It is all planned down to the last item. Maud knows exactly where the lady keeps her treasures and you have helped her to gain access to the soirée this evening. I will be there to keep Sir James occupied in a card game with the other gentlemen, including Eldon.'

Eldon nodded. 'Sir James was in the game here last evening. No doubt he plans to win back the sum

263

he lost.'

'This is madness. You won't get away with it,' Patricia said breathlessly. 'I refuse to be part of such a scheme.'

'But you are already, my dear,' Ewart said smoothly. 'And you are going to assist Maud this evening.'

'I will do no such thing.'

'Your part is quite straightforward, Patsy.' Eldon laid his hand on her shoulder. 'All you have to do is keep Colette and the other ladies amused, while Maud does her work. You will sing to them with Nancy accompanying you at the pianoforte.'

'No. This is beyond belief. Why would I do such a thing? What is to stop me from going to the police here in Paris?'

'Because your family name will be disgraced for ever if you are implicated in such a grand theft,' Ewart said with a sly grin. 'You, Lady Greystone, will go to prison for a very long time, while we retire to the South of France and live royally off the proceeds of the robbery.'

'I would tell the police everything.'

'To begin with, I understand that you don't speak the language, and you have been travelling with a man who has taken the identity of your late husband,' Ewart said smoothly. 'Eldon is not known here in Paris, nor is Maud Grubb. We will disappear like morning mist, leaving you and the child to take the consequences.'

Eldon reached out to lay his hand on hers as it rested on the arm of her chair. 'Patsy, my love, all you have to do is entertain the ladies. We will keep the gentlemen occupied with a game of poker. Maud will do the rest.'

'This is all wrong, Eldon.' Patricia shook free from

his grasp and stood up, facing them both with a defiant lift of her chin. 'I won't be party to this.'

'I'm afraid it's too late for you to back out now, my dear. You left England willingly and accompanied us to Paris. You knew that I had taken Greystone's identity and you also knew that Maud had been in trouble with the police in London. Even if a judge was lenient, you would still have dragged the family name through the mire. Do you think you would be welcome home after that?'

'My family know me. They wouldn't blame me,' Patricia said doubtfully. Of course Rosie would be on her side — she knew she could trust her sister implicitly — but as to her stepdaughters, they would be only too happy to believe anything against her. Mama would never speak to her again. The future had never looked so fraught with difficulties.

'You know better than that.' Ewart moved a little closer, his eyes narrowed and his lips pulled back in a sneer. 'The proud Miss Carey would be the disgraced daughter, sister and stepmother. You would end your days sitting in a corner while the rest of the family cavorted around you. You would be nothing.'

Patricia shot him a look of loathing. 'You are a devious snake, Ewart. I want nothing to do with you.'

'After tonight you may do what you please,' Ewart said through clenched teeth. 'You can go to the police if you wish, but do you really think they would believe your innocence? You are in this with us, Patricia, whether you like it or not.'

Eldon nodded. 'I'm afraid he's right, Patsy. But despite everything my offer still stands. If you come with me I will give you my protection and you will want for nothing. You scorned me once — I suggest you give this more thought than you did previously.'

Patricia was tempted to tell him exactly what she thought of him and his offer, but she turned on her heel and marched out of the salon. She could hear them laughing as she closed the door behind her, and she made her way upstairs to the room she shared with Nancy. However, she stopped outside the door and took several deep breaths. Having calmed down, she went inside.

'Are you all right?' Nancy asked anxiously. 'You look upset, Patsy.'

'I've just had a slight difference of opinion with Lord Eldon and that hateful man Blease Ewart.' Patricia sank down on the bed. 'I can't believe that they are working together.'

Nancy sat beside her, slipping her arm around Patricia's shoulders. 'Let's run away. You said we had enough money to get back to England. We can sing on street corners if necessary.'

Patricia smiled and gave her a hug. 'It isn't that easy, Nancy. I'll think of something but for now we have to go along with their plan. I don't like it, but I can't see any alternative.'

'Are they going to steal more of Lady Oakley's jewels?'

'What put that in your head?'

'Maud took the brooch and you wouldn't have sent me out of the room if you'd wanted me to hear what Ewart had to say.'

'You're a clever girl, Nancy. Far too clever, in fact, but you're right. They are planning to steal the rest of Lady Oakley's jewels. You and I are to entertain the ladies while Eldon keeps the gentlemen occupied in a game of poker. It all sounds so simple but it's what happens afterwards that worries me.'

'We can leave in the middle of the night. There must be a way.'

'If there is I'll work it out, Nancy. In the meantime we must go along with their plans. I know Eldon isn't dangerous, but I don't trust Blease Ewart. He's a bad man and I wouldn't like to cross him, particularly now.'

'All right, I'll do as you say, but I don't like it either. I really don't.'

'Let's be practical,' Patricia said firmly. 'We have to pick the songs I'm to sing this evening, and decide on the order.'

'Maybe you could pretend to be ill or lose your voice?' Nancy suggested tentatively.

'That wouldn't work. Eldon knows me too well and Ewart would probably drag me there even if I was unconscious. They are after a fortune and they won't allow us to foil their plans.'

'We could warn the police.'

'Even if we could get out of the hotel without being seen, neither you nor I speak enough French to make ourselves understood. They would think we were mad Englishwomen and send us away. I will try to think of a way out, Nancy. I promise.'

★　★　★

There seemed to be little chance of escape. Patricia and Nancy went down to the dining room to order food, but wherever they went in the hotel they bumped into either Ewart or Eldon. Even the waiters seemed to have been primed to keep an eye on them, and the rest of the day passed all too quickly. Patricia had racked

267

her brains in an attempt to solve the problem but the only solution she could come up with was to leave in the middle of the night, as Nancy had suggested. Such a plan posed more problems than it solved, but she could think of nothing else. Whatever happened, Patricia was determined that she and Nancy would get away somehow. They would not accompany the others to Grasse or anywhere else, for that matter. She was worried but she did not share her concerns with Nancy, and they passed the rest of the afternoon by taking a walk. However, as they returned to the hotel Nancy came to a sudden halt.

'What's the matter?' Patricia followed Nancy's gaze but she could see nothing out of the ordinary. 'I'm sure we were followed,' Nancy said anxiously.

'I had the feeling several times, but when I look round there's no one there.'

'We're both nervous and agitated.' Patricia took Nancy by the hand and led her into the hotel foyer. 'We'll get through this and be on our way home before you know it.'

Nancy shook her head. 'I wish I could believe that. I really miss Rockwood and all the family. I realise now how lucky I was to have such a good home.'

'We all take family for granted. I know I'm just as guilty of that as you are, Nancy.' Patricia walked over to the concierge to collect the key to their room. 'We'd better get ready for whatever it is we have to face later on.'

* * *

Lady Oakley greeted Blease Ewart as if he were an old friend. It was only then that Patricia realised he

268

must have been planning the robbery for some time. He had admitted that his desire to involve her in his crime was motived by his wish to punish her family for bringing him to justice several years ago, even though he had escaped and gone into exile. She could only wonder what had twisted Ewart's mind to make him want to seek his revenge on innocent people. She watched him charming Colette Oakley with his flagrant flattery, and she wished she could warn Lady Oakley what was about to happen, but that would put herself and Nancy in danger. Patricia suspected that beneath the veneer of respectability and good manners, Blease Ewart was a man who would go to any lengths to get what he wanted. She did not relish the idea of taking him on single handed.

Colette greeted Eldon with a polite smile and motioned to one of the footmen to show the gentlemen to the billiard room, where a table had been set up for the card game. Having sent them on their way, she led Patricia, Maud and Nancy to the drawing room.

'It isn't usual to entertain a servant like this,' Colette said in a low voice, 'but Blease assured me that you needed Nancy to accompany you on the pianoforte.'

'Yes, that's right.' Patricia gave Nancy an encouraging smile. 'Nancy is quite happy to sit quietly until such time when you wish us to perform.'

'Excellent. Come and meet my friends. I'm afraid none of them speak English, but they will make you very welcome, and of course Valentina can make herself understood in our language.'

'I should say I can,' Maud said, smiling proudly. 'I lived in Paris for more than a year, so I learned a bit of the lingo.'

Patricia said nothing. She was feeling faint with nerves as she looked for away of escape. Maud was clearly excited at the prospect of executing a robbery on such a scale, and was bubbling over with suppressed energy. Nancy slipped her hand into Patricia's.

'Don't worry. We'll be fine.'

'Of course we will,' Patricia said with more conviction than she was feeling. She had toyed with the idea of pretending to faint, but even if she was sent back to the hotel it would still leave Maud and the others to carry out the crime. She and Nancy would be implicated by association and nothing would have changed, except the fact that she would have angered both Eldon and Ewart.

The other ladies were already in the drawing room, which was ablaze with light from crystal chandeliers and dozens of candles in silver candelabras. A fire had been lit in the magnificent marble fireplace and the ladies sat around resplendent in their brocade, satins and silks. After the introductions, Patricia sat on the sofa while Nancy was relegated to the piano stool, where she was expected to sit until Colette gave them the signal to start their performance. Refreshments were served in the form of tiny glasses of ratafia wine and small almond-flavoured biscuits. Patricia sipped her drink slowly, wanting to keep a clear head, and she sat in silence, finding it impossible to follow the conversation. She was beginning to relax a little when Maud rose to her feet and left the room after a brief conversation with Colette, who nodded and smiled. Patricia's heart began to beat faster: Maud was about to put her plan into action, leaving her friend in blissful ignorance of her treachery.

Colette rose from her seat. 'I think now is the time

for our entertainment to begin. Patricia, would you care to delight us with your lovely voice?'

Patricia nodded and forced her lips into a smile. 'Of course.' She stood up and walked over to stand by the pianoforte while Colette introduced her to the audience. She finished to an enthusiastic round of applause and launched into her second choice, which went down equally well. It seemed that the ladies could not get enough of the English folk songs, sad ballads and even a sea shanty, and Patricia was at the end of her repertoire when Maud burst into the room followed by a maid, who was screaming hysterically.

Sir James, Eldon and several other gentlemen followed them, but there was no sign of Ewart. Nancy jumped to her feet and hid behind Patricia, who found she could not move. The room was in uproar and one of the footmen grabbed Maud by the arms, struggling to hold her as she fought and kicked, shouting obscenities in English. Jewels fell from the pockets that she had sewn into the folds of her wide skirts, and the maid fell upon them, gathering them up in her hands. Colette stepped forward and slapped Maud so hard that her head jerked back and her eyes widened in shock.

Suddenly the room filled with gendarmes waving batons, and in the midst of the chaos Patricia thought she was hallucinating as she recognised the gentleman who broke away from the party and strode towards her.

'Come with me, Patricia. You, too, Nancy.' Leo Wilder wrapped a cloak around Patricia's shoulders and propelled her towards a side door, used only by servants, with Nancy following them. Outside the overheated drawing room the air was chilly and cooking aromas floated up from the basement kitchen.

'Wilder, what are you doing here?' Patricia gasped.

'I'm saving you from arrest. Don't say anything; just do what I tell you.' He led them down narrow corridors and a flight of stone steps, which ended in a maze of lamp-lit passages. Eventually they emerged into the fresh night air. It was dark except for the reflected light from what appeared to be the servants' hall, and they were in the back garden of the Oakleys' mansion. 'Follow me and don't make a sound.'

Patricia could see very little in the darkness but she clutched the tails of Wilder's frock coat and grasped Nancy by the hand. Their feet crunched on a gravel path. Somewhere close to the house, dogs had started to bark, but Wilder kept going until he unlatched a gate that led into a narrow alley at the rear of the buildings. A carriage was waiting for them in the adjacent street and he bundled them into it, giving the coachman a curt instruction in French. Wilder climbed in after them, closing the door as the cab lurched forward.

'We made it,' he said with a sigh. 'For a moment I thought we were going to be arrested with the others.'

Patricia sank back against the leather squabs. 'What are you doing here, Wilder? I thought you'd been arrested.'

'The Metropolitan Police had been after Ewart for some time, but it was Eldon who unwittingly gave him away. Your friend talks too much, especially when he's drunk.'

'But they arrested you.'

'I'm no saint, Patricia. I've done things I'm not proud of, but I wasn't going to allow Eldon and Blease Ewart to lead you into danger. I agreed to help the police providing they dropped all charges against me.

They made the arrangements for me to travel to Paris with a detective.'

'But how did you get into the Oakleys' mansion tonight?' Patricia eyed him curiously. 'We were only invited yesterday.'

'The detective was working with the gendarmerie. They had been watching Ewart and Eldon, too. I simply went along with their plan to catch the thieves red-handed.'

'What now?' Patricia asked anxiously. 'Will we be in trouble?'

'You were duped by Eldon. The authorities have no interest in you or Nancy, but Maud is wanted for a series of thefts, and now she has been caught red-handed. I imagine that Eldon, Ewart and Maud will get hefty prison sentences.'

'Ewart wasn't there when the police burst in. Do you think he got away?'

'He won't get very far. The French police are keen to arrest him for crimes he's committed while living here, but until now he's managed to evade them.'

Patricia glanced at Nancy in the semi-darkness. 'You're very quiet. Are you all right?'

'It was so exciting,' Nancy said dazedly. 'But I can't wait to get home to Rockwood to tell them what happened. I can just imagine Tommy's face. He'll be so jealous because I've had all these adventures and he's had none.'

Patricia reached out to pat Nancy on the hand. 'You've done so well in all this. I'm really sorry that I've dragged you into such a mess.'

'Nonsense. I've never had so much fun. I'm almost sorry it's over. What are we going to do now?'

'The first thing is to get you two back to England,'

Wilder said slowly. 'I don't think the French police will need you as witnesses. They have all the evidence they need against Maud and Eldon. They'll catch Ewart sooner or later.'

'Are we going back to the hotel now?' Patricia asked anxiously. 'All our things are there.'

Wilder shook his head. 'I bribed a chambermaid to pack your bags and leave them out for me to collect, which I did soon after you left this evening.'

'Was that you who followed us this afternoon?' Nancy leaned forward.

'Yes, it was me. I wanted to make sure you were safe.'

'You could have made yourself known to us,' Patricia said slowly. 'Why didn't you warn us what was going to happen?'

'Would you have been able to follow through their plan had you known I was going to attempt a rescue? Could you have sung so sweetly knowing that any moment all hell was about to break loose?'

She shook her head. 'No, I don't think I could.'

'Then that answers the question.'

'What happens next?'

'I'm taking no chances. I have a safe place for you to spend the night and tomorrow we'll sail for England.'

'But you said that the police aren't interested in us. Why can't we use our room at the hotel?'

'Because we're on our way to Le Havre, where a fishing boat will pick us up late tomorrow evening.'

'You've thought of everything,' Patricia said slowly. 'How did you know I would come with you? I might have been party to Eldon's plans.'

'I think I know you well enough to say that would be

274

an impossibility, Patricia. I also know that you would have nothing to do with Ewart.'

She was silent for a moment. 'You say that, but you were the one who asked Ewart to keep us safe in London.'

'I wasn't fully aware of his past when I asked him to escort you, but now I think he's not in his right mind. I certainly didn't know that he harboured a grudge against your family. I mistakenly thought that, despite everything, he was a gentleman.'

'You were wrong there, Wilder.'

'Yes, I see that now, and I realise that he's a danger to you and your family. While he's on the run from the police it's more important than ever for us to leave France as soon as possible.'

18

They drove on into the night and Nancy nodded off, leaning her head against Patricia's shoulder. Eventually, after two hours of bumping along country roads, the carriage drew to a halt and Wilder opened the door. He climbed out and spoke briefly to the coachman before proffering a hand to help Nancy to alight, followed by Patricia. She moved slowly as her cramped muscles came back to life shooting pain like darts from her feet to her fingers. Nancy yawned and stretched.

'Where are we?'

'The coachman assures me that this is as good a place as any to spend the rest of the night. The landlord is his brother so I believe him.' Wilder led the way up a narrow path to a small cottage at the side of the road.

'Where is he going?' Patricia demanded as the carriage was driven off into the night.

'Don't worry. The fellow is taking the horse back to the stables, but he'll be here first thing in the morning to take us to the coast.'

'We're really going home?' Nancy's voice broke on a sob. 'I know I was eager to leave Rockwood, but I really miss everyone.'

'Come inside and get warm. I gave instructions for a fire to be lit before we arrived.' Wilder opened the front door and ushered them into the main living room where, as he had predicted, a fire burned in the range and a kettle bubbled on the hob. He lit an oil lamp with a spill and placed in the middle of a table. 'Good, he left food for us. I don't know about you but I'm starving.' Wilder slipped off his coat and pulled up a chair. 'Take a seat, ladies. It's not the sort of meal you might have enjoyed at the Oakleys' mansion, but it's good enough.'

Nancy sat down and seized a knife, inexpertly hacking a slice from a large round loaf of bread. 'I'm really hungry and thirsty.'

Patricia was busy investigating the cupboards and she found some coffee beans and a grinder. In minutes she had made a pot of coffee, which she placed on the table. 'How did you manage to arrange all this, Wilder?'

He swallowed a mouthful of food. 'I arrived in France two days ago, which gave me time to get the lie of the land and make the necessary arrangements.'

Patricia sat down and poured the coffee. 'Did you know that my mother had been appearing at the opera house in Paris?'

'Yes, I discovered that by accident. I also found out that she and her husband had left for the South of France. You didn't accompany them so that told me all was not well with you.'

'You really have been busy.' Patricia buttered a slice of bread and helped herself to cheese. 'I can't thank you enough for this, Wilder. You've gone to so much trouble on our behalf.'

He smiled. 'I've cleared my debt to society by assisting the police, and in doing so I've saved you from Eldon and Maud. They belong together.'

'You're right, of course.' Patricia poured the coffee. 'But you didn't have to do all this. I can't repay all the money you must have spent.'

277

'I dare say I owed you more for the trade you brought to the Goat and Compasses.'

'Will you go back there now?'

'I doubt it. My reputation with the locals will be ruined when they discover I've helped the police.'

'What will you do then?' Nancy asked. 'Maybe you could take over the Black Dog in Rockwood village.'

'I don't know about that, Nancy. I think the present landlord might object.'

'You could live with us at the Castle. There are plenty of rooms.'

He laughed. 'I don't think I'm a castle sort of person, Nancy. But thank you for the thought. I just want to see you safely home.'

'Do you think Ewart might try to find us?' Patricia asked anxiously.

'Not if he has any sense because the police wouldn't be far behind, but you never know with a man who is deranged.'

'Are you saying he's mad?'

'He certainly isn't sane. Something has twisted his mind and it involves your family, Patricia. You probably know more about that than I do.'

Nancy yawned. 'I think I should go to bed. I can hardly keep my eyes open.'

'There's just one bedroom. I'll sleep down here,' Wilder said firmly.

'Good night then.' Nancy rose from her seat and made her way up the rickety staircase to the first floor.

'I'll be up soon.' Patricia yawned. 'I suppose it will be an early start tomorrow?'

'We still have quite a way to go, so I've arranged for the carriage to be brought round at six.'

'You've thought of everything, Wilder.'

'We've known each other for a while now, Patricia.'

She shot him a curious glance. 'Why do you say that?'

'It's just that you insist on using my surname. Don't you think you might call me Leo?' He met her surprised gaze with a winning smile. 'After all, we are sleeping in the same house.'

'My reputation is already in tatters, Leo,' Patricia said with a sigh. 'I don't suppose one more infringement of the rules will make any difference.'

He sat back in his chair, his eyes alight with amusement. 'You don't strike me as someone who cares about what others might say.'

'I used not to care about what people might think of me, Leo. But perhaps now is the time for me to change. I would like to be well thought of by those who are important to me.'

'Does that include me?'

'Yes, as a matter of fact it does. You've never criticised me or questioned my decisions. I value you as a friend.'

'Is that all?'

Patricia rose to her feet and began to gather up the dirty crockery. 'I'd better wash the dishes before I go to bed as we've an early start tomorrow.'

'Leave that.' Wilder reached out to lay his hand on hers. 'I'll see to it. You need to get some rest.'

She hesitated, looking away. The intensity of his gaze was too much to bear, particularly now, when she was tired and at a low ebb. The warmth of his hand on hers was comforting and somewhat disturbing, but she could not bring herself to break away.

'I'd better go and see if Nancy has settled.'

'You don't have to be afraid of me, Patsy. I wouldn't

do anything to harm you.'

'I know that,' she said softly.

'You are an amazing woman and I have the greatest respect for you.' He withdrew his hand quickly. 'I promise to get you home where you belong.'

'Good night, Leo. Thank you for everything.' Patricia left him to finish his coffee and made her way up the narrow staircase. She found that Nancy had fallen asleep, fully dressed.

Patricia snuffed out the candle and lay down beside her, pulling the coverlet over both of them. She was exhausted, but when she closed her eyes her emotions whirled around in her head, confusing her to such an extent that she felt as it the world was spinning out of control. She had not wanted to return to Rockwood having failed to make her mark on the world as she had hoped, but now all she wished for was the comfort and security of the crumbling old walls and the echoes of ancestors long dead. She tried to put Wilder from her thoughts but every time she closed her eyes he was there, gazing intently at her. No man had ever had such an effect on her before, although several times she had fancied herself to be in love. The blacksmith's son had caught her eye, and she had eloped with him even though his fiancée was pregnant with his child. Rosie and Piers had put a stop to that, and thank heavens they had. When Patricia had last seen Barnaby Yelland he had lost the romantic appeal of youth and was the hard-working father of three healthy young children with another baby on the way.

Then there had been Alex, a dashing captain in the 32nd Foot at the time. Their romance had been doomed from the start and deep down she had known that Rosalind was his true love. It had appealed to Patricia's vanity to win him over, but fate had intervened, which was fortunate for all of them. She realised now that she and Alex were far too alike to have been happy together.

The attention lavished upon her by Sir Michael had been flattering and his fortune had been tempting, but they had confounded the gossips by having a good relationship, although hardly a romantic one. Now, for the first time in her life, Patricia felt herself falling headlong in love with a man who could not have been more unsuitable, as far as her family were concerned. Wilder had a disreputable past and an even more uncertain future. If she threw her lot in with such a man she might end up singing for her supper in public houses for the rest of her days. It was not an encouraging thought, and yet she wanted desperately to trust him and enjoy the excitement that simply being in his company generated.

She could hear him moving around in the room below and then there was silence. The darkness of night surrounded her, calming and oddly comforting in the isolated cottage with the two people whom she cared about most, and finally she fell asleep.

★ ★ ★

Someone was shaking her but Patricia was warm and comfortable in the dream of home and she did not want to wake up. However, Nancy was persistent, and reluctantly Patricia opened her eyes to find the soft light of dawn filtering through the bedroom window.

'Come on, Patsy. Wilder has been up for ages. He's made coffee for us and he's toasting the bread that

281

was left from supper. He wants you to come downstairs now. We have to leave soon.'

'Give me a minute and I'll come downstairs.' Patricia sat upright in the bed and stretched. Last night she had been too exhausted to bother about the hard mattress and the slightly damp bedding, but this morning she was stiff and aching. Nancy clattered noisily down the wooden stairs, and Patricia swung her legs over the side of the bed. There was a shard of broken mirror on the top of the chest of drawers, and she managed to tame her unruly blond curls into a knot at the back of her neck before following Nancy down to the kitchen.

'Good morning.' Wilder filled a cup with strong coffee and handed it to Patricia. 'Did you sleep well?'

'I think so.' She sipped the scalding brew, secretly wishing she could cool it with a little milk or cream. A touch of sugar would have been more than welcome, but she realised that Wilder had gone to a lot of trouble to make them breakfast and she took her seat at the table.

'The carriage will be here soon, and we'll leave immediately.' Wilder passed the basket of slightly burned toast to Nancy. 'Have another slice. I don't know when we'll get a chance to stop and eat.'

'Are we really going home?' Nancy jabbed her knife into what was left of the pat of butter. 'I can hardly believe it. We seem to have been away for months.'

'You could have returned to Rockwood sooner,' Patricia said guiltily. 'I shouldn't have kept you away from the family for so long.'

'No, I chose to be with you, Patsy. I wouldn't have had it any other way, but now I'm glad we're going home together.'

'Eat up,' Wilder said cheerfully. 'I can hear the sound of horses' hoofs and rumbling wheels. We've got a long journey ahead of us, but at least we're on our way.'

Nancy grabbed her slice of toast and jumped to her feet. 'I'm just glad to be away from Lord Eldon and Maud. I much prefer you, Wilder.' She snatched up her bag and went to open the door. 'Come on, Patsy.'

Patricia drank the rest of her coffee and stood up. 'I can't thank you enough for this, Leo. I really do appreciate what you're doing for us and I'll make sure you are sufficiently rewarded.'

He silenced her with a kiss on the lips. 'My reward will be to see you safely back with your family. I've lived a selfish life so far. Maybe this is my chance to do something for someone else. Someone I care about deeply.' He picked up her valise and strode out of the cottage before she had a chance to recover.

★ ★ ★

They travelled for hour after hour, stopping only to change horses at country inns. Wilder bought them food and drink, but they had very little time to enjoy the break before they were on the road again. Sometimes Wilder rode up with the coachman, and at other times he sat opposite Patricia. Something had changed between them since their conversation the previous evening and the brief kiss that had sent Patricia's senses whirling in circles. She found that she could not look at him without the colour rising to her cheeks and she spoke only when absolutely necessary. For once she was thankful for his silence, which was filled by Nancy's eager chatter, but as the day wore on even Nancy ran out of conversation and she fell asleep.

Eventually the movement of the carriage stopped and Patricia opened her eyes to the darkness of the interior. Outside she could just see a glimmer of moonlight on the water and as the door opened she could hear the sound of the waves beating against the rocks.

'Where are we?' she asked sleepily.

'We're on the outskirts of a fishing village close to Le Havre.' Wilder helped her to alight. 'We've made good time but I have to go down to the quay to make sure the boat is ready for us.'

The night air was chilly and a cool easterly breeze made Patricia shiver. 'What do we do now, Leo?'

'Best wake Nancy. She would sleep through any-thing. I'll take you both to the village inn where you can wait in comfort.'

'What do we do if the boat isn't there?'

'I paid enough for our passage so I hope the skip-per keeps his word. Don't worry, I'll get you home, even if I have to steal a boat and row you to Rock-wood myself.'

'I believe you would, too,' Patricia said, laughing.

'That's better. I know you must be tired and hun-gry. You're a brave woman, Patsy.'

'I'd better wake Nancy. It looks as if the coachman is eager to go home.'

'Yes, poor chap, he lives nearby and I've paid him handsomely.'

'You will be repaid, Wilder. I promise.'

'It was worth every penny to be with you again and make sure you are safe. I know we will part as soon as I get you back to Rockwood, but I will remember the time I've spent with you for ever, Patsy.'

Wilder walked off to speak to the coachman as he was about to climb back on the box.

Patricia took a deep breath. Wilder was wrong. This was not the end — it was simply a new beginning. She walked round the carriage to wake Nancy.

★　★　★

It started to rain just as they arrived at the inn. The landlord was about to close up, but even with the difficulty of communication, they managed to make him understand that they needed shelter, if only for a short while. Grudgingly he allowed them to sit by the fire while Wilder went down to the quay. The land-lord stood glowering at Patricia and Nancy until his wife bustled into the parlour. She took one look at her guests and shooed her husband out of the room. She returned moments later with two bowls of onion soup and chunks of bread, chattering volubly and accompanying her words with fluttering hands. All Patricia could do was to smile and nod, which seemed to be enough. The soup was hot, delicious and more than welcome after such a long journey. Wilder joined them later and this sent the landlady off to the kitchen again to fetch another bowl of soup and yet more bread.

'Is the boat there, Leo?' Patricia asked wearily. 'It must be very late.'

'It is moored alongside the quay, but unfortunately we've missed the tide. We will have to sleep on board.'

Patricia glanced at Nancy, who was nodding off by the fire. 'I have enough money to pay for a room for tonight. It doesn't seem fair to make the poor child walk down to the quay.'

The landlady reappeared with the food for Wilder. '*Merci, Madame.*' Wilder glanced at Patricia and smiled. 'That's all the French I know.' He cleared his throat. 'Madame, have you a room for the ladies just for tonight?'

The landlady threw up her hands, shrugging and shaking her head as if to indicate that she did not understand.

Wilder pointed to sleepy Nancy and then at Patricia, making a mime of sleeping, and the woman began to giggle like a schoolgirl. She seemed to find his antics hilarious, but she also understood. She pointed to the ceiling and closed her eyes, holding her hands to her cheek like a child pretending to sleep.

Patricia nodded. 'Thank you, Madame.'

The landlady held out her hand, indicating that she wanted payment in advance, and Patricia took some coins from her purse. The landlady took them but she shook her head, holding her hand out for more. Eventually they settled on a price and their hostess opened the door, holding it and beckoning to them.

'I think she wants us to go upstairs,' Patricia said, gently shaking Nancy awake. 'Will you be all right down here, Leo?'

'Don't worry about me. Get a good night's sleep and I'll come for you in the morning. I think the tide turns at about half past seven.'

'We'll be up and ready.' Patricia hesitated, meeting his gaze with a steady look. 'I can't thank you enough for what you're doing for us, Leo.' Something passed between them like a flash of summer lightning, and she thought that he was going to kiss her again, but the moment passed and she hurried from the room, wondering if it had been real or imagined.

They sailed next morning on a damp day when visibility was poor and the swell made the fishing boat rise and fall into the trough of the waves with uncomfortable monotony. Fortunately both Patricia and Nancy were good sailors, although they spent most of their time sheltering in the small accommodation. Wilder, on the other hand, stayed on deck to assist the skipper and the mate, and he seemed to be in his element, which surprised Patricia as she had thought of him as a landsman through and through. It was not luxury travel. The smell of fish permeated everything they touched and was soon in their clothes and hair. Although, after their first night on board the smell seemed to wear off, or they might have grown accustomed to it. Patricia knew she would never get used to sleeping on a hard, narrow bunk, and she longed for a comfortable bed and hot food. However, each hour that passed brought her closer to home. She had never thought that she would be so eager to return to Rockwood Castle, but now she could not wait for the sight of the red cliffs and rolling hills of Devonshire.

Although they were living in such close proximity, Patricia saw very little of Leo during the time they were on board. They shared meals in the tiny cabin, but these consisted mainly of bread, cheese and slices of ham carved off the bone. They drank water that tasted of brine from a keg, and only occasionally were they able to boil water on a small spirit stove to make tea. The only treat they had each day was a rather wrinkly and bruised apple, which they gnawed down to the core. Nancy laughed and said they looked like rabbits eating a juice carrot, but Patricia could only think of the fine dining she had enjoyed as Lady Greystone with one of the best chefs in London presiding over her kitchen.

After several days and nights at sea Patricia was clearing away the remains of their evening meal when Leo beckoned to her from the cabin door. She glanced round and saw that Nancy was busy darning a hole in one of her stockings, using a needle and thread from the *étui* that Hester insisted that a lady should always have packed in her luggage.

'I'm just going on deck for a minute or two, Nancy.'

Nancy barely looked up. 'That's all right. Please don't fall overboard.'

Patricia laughed. 'I'll try not to.'

She went out into the fresh, salt-laden air and took deep breaths. The sky to the west was bruised with dark clouds and vivid streaks of purple and scarlet as the sun plummeted beneath the horizon. 'What is it, Leo?'

He pointed to the dark shoreline. 'The skipper says we'll reach Exmouth tomorrow morning and by noon we'll land at Rockwood.'

She clutched his arm as the boat tacked to starboard. 'Really? I can hardly believe it.'

'I'll see you to your home and then I'll say goodbye. I think it's best if I leave then.'

Patricia's grip tightened on his wrist. 'Why? I mean, no. You can't just walk away, Leo. I want you to meet my family. They'll want to meet you.'

He shook his head. 'I doubt it, Patsy. Apart from the fact that I need a shave and I smell of rotten fish, they won't want to know someone like me. You're going home to a different life.'

'That's nonsense,' Patricia cried angrily. 'My family will want to thank you for everything you've done for me and Nancy. My brothers and my sister will expect you to stay with us until you've decided what to do next.'

'I doubt it.' Wilder laid his hand over hers. 'This is goodbye, Patsy. This is where our lives go different ways. I will have to go back to London. I need to find a new way of earning a living.'

'This is crazy talk,' Patricia said in desperation. 'We've been so close, Leo. You saved us from Eldon and Blease Ewart. You can't just leave me at the gatehouse.'

A wry smile curved his lips. 'You even have a gatehouse? How can I live up to that when I'm homeless? It doesn't matter how I feel about you, Patsy. I have nothing to offer any woman, least of all someone who was brought up to be a lady.'

'You gave up your home and your living to help me.' Patricia's voice broke on a sob. 'How can you think of abandoning me now?'

'That's not fair and it's not true. I'm taking you home to be with the people you care about most. You are a lady in all ways, and I am certainly not a gentleman. I have a past, Patricia. Even the most broadminded of your family will disapprove of some of the things I've done.'

She broke away from him and made her way along the heaving deck to the cabin. She went inside and slammed the door.

Nancy looked up. 'What's the matter?'

'Wilder says he's going to leave us the minute we get home to Rockwood. He's a stubborn, pig-headed fool.'

The excitement of returning home was dulled by Wilder's insistence that he would not intrude on the family. He remained adamant, no matter how many times Patricia tried to convince him that he would be welcome, and when they eventually dock at Rockwood quay they were barely on speaking terms.

'Nancy and I know the way home,' Patricia said coldly as Wilder extended his hand to help her ashore.

Nancy tugged at her sleeve. 'Don't be cross, Patsy. We wouldn't be here now but for Leo.'

'I know that.' Patricia went to take her valise from Wilder but he shook his head.

'I'll see you safely home. It's what I promised and I'll do it even if I have to follow you at a distance.'

'I can't stop you.' Patricia faced up to him. 'Is there nothing I can say that will make you change your mind?'

He met her troubled gaze with a steady look. For once there was no gleam of humour in his eyes, which seemed to change colour according to his mood. They were a darkened blue now, like the overcast sky.

'Come on, Patsy. Let's get you and Nancy home before it rains again.'

Patricia sighed. She knew in her heart that he meant what he said and she turned away. 'All right, but you're wrong, Leo. Very wrong.' She walked off but she had not gone more than a few paces before she was met by a friendly face.

'Welcome home, my lady.' Minnie Jarvis, the elderly sister of the butler at Rockwood, was in the tiny front garden of her cottage. 'Mary,' she called, waving to her neighbour, who was sending her younger children off to the village school. 'Look who's here.'

Mary Tucker bobbed a curtsey. 'It's good to see you, Miss Patricia. I mean, Lady Greystone.'

'Thank you both,' Patricia said, smiling. 'I hope

you are keeping well.'

'Yes, thank you.' Minnie nodded to Mary. 'Nothing much changes in Rockwood, do it, girl?'

'No, my dear. We get by as well as we can.' Mary caught the hand of her seven-year-old son, who tried to escape without his slate. 'You'd forget your head if it weren't screwed on, Billy Tucker. You'd better run or Mrs Carey will be angry with you. And don't forget to drop that order of pilchards off at the castle on your way.'

Patricia was about to walk on, but she hesitated. 'Is my sister-in-law teaching at the village school, Mrs Tucker?'

'Yes, my lady. She's been there for a few weeks now.'

'She should be at home resting,' Patricia said, frowning. 'Her baby is due in a couple of months.'

'We should hurry.' Nancy glanced up at the lowering clouds. 'It's going to rain and I can't wait to see everyone.'

'Of course.' Patricia smiled and nodded at Minnie and Mary. They were sending covert glances in Wilder's direction, but Patricia was not in a mood to introduce him. He had chosen to abandon them, although she was hoping against hope that he might relent at the last moment. 'Good day, ladies.' She walked on, following Nancy, who was hurrying on ahead.

'You can see what I mean now,' Wilder said, matching his stride with hers. 'I don't belong here, Lady Greystone. You've come home.'

Patricia came to a halt at the end of the row of fishermen's cottages. 'Yes, I understand, Leo. You don't have to keep on about it. If you want to go I am not stopping you. In fact it's probably better if we say goodbye now. Thank you once again for everything.'

She hurried on, catching Nancy up as they reached the lane that led to the castle. 'I won't give him the satisfaction of begging him to change his mind. Is he following us, Nancy?'

19

The tall iron gates groaned in protest as Nancy pushed them open, and they swung shut behind them as they crossed the cobbled bailey. Patricia paused for a moment, looking up at the mellow stone of her family home. It was a bitter sweet moment, but a sudden rush of longing to be in the comfort of her family overcame her doubts about returning with nothing to show for her marriage and her months of independence. She put all thoughts of Leo Wilder out of her mind as she approached the front entrance. The heavy oak door opened as if by magic. Jarvis stood there, his normal stony expression replaced by a wide smile.

'Welcome home, my lady.' He beckoned to James, the footman, who stepped forward to take the luggage from Patricia and Nancy.

'Were you expecting us, Jarvis?'

'Mary Tucker's eldest boy came with the glad tidings, my lady. He delivered it with some fish for the kitchen.'

'News travels fast in Rockwood,' Patricia said, smiling. 'That boy must have run like the wind to get here before us. Anyway, it's good to be home.' She looked around the panelled entrance hall and she realised that she meant what she said. The old building wrapped its arms around her and the musty smell of old wood and ancient stones was more fragrant than the most expensive French perfume. The visor on Sir Denys's suit of armour seemed to be smiling a welcome, and it seemed that the ancestors gazed from their gilt frames with more benign expressions than usual.

'Where will I find my sister, Jarvis?'

'Mrs Blanchard is usually in the nursery at this time in the morning, my lady. Shall I have your baggage taken to your old room?'

'Yes, thank you, Jarvis. And will you send a message to the kitchen for hot water, plenty of it. I wish for a bath, as does Nancy.'

'I can have the water after you,' Nancy said eagerly.

'Nonsense. Don't start feeling sorry for yourself again.' Patricia tucked Nancy's hand in the crook of her arm and gave her a hug. 'You are one of us. Never forget that.'

'Yes, Patsy.'

'That's better. Now you do whatever you want to. I'm going to have a word with Rosie about your position in the household, and I know she'll be horrified to think that you felt so left out of things.'

'I'd like to come with you to the nursery. It seems ages since I last saw the little ones.'

'Of course, and they love you, too. You can keep them amused while I tell my sister everything that's happened to us.' Patricia led the way up the great staircase to the nursery suite, where she found Rosalind with baby Phoebe on her lap. Dolly was hugging a large doll with a painted china face and luxuriant hair, and Rory was having a tantrum, drumming his heels on the floor.

Rosalind shifted the baby to a more comfortable position and rose to her feet. 'Patsy. Good heavens, this is a lovely surprise. And Nancy, too. I wasn't expecting you.'

Patricia hurried to her side and kissed her on the

cheek. 'You seem to be the only one who didn't know we'd landed at the fishermen's quay. The servants were primed by Billy Tucker, who just happened to be delivering an order of fish to Cook on his way to school.'

Rosalind sank back on her seat. 'Molly, can't you do anything to stop Master Rory from crying?'

'He wants to play with Miss Dolly's toys, ma'am.'

Nancy scooped the howling child up in her arms. 'What's all this, Rory, my boy? Why are you being naughty?'

Rory's hazel eyes opened wide and he pointed to his sister's doll. 'Mine,' he sobbed.

'It's not his.' Dolly pouted ominously. 'It's mine. Tell him, Nancy.'

Nancy smiled. 'Let's find him something else to play with. Will you help me, Dolly?'

'Maybe I should make Nancy the children's nanny,' Rosalind said thoughtfully.

'I wanted to talk to you about that, Rosie.' Patricia lowered her voice. 'Nancy is not a servant. Don't forget it was you who sent her to a good school. We've adopted her into the family and I think you should treat her as you would me.'

Rosalind's eyes lit with humorous glint. 'You are a fine one to talk, Patsy. Where have you been and what have you been doing? And if you don't mind me saying so, you look a terrible mess and you both stink of rotten fish.'

'Well, it's a long story and I think for my own sake I'll wait until we're all together before I start going through all the events of the past few months.'

'So you are not the operatic star you hoped you would be?'

295

'No, sadly not, but I have discovered that I can entertain people by singing, although not in the classical way.'

'All right, I suppose I'll have to wait for you to tell us what you've been up to, but why are you in such a state?'

'We sailed from France almost a week ago on a fishing boat, which would make anyone look and smell awful.'

'You've been in France?' Rosalind stared at her sister in amazement. 'You have a lot of explaining to do, Patsy.'

'You won't believe what we have to tell you, Rosie.' Nancy whirled Rory round until he stopped crying and began to chuckle. 'That's better, young man. Now where are your toy soldiers? You want to be like your papa, don't you?'

'I want to be like you, Auntie Patricia.' Dolly tugged at Patricia's skirt. 'I can sing. Grandmama said I have a very nice voice, but I don't want to be old like her. I want to be a pretty lady like you.'

Rosalind sighed. 'You are already being a bad influence on my child, Patsy, and you haven't been home for an hour yet.'

Patricia stroked baby Phoebe's plump cheek. 'I wasn't sure what sort of welcome I would get, Rosie. I have no home of my own and no money. My fine plans for a career in opera did not work out as I'd hoped. I am your pauper sister.'

'Since when did money matter to us, other than having enough to live on and keeping a roof over our heads? We've been rich and we've been poor. We're managing quite nicely now, but we'll never have the grand balls and hunting parties that I remember as a child.'

'I know you're happy to welcome me home, but what about Alex? How will he feel if I have to live with you?'

'Alex is fond of you, and don't forget Bertie and Walter. They'll be delighted to have you back with us. The Careys of Rockwood will band together, as always.' Rosalind reached out to pat her sister on the shoulder. 'Now please, do go and have a bath. And change your clothes before you see anyone else, or you might find your welcome a little strained.'

'Hester never did approve of me. How is she?'

'Hester never changes, but she won't be very happy to see you in this state.' Rosalind turned to Nancy. 'I think you'd better do the same. You both smell like fishwives.'

Patricia hesitated in the doorway. 'When will we all be together?'

'I'll send word to the kitchen to prepare a special dinner this evening to celebrate your homecoming. You can tell us your story after we've eaten. I can't wait to hear it.'

'Thank you, Rosie. You're the best sister a girl could have.'

'It took you long enough to acknowledge it,' Rosalind said, laughing. 'Please go and get clean. I can't bear the smell.'

'All right, I'm going. Come along, Nancy. We'd better do as my older sister says.'

Patricia made her way to the room she had shared with Rosalind when they were children. The floral chintz material in the curtains and bed cover were faded now, but still pretty and welcoming. The view from the window looked out over the rose garden to the cliffs and a blue stripe of the estuary beyond. The rain clouds had been blown away and the sky was pure azure with a few fluffy clouds floating on the horizon. The breeze from the sea was tangy with brine and softened by the scent of the roses and honeysuckle that clambered up the castle walls.

Jennet had just poured the last pitcher of water into the copper bath, lined with a large white sheet. She bobbed a curtsey. 'Welcome home, my lady.'

'Thank you, Jennet. I can't tell you how much I need this.' Patricia slipped off her soiled garments and stepped into the bath. 'My clothes will have to be washed thoroughly, and everything in my valise. Will you make sure they go to the laundry room?'

'Yes, my lady.' Jennet handed her the soap and stood back while Patricia washed her hair and rinsed it clean. 'Are there any of my old gowns in the clothes press, Jennet? I've been travelling light and have nothing to wear. Look for something simple, not one of my London gowns.'

Jennet walked over to the large oak clothes press and opened the cupboard and then the drawers, one by one. She pulled out a couple of cotton print gowns that were faded and definitely not this year's fashions, but at least they were clean.

'Will either of these do, my lady?'

'I'll look like a milkmaid, but at least they won't smell of fish. You may go, thank you, Jennet. I can manage now.'

Jennet's fine eyebrows arched in disapproval. 'You surely don't mean to dress yourself, my lady?'

Patricia stifled a giggle. 'I've grown accustomed to looking after myself, Jennet. It will take a while to get used to being waited on, but I'll certainly try. You may go now.'

Patricia sat back in the bath, luxuriating in the warm scented water. Despite her efforts to put Leo Wilder out of her mind, she was regretting the way they had parted. He had saved them from possible arrest by the French police and he had gone to enormous trouble to bring them safely home. She had thanked him but she had also berated him for not doing as she wished, and for that she was sorry. She wondered what he would do now and where he would go. Suddenly she could bear it no longer and she rose from the water, sending rivulets onto the floorboards as she stepped out and reached for a towel. Having dried herself she dressed in the clean clothes and tied her damp hair into a knot at the back of her neck. There was probably an hour or so before luncheon would be served and that would be just enough time to walk back to the quay and make enquiries as to Wilder's whereabouts. He could not have gone far without some means of transport. She had to find out.

★ ★ ★

With a shawl wrapped around her shoulders Patricia left the castle by a side door and made her way through the postern gate, taking the path that ran alongside the backwater until she came to the bridge. After than it was a reasonably short walk along the edge of the woods to the fishermen's quay. However, no matter who she asked no one knew where Wilder had gone and the fishing boat had already set sail. She could have wept with frustration. If he had gone with it she would never be able to find him and apologise for her lack of understanding and ungrateful behaviour.

She turned back and made her way along the lane, past Greep Farm, the sawmill and the wheelwright's premises. She paused briefly at the smithy to acknowledge a greeting from Barnaby Yelland, and then hurried on, being in no mood to stop for polite conversation. It occurred to her that the obvious place for anyone who was a stranger to the area would be the village pub. When she was a child she had tagged on to the older children in the village, Ben Causley, the innkeeper's son, being one of them, but she had been the youngest and none of them had taken her seriously. It would be different now. She was still Lady Greystone and they would have to take notice of her. Perhaps Ben or his father would know something. She hurried along the main street, acknowledging greetings from everyone she saw, although she did not stop to talk. If they thought it was odd to see Lady Greystone bareheaded, wearing a simple cotton gown and shawl, unaccompanied even by a maid, they were not given a chance to make any comments.

Hot, windswept and breathless, Patricia marched into the taproom of the Black Dog. Ned Causley approached her from behind the bar.

'Lady Greystone. This is very irregular. Ladies are not allowed in the bar unaccompanied.'

'My family own the land this public house is built on, Ned. Besides which, I am not here as a customer. I'm looking for someone.' Patricia glanced over his shoulder and to her intense relief she saw Leo Wilder standing at the bar.

'Even so,' Ned said urgently. 'This isn't the sort of place you should be seen, ma'am.'

'Patricia! What on earth are you doing here?' Bertie's voice rang out in the silence as the locals stared

300

in amazement at Patricia.

She looked round and saw her brother seated on a wooden settle by the inglenook. Wolfe was already on his feet, glowering at her. Patricia held up her hand. 'It's all right, Bertie. I'll explain later.' She moved towards Wilder. 'Please come outside. We need to talk.'

'Who is that?' Bertie demanded, glaring at Wilder.

'Leo is a friend of mine, Bertie.'

'Wolfe, fetch my Bath chair,' Bertie said firmly. 'We're going home and you're coming with us, Patsy. And you, sir, will come outside and explain yourself.'

Ned shook his head. 'Sir Bertram, I'll thank you to keep your voice down. This is a respectable ale house.'

'Remember who you're talking to, cully,' Wolfe growled. 'Sir Bertram owns this pub and you're late with the rent.'

Ned clenched his fists but Wolfe was head and shoulders the taller of the two and Ned retreated behind the bar.

'Leo, please.' Patricia sent him a meaningful look and he followed her out into the sunshine. 'I'm sorry about that. I didn't know my brother would be in there.'

'What's the matter? Why have you followed me?'

'Because I'm sorry if I was sharp with you. You've done so much for me and I didn't mean to be ungrateful.'

Leo smiled and laid his finger on her lips. 'Being humble doesn't suit you, Patricia. But I decided to leave, and it looks as if your brother is about to agree that I made the right choice.' He glanced round as Wolfe pushed the Bath chair towards them. Bertie opened his mouth to speak but Patricia stepped in between them.

'Bertie, before you say anything I want you to meet Leo Wilder. He is the person who saved Nancy and me from being arrested by the French police.'

Bertie's angry expression was replaced by a puzzled frown. 'You were in France?'

'It's a long and complicated story, Bertie. I was going to tell the family at dinner tonight. That was Rosie's idea. At least she was pleased to see me.'

Wilder took Patricia's hand and raised it to his lips. 'You need to be with your family now. I should be going.'

'No, Leo. You can't just walk away like this. Where will you go? What will you do?' Patricia turned to Bertie. 'Wilder gave up his pub in London to take Nancy and me to Italy. I thought if I could find Mama she might help me with my career. That was a mistake I won't repeat, but you have no idea what we went through. However, I wouldn't be standing here now if it weren't for Leo.'

Bertie gave Wilder a searching look. 'It seems that I'm in your debt, Wilder. Although I have no idea what my sister is talking about. However, she's right about one thing. We can't allow you to leave Rockwood without thanking you properly.'

'There really is no need.' Wilder shook his head. 'I'm going to look for work and lodgings in the nearest large town.'

'You're a fair way from Exeter or Newton Abbot,' Wolfe said gloomily. 'Best start now if you're on foot.'

'You'll do no such thing.' Bertie shot an angry look in Wolfe's direction. 'Mr Wilder will be our guest at Rockwood for as long as he wishes. Were you a military man, Wilder? You have the disciplined look of

302

someone who served his country.'

'I ran away to sea when I was a boy and served my time in the navy, Sir Bertram.'

Patricia stared at him in surprise. 'You never told me that, Leo.'

'You didn't ask. You took it for granted that I'd always been a tavern keeper.'

'This is getting us nowhere,' Bertie said impatiently. 'I'm hungry and it's time for luncheon. Come with us, Wilder. At least allow us to offer you some hospitality in recognition of the service you've done for my sister.'

'Yes, Leo,' Patricia added. 'Please come with us now. You may leave later if you so wish, but I want you to meet the rest of my family.'

'How can I refuse?' Wilder proffered his arm to Patricia. 'It seems we are not destined to part yet.'

★ ★ ★

Apart from a brief period when Lady Pentelow had presided over the table, luncheon had never been a formal affair at Rockwood Castle, and today was no exception. Alex and Rosalind were already seated at the dining table with Hester and Nancy when Patricia and Wilder joined them. Wolfe pushed the Bath chair into the room and settled Bertie at the head of the table.

Patricia cleared her throat. She wanted desperately for Wilder to be accepted by her family and that made her suddenly nervous.

'I want you all to meet my good friend, Leo Wilder. He took care of Nancy and me when we were homeless in London and he travelled all the way to France to rescue us from almost certain arrest.'

Hester acknowledged Wilder with a look that would have scared a lesser man, but Alex jumped to his feet and shook Wilder's hand.

'Rosie has told me the little she knows of your exploits, Mr Wilder. I look forward to hearing the rest of it.'

'It's so nice to meet you, Leo,' Rosalind said, smiling. 'Do take a seat. Molly will bring the soup in a moment.'

Wolfe lifted Bertie from the wheeled chair and set him down at the head of the table. Patricia took her old place opposite Hester and she patted the seat beside her.

'Please sit next to me, Leo. My family might look fierce but I promise you they are really nice when you get to know them.'

'It's very good of you to invite me into your home, Sir Bertram.' Wilder unfolded the linen napkin and laid it on his lap. 'We've been living off bread and cheese for a week or so, but at least the fishing boat brought us here safely.'

'Why were you three skulking around like criminals?' Hester demanded. 'Why didn't you travel by packet boat and train like other folk?'

'That's not fair, Hester,' Patricia said hastily. 'You don't know the circumstances.'

'We're eager to hear about your adventures, Patsy.' Bertie reached for a bread roll and put it on his plate where he began to break it into small pieces. 'Where's Molly with the soup? I'm starving.'

As if on cue Molly entered the room bearing a weighty tureen filled with savoury-smelling soup. She walked round the table offering it to each one in turn before leaving the dish in front of Rosalind. She stood back, hands folded neatly in front of her as the family began their meal.

'Well?' Hester demanded. 'You haven't answered my question, Mr Wilder.'

'We had to leave Paris in rather a hurry,' Wilder said casually.

'And there was the matter of Blease Ewart as well,' Patricia added. She glanced round at the surprised faces at table. 'You all thought you'd heard the last of him, didn't you? Well, apparently he's been living in France for some years, having escaped the law. I really hope the French police catch him this time.'

Alex dropped his spoon in his bowl with a clatter. 'How did Ewart come into this? I thought he had gone for ever.'

'He was part of Lord Eldon's plan to rob a very wealthy woman of all her jewels.' Wilder gave Patricia a reassuring smile. 'He and Maud Grubb, or Signora Gandolfi, as she prefers to be known, were in it together, and I suspect that Ewart planned the whole thing.'

Rosalind gazed at her sister in amazement. 'Patsy, how did you become involved in all this?'

'My career in the opera company had faltered and I wanted to see Mama. I thought she might help me to better my chances. I wanted to join her in Italy but I ended up travelling with Eldon and Maud. I thought it was by chance, but I know now it was part of their plan to rob a wealthy woman of her jewels. Nancy and I were to be the unsuspecting cover they needed to carry out the robbery.'

'But how did Ewart come into it?' Alex demanded, frowning. 'That man has been nothing but trouble.'

305

'We met Ewart in Leo's pub,' Patricia said wearily.

'What I want to know, Patricia, is how did you get yourself involved with criminals?' Hester gave her a stony stare. 'You always managed to get into trouble one way or another, even as a child.'

'That's not fair, Hester,' Rosalind protested. 'Patsy was the youngest and Mama went off to follow her career. After Papa died abroad Patsy only had me to look after her.'

'I suppose you're going to tell me that I was simply the housekeeper in those days,' Hester said sharply.

'No, Hester. You took care of us devotedly — no one can deny that — but Patsy was very young and she needed someone to give her all their attention.'

Bertie held up his hand. 'We're getting away from the main topic. You said you were going to Italy to find Mama. How did you end up in Paris, Patsy?'

'Well, if you'll all stop interrupting I'll tell you what happened, and how we came to travel home on a dirty old fishing boat.' Patricia launched into a detailed description of the times he and Nancy had spent in Paris, and she finished by thanking Wilder once again for bringing them home.

'What I don't understand is why Blease Ewart would want to work with Larkin Eldon and Maud Grubb.' Alex turned to Wilder with a questioning look. 'Do you know any more than Patsy just told us?'

Wilder shook his head. 'Ewart walked in to my pub a couple of months ago. He'd come off a ship, so he said, and had lodgings in Bleeding Heart Yard. I used to get all sorts of characters coming into my taproom, but I did think it odd that he knew Starlina Beaney. She is a fortune-teller and some suspect she is also a fence for stolen goods.'

306

'You know her sister, Alex,' Patricia added quickly. 'Ewart must have met her while he was here in Rockwood.'

Alex shook his head. 'I don't know anyone of that name.'

'Yes, you do,' Rosalind said, smiling. 'Squire Cottingham's wife, Glorina, is Starlina Beaney's sister. Blease Ewart must have met Starlina through her or vice versa.'

'I wouldn't put it past Glorina to have persuaded Ewart that he was heir to the Rockwood Estate.' Hester sniffed, sending a defiant look in Bertie's direction. 'That woman likes to make mischief.'

'True or not, Blease Ewart is a common criminal,' Bertie said firmly. 'You were lucky to get away from him and his cronies, Patsy. Thanks, it seems, to you, Wilder. I'm in your debt.'

'Not at all.' Wilder turned his attention to Alex. 'Ewart claimed to have committed some of the crimes for which your brother, Piers, was convicted and transported to the penal colony in Australia.'

Rosalind frowned. 'If that's true, Alex, someone ought to tell Lady Pentelow. I know that Piers did do things he regretted bitterly, but maybe his grandmother could get her solicitor to appeal to the courts for clemency.'

'I'll think about it, Rosie,' Alex said gently. 'Piers did wrong, but he's paid for it with four years' hard labour. I believe he's a ticket of leave man now.'

'You've heard from him?' Rosalind gazed at her husband in surprise. 'You didn't tell me.'

'I had a letter a few weeks ago. I didn't want to drag up the past, so I didn't tell you.'

'But it sounds like good news,' Rosalind said

thoughtfully. 'What does ticket of leave mean exactly?'

'It gives the convict the right to seek employment in a specified district and earn his living. He or she can even marry or bring their family from England.' Alex gave her a reassuring smile. 'I'll go to Cornwall and visit Trevenor. With this information we might even get a pardon for Piers and he can go home. I've never been entirely happy about Martin Gibbs running the mine on his own, especially as we own a few shares.'

'That's all very well, Alex,' Bertie said hastily. 'But if you go to Cornwall I'll struggle to manage the estate, even with Wolfe's support.'

'Alex must do what he thinks is right, Bertie.' Rosalind gave her brother a stern look. 'I'm sure we can manage without him for a couple of weeks.'

'Why don't you ask Leo to stay on and help you, Bertie?' Patricia suggested sweetly. 'He hasn't any plans for the time being.'

'I know nothing about country matters,' Wilder protested.

'Bertie could tell you what he needed you to do.' Rosalind turned to her brother with a persuasive smile. 'I could go with Alex and take the children to see Dolly's great-grandmother. Patsy and Hester can manage the household. Do say yes, Bertie.'

'I need a strong fellow to keep the tenants in order,' Bertie said slowly. 'You look as though you're used to handling men, Wilder.'

'I've done my share.'

'Please say you'll stay for a while at least.' Patricia laid her hand on his sleeve. 'I owe you a lot for bringing Nancy and me safely home. I might have been languishing in a French prison if you hadn't intervened.'

'Yes, I agree.' Bertie pushed his soup plate away. 'Give me a portion of cold ham and beef, Rosie. I've developed quite an appetite. Eat up, Leo Wilder. You and I will have a talk after luncheon. I won't hold you to anything you don't wish to do. Just ignore my sister's pleas. Patsy is used to having her own way.'

'She was a spoiled child,' Hester said, frowning. 'Your late husband gave you whatever you wanted, Patricia. You are too used to getting everything you want.'

'That might have been true once, Hester.' Patricia bowed her head meekly. 'But that ended when Greystone died. I do owe you a debt of gratitude, Leo. You took me and Nancy in when we were almost destitute. Please allow me to help you now.'

20

Cora Fletcher towered over Jim Gurney as he super-vised packing the family's luggage into the second carriage. Her tattooed, muscular arms were bare to the elbow as she waved them like the conductor of an orchestra, pointing this way and that as Jennet and Tilly attempted to stow the children's toys. Patricia watched from a safe distance. No one was allowed to interfere when Rosie's faithful servant was in charge. Jennet was to travel in the carriage with Rosalind and the three children, while Alex had chosen to take the reins, leaving Gurney to bring up the rear with Fletcher and the luggage in the smaller carriage. Patricia was glad that she was not part of this entourage. It would take them several days to get to Trevenor, stopping often to rest the horses and sleeping at wayside inns. Travel had lost some of its appeal for Patricia after her flight from Paris and the uncomfortable voyage home on the fishing boat.

Rosalind emerged from the main entrance holding Dolly and Rory by their hands, while Molly carried baby Phoebe. Alex came striding from the direction of the stables, followed by Wilder.

'Are you ready to leave, Rosie?' Alex picked up Dolly and gave her a kiss. He put her down again and ruffled Rory's curly golden hair. 'You will be good for Mama, won't you? I'll be outside on the box so I'll know if you're naughty.'

Dolly smiled sweetly. 'Of course, Papa. We are always well behaved. Mama says so.'

Rosalind reached up to brush her husband's cheek with a kiss. 'You have been told, my love. Dolly has a way with words, but it's time we were on our way.' She turned to Patricia. 'I'm trusting you to keep everyone in order. Just remember that Walter and Louise are living in the old keeper's cottage, so they are near if you need any assistance.'

'Walter comes almost every day to use the library, so please don't worry.'

'Yes, I know he does. He can be quite practical when it suits him, but don't allow Hester to bully you. She means well but she still thinks you are ten years old.'

Patricia pulled a face. 'Yes, I know it. Anyway, don't worry. You go to Cornwall and enjoy the trip.'

'We'll be back in a week or two, depending on how Lady Pentelow takes the news and if Alex has to deal with the solicitors.'

'How would you feel if Piers did return from Australia, Rosie?'

'We were very young when we first met. We thought we were in love and perhaps we were, at first, but he couldn't get Cornwall from his heart, and that's where he's happiest. I am part of Rockwood and that's just the way it is. We're both older and, I hope, wiser now.'

'But Dolly is his daughter. Won't he want to see her?'

'He's never shown any interest in her, Patsy. It's a little late to start now.'

'Are you coming, Rosie?' Alex demanded. 'Or are you going to chat with Patsy all morning?'

'I'm coming. Goodbye, Patsy. I'll see you again soon.' Rosie handed the children into the carriage before climbing in herself.

'They'll be back soon,' Wilder said, as if reading Patricia's thoughts.

311

'Yes, I hope so, but I know what Lady Pentelow is like. Once she gets a hold on Alex she'll want him to remain at Trevenor for as long as possible.'

'I think your sister would have something to say about that. Rosalind seems very patient but I wouldn't want to push her too far.'

Patricia laughed. 'Perhaps that's a family failing. I am very stubborn.'

'I noticed.' Wilder started off in the direction of the stables. 'I will see you later.'

'Where are you going?'

He came to a halt. 'Sir Bertram is visiting his tenants and I'm going with him.'

'Wolfe won't like that.'

'He doesn't have much choice. If I am to be of any use I need to meet the tenants and get to know them.'

'Don't turn into too much of a countryman, Leo. It wouldn't suit you.'

Patricia turned away and walked slowly into the entrance hall, which seemed even larger than normal and unusually silent. She had wondered how Wilder would cope with living in such a rural setting, but if she were honest it was herself she was worried about. When she was a girl she had longed to escape from Rockwood Castle, and that feeling was creeping up on her again. After the excitement of living in London, be it in the smart West End or the impoverished East End, she was already experiencing that old familiar sense of boredom and the longing to get away.

'So she's gone.'

Patricia jumped at the sound of Hester's voice and she spun round to face her. 'Yes, they've just left.'

'Don't imagine you can take over from your sister, Patricia. I am in charge of the household while

Rosalind is away.'

'Are you saying that I am incapable of taking care of things, Hester?'

'If the cap fits, wear it.'

'You may have married my grandpapa when he was in his dotage, but that doesn't alter the fact that you were our servant for as far back as I can remember.'

'Your grandpapa was as sane as you or I. You shan't defile his memory.'

'I loved him, but he was definitely off his head most of the time. Do you really think he would have married you had he been completely sane?'

Hester's cheeks flamed and her eyes narrowed. 'How dare you speak to me like that? I am your step-grandmother and I demand respect.'

'I didn't mean to be so harsh, Hester. You looked after us all when we were children, but Rosie left me in charge, not you. If we are to get along together I suggest you leave me alone.' Patricia stormed off. She knew that Hester was staring after her, but she did not look back. Perhaps coming home had been a mistake, but where else was she to go? She came to a halt and turned round to see Hester standing like a statue next to Sir Denys's suit of armour. Patricia hurried back to fling her arms around Hester's portly body.

'There, there, Hester. You know me: I say things without thinking sometimes. Of course you are part of the family and always have been. You do what you always do and I won't interfere.' Patricia glanced over Hester's shoulder as a shadow fell across the flagstones and Walter rushed into the entrance hall. 'Walter? What's the matter?'

'It's Louise,' he said breathlessly. 'She was taking a class at the village school when she was taken ill. She's

313

at home now but she's in terrible pain.'

'The baby isn't due for a couple of months,' Hester said anxiously. 'I'll come right away, Walter.'

'Have you sent for the doctor?' Patricia asked urgently.

'He's at Greystone Park attending Sylvia, who has taken to her bed, so his wife said.' Walter brushed a lock of hair from his brow.

Patricia thought quickly. 'I'll get Hudson to saddle a horse for me and I'll ride to Greystone Park. It's probably Sylvia having one of her megrims. You go with Walter, Hester. I'll fetch the doctor and be with you as soon as possible.'

Hester nodded. 'Have you told Louise's parents, Walter?'

'No. I came straight here.'

'That's a relief. I never could stand the vicar's wife. Dreadful woman. Come on, Walter, don't stand there gawping. We should hurry.' Hester waddled after Walter, who raced on a head, leaving Patricia to make her way to the stables.

Hudson listened to her request for a suitable mount. 'There's only Sultan, the captain's horse,' he said reluctantly. 'I could saddle him for you, my lady, but he's hard to handle.'

'What about Sheba, my sister's bay mare?'

'She's at the farrier's, my lady. She cast a shoe yesterday and Pip took her to the smithy this morning.'

'Saddle up Sultan. This is an emergency.'

'He's mettlesome and very powerful, my lady.'

'I can handle any horse, and there's no time to wait for Sheba to be brought back. I'm a competent rider, Hudson.'

'Very well, if you're sure, my lady.' Hudson disappeared into the stables and minutes later he led Sultan out into the summer sunshine.

Patricia climbed onto the mounting block and with a determined effort she mounted Sultan. The horse pranced about even though Hudson was still holding the reins.

'It's all right, Hudson. You can let him go. I'll be perfectly . . .' Patricia's words were lost as Sultan surged forward, leaving the stable yard at a swift trot, breaking into a canter. Patricia kept her seat and eventually reined him in. 'You won't get the better of me, Sultan. But we need to get to Greystone quickly.'

Sultan twitched his ears and snorted.

'Giddyap,' Patricia said through clenched teeth, and Sultan needed no second bidding. If she had not been so desperate to seek help for her sister-in-law, Patricia would never have attempted to ride such a spirited animal, but she managed to hold on when Sultan broke into a gallop. With her hair flying behind her like a pennant and her skirts above her knees she was attracting astonished stares as they flew through the village streets, but all she could do was concentrate on staying in the saddle. Her lungs felt as though they might burst by the time they reached Greystone Park and the gatekeeper hurried out to let her in. Patricia had no breath left to thank him but she managed to control Sultan's exuberance so that they slowed to a trot as they approached the house. A stable lad rushed out to hold the reins while Patricia dismounted and she walked somewhat shakily to knock on the door, which opened almost immediately.

Foster stared at her and for a moment he seemed at a loss for words but he recovered quickly. 'Good morning, my lady.'

'Is Dr Bulmer here, Foster,' Patricia asked breathlessly.

'Yes, my lady. He's with Miss Sylvia.'

'Is she unwell?'

'She's been confined to her room for several days, my lady.'

'Then I'd better go upstairs and see her. Thank you, Foster.' She could see that he was torn between loyalties and she smiled. 'Don't worry, Foster. If Miss Sylvia protests I'll say I pushed past you.' She hurried across the magnificent marble-tiled hall and took the stairs two at a time. She hesitated outside Sylvia's room but before she had a chance to turn the knob the door opened and Dr Bulmer stepped out onto the landing.

'Lady Greystone? I didn't expect to see you here.'

'I'm staying at Rockwood Castle at the moment. Is my stepdaughter ill?'

Dr Bulmer looked down at his highly polished boots. 'I'm afraid she's been suffering from consumption for some time, Lady Greystone.'

'Consumption?' Patricia gazed at him in horror. 'Surely not? Sylvia is younger than me.'

'The disease attacks people of all ages and from all walks of life, my lady.'

'Is there anything to be done for her?'

'Rest, good food and fresh air are the only things that might help. She needs someone living here to look after her.'

'Christina should come home. Why isn't she here?'

'I believe that Mrs Cottingham is in the family way, my lady. She has been advised of her sister's illness, but she has decided to remain at home.'

'I see.' Patricia sighed. 'Miss Sylvia won't countenance my return. I suppose you know that my late husband left everything to his daughters?'

'I did hear something of the sort.'

'Anyway, I didn't come here to discuss my problems. You are needed urgently at the Keeper's cottage on the Rockwood estate, Doctor. My sister-in-law might be in early labour. Her baby isn't due for a couple of months, so I've been told. Please will you go there right away?'

'Of course, my lady.' Dr Bulmer made as if to walk away but he stopped, turning his head to give Patricia a steady look. 'Might I suggest that this is not the time to continue family feuds? Miss Sylvia needs you.' He strode off in the direction of the stairs.

The faint sound of coughing from the sickroom underlined his words and Patricia opened the door. 'Sylvia, may I come in?'

'Patricia?' Sylvia said faintly. 'I'm rather unwell.'

'Yes, so the doctor said.' Patricia walked slowly towards the bed with its carved posts and ornate tester. 'How do you feel?'

'I'm tired all the time and I have this wretched cough. Did you come here to see me?'

'Of course,' Patricia said firmly. She could not bear to see her old friend looking so poorly. Sylvia looked drained even though she had pink cheeks and suspiciously bright eyes.

'You will stay for a while, won't you?' Sylvia reached out to grasp Patricia's hand.

'I could visit you every day if you wish.'

Sylvia's eyes darkened. 'I am so sorry, Patsy. We treated you very badly after Papa died.'

'That doesn't matter now. You must concentrate on getting better.'

'I don't think that's going to happen. Dr Bulmer

317

won't tell me the truth, but I think I'm dying.'

'That's nonsense. You're imagining things, Sylvie. You always did make a big fuss about the smallest things.'

'I used to make you laugh in the old days.'

'And you will again. You just need to do what the doctor tells you. He prescribed rest and fresh air.'

'Christina won't visit me, so I know I must be very ill. She's in that way again, if you know what I mean.'

'That's probably why she wants to stay at home. Don't take it personally, Sylvie.'

'I wish we hadn't sent you away. Do you live in the London house now?'

Patricia had not the heart to remind her. 'Yes, of course, although I think I prefer the country. London is so very crowded and noisy. You can't hear the birds singing or see the flowers growing in gardens. I'm staying with the family for a while.'

'I should so like to go outside. Do you think you could take me?'

'Of course I will, but not at the moment. I have to return to Rockwood because Rosie and Alex have taken the children to Cornwall for a short stay.'

Sylvia's mouth drooped at the corners and her eyes filled with tears. 'I wish you would come home, Patsy. It would be such fun if we were together again. I could still beat you at croquet.'

'Then when you are stronger we'll have a match and see who's best. But until then I want you to do what the doctor says.'

'You will come again tomorrow, won't you?'

'Who is looking after you, Sylvie? Where is Miss Martha? I haven't seen her today, or Miss Moon.'

'They went on one of their visits to relations in the

North. Ivy does her best, but the other servants keep away. I don't know what is going on below stairs.'

Patricia frowned. Christina and Sylvia had rejected her claim on the property and now Sylvia was begging her for help. The irony of the situation was not lost on Patricia. However, she could not stand by and see her old friend suffering, nor could she allow the servants to do as they pleased.

'I have to go home now, but I'll return this afternoon.'

'I'm really sorry, Patsy,' Sylvia said in a small voice. 'We treated you so badly.'

'It doesn't matter now. You must concentrate on getting better and leave everything else to me.'

'Yes, Patsy,' Sylvia said meekly.

'I'll be back before you know it.' Patricia patted Sylvia's thin hand as it lay on the coverlet. She noticed that the pillowcases needed changing and the sheet was stained where Sylvia must have been trying to eat or drink when only partly propped up in bed. Patricia was suddenly angry, and she left the room to make her way down the main staircase. Foster was waiting in the entrance hall and he was about to open the main door when she held up her hand to stop him.

'Foster, I'm going below stairs. I want words with Mrs Simpson. I assume she is still the housekeeper.'

'Yes, my lady. Is there anything wrong?'

'From the little I've seen today I think something has gone awry in the household since Miss Sylvia was taken ill.'

Foster cleared his throat nervously. 'Any complaints should be passed on to me, my lady.'

'I agree. I don't know what you've been doing, Foster, but I'm about to find out. You'd better accompany me.' Patricia marched off in the direction of the green baize door that led to the servants' quarters. Foster followed her at a respectful distance.

Patricia went straight to the housekeeper's office. She entered without bothering to knock and found Mrs Simpson seated behind her desk enjoying a cup of tea with a plate piled high with cakes in front of her.

'I see you are busy, Mrs Simpson,' Patricia said coldly. 'Is this why the housekeeping has become so incompetent since I am no longer here to keep an eye on things?'

Mrs Simpson put her cup down and rose to her feet. 'It's not how it appears, my lady. I am entitled to have a break every now and then, am I not, Mr Foster?'

'Undoubtedly, Mrs Simpson, but Lady Greystone has concerns that need to be addressed.'

'I can speak for myself, thank you, Foster.' Patricia stood her ground. 'Miss Sylvia's room is in need of a thorough clean, Mrs Simpson. Her bedding doesn't appear to have been changed for a while and she's obviously not eating properly.'

'You need to speak to Mrs Banks about that, my lady.'

'And I shall, but you and Foster will accompany me.' Patricia left the room with Foster and Mrs Simpson following her.

The kitchen was reached by a series of passages with doors leading to the various pantries, larders, the still room, flower room and linen cupboards. At the very end of the corridor was the kitchen and scullery. The steam and smell of boiling mutton almost knocked Patricia off her feet as she entered. Mrs Banks was seated by the range with her feet resting on the brass rail, while two of the kitchen maids were playing some sort of childish clapping game, and the scullery maid was sobbing in a corner. The huge pine table was piled high with vegetables covered in mud and rotting leaves, empty beer bottles and a large wheel of cheese, which had been hacked into and was now developing green mould.

'What is the meaning of this?' Patricia demanded loudly. 'This is a disgrace. Look at the mess in this kitchen.'

The maids froze with their hands still poised and Mrs Banks rose unsteadily to her feet. The sobbing maid ran and hid in the scullery.

'What a disgusting sight,' Patricia said angrily. 'You are the housekeeper, Mrs Simpson. You should have been keeping your eye on the kitchen servants. As to you, Cook, I am at a loss for words.' Patricia turned to Foster, who had paled to an alarming shade of grey, green-tinged at the sides of his nose. 'You used to be so efficient, Foster. You've allowed the servants to do exactly as they please.'

'You will be in your rights to send me away without a character, my lady.' Foster bowed his head.

'You aren't getting away so easily.' Patricia picked up a rotten cabbage and tossed it on the floor. 'I want this kitchen cleaned and scoured. Your mistress is confined to her sickbed and you have all taken advantage of the fact. Mrs Banks, you will prepare tasty and nourishing food, as I know you can when you put your lazy mind to it. Mrs Simpson, you will organise the housemaids to spring clean every room in this house, starting with Miss Sylvia's bedroom. Her bedding will be changed, aired and the carpets taken outside and beaten.'

'It's not my fault,' Mrs Banks protested.

'I do my best,' Mrs Simpson added plaintively.

'I blame all of you equally. You ought to be ashamed of yourselves. But I am giving you a chance to make things right. You will start now and work hard until Greystone Park is in the condition it was when I left. Sir Michael would be turning in his grave if he could see the state of his beloved home now. Do I make myself clear?'

A muffled murmur of assent rippled round the room. Patricia beckoned to Foster as she left the hot, steamy atmosphere of the kitchen. 'I am going back to Rockwood now but I will return later and I will move back into my old room, which I want cleaned thoroughly. I expect the bed to be aired and I want clean bedding. You will speak to Mrs Banks and inform her that I expect dinner to be of the standard required. I might be accompanied by one other, so let that be known, and have the room next to mine made up to accommodate a guest.'

'Yes, my lady. I assure you that it will be done,' Foster said humbly.

'You may start by sending instructions for my horse to be brought from the stable. I'm leaving now, but I expect to be back in the middle of the afternoon.'

'Yes, my lady. I understand.'

★ ★ ★

Patricia now had the measure of Sultan and instead of going straight to the castle she rode to the keeper's cottage at the edge of the woods. She dismounted and looped the reins over a tree stump before letting herself into the main living room. Walter was pacing the

322

floor, pale faced and visibly upset by the cries emanating from the bedroom upstairs.

'How is she, Walter?' Patricia asked anxiously. 'What did the doctor say?'

'He's with her now, Patsy. The baby is coming almost two months early. I'm afraid I will lose both of them.'

Patricia wrapped her arms around him in a hug. 'Nonsense, Walter. Women have babies all the time. Louise is young and healthy. You have to be strong for her.'

'I can't bear to watch her suffer so.' Walter sank down on a wooden chair, holding his head in his hands. 'I didn't know it would be like this.'

'Rosie has had three babies and look at her now. She's the picture of perfect motherhood and her little ones are fit and healthy. There's no reason why Louise won't do just as well.'

'Hester is with her now.'

'She will take care of Louise, and the baby when it comes. Have you told the vicar that his daughter is about to make him and Tabitha grandparents?'

'No. Not yet. I don't want either of them here just yet.'

'Would you like me to call in on them on my way home?'

'Would you?' Walter met he gaze with an attempt at a smile.

'Yes, of course. It's on my way, more or less. But there's another thing, Walter.'

'What is it? I can't think about anything else at the moment.'

'It's nothing for you to worry about. I'll be moving back to Greystone Park — for awhile, anyway. When I

323

went there to fetch Dr Bulmer I found out that Sylvia is very ill. Christina won't look after her because she is in the family way, and that left Sylvia at the mercy of the servants, who have become very lax.'

'The girls took your inheritance, Patsy. Why would you bother with either of them?'

'I was mistress of Greystone Park for four years, Walter. Sylvia is my stepdaughter and she was my best friend when we were younger. This isn't the time to bear grudges. I'll stay there until Sylvia is well again, or at least until Christina does her duty by her sister.'

'You have changed, Patsy,' Walter said, smiling. 'I'm impressed.' He shuddered as a fresh howl from the bedroom echoed round the room. 'I can't bear this much longer.'

'It will be over soon and you'll have a son or daughter to carry on the family name. I must go, Walter. I'll look in again before I return to Greystone Park.'

Patricia left before Walter had a chance to beg her to stay. She mounted Sultan by standing on a log and climbing onto the saddle, and rode off in the direction of the castle, planning to stop at the vicarage on the way. She had just ridden past the smithy when she saw Wilder chatting to Ben Causley at the side of the road. She reined in.

'Good morning, Ben.'

He tipped his cap. 'Morning, my lady.'

'I'm sorry to interrupt but might I have a word with you, Leo?'

'I was just on my way, ma'am,' Ben said cheer- fully. He slapped Wilder on the shoulder and strolled off in the direction of the sawmill, where he was now manager.

'What was all that about?' Patricia demanded.

324

'I could ask you the same,' Wilder said, grinning. 'What is so important it can't wait until we meet up at luncheon?'

'What would you say if I offered you a position at Greystone Park, Leo?'

'What are you talking about, Patricia?'

'It might not be permanent, but I'm returning to my home, Greystone Park. Sylvia is very ill and her sister won't look after her. You could help me run the estate.'

21

Wilder shook his head. 'I'm not your lapdog, Patsy. I appreciate what you've tried to do for me, but the life of a country squire doesn't appeal to me. I don't fit in here and everyone knows it, except you.'

'That's not true.'

'But it is. I've just had this conversation with your brother, and he understands. I'm glad if you're getting your home back, but as soon as your sister and her husband return I think it will be time for me to move on.'

'You can't just leave, Leo. Where will you go?'

'I haven't decided exactly, but I'm heading for London.'

'You gave up your pub. Are you sure the police aren't after you now?'

'I did what they wanted and delivered Eldon and Maud into their hands. If all else fails I'll go back to sea.'

Patricia stared at him in dismay. 'I've grown used to having you around, Leo. You could make a good life here. I saw you talking to Ben — maybe his father will retire and you could take over the Black Dog.' She held on to the reins with difficulty, but Sultan was growing restive. He put his head down unexpectedly, tipping Patricia from the saddle but Wilder caught her before she hit the ground.

'I didn't think you were as expert in the saddle as you claimed, Patsy,' he said, laughing.

'Put me down, Leo. People are looking.' Patricia

met his amused look with a frown. 'Let me go, please.'

He answered by kissing her soundly on the lips until she was breathless and dizzy with shock.

'You could come with me, Lady Greystone. Leave Rockwood and the home that your stepdaughters took from you once and will probably do so again. Take your chances with me.'

Patricia broke away from him, her emotions in turmoil. Her first instinct had been to return the embrace as wholeheartedly as it had been given, but she was furious with him for making a spectacle of her in such a public place. She raised her hand to slap his face, but he caught it and kissed the palm.

'How dare you?' Patricia said angrily. 'Who do you think you are, Leo Wilder?'

'I'm the man you love, Lady Greystone. Although I know it's against everything you hold dear.'

'I don't love you. In fact I hate everything you stand for. I wouldn't go with you if my life depended upon it.'

'And yet you did exactly that. You were pleased enough to allow me to rescue you in Paris, and you were very quick to move into the attic at the pub when you needed somewhere to lay your head.'

'I don't have to stand here and listen to this.'

'I'm sorry, my lady.' Wilder released her hand and bowed from the waist. 'Forgive me for speaking out of turn. I'll leave you to try to go back to the life you once led, but you're not that person now. You and I belong together and one day you'll come to realise it.'

Wilder walked off in the direction of Rockwood Castle, leaving Patricia standing in the middle of the road while Sultan munched grass from the verge. She had to restrain herself from stamping her foot as she wiped tears of rage from her cheeks. Wilder knew exactly what to say to make her angry and to see herself for what she was, and she did not like what she saw. It was only then that she realised Barnaby Yelland was standing outside the smithy, staring at her with a worried frown.

'Are you all right, Patsy? Shall I give the fellow a wigging?'

'No, thank you, Barnaby. I can handle Wilder, there's no need to worry.'

'You shouldn't be out on your own.'

'Yes, I know, but I must move on, Barnaby. I have important news for the vicar and his wife.'

Barnaby nodded, grinning. 'Aye, I heard that Mrs Carey was about to give birth.'

'There is something you can do for me. Will you hold Sultan while I call in at the vicarage? I won't be long.'

'Yes, I'll tether him to our railing. He'll be fine there.' Barnaby took Sultan's reins and led him into the yard, leaving Patricia free to walk the short distance to the vicarage, where she passed on the news and left as quickly as good manners allowed. She was much calmer by the time she collected Sultan and the ride back to the castle gave her time to think more clearly. Rosalind and Alex would be home in a week or two and although she knew she was welcome to remain at Rockwood, Wilder was right in saying she had changed. However, he was the same arrogant person who believed that he only had to crook his finger and she would follow him to the ends of the earth. She was still Lady Greystone of Greystone Park and she would take up her rightful position.

With that in mind Patricia left Sultan in Hudson's

capable hands and made her way into the castle where she changed out of her soiled gown. She gazed critically at her reflection in the cheval mirror. Unless she could find something more suitable to wear, a trip to Exeter and a visit to Meggie Brewer was essential. Lady Greystone must not be seen to look like a drab. A whole new wardrobe was called for, and the cost would come out of the housekeeping allowance at Greystone Park. She would return there and take over the role she had married into.

The family and Wilder were assembled round the table when Patricia entered the dining room. She had intended to tell them of her decision to move back to her old home, but before she had a chance to speak Walter burst into the room, grinning from ear to ear.

'It's a girl,' he said gleefully. 'A beautiful baby girl. She's very small but Dr Bulmer says she's strong and healthy.'

'How is Louise?' Bertie asked anxiously.

'She is doing well, so the doctor said. I'm just relieved that she survived such an ordeal and the baby is safely delivered.'

'Congratulations, Walter.' Patricia gave him a hug. 'Have you decided on a name for her?'

'Charlotte Louise,' Walter said proudly. His smile faded and he turned to his brother. 'Bertie, I need to earn more than I can make from writing. I know I haven't done much towards running the estate in the past, but there must be some work I can do for you.'

Bertie frowned. 'I'm not sure I can afford to pay you, Walter. I thought your latest book was doing well.'

'It's not too bad.' Walter took a seat. 'But Louise and I need somewhere better to live than the gamekeeper's cottage. It's been fine until now, but with the baby and a nursery maid we find ourselves very cramped.'

'Abe Coaker's family lived in that cottage until Abe went to live with his daughter.' Hester sent him a disapproving look. 'Joseph Coaker and his wife raised six children there without cause for complaint.'

'Are you saying you want to come home, Walter?' Bertie asked, smiling.

'It would be more convenient,' Walter said hesitantly. 'I know we wanted our own residence, but if we returned to Rockwood it would only be temporary — until I can afford to purchase somewhere more suited to our needs.'

'Of course you can come home.' Bertie reached for a slice of cold pie. 'Charlotte will be brought up in the nursery with Dolly, Rory and Phoebe. I know Rosie will agree with me.'

'I suppose my opinion doesn't count.' Hester glared at him. 'I am the person who has to balance the housekeeping books, Bertie.'

'Which you do excellently, Hester,' Bertie said hastily. 'But we Careys must stick together.' He turned his attention to Patricia with an apologetic smile. 'Did you want to say something, Patsy?'

'Yes, Bertie. I've decided to return to Greystone Park. Sylvia is very ill and the servants aren't looking after her properly. They need taking in hand, and I intend to claim my rightful inheritance.'

Hester snorted. 'You'll be back in a week, Patricia. As soon as Christina finds out what you're planning she'll make your life a misery until you pack up and leave. You'll also have that dragon Martha Collins to deal with.'

'That's a bit harsh, Hester.' Walter sat down next

to Patricia. 'I think you are within your rights, Patsy. Don't let them bully you.'

'I'm sure that Sir Michael would approve,' Bertie added hastily. 'He should have made a new will so that you were provided for.'

'I agree, and I'm going to Exeter to speak to Mr Mounce, our solicitor. I will contest the will in court, if necessary.' Patricia met Wilder's amused gaze with a questioning look. 'Do you find this funny, Leo?'

'You are ready to take on the world, Patricia. Good luck, that's all I can say.'

'When are you leaving?' Walter asked plaintively. 'Don't you want to see Louise and the baby?'

'Of course I do, Walter. I intend to pack my things and move back to Greystone Park this afternoon, but I'll visit the cottage tomorrow when Louise has had time to rest.' Patricia glanced at Nancy, who had so far not said a word. 'Will you come with me, Nancy?'

'I don't know,' Nancy said cautiously. 'I've only met Sylvia and her sister a few times. They weren't very friendly.'

'Sylvia is confined to her bed and Christina refuses to visit while she's in the family way, so that won't be a problem. I'd like you to come with me, Nancy.' Bertie shook his head. 'Don't keep on at her, Patsy. Nancy can make up her own mind.'

'Tommy will be home from school in a week or so,' Nancy said awkwardly. 'I'd like to be here when he arrives.'

'Oh, well, you can always change your mind. Anyway, I dare say I'll be fully occupied.' Patricia helped herself to slices of cold roast chicken. 'My offer to you still stands, Wilder. I hope you'll think it over carefully.'

Patricia ignored all the advice handed out by Hester, who clearly disapproved of her move. Walter barely had time to digest his meal before returning to the cottage in the woods, and Nancy seemed happy to remain at Rockwood Castle. Accompanied by Wilder, Bertie and Wolfe set off on a visit to the sawmill. Patricia was surprised to discover that Wilder had suggested a way of expanding business there, and Bertie was eager to explore the possibilities.

Patricia felt a little piqued by their lack of enthusiasm concerning her plan to reclaim her rights at Greystone Park. No one seemed to think it would work out well, nor did anyone hold out much hope for the outcome of her visit to Mr Mounce's chambers. In fact, she realised that nobody in the family had any faith in her judgement or her ability to stand up to her two stepdaughters, even if one of them was laid low with a wasting disease. When everyone had left the dining room Patricia caught up Nancy, who was about to go for a walk on the cliffs.

'Won't you change your mind about coming to Greystone Park with me, Nancy? We've been through so much together.'

'If you want my opinion I think you ought to wait until Rosie comes home. She always knows what to do.'

Patricia threw up her hands. 'Everyone worships my sister. I am always in the wrong, but this time I'm going to stand up for myself. Greystone Park was my home and I intend to contest the will.'

Patricia stormed off, making her way to her room. She flung a few garments into her valise and carried it downstairs without waiting for a servant to help her. She was on a mission and she was determined to succeed. Patricia Greystone was not someone who would allow people to walk all over her. They could all go to hell, including Leo Wilder. He was just as bad as Hester and the rest of her family.

★ ★ ★

Sylvia was pathetically pleased to see Patricia when she walked into the stuffy bedchamber. The smell of sickness was suffocating, and Patricia was shocked to see that the bed had not been remade as she had ordered. There was a bowl of congealing porridge on the side table and a glass of sour milk. Sylvia herself was feverish and her auburn hair was plastered to her head with sweat. Her brown eyes were underlined in dark bruise-like smudges.

Patricia tugged at the bell pull. 'Have any of the servants visited you this afternoon?'

'I can't remember,' Sylvia said faintly. 'I feel very uncomfortable.'

'This is going to stop now. I'm going to sort your servants out if it's the last thing I do. I'll be back in a minute.' Patricia left the room and headed for the servants' quarters where she found Mrs Simpson and Cook taking tea in the housekeeper's office.

'You should be ashamed of yourselves.' Patricia glared at them. 'I've just been to see Miss Sylvia and her room is still a disgrace. I want it cleaned immediately and her bedding changed. I will need hot water, soap and clean towels and I will wash her myself.'

Mrs Simpson stood up, brushing cake crumbs from her black bombazine skirt. 'I will have words with the

333

chambermaid, my lady. She was instructed to do as you asked this morning.'

'I'll make sure there's enough hot water, my lady.' Mrs Banks rose from her seat.

'I want you to make some nourishing broth for Miss Sylvia,' Patricia said firmly. 'And for breakfast she needs thin gruel, sweetened with sugar and cream. She might be able to eat that. Her appetite needs tempting with delicate food. I will dine at seven.'

'Yes, my lady. I'll see to it immediately.' Mrs Banks scuttled from the room before Patricia had a chance to say anything further.

'I will select clean sheets and pillowcases myself, my lady.' Mrs Simpson walked to the door. 'Forgive the oversight. It has been difficult to keep things going without a mistress to guide us.'

'That difficulty is over now, Mrs Simpson. I am moving back into my old suite of rooms today. You will answer to me in future. You may notify Foster of the change in circumstances.'

Mrs Simpson bobbed a curtsey. 'Yes, my lady.' She shot a sly glance in Patricia's direction. 'Does Mrs Cottingham know about the changes?'

'She will be told, but I don't want any gossip to reach her ears before I have a chance to speak to her. Is that understood?'

'Perfectly, my lady.'

Patricia walked away. She was aware that she had made an enemy of the housekeeper and Cook, but they depended on their positions at Greystone Park, and would be unlikely to give her trouble. It was Christina who might make things difficult.

Patricia went to her old room and was pleased to see that an attempt had been made to make it habitable. Despite the fact that it was a hot day, a fire had been lit in the grate and the bed appeared to have been made up with fresh linen. She opened the clothes press and was surprised to find that all the garments she had left behind because they were last season's fashion were still there. She took the gowns out one by one and held them in front of herself, taking a critical look in the tall mirror. Perhaps they were not the very latest style but they were still far grander than most clothes worn by the county set. She rang the bell to summon a maid and minutes later Ivy Lugg appeared in the doorway.

'Ivy, I expect you already know that I am taking up my position as mistress of the house. I want you to be my personal maid.'

'Does Mrs Simpson know, my lady?'

'Mrs Simpson will do as I say, Ivy. I am not asking her permission. If she needs more servants she must ask Foster, who will consult me.'

'Yes, my lady.'

'I want you to unpack my clothes from the press and make sure they are clean and aired. That's all for now. I'm going to take care of Miss Sylvia myself.'

★ ★ ★

During the next week Sylvia's condition slowly improved. Dr Bulmer was pleased with her progress but he warned Patricia not to expect a miracle. However, he praised her for the way she was taking care of her stepdaughter, and he left a bottle of tonic and one of laudanum. Patricia took some comfort from his words, but she could see that Sylvia was a very sick young woman.

She also managed to take the time to visit Mr Mounce's chambers in Exeter, although in his opinion her chances of overturning her late husband's will were so slight that it was hardly worth the expense such a procedure would incur. He suggested that she approach Christina and sort the matter out between them, as it seemed the only way to ensure that Patricia was able to remain in her former home. Patricia was not convinced.

Matters were taken out of her hands a day later when a carriage pulled up outside the house and Christina stepped out, followed by her husband. Patricia happened to be crossing the vast entrance hall when she spotted her stepdaughter, looking more like a grand duchess than a vicar's wife. A flowing garment together with a skilfully draped lace shawl concealed her pregnancy, and a bonnet trimmed with ostrich feathers, flowers and bows drew attention away from her swollen body. Oscar followed her, dressed soberly in black, except for a white neck tie.

'Show them into the drawing room, Foster,' Patricia said hurriedly. She quickened her pace and by the time Foster announced them Patricia was seated primly in a chair by the ornate marble mantel-piece. She rose to her feet as Christina entered the room like a ship in full sail.

'How dare you!' Christina said angrily without giving Patricia a chance to speak. 'You have no right to be here.'

'I have every right. You stole the inheritance I should have received from your father. He would be turning in his grave if he could see the way you've treated me.'

'Papa knew that you only married him for money and position. He left the estate and what remained of his fortune to Sylvia and me.'

'Your father and I had a good marriage, Christina. We were a happy couple until the accident that took him from us. He would never have left me penniless but for an oversight in revising his will. You know that as well as I do.'

'Nevertheless, we have the law on our side. I want you to leave this house. Oscar agrees with me, don't you, my dear?'

Oscar took off his hat, gazing at Patricia with soulful eyes. 'It is not a pleasant duty, but you should listen to Christina.'

'You are a man of the cloth now, Ossie. But you were my friend when we were younger. Will you really stand by and allow me to be thrown out onto the street?'

He cleared his throat nervously. 'Patsy, this is painful for all of us. Please consider my wife's delicate condition.'

'Christina is a picture of good health,' Patricia said acidly. 'Unlike poor Sylvia, who is dying from consumption in the room above this, and yet her sister refuses to care for her.'

'Sylvia has lung fever, but she will recover without your help. She has a house filled with servants to wait upon her every need.'

'Have you been here lately to make sure that is happening?' Patricia demanded. 'No, you have not. I had to take the servants to task for the slack way they have been behaving. I had to bathe your sister myself when I first returned to my rightful home.'

'This is not your home,' Christina insisted. She fanned herself vigorously. 'Oscar, bring me a chair — I'm feeling faint.'

Oscar rushed forward, placing a chair behind his wife so that she could collapse onto it with a theatrical sigh. 'Are you all right, my dear?' Oscar sent a pleading look in Patricia's direction. 'Think of the child, Patsy. My wife does not need all this to-do.'

'Let me be clear about one thing, Ossie,' Patricia said firmly. 'I have spoken to my solicitor with a view to contesting the will. For one thing, Sylvia needs someone to take care of her, and I refuse to be cheated from what should be mine by rights.'

'You have no choice.' Christina sat upright, glaring at Patricia. 'Our solicitor told us that the will is perfectly legal. Papa had every right to leave the estate to us if he so chose. You will leave here at the end of the week. I think I am being very generous in that. As to my sister, Cousin Martha will take care of her until after my confinement. Oscar and I have discussed the matter and as soon as I am well enough we will move back here. It isn't too far from Oscar's parish. Is that not the case, Oscar?'

He nodded dutifully. 'Yes, my dear.'

'Martha Collins and her friend seem to spend more time visiting their other relatives than staying here and looking after Sylvia,' Patricia said angrily.

Christina rose to her feet, holding on to the back of the chair as if it was an effort to stand. 'That is none of your business, Patricia. I insist that you leave Greystones at the end of the week.'

'I am not going anywhere, at least while Sylvia is so ill.' Patricia faced them with a stubborn lift of her chin. 'You can't make me.'

Christina laughed. 'You've met my cousin Martha. She will make your life a misery until you move out. You won't stand a chance against her and her

338

companion, Miss Moon.' Christina moved toward the doorway. 'I have instructed Foster to tell the servants that if they allow you to remain here after Friday, they will find themselves looking for new positions. Door, please, Oscar.'

Oscar rushed past her to open the door. He shot an apologetic look at Patricia. 'I am sorry, but we mustn't upset Christina in her condition.'

Patricia picked up a particularly ugly china figurine and hurled it at the door, but Oscar had already closed it and the china shattered into shards, falling harmlessly to the floor. Patricia strode over to the window that overlooked the carriage sweep. She clenched her fists at the sight of Christina being helped into the carriage. At the last moment, as if knowing that she was being watched, Christina turned her head, smiling triumphantly. Patricia clutched the window-sill to prevent herself from hammering on the glass with her hands. She knew that she was beaten and nothing would prevent Christina from carrying out her threat. She knew that the servants would do as they were told for fear of losing their positions. Even faithful Ivy Lugg would crumble beneath such pressure.

Patricia packed her valise. Having made sure that Sylvia understood the situation and that the servants knew that Miss Martha would be arriving very soon, Patricia had one of the horses in the stables saddled up and she rode to Rockwood. She had taken considerable trouble with her appearance and was wearing a dark blue velvet riding habit with her hair confined to a neat chignon at the back of her neck. She had no intention of telling her family about Christina's dire promise to have her evicted by the end of the week, but she wanted to see Rosalind and she could only hope that she had returned from Cornwall.

22

'We arrived home last evening,' Rosalind said, smiling. 'It's such a long journey, but it was worth it for Alex to see Lady Pentelow again. He's very fond of her.'

'I don't know why.' Patricia rolled her eyes. 'She's a domineering old woman and she doesn't like me.'

'Fortunately for us she is devoted to Trevenor and wishes to spend the rest of her life there, but we discovered that the mine isn't making as much money as it should. Martin is doing quite well organising the mine itself, but he has little idea how to run the business.'

'I'm really sorry for Aurelia's sake. Is she all right?'

'She's living with her grandmother. I don't think life as the mine manager's wife was as exciting as she had hoped.'

'Has she left Martin? I thought they were madly in love.'

Rosalind shrugged. 'She said she was concerned for Lady Pentelow's health, but I think there's more to it than that. However, it wasn't my place to question her, and Aurelia obviously didn't want to talk about personal matters.'

'What did Lady Pentelow say about Piers? Does she want to clear his name?'

'She knows that Piers was involved with Blease Ewart — or Ewart Blaise, as he presented himself in the beginning — but she never really believed that her grandson could have done wrong. She's longing to see him again.'

'But he did get involved with Ewart, and now he's paying for it while Ewart is enjoying a life of crime in France.'

'I think that is so unfair. Piers had his faults but his grandmother loves him and she wants him to come home. If Piers was able to return to Trevenor he might be able to turn the business around.'

'So what next?'

'Only a court of law could clear Piers, or at least commute his sentence. He's already served over four years in the penal colony, but any appeal for clemency would depend on the French police catching Ewart and making him confess.'

'But how would you feel if Piers returned to Cornwall?'

'Alex and I are happily married, Patsy. Nothing can alter that. Alex would rest easier if he knew that his family in Cornwall were taken care of. I'm not sure that Aurelia will go back to Martin. I think she realises that it was a mistake to marry out of her class.'

'I'd go there myself and see Aurelia, but I have problems of my own.'

'Is Christina being difficult?'

'You know her as well as I do. She won't live in the house while Sylvia is ill for fear of catching the disease, but she doesn't want me there either. Martha Collins and her friend Miss Moon will return soon, and Christina wants me to leave by the end of the week.'

'I did warn you, Patsy,' Rosalind said sadly. 'You must come home. We all want you to live here with us. We'll be a whole family again.'

'It doesn't seem that I have much choice.'

'You tried, that's all that matters. It's not worth making yourself miserable or suffering the insults that Martha will heap on you. I remember meeting her once and she's not the sort of person one would forget. The only good thing is that she will take care of Sylvia. She's that sort of woman.'

'I suppose so,' Patricia said reluctantly. 'Although she doesn't seem to have been very efficient in the past. I've done my best to look after Sylvia.'

'I'm sure you have, Patsy. It was fortunate for her that you returned to Greystone Park when you did.'

'I'm not abandoning her. I'm not like Mama.'

'Of course not,' Rosalind said hastily. 'What put that idea in your head?'

'When I left London I thought that Mama might take an interest in me because I can sing, even though I have not her operatic style.'

Rosalind smiled. 'You should have known better after all these years. You know what Mama is like. She'll never change.'

'You really don't think I'm like her, do you, Rosie?'

Rosalind gave her a hug. 'Of course not. Well, maybe a little, but if you had children I don't think you would abandon them for a career onstage, would you?'

'I don't know. I never wanted children, so maybe I am like Mama.' Patricia gazed at Dolly, who was sitting on the nursery floor playing with a rag doll, which Rory was trying to take from her. Baby Phoebe slept in her cradle, while Jennet bustled about tidying the mess the children had created. 'They are lovely,' Patricia added carefully. 'But I don't have to look after them.'

'Of course not, but it's different when they are your

own children.'

'I suppose so. Anyway, I don't intend to marry again so the situation won't arise. I can enjoy my nieces and nephews.'

'That reminds me, Patsy. I must go and see Louise and baby Charlotte. Have you been to the cottage recently?'

Patricia shook her head. 'I haven't seen the baby yet.'

'Then we'll go together. Why not move your things back here today? If the servants are looking after Sylvia properly now there's no need for you to remain at Greystone Park until the end of the week.'

'You make it sound so final.'

'You have to face facts, Patsy. That part of your life is over and done with. It's time to start afresh. You're young, beautiful and talented. You'll find someone else to love you just as Sir Michael did.'

'I told you I'm not looking for another husband. I don't think marriage is for me, Rosie. I really don't know what I want.'

'I'm sure it will come to you eventually. Pack up your things and come home, Patsy. It will be like old times and we can enjoy being together again.'

'That wouldn't last long,' Patricia said, laughing. 'We'll end up arguing, as we always did. Besides which, you can't tell me what to do now I'm a grown woman and a widow into the bargain.'

'Maybe not, but I expect I'll try. Being the older sister gives me certain privileges.'

Dolly gave Rory a shove as he attempted to take her rag doll from her and he toppled over. He screamed loudly and began to sob, which was Patricia's cue to leave. She jumped to her feet and leaned over to kiss her sister on the cheek.

'I must go now but I'll see you soon, Rosie.'

'You will seriously consider returning home, won't you?'

'Of course. I really don't see any alternative at the moment.' Patricia left the nursery and made her way downstairs to the great hall where she almost bumped into Wilder, who had just placed his carpet bag by the door. She gazed at him in surprise. 'You're leaving?'

'I'm returning to London. There's a train at three o'clock.' Wilder met her gaze with a smile. 'I told you I would go when Alex and Rosie returned from Cornwall.'

'What will you do in London? Where will you stay?' Patricia made an effort to sound casual, but her heart was pounding and the danger of losing him for ever was suddenly all too real.

'What does it matter to you, Patsy? You made it clear you want nothing to do with me.'

'I'm sure I said nothing of the sort.'

'Go back to your mansion, Lady Greystone. You made your choice.'

'Yes, I did.' Patricia sighed. 'You're right, Leo. I am free to choose which way I go next.' She marched past him, forgetting to pat Sir Denys's visor as she headed for the doorway. She did not look back but she sensed that Wilder was standing in the entrance watching her until she was out of sight.

She went to the stables and instructed Hudson to saddle her horse. Nothing had changed and yet she suddenly felt liberated. There were no ties for her now at Greystone Park and very little to be gained by moving back with her family. At least she knew they were there if she needed them. Whatever happened in the future she was not going to sit back and allow herself to be bullied, cajoled or forced by circumstances to live like a nun or to marry a man she did not love purely for the sake of convention and keeping a roof over her head. The world was out there to conquer and she knew exactly who would help her to achieve her ambition.

★ ★ ★

A minute before three o'clock in the afternoon, Patricia strolled onto the station platform and deposited her valise at Wilder's feet.

'What's all this?'

'I'm coming with you.'

'I haven't got anywhere to stay in London, Patsy. I'm prepared to take my chances, but that isn't good enough for you.'

'Why not? I'll sleep under a railway bridge tonight, if necessary. Anyway, it won't come to that. I have enough money to pay for rooms at a respectable inn and dinner at one of the best chop houses.'

'I can't take you away from your family and everything you hold dear, especially now I've met them all. You came to me for help in the first instance, but this is different.'

Patricia glanced over his shoulder. 'The train is coming. If you don't want me to go with you I will manage on my own. Perhaps I can get a small part in one of Garson Thorne's productions.'

'You really mean it, don't you?'

'Yes. I do.' Patricia picked up her case as the train roared to a halt. 'Are we travelling together or must I find a carriage to myself?'

He took her valise from her. 'It looks as if we're in this together. Although I think after a few days you might change your mind.'

'Not I,' Patricia said stoutly. 'When I decide to do something there's no stopping me, Leo.' She opened the nearest carriage door and climbed into the compartment. 'Come on.'

He followed her, shaking his head. 'This is madness. Your reputation will be in shreds simply by travelling to London with me.'

Patricia settled herself in a corner seat. 'I don't care. I'm done with all that, Leo. I've thought how I will keep myself and it's quite simple.'

He placed the cases on the shelf and sat down opposite her. 'Go on. Tell me.'

'I will sing in public houses or perhaps the Grecian Theatre, as the Grecian Saloon has become. I do read the newspapers occasionally, Leo.'

'You have it all thought out, but where will you stay?'

She smiled. 'With you, of course. I can't live on my own. That would be courting disaster.'

'You don't think that by living with me you would be making even more trouble for yourself?'

'That's a detail. We'll think of something. You could be my brother or my guardian.' Patricia laughed at the horrified expression on his face. 'I know you are a bit young to be my guardian, but we will think of something. As a matter of fact, I really don't care what people say.'

'Have you thought how this might upset your sister, not to mention your brothers?'

'They have their lives to lead, Leo. I have mine. Our mother successfully defied convention and I'm going

347

to do the same.' Patricia eyed him curiously. 'Anyway, never mind me. How do you propose to earn your living without the pub to support you?'

'I'm not entirely sure. Maybe I ought to visit Starlina Beaney and she could tell me.'

'Now you're laughing at me.'

'No, indeed I am not. As a matter of fact I was hoping to lure Ewart back to London. I saw what he had done to your family and for once I was thinking of others rather than myself. My brief time working for the Metropolitan Police was instructive and oddly satisfying.'

'Does that mean you're going to France to look for him?'

'I rather think he might come looking for me. I have contacts in the criminal underworld that were useful once, and might prove so again. But it mustn't be known that I had anything to do with assisting the police. It would ruin my reputation. You do understand that, don't you, Patsy?'

'Yes, of course. Not a word from me. How exciting! Do you think he might come looking for us?'

Wilder frowned. 'He might come for me. You are to keep well away from him and his associates.'

'Why do you want to help my family? Do you want to see Piers pardoned?'

'They were good to me. I was welcomed into your family without any questions, except from Fletcher, who acts like a guard dog, together with Wolfe, and Hester. She is a difficult woman to gauge, but I think she acts out of loyalty.'

'You are probably right, but I come in for criticism from Hester whatever I do. In fact I've given up trying to please her.'

'She's not a bad sort, Patsy. But she certainly won't approve of what we're doing now.'

'She might change her mind if I become famous like Mama. One day Hester will smile at me and mean it, and she'll acknowledge the fact that I am no longer a child.' Patricia sat back in her seat and closed her eyes. 'Wake me up when we get to London, Leo. I'm going to take a nap.'

★ ★ ★

Patricia had slept much longer than she intended and she was still only half awake when Wilder helped her into a hansom cab at the station.

'Where are we going?' she demanded, yawning.

'An old friend of mine runs a lodging house in Wellclose Square. She might have a couple of rooms for us.'

'I'd prefer somewhere a little more exclusive.'

'You may move on whenever you please, Patsy. I have no hold on you, but I suspect that despite what you say, you are rather short of funds, as am I at present. Bridie Salmon's rates are reasonable and the place is clean. You won't have to worry about bed bugs and lice.'

'I should hope not,' Patricia said, shuddering. 'It's getting late so I suppose it won't hurt to spend one night there, but tomorrow I will look for something more suitable.'

'Very well, my lady. As you wish.'

'It's not funny, Wilder. You may be used to living in a slum, but I was brought up in a — '

'In a castle that needs hundreds of pounds spent on it just to keep it from crumbling into the dust,'

349

Leo finished the sentence for her. 'Shall I ask for one room or two?'

'You are laughing at me, Leo Wilder. But I don't care. I am a free woman and I make my own decisions.' Patricia sank back against the stained leather squabs. The familiar noxious smells of London in the summer assailed her nostrils, making her reach into her reticule for a handkerchief. She covered her nose and mouth, inhaling the lavender scent that imbued all the clean linen at Greystone Park.

When they finally arrived in Wellclose Square Patricia was pleased to find that most of the four-storey terraced houses seemed well kept and respectable. The area was a strange mix of faded gentility and downright shabby. A couple of wooden cottages looked oddly out of place next to the courthouse and an ancient lock-up. A fine church commanded the central position in the tree-lined square. However, there was a definite and slightly strange smell of burning sugar emanating from the sugar refineries in Well Street and Dock Street, which did not quite overcome the stench from the river in high summer. Wilder helped Patricia to alight from the cab and he paid off the cabby before mounting the pavement and knocking on the door of a house in the middle of a terrace. The woman who answered his knock bore a striking resemblance to Maud Grubb, and for a minute Patricia thought that it was Maud who had returned from France. However, the landlady smiled a welcome and opened the door wide enough for them to step inside.

'Well, if it isn't my old pal Leo.'

'Bridie, this is my good friend Patricia Greystone.'

'Patricia Carey,' Patsy said hastily. 'I am a widow, Mrs, er . . .'

350

'Salmon, love. I'm Bridie Salmon. What have you to do with this rogue?'

Patricia recoiled slightly, startled by the direct question. 'We're friends of sorts.'

Bridie cackled with laughter. "Of sorts' can mean a lot, dearie. Do you want one room or two, Leo?'

'Two rooms, Bridie.'

She eyed him curiously. 'I heard you'd been arrested, and the pub has gone to another landlord.'

'It's true. Although I was let off with a caution. Unlike your sister and Blease Ewart.'

'What's Maud got herself into now?' Bridie's smile faded and was replaced by a frown. 'She's not up to her old tricks, is she?'

'Not exactly. She tried to rob a rich woman of her jewellery and she was caught by the French police.'

Bridie's jaw dropped. 'What's she doing in France?'

'I suspect she'll end up in a French prison, but Ewart got away.'

'He's a bad lot and my sister was always gullible. Serves her right, but I'd like to get my hands on him.'

'So would I.' Wilder lowered his voice. 'We could work together to trap him and see he gets his deserts, Bridie. I reckon he'll return to London to get away from the French police.'

Patricia gazed at Wilder in dismay. 'Are you sure of that, Leo?'

'I'm certain of it. Ewart has a score to settle with me now. He's not the sort to forgive easily.'

'I don't see how I can help, Wilder.' Bridie hesitated in the doorway. 'I don't want to get involved with him.'

'Just put the word out where I can be found, Bridie. I'll deal with Ewart.'

'I think you ought to leave it to the police,' Patricia said anxiously.

'I'll put the word out, Wilder.' Bridie nodded emphatically. 'But if I hear that Ewart is back in London you will have to deal with him.'

'It will be my pleasure,' Wilder said grimly. 'Now about those rooms . . .'

'I got two next to each other on the third floor. That should be nice and private and convenient.' Bridie winked at him and turned away. 'Follow me, if you please.'

Patricia caught hold of Wilder's sleeve. 'I'm not sure about this, Leo.'

'Don't worry. Bridie is all right when you get to know her. She's not a criminal, unlike her sister.'

'I spotted the likeness immediately.'

'That's where it ends. Bridie is a hard-working businesswoman. She doesn't stand for any nonsense nor does she take in members of the criminal fraternity. This might not be luxurious but you'll be safe here, even if I am not around.'

Bridie mounted the steep staircase, stopping to peel off a long sliver of damp wallpaper. 'I ain't got all night, you two. Come if you're coming; if not, I got supper to make for my gents.'

Wilder gave Patricia a gentle push in the direction of the stairs. 'Go on, she won't bite.'

'I heard that, Leo Wilder.' Bridie uttered a throaty laugh and continued to ascend the stairs with Patricia following her and Wilder close behind.

The room that Patricia was allocated was large enough to take a double iron bedstead, a chest of drawers, a wooden chair and a washstand, complete with china jug and bowl, gaudily decorated with pansies and violets. A crimson coverlet on the bed provided a splash of colour but the rest of the room was whitewashed, which needed retouching. The curtains could also do with a wash, but Patricia was too tired to complain.

'I trust this will suit you, my lady?' Bridie said with a sarcastic grin.

'It's fine, thank you.' Patricia tried to sound enthusiastic but she knew that Wilder was watching her with that familiar amused twinkle in his eyes.

Bridie held out her hand. 'That will be seven bob, miss. And another seven bob deposit just to make sure you don't do a moonlight flit without paying.'

'You can trust us, Bridie,' Wilder said calmly. 'You know me.'

'I do, love, but I don't know the lady. So like I says, I want fourteen shillings or off she goes.'

Patricia handed over the money with great reluctance. 'There you are, Mrs Salmon.'

'It's Bridie to my friends and those who pay up on time, dearie.' Bridie hustled Wilder out of the room. 'You're next door, love. What you get up to after dark is your business, not mine.'

Patricia sank down on the bed and, as she had suspected, it was hard and lumpy. She sighed, thinking of the luxury she had left at Greystone Park and the love and comfort she had turned her back on at Rockwood Castle. But she was not allowed to rest for long. Wilder put his head round the door. 'Bridie and I are going to the old Mahogany Bar at Wilton's. Come with us and we'll get a bite to eat.'

'I don't know about that, Leo. You go and enjoy Bridie's company.'

'You have to eat, Lady Greystone, even if it isn't

353

up to your West End standards.' Wilder held out his hand. 'Come on, Patsy. You might learn something to your advantage. Wilton has a grand new theatre so you might even get a spot in one of his shows.'

Patricia leaped to her feet. 'That's different. I'm coming, but you'll have to pay because I gave Bridie about half the money I took from the housekeeping at Greystone Park.'

'Are you telling me you stole money from your stepdaughters?' Wilder gave her a quizzical smile. 'And you call me a criminal.'

'You're laughing at me again, Leo. Yes, I did. I admit it, but they owe me a fortune, quite literally. Anyway, I am hungry, so let's go.'

★ ★ ★

Behind the double doors in Graces Alley, the Mahogany Bar was packed with men enjoying a drink or a simple meal. Bridie was obviously well known and accepted, even though she was a single woman. She ordered food and drink and went to join Wilder and Patricia at one of the tables in a dark recess. She sat down and raised her hand to attract the attention of a gentleman in a frock coat.

'Wilton, come here. I have someone you might want to meet.'

'Bridie. My best customer. How are you today?' John Wilton strolled over to their table. He eyed Wilder curiously. 'You look familiar. Do I know you, sir?'

Wilder rose to his feet. 'Leo Wilder. We've met a couple of times.'

'Ah, yes. I never forget a face. The Goat and Compasses at Puddle Dock. Am I right?'

354

'You are indeed, sir.'

Wilton turned to Patricia with a beaming smile. 'Now here's a face a gentleman would never forget.' He bowed over Patricia's extended hand.

'Patricia Carey. How do you do, Mr Wilton?'

'Nicely, thank you, miss. I see we have a lady in our midst, Bridie.'

'Actually I am a performer.' Patricia spoke before Bridie had a chance to reply. 'I am operatically trained by Garson Thorne, but I decided that opera was not for me. I prefer more popular songs.'

John Wilton pulled up a chair and sat down. 'Well, now. Have you any experience of entertaining the masses?'

'Patricia sang for me every night at the Goat and Compasses,' Wilder said casually. 'She was very popular.'

'I heard that you'd been arrested, Wilder.' Wilton turned to him, frowning. 'What did you do to get on the wrong side of the law?'

'A bit of this and that, Wilton. Nothing of particular note.'

'This isn't about Wilder, John.' Bridie reached out to lay her hand on his. 'I think this young lady could do well here.'

'You're certainly worth considering, if only for your looks and bearing,' Wilton said critically. 'We don't often get ladies of quality wanting to entertain common people, so let's hear you sing, Miss Carey.' He turned in his chair and beckoned to a young man who was drinking at the bar. 'This lady says she can sing, Freddie. Will you accompany her?'

Freddie came slowly towards them. 'Certainly, boss.'

'We'll go into the old concert room. There's a grand piano which I keep tuned at all times. We don't cut corners here.' Wilton rose to his feet and headed for a door at the back of the bar with Freddie at his side.

Bridie jumped to her feet. 'He don't take to everyone, girl. This is your big chance.'

Slightly dazed by the sudden change in her fortunes, Patricia stood up and followed them more slowly. Freddie took his seat at the piano, looking up at her with a wide smile.

'What shall I play, miss?'

'Do you know 'The Last Rose of Summer'?'

'I know all the popular ballads and some of those less well known as well.' Freddie played the introduction with a flourish, nodding to Patricia at her cue to begin. She clasped her hands in front of her and sang the sentimental ballad. Her voice soared to the high ceiling, coming back in a faint echo as a refrain. She was barely aware of the people who crept in from the bar, standing quietly at the back of the room, and it was not until the final chord had been played that she realised she had an audience. Their clapping drowned whatever it was that John Wilton was trying to say, but Patricia could tell by his smile that she had triumphed. Freddie was eyeing her with greater respect and Wilder patted her on the shoulder.

'That brought tears to my eyes, Patricia,' Bridie said, wiping her face on a tattered scrap of cloth. 'I reckon you're good for the rent. I might even throw in breakfast.'

Wilder laughed. 'You sang like an angel. I'm proud of you.'

'Yes, you say that now, Wilder. In another minute you'll be telling me I've made a terrible error. I

356

know you.'

John Wilton slipped his arm around her shoulders. 'My dear, anyone who sings like a nightingale can do no wrong for me. When can you start?'

23

Wearing a rather flamboyant gown that Maud had
worn on stage when she sang at Wilton's, Patricia appeared that evening as a surprise addition to
the entertainment. The audience had thrown rotten
tomatoes and bad eggs at the previous performer,
much to Wilton's annoyance, and they had ignored
calls for order. Patricia watched from the wings and
was tempted to walk away, but Freddie was at her
side and he gave her hand a squeeze.

'Don't worry, duck. When you go on stage they'll
love you.'

'They didn't love the last act and he was a conjuror.
He showed them magic tricks.'

'That's just it, Patsy. They knew they was being
fooled. To be fair, he's a very bad magician. Anyone
could see that he had pigeons tucked inside his waistcoat. There was feathers flying all over the place.'

'I haven't had a rehearsal. What if I forget the
words?'

Freddie grinned. 'I'll do a few dramatic chords and
they'll think it's all part of the performance. Believe
me, love, I've accompanied some performers who are
so awful they make me blush, and that's an almost
impossible thing to do in this business.'

Patricia took a deep breath as Freddie led her onto
the stage. He took his seat at the piano and she walked
into the centre of the stage. Her mouth was dry and
her hands were shaking so much she had to clasp them
tightly together. She could feel the audience waiting

to boo and hiss or, even worse, to throw things at her. However, it was too late to run. Freddie played the introduction, gave her a cheeky wink and a nod, and she began to sing. She forgot about the audience, who were no worse than the crowds in Clare Market or the drunks in the Goat and Compasses, and she sang as she had never sung before. The last words had barely left her lips when there was a roar, but this time it was accompanied by clapping and stamping of feet. The audience called for more and Freddie played the first few bars of 'Home, Sweet Home', which Patricia knew to be an all-time favourite. She sang again to rapturous applause and in the end it was Freddie who rose from his seat to escort her from the stage, ignoring their raucous cries for more. John Wilton walked on holding up his hands to call for quiet and to assure the noisy crowd that Miss Carey would be performing again the following night. He left the stage beaming from ear to ear.

'Well done, Patricia. You have surprised even me, and I thought I was beyond that sort of emotion. I've been in the business for a long time, but you have the common touch, which is very rare.'

'I'm to perform again?' Patricia asked breathlessly.

'With a reception like that I'm signing you up for a whole season. I don't want Garson Thorne to have second thoughts about giving you a part in his next production. We will talk about your repertoire tomorrow morning. Meet me here at eleven, and we can discuss your programme with Freddie.'

'I'll be here at eleven,' Patricia said dazedly.

'I think this calls for a glass or two of Champagne to celebrate our forthcoming partnership, Patricia.'

Wilder came to join them. 'That was your best

performance yet, Patsy. I think you ought to double her pay, Wilton.'

John Wilton laughed and walked away. 'I'll see you in the morning, Patricia.'

'May I escort you home, Miss Carey?' Wilder proffered his arm, smiling.

'Thank you, Leo. I must confess I'm exhausted.'

They had to push their way through a crowd of admirers who were lying in wait outside in the alley. Patricia smiled and thanked people for their comments but Wilder led her away without stopping.

'They'll keep you standing in the chilly night air, Patsy. We can't allow the star of the concert room to catch a cold.'

'I wasn't the star,' Patricia said, smiling.

'I have a feeling that you will be much in demand.'

'What about you, Leo? What will you do now?'

'If you want the truth, I'm not going to rest until I have Blease Ewart arrested and sent for trial. I want him to give a full confession as to his part in the crimes that Piers Blanchard paid for in the penal colony.'

She turned her head to look at his profile as they walked briskly towards Wellclose Square. 'Why do you care what happened to Piers? You've never met him.'

'Your family accepted me without question, and Alex trusted me enough to ask me to help Bertie run the estate while he was away. I don't suppose you can understand what that means to someone like me, who has spent his whole life teetering on the edge of respectability.'

'You had to live your life as it presented itself to you, Leo. You took Nancy and me in when we had nowhere to go. I don't think you owe my family anything, least of all by putting yourself in danger.'

They came to a halt at the front step. Leo laid his hands on Patricia's shoulders, gazing at her in the light of the streetlamp. 'You really don't understand, do you?'

She shook her head. 'No, I don't.'

'I cooperated with the police and I intend to do so again. I don't want a man like Ewart on the loose. It's only a matter of time before he thinks of something else to put your family through. The man is twisted and he's dangerous.'

Wilder's face was in shadow, but Patricia felt the intensity of his gaze. 'What do you think he might do?'

'What do your sister and her husband hold most dear?'

Patricia gasped in horror. 'The children? No, even Ewart wouldn't stoop so low.'

'Wouldn't he? I think that's exactly what he might consider next. He harbours a grudge against your family, Patsy. I'm going to stop him doing anything to harm them even more.'

'We must warn Alex and Bertie. They will alert the groundsmen and outside workers to keep an eye open for a stranger.'

'I don't want to scare them unnecessarily. If Bridie does what I asked her to do, Blease Ewart will come looking for me first. That will be his downfall.'

'But you'll put yourself in danger.'

'Does that worry you, Patsy?'

She nodded, unable to put her feelings into words, and with a swift movement he swept her into his arms. She resisted his kiss at first, but the aching intensity she had experienced in their previous embrace was doubled by the danger Ewart posed to those she loved the most. She abandon all pretence of indifference and kissed him back.

'I must go.' Wilder released her reluctantly. 'You're safe here, Patsy. Go to your room and get a good night's sleep.'

'Where are you going? What are you planning, Leo?'

'There's a card game at a pub in Cable Street. It's the sort of place where Ewart's cronies are likely to be found. I'm not going to do anything other than play a hand or two of poker. I just want my name to get round. When Ewart returns to London, if he isn't already here, he will know where to find me.'

Patricia caught him by the sleeve as he was about to walk away. 'Leave it to the police. You've done enough.'

He grasped her hand and lifted it to his lips. 'I haven't even begun yet. Go inside and lock your bedroom door. I'll see you in the morning.' He strode off without giving Patricia a chance to argue.

Patricia was determined not to allow the shadow of Ewart to scare her, but she did as Wilder had suggested and went straight to her room in the lodging house. The events of the day had suddenly overtaken her, not least the kiss that had left her feeling even more confused than ever about her feelings for Leo Wilder. She had imagined herself to be in love many times, but somehow this was different. He maddened her often, and yet she could not imagine living without seeing him every day. However, trusting her heart to someone else was another matter and she was wary of allowing him to get too close.

She locked her bedroom door and lit a candle, which she placed on the washstand. Having taken off her bonnet and shawl she went over to draw the curtains and, for a brief moment, she thought she saw a man standing by the railings on the opposite side of the street. He was looking up at her window and in the flickering yellow light of the gas-lamp she thought she recognised Blease Ewart. But he turned and walked away and she drew the curtains together. It was probably her imagination. Leo had put the thought in her head when he talked about Ewart coming for him. She sat down on her bed and unlaced her boots. Tomorrow she would have a long talk with Leo and she would make him promise to give up his attempts to entrap Ewart. The police were paid to deal with such matters. Leo Wilder needed to find a respectable occupation that would keep him safe.

She undressed and slipped on her nightgown before climbing into bed. She could still hear the sound of applause ringing in her ears, but that was a minor consideration when her whole body ached to be held again in a tender embrace. Leo's kisses had awakened physical longings that she had resolutely suppressed since the death of her husband. It occurred to her suddenly that she had never felt jealous of the mistress she was certain Sir Michael had kept, but she knew instinctively that if Wilder looked longingly at another woman it would tear her heart out.

Patricia closed her eyes, and despite her fraught emotional state she drifted into a deep sleep of sheer exhaustion.

★　★　★

Next morning there was no sign of Wilder at breakfast in the shabby dining room. Patricia was late rising and by the time she went downstairs there was only one travelling gentleman still at the table. He was thin and balding with a starched white collar that threatened to chop off his earlobes every time he turned his head. His black jacket and trousers were tinged with green and threadbare at the elbows and knees, but he had a pleasant enough smile. He wished her 'Good morning' as he left the room.

The young maid brought a pot of strong coffee and a jug of milk to the table, as well as a laden toast rack and a slab of butter. Patricia was hungry and she ate heartily, hoping that Wilder would come to join her, but when he finally put in an appearance she had finished her meal and was about to leave the table. She sank back in her seat.

'The coffee is cold. I suppose you could ring for the maid to bring some more.'

He pulled up a chair and filled a cup with cold coffee. 'That's all right, I need something to drink. My throat is parched.'

'You look as though you were up all night, Leo.'

He smiled ruefully. 'I had an hour or two of sleep. But I met a lot of old acquaintances and I put it about that I was looking for Ewart, when in fact I hope it's the reverse.'

'I've been thinking, Leo. Perhaps if we warn Alex and Rosie to look out for Ewart or anyone who looks suspicious, we should let the law take its course. You don't need to risk your life to bring Ewart to justice.'

Wilder refilled his cup. 'I hate to say it, but Ewart is too clever for the French police and the Metropolitan force hasn't done any better. If it weren't for you and Nancy we might never have got as close to him as we did in Paris. I don't like it, but this is the only way.'

Patricia eyed him warily. 'I was probably mistaken, and I was very tired last night, but . . . ' she hesitated.

364

Wilder looked up. 'What are you trying to tell me?'

'I saw a man who looked a bit like Ewart. He was standing on the opposite side of the road and he seemed to be staring at my window. As I said, it was probably my imagination. He walked off when he realised I'd seen him.'

'Dammit!' Wilder leaped to his feet, almost spilling what was left of his coffee. 'Why didn't you tell me this before?'

'You've only just come down to breakfast. What good would it have done anyway? He simply walked away, and I might have imagined the whole thing.'

'If it was Ewart it means that you are in danger, Patsy. You will go nowhere unless I am with you.'

'I have to be at the theatre at eleven, Leo.'

'Then I'll wait and see you there safely.'

'It's just a short walk away. Is that really necessary?'

'This is London, Patsy. You could be abducted in broad daylight and nobody would blink an eye.'

'They might if I screamed at the top of my voice,' Patricia said, laughing.

'This isn't funny. I don't want that man to get anywhere near you. In fact I can't believe that I recommended him as a suitable escort when you lived with me at the pub.'

'Please stop worrying, Leo. I will be very careful, I promise. But I'm more concerned about Rosie's babies. You don't really think that Ewart would try to kidnap them, do you?'

'I think he is capable of anything. In fact, when I've seen you safely to Wilton's I'm going to the police. This time we'll get Ewart before he can do any real damage.'

'I do hope so. I'll do anything I can to help.'

'Just take extra care, that's all I'm asking.' She smiled. 'I will. I promise.'

Wilder glanced at the clock on the sideboard. 'It's still quite early. I'll get a cab to the police station and I'll be back in time to take you to Graces Alley.'

'You haven't had any breakfast,' Patricia protested.

'I'll get something later. This is more important.' Wilder rushed from the room.

Moments later Patricia heard the front door open and close. She rose from her seat and went in search of Bridie.

Below stairs was a maze of narrow passages and small rooms, leading eventually to a much larger kitchen and scullery. After opening several doors Patricia found Bridie in a room little bigger than a cupboard, which was filled almost completely with a desk. Bridie sat behind it on the only chair in the room. She looked up, frowning.

'What are you doing here, miss? This is my private office.'

'Yes, I'm sorry, but I need your help.'

Bridie raised a thin eyebrow. 'How may I help you, Miss Carey?'

'Do you know a man called Blease Ewart? Sometimes he calls himself Ewart Blaise.'

'I might,' Bridie said cautiously.

'I'd better start at the beginning then.' Patricia perched on the edge of the desk. She told Bridie everything that she knew about Blease Ewart, eyeing her expectantly when she came to the part where Wilder had gone to the police station.

Bridie pursed her lips. 'Ewart must be dangerous if Leo had gone to the police. I remember a time when none of us round here would have anything to do with a peeler.'

'Is there anything you know about Ewart that the police do not?'

'Possibly, although who's to say what they've found out about him? I didn't know he was in France. He just disappeared off the face of the earth, and he wasn't much missed. I'll tell you that for nothing.'

'I wouldn't swear to it but I think he was in the street last night, staring at this house.'

Bridie's eyes widened and she whistled between her teeth. 'The bastard — excuse my language — I knows you're a lady and not used to uncouth speech.'

'Never mind that, Bridie. I don't care. If you know anything please tell me. I'm not afraid for myself but Leo thinks that my sister's children might be Ewart's target.'

'Leave it with me, ducks. I got contacts. If Ewart is back in London they'll know.'

'Thank you, Bridie. I'll be forever in your debt. Ewart has a score to settle with Leo, too.'

'And I'll have words with Ewart if I find him. I know my sister has a problem with light fingers, but in the past she's only pinched small items. The jewel robbery would have been Ewart's idea, not Maud's. It sounds as if she's languishing in a French prison while Ewart is a free man. That ain't fair and it ain't right.'

'I agree entirely. I think you and I together could do more to entrap Ewart than the whole of the Metropolitan Police force.'

Bridie chuckled. 'I'm sure of it, ducks. Leave it with me and I'll put the word round.'

'Best not tell Leo,' Patricia said thoughtfully. 'It will only worry him.'

'We'll allow him to think he's in charge. No need to let him know that we can do just as well without him.'

* * *

Wilder returned in time to escort Patricia to Wilton's, but he left as soon as he had seen her safely inside. She did not ask him where he was going, although she assumed that it was something to do with the police and their hunt for Ewart. However, she had little time to worry about criminal activities as she was met by Freddie, who took her through to the concert hall where they went over their programme for that evening. Patricia was flattered to find that she had been given star billing second only to 'Pompom, the amazing performing poodle from Germany'. Freddie assured her that this was almost unheard of and by the end of the coming week he expected Pompom to be downgraded to second billing with Patricia the number one.

They had just finished selecting the songs that she would sing when John Wilton came to join them. He sent Freddie off to get coffee for them while he and Patricia talked business. She was secretly delighted by the offer of a weekly salary much larger than she had dreamed of, but she managed to appear casual.

After they had toasted her acceptance of Wilton's terms with cups of strong coffee, it was time for rehearsal. Freddie was a brilliant accompanist and by mid-afternoon they were both satisfied that their performance would be faultless. Freddie offered to escort Patricia back to Wellclose Square and she agreed, although she was sure that Ewart would not try anything in broad daylight, as Wilder had feared.

368

She thanked Freddie and said goodbye to him on the doorstep, having promised to be at the theatre in good time before she was due to go on stage. He sauntered off and Patricia hurried into the entrance hall to find Bridie waiting for her with a satisfied grin.

'Come into the parlour,' Bridie whispered, catching hold of Patricia's arm and dragging her into the room. She closed the door. 'You were right, ducks. He's here in London. I reckon that was Ewart you saw last night.'

'How did you discover that?'

'Like I told you, I got contacts. I've lived here for a good part of my life and I know most folk in the square, and I know the pubs where Ewart and the gangs drink, so all I had to do was to put out a few feelers and the news come running to meet me.'

'So where is he living? Did they tell you that?'

'Not exactly, but he's lying low somewhere round the docks. I don't think that's important. We need to lure him out with bait, like we was fishing in the river.'

'And I suppose I am the worm you mean to fix on the hook?'

'I couldn't have put it better, but if I was you I wouldn't breathe a word of this to Leo.'

'I agree. How do you think we should proceed?'

'Just do what you need to do. I mean you'll be going to and fro from the theatre. He might try to drag you into a cab or something. I dunno, but I'll be watching you and I'll pay some of the young street Arabs to follow you at a safe distance, too.'

'You think of everything, Bridie.'

Bridie puffed out her chest. 'I got brains, ducks. Men think they know it all but women are far cleverer, in my opinion.'

Patricia laughed. 'We are smart enough to allow them to imagine they are the superior beings, isn't that so?'

'You have a point there. Now I've got work to do. My gents demand supper at six, so if you want to eat then you can join them. It's boiled beef and carrots, one of their favourites.'

'Thank you, that sounds delicious, but it was very late when I ate luncheon.'

'Your loss, ducks. If Leo doesn't turn up to take you to the theatre, I'll follow you at a distance. Then if Ewart tries anything I'll be able to send help.'

'Thank you.' Patricia was not sure she liked the sound of this arrangement, but she was not going to argue. Bridie was an invaluable spy and she did not want to offend her. She decided to go to her room and rest before the performance. If only Nancy were here she could talk matters over with her. Nancy might only be fifteen, but she had the mind of a grown woman and Patricia missed her company.

She made her way upstairs and lay on her bed fully clothed. Ewart might be living in London, but that would not prevent him from travelling to Devonshire. She was worried for Rosie's children, and then there was Tommy, who was Bertie's heir. If Ewart discovered that, he might try to kidnap Tommy and hold him for ransom. There was no knowing what that man might do, and the sooner the police caught him the better. Despite her initial success at Wilton's she was prepared to drop everything and catch the next train back to Devonshire if she heard that Ewart had left London.

* * *

The performance that evening went even better than Patricia's debut. It seemed that word had gone round and the concert hall was packed. Wilton was rubbing his hands with glee when he came to congratulate Patricia and, for a moment, she thought he was going to wrap his arms around her in a fond embrace, but he managed to control himself. Wilder came to the bar to take her home after the show, but he was evasive when she questioned him about his activities that day. They parted at the foot of the stairs in Bridie's lodging house and he left quickly. There was no repeat of the passionate embrace they had shared previously, which left Patricia feeling very much alone and oddly unhappy, despite her triumph at the theatre. She went to her room and sat by the window for a while, staring into the shadows half-hoping to see Ewart and yet dreading what a definite sighting of him would mean. She had undressed and was about to slip into bed when there was a knock on her bedroom door.

'Patricia, it's me. Bridie.'

Patricia unlocked the door and opened it. 'What's the matter? Is anything wrong?'

'I know where Ewart is.'

'Come in and tell me.'

Bridie shook her head. 'No need. I'm going to tell Wilder and he can pass it on to the police, if he so wishes. Not that I got much time for the peelers, but sometimes you need them.'

Patricia thought quickly. 'No, don't tell him yet. I want to have a word with Blease Ewart in private.'

'You want to speak to him in person?'

'That's what I said. Maybe I can put a stop to all this before it gets out of hand. I don't want him to hurt anyone I love, but I do want him to write a

371

confession which will clear Piers' name.'

'Who is this Piers person?'

'He was married to my sister, but he was convicted of a felony and sent to the penal colony in Australia. He's served more than four years now and has earned a ticket of leave, but if Ewart signs a confession it might get Piers a pardon.'

'You're risking a lot if you get involved with that man.'

'I've a lot to make up for, Bridie. I took my family for granted and I wasn't a very nice person. If I can do anything to atone, I will.'

'Are you sure, ducks? I don't think you know what you're letting yourself into. If I was you I'd let Wilder take all the risks.'

'No, Bridie. This time I want to do something not just for myself but for the rest of the family. Tell me where to find Ewart, I'm begging you, Bridie. Please . . .'

24

Patricia knew the way only too well. She arrived at the Goat and Compasses early next morning. Jonas Beaney, the potman, recognised her instantly. He put down the cloth he had been using to polish the bar counter and walked towards her.

'What d'you want here, miss?'

'I want to see Mr Ewart. I know he's lodging here.'

'Starlina warned me about you,' Jonas said crossly. 'Why can't you leave us in peace? For your own good, go away.'

'I won't leave until I've spoken to Mr Ewart.'

Jonas advanced towards her but the inner door opened and Ewart stepped into the taproom.

'I thought I recognised that voice. The star of Wilton's has come to visit us, Beaney.'

'I want a few words with you, that's all,' Patricia said firmly. 'In private.'

Ewart laughed. 'It's not often that I get a young lady wanting to be alone with me. We'll be in the parlour, if anyone wants me, Beaney.'

'Right, boss.' Beaney nodded and went back to his work.

Ewart ushered Patricia into the parlour and closed the door. 'Do take a seat, my dear.'

Patricia shook her head. 'I prefer to stand. What I have to say won't take long.'

'As you wish.' Ewart sprawled in a chair by the empty grate. 'This will be very interesting.'

'I want you to leave me and my family alone.'

'And what if I don't, Patricia?'

'Did you know that Leo Wilder is determined to bring you to justice, Ewart?'

'Of course I did. How do you think I've managed to evade the police here and in France? I am extremely resourceful.'

'And yet you seem to have taken over Leo's pub. Doesn't that make you fair game for the police?'

'Obviously I keep out of sight of the police and public. But I have always had a fancy to own a dockside pub. I don't suppose that sounds very interesting to someone like you, who was born with the proverbial silver spoon in her mouth.'

'You know that's not true. We aren't rich.'

'Compared to most people you live a life of luxury, you just don't know it. However, I intend to put a stop to that.'

Patricia stared at him in horror. 'What are you saying?'

'I think it would be amusing to bankrupt your family properly this time. I managed to get Piers transported and disgraced. I fancy owning a castle in Devonshire.'

'Haven't you done enough harm to my family?' Patricia controlled her anger with difficulty. Ewart seemed totally unrepentant and irritatingly arrogant, but she needed to find out exactly what he intended.

'I haven't even begun. I once had proof that I was the heir to Rockwood Castle, but Piers came between me and my inheritance.'

'You were never the heir. I was very young, but even I understood that you were the son of a shepherd and a maidservant. You are an imposter, Ewart.'

His smile faded and he jumped to his feet. 'You will end up at the bottom of the river if you persist

374

in telling such lies. You are the one at fault. None of you Careys belongs in Rockwood. I know for a fact that Alexander had a loan to carry them through last winter after a poor harvest.'

'How could you possibly know that?'

'I can't tell you that, but if you ask him he'll say it's true. They have defaulted on the repayments and the castle will be put up for sale. I will step in and take back my rightful home.'

'You are mad,' Patricia said slowly. 'Where did you get so much money to lend them in the first place?'

'The jewel robbery was very profitable, but it was just one of many. I've worked hard during my years in France, and I've travelled to other countries, so that the police are always one step behind me. A madman would not be so clever. Think about that, Patricia.'

She backed towards the door. 'I can see I've wasted my time.'

'Aren't you afraid that I will detain you at my pleasure?'

Patricia faced him, hoping she appeared fearless, although inwardly she was terrified. 'Bridie knows where I am, and I recognised a couple of the customers sitting in the inglenook. This is hardly a private place. I think you might have made a mistake in coming here.'

'You've got a nerve, I'll give you that, Miss Carey. Tell me why I shouldn't simply wring your neck now and dispose of your body quietly.'

Patricia put her hands behind her as she felt for the door handle. 'Because if you come a step nearer I will scream so loudly they will hear me in Clapham. Believe me, I'm opera trained.'

Ewart hesitated and then he laughed, but there was no humour in the sound and his eyes glinted maliciously. 'Go then. You'll be sorry you got on the wrong side of Blease Ewart. When I own Rockwood Castle I'll make you work for me in the kitchens. You'll know your place then.'

Patricia twisted the handle and opened the door to the taproom. Once inside she walked briskly to the door and let herself out into the street. It was only then that she gasped for breath. No matter how evil the smell from the stinking mud or the stench from the manufactories on the riverbank, the air was sweeter than wine compared to the odour of Ewart's evil body. She had seen madness first hand and she knew now what they were fighting. Wilder needed to be warned first but then she must go home to Rockwood and give Alex, Bertie and Rosie the bad news. She walked towards Doctors' Commons where she was certain she would find a cab, and within minutes she had flagged one down and was heading towards Wellclose Square.

★ ★ ★

Bridie listened to Patricia's account of her meeting with Ewart in shocked silence. 'You shouldn't have gone there on your own,' she said when Patricia finished speaking. 'Lord have mercy on him but that man is as mad as a March hare, and he's dangerous. You was lucky to get out unharmed.'

'I need to find Leo. Where might he be at this time of day, Bridie? He won't tell me what he's been doing or where he's been going.'

'I dunno, ducks. Why would he tell me anything?'

376

'You seem to know everything that's going on in this area, Bridie.'

'I'm flattered, but Leo Wilder keeps hisself to hisself. He must know that Ewart has taken over his old pub.'

'Maybe he doesn't,' Patricia said slowly. 'In which case I must go to the nearest police station and tell them where to find Ewart.'

Bridie shook her head. 'That might be a bad idea, ducks. Leo is sure to have that information. I know from experience that the peelers wait until they have firm evidence before they leap in an arrest a criminal. I'm not saying as how I mix with the likes of them, but with me sister a light-fingered lady I have some experience of dealing with the law.'

'Do you really think that Leo knows where to find Ewart?'

'I'd bet my life on it, love. If you ask me I think the best thing you could do is to go home to Devonshire and tell your family what Ewart is up to. Maybe you can save them from losing their home.'

'I know you're right, but I have a verbal contract with Mr Wilton. I'm doing so well there, Bridie. I could be top billing next week.'

Bridie shrugged and sniffed. 'You've got to decide who to put first, yourself or your family. I can't help you there.'

'You're right. I'll go to the theatre and tell Mr Wilton that I have to go to Devonshire for a few days. I'm sure he'll understand when I explain that it's an urgent family matter.'

★ ★ ★

Two hours later Patricia was on the train heading for Exeter. Mr Wilton had not been accommodating and he had cancelled their contract on the spot. Freddie had tried to intervene but there was little possibility that the angry theatre owner would change his mind. Singers were ten a penny, Patricia was told, and she found herself out of a job with two days' pay in her pocket. She considered herself lucky to have that; at least it would cover her fare home. She had not been able to contact Wilder, but after all, Wilder did not own her. Their brief romance seemed to be at an end, if indeed it had ever really begun. Patricia put her own feelings resolutely behind her. Given time she would forget her emotional involvement with a man who did not seem able to decide whose side he was on. Wilder had been rubbing shoulders with criminals in Puddle Dock, as well as working with the police. She was totally confused and eager to go home to where life in the country continued as it had done for centuries. When she left the station at Exeter she was fortunate to see a city gentleman alighting from a cab, which she hired at ridiculously above the going rate, but she was desperate to get home. Nothing mattered now other than to be with her family and warn them of the danger that Ewart posed.

The cab was old, probably having been bought cheaply, and the cracked leather squabs seemed to have inhaled the dubious aroma of tobacco, farm manure and wet dog. In the old days Patricia would have complained vigorously, if she had deigned to get into the carriage at all, but she was past all that.

The important thing was to get home as quickly as possible. She looked out of the window, welcoming the familiar streets of Exeter with a smile. She wondered why she had not noticed the beauty of the old buildings before, or the rolling green hills and the lush farmland when they left the city. Farm workers were toiling in the fields during haymaking, and would labour on until dusk or even later. Patricia had never taken much notice of country activities before, but suddenly they seemed the most welcoming sight she had seen in a long time. Life in the city was brutal and although there was hardship and poverty in the country, it seemed to her now that anything was preferable to some of the things she had seen in London.

It was early evening when Patricia alighted in the bailey of Rockwood Castle. The sun was low in the sky, casting purple shadows on the grassy banks outside the castle walls. Patricia took her valise from the driver, ignoring his outstretched hand. The cost of the fare would be sufficient to feed him and his family for a week, and she was not about give him a tip. He stomped off and climbed onto the driver's seat, muttering beneath his breath.

The great iron-studded door opened and Jarvis welcomed her with a creaky smile, something that did not happen very often, and the effort appeared to crack his lined face into two. He took the valise from her.

'Welcome home, Lady Greystone.'

'It's good to be here, Jarvis,' Patricia said, returning his smile. 'Where will I find everyone?'

'The family are assembled in the drawing room, my lady.'

'Thank you, Jarvis.' Patricia entered the hall, breathing in the scent of roses crammed into a silver rose bowl, their petals reflected in the highly polished surface of an ancient coffer. She gave Sir Denys's visor a

379

casual pat as she walked past the old suit of armour and for a moment she thought the mail-covered fingers twitched in response, as if Sir Denys was also welcoming her home.

Patricia entered the drawing room to find the whole family seated in a large group, including Wolfe, who was standing dutifully behind Bertie's Bath chair, and Fletcher, who was standing beside Hester, arms folded with a martial look on her face. Nancy was the first to react and she rushed to greet Patricia, almost smothering her with a hug and a kiss on the cheek.

'I've missed you, Patsy. I wished I'd come with you.'

Patricia returned the embrace. 'Well, I'm home now, but I really missed you, too.'

Rosalind leaped to her feet. 'Patsy, why didn't you let us know you were coming?'

'It was a spur-of-the-moment decision.' Patricia held her sister at arm's length. 'You've been crying. What's going on?'

'We've had some bad news,' Rosalind said slowly. 'Tell her, Bertie. If I try to explain it will start me off again.' She walked back to the shelter of her husband's arms.

'You're like a bird of ill omen, Patricia.' Hester shook her head. 'You always turn up when there's trouble.'

'That's not fair,' Patricia retorted angrily. 'Why do you always have to blame me for everything, Hester? I came all the way from London to try to help you all. I gave up the chance of a lifetime at Wilton's Theatre to come here.'

Bertie raised his hand. 'Calm down, everyone. I'm pleased to see you, Patsy. But the truth is I've just had to tell the family that we're almost bankrupt.'

Walter had been sitting next to Louise, but he rose

to his feet. 'You've come home at a bad time, Patsy. But if it's any consolation, I'm delighted to see you.'

'Me, too.' Louise smiled up at her. 'You're here in time for Charlotte's christening. We'd love you to be one of her godmothers.'

'She's a really beautiful baby,' Nancy added excitedly. 'You'll adore her, Patsy.'

'I'm sure I will, and at the first opportunity I'll come and see you and we can talk about it.' Patricia looked round at their downcast faces. 'Perhaps someone would tell me what's happened to upset you all so much.'

Bertie cleared his throat. 'We had a bad harvest and our investment in the sawmill hasn't paid off. In fact, we've lost money on it.'

'I'm to blame for that,' Alex said hastily. 'I don't know the first thing about that sort of business. I was a good soldier but I'm a rotten businessman.'

Rosalind patted his hand. 'It was bad luck, darling. It wasn't your fault.'

'Anyway, whatever the cause, I took out a loan secured on the castle itself. I know it was rash but I was desperate. They called in the loan when we couldn't keep up the repayments.'

'So you see why this is a difficult time,' Hester added, frowning. 'You can go back to your career, just like you mama always does.'

'That's enough, Hester,' Rosalind said angrily. 'I won't allow you to speak to my sister in that tone. Patsy is one of us and she deserves to be treated with respect. You should be ashamed of yourself.'

Hester bowed her head. 'I'm sorry, Patsy. I'm just worried, that's all.'

Patricia nodded her acceptance of the apology but

she turned to Bertie. 'Do you know who it was who loaned you the money?'

'It was a company in London. I have the name in my study.'

Patricia peeled off her lace gloves and undid her bonnet. 'I've just travelled all the way from London. Do you think I might have a glass of lemonade or a cup of tea?'

Hester rose to her feet and tugged at the bell pull. 'I am sorry, Patsy. Manners fly out of the window when there's a crisis.'

'So it seems.' Patricia took a seat facing the rest of her family. 'None of you has asked why I came here in such a rush. I'll tell you anyway because I know who loaned you the money. It was Blease Ewart.'

There was a moment of stunned silence. Bertie was the first to recover. 'How do you know that, Patsy?'

'Because he told me so just this morning. Ewart has been back in London for some time. My land-lady tracked him down and discovered that he had bought Wilder's old pub, the Goat and Compasses. I went to see him this morning and he told me that he set out to bankrupt our family. He is quite mad. He still thinks he is heir to Rockwood and he won't stop until he has secured the castle for himself.'

'He is crazy,' Rosalind said breathlessly. 'I knew that years ago, but I thought we would never see him again. But why did you seek him out, Patsy? You know he's dangerous.'

'I went to him to try and make him confess to his part in the crimes that he and Piers committed. You told me that all is not well at Trevenor, and Aurelia is my dear friend. I thought if Piers could come home he would be able to resurrect the mine and maybe

382

Aurelia and Martin would be happy again.'

'Good for you,' Walter said earnestly.

'Yes, indeed.' Louise clutched her husband's hand and held it to her cheek. 'You are a true friend, Patsy.'

Patricia could feel her cheeks burning at such unexpected praise and a warm feeling in the pit of her stomach was something of a surprise. 'Thank you, but anyone would do the same. Anyway, Ewart is wanted by the Metropolitan Police as well as their counterparts in France. Wilder is determined to bring him to justice.'

'And you came all the way from London to tell us?' Bertie grinned at her. 'Thank you, little sister. You might have saved us from having to sell up and move out of the castle.'

'I'd barricade myself and my family in before I'd give up,' Rosalind said firmly. 'This is our home and always will be. You were very brave to face Ewart on your own, Patsy, but please don't ever do that again.'

Patricia smiled. 'Don't worry. It's not something I would like to repeat. I just wish I'd been able to talk to Leo before I left London. Heaven knows what he'll be thinking now.'

'Didn't you leave a note explaining things?' Rosalind smiled, shaking her head. 'How like you, Patsy. You act first and think later.'

'I've a good mind to go to London and help Wilder bring Ewart to justice,' Alex said thoughtfully. 'Maybe between the two of us we can persuade him to write a confession that would stand up in court. I'd like to see my brother pardoned and brought back to Trevenor.'

'Your cousin, darling.' Rosalind smiled up at him.

'We didn't know that when we were brought up together. To me he'll always be my brother and family comes first in my mind.'

Hester rose to her feet. 'Where is that maid? I rang the bell a good five minutes ago. I'm going below stairs to give them all piece of my mind.'

'Dinner should be ready soon.' Rosalind turned to Fletcher. 'Cora, dear, would you go downstairs and see what's happening? They won't argue with you.'

'I could run this household with me eyes shut,' Fletcher muttered as she left the room.

'Sauce-box!' Hester said explosively. 'The nerve of the woman.'

Patricia stifled a giggle but Rosalind managed to keep a straight face and she slipped her arm around Hester's shoulders.

'My dear, don't you think it's time you allowed someone else to take over the housekeeping duties? Fletcher really does know how to manage the servants. Most of them are too scared to argue, although she gets along very well with Cook. Might we not give her the opportunity to prove herself, and for you to relax a little?'

Walter rose to his feet, holding out his hand to his wife. 'I think we ought to return to the cottage. We left Charlotte with Mrs Madge's daughter, Flossie,' he added hastily. 'She's only thirteen.'

'Yes, of course,' Louise said hurriedly. 'It's good to have you home, Patsy. Do come and see us tomorrow. You must see how Charlotte has grown in such a short time. She's such a lovely baby.'

'I'm sure she is. I will come, I promise.' Patricia sighed. She was pleased that Walter, whom she loved dearly, was happily married, but she was slightly envious. Rosie and Alex were a perfect couple also, but that left her, Patricia Carey, the spoiled darling of the family, widowed and alone yet again. Perhaps she was destined never to be happy in a relationship. Rosalind laid her hand on Patricia's shoulder. 'You were so brave, Patsy. I'm proud of you. Alex will travel to London tomorrow and he'll help Leo to bring Ewart to justice. Maybe then our family will get some peace.'

'I do hope so,' Patricia said with a heartfelt sigh.

★   ★   ★

Dinner was a subdued meal that evening but Fletcher had the kitchen and housemaids under control and everything went smoothly. Even so, despite everyone trying to appear as if nothing was wrong, there was an undercurrent of anxiety. Later, when the meal was over and conversation lagged, Patricia went to her old room and was comforted by the familiar if slightly shabby surroundings. Memories of her happy childhood were everywhere and the view from the window had never changed. The feather mattress seemed to mould itself round her body and she slept with the window thrown open to allow the summer breeze to waft round the room, bringing in the sweet perfume of night-scented stocks, roses and honey- suckle. The distant sound of the waves lapping on the shore was better than a lullaby and she drifted off to sleep.

★   ★   ★

Patricia was awakened by someone shaking her and she opened her eyes. 'What's the matter?'

Nancy tugged at her arm. 'Get up, please. There's bad news.'

'What is it?' Patricia snapped to a sitting position.

385

'Calm down, Nancy. Tell me slowly what's happened.'

'Tommy's been kidnapped. A messenger arrived just now to give Bertie a note from the school. Tommy should have been leaving there today to travel to Exeter where someone would pick him up from the station. But he was walking back to the main building after a game of cricket when he was dragged into a carriage and driven off.'

'Ewart! He made threats against the family and now he's done his worst.' Patricia rose from her bed and stripped off her nightgown, allowing it to fall to the ground. 'Pass me my chemise and gown, please. I need to speak to Bertie.'

'Are you sure it was Ewart who abducted Tommy?' Nancy plucked Patricia's clothes from the chair and handed them to her.

'I don't see who else it could be.' Patricia dressed hurriedly, and ran a brush through her tangled hair, which she tied back with a ribbon. 'Come on, Nancy. I'm going to find Bertie. We have to do something.' She left her room and ran down the narrow spiral stairs to the main landing and the grand staircase.

Bertie was in the entrance hall, talking to the messenger. The man tipped his cap and left, ushered out by James, who had not had time to button his tunic. Such a transgression would have earned him a stern rebuke from Jarvis in ordinary times, but this was definitely not an ordinary day. Wolfe pushed Bertie in his wheeled chair, coming to a halt in front of Patricia.

'Nancy told you what's happened?'

'Yes, Bertie. I'm so sorry. I did try to warn you last evening. Ewart is a lunatic and he'll do anything to get his hands on Rockwood. I don't know of anything that would persuade him otherwise.'

'You're right. He has a crazed mind. I remember the trouble we had with him before. Piers is still paying the price, although he was far from innocent himself. But Ewart was the chief transgressor.'

'We need Wilder,' Patricia said flatly. 'It's no use going to the police: they've failed miserably. Wilder is the only one who understands the workings of Ewart's sick mind.'

Bertie shook his head. 'I don't care about anything other than getting my son back unharmed. If it means giving in to Ewart I'm prepared to do so.'

'Never, boss!' Wolfe's deep voice echoed off the stone walls of the entrance hall. 'You can't give in to blackmail.'

'I know that, Wolfe, but what else can I do? Tommy is just a boy and he's in the hands of a maniac. I blame the school. They didn't take proper care of him.'

'No one could have foreseen such an event,' Patricia said gently. 'I'll get the next train back to London and I'll see if Leo can help. It's our only chance unless you give in to Ewart's demands. Has he contacted you?'

'No, not yet. But he will.'

James had been standing stiffly to attention but at that moment Jarvis opened the secret door beneath the staircase that was used by the servants. He marched up to James but if he had intended to berate him for his untidy appearance he was fore-stalled by the arrival of a horseman.

'Another messenger?' Bertie said anxiously. 'This will be the ransom demand, no doubt. Open the door, Jarvis. Don't let the fellow escape.'

Wolfe rolled up his sleeves. 'Let me, sir. I'll make the fellow talk.'

25

'Wait a minute, Wolfe,' Patricia said urgently. 'Find out who it is before you go in for a fight.' She ran to the doorway and over Jarvis's shoulder she saw a familiar figure dismount, tossing the reins to Pip, the stable boy.

'Leo!' Patricia pushed past Jarvis and ran to greet him. 'I'm so glad to see you. We're in an awful state. Ewart has kidnapped Tommy.'

Wilder held her briefly in the circle of his arms, and he rested his cheek on her hair. 'I had to find you, Patsy. I had to know you were safe.'

'I'm fine. I'm sorry I couldn't let you know that I was leaving, but I had to warn my family that Ewart planned to bankrupt them, and now he's got Tommy. Ewart is a madman, Leo. Heaven knows what he'll do to the poor boy.'

Wilder laid his finger on her lips. 'Don't worry. We'll get the boy back safely. I've travelled all night to be here, and now I need to speak to your brother.'

Jarvis was standing stiffly to attention, gazing into the distance as Patricia took Wilder by the hand and dragged him into the entrance hall. 'Leo will get Tommy back safe and sound, Bertie.'

Bertie leaned forward in his chair, his face ashen with worry. 'What can you do, Leo? I'm at a loss.'

'Have you had a ransom note? We can't do anything until Ewart gives us a clue as to his whereabouts, however small.'

'Not yet. I thought maybe you were the messenger

388

from Ewart.'

'I'm out to catch the devil and see him safely behind bars.'

'Leo has been travelling all night, Bertie,' Patricia said firmly. 'The least we can do is to offer him some rest and refreshment. As he says, we can't do anything until we hear from Ewart.'

'She's right, boss,' Wolfe said gruffly. 'Do you want me to take you to the drawing room? You'll be more comfortable there.'

'Yes, I suppose so, but it's hard to be stuck here like the cripple I am while my son is in danger.'

'We'll find him, boss,' Wolfe said grimly. 'Heaven help that man if I gets my hands on him first.'

'All I care about is my son.' Bertie turned to Patricia. 'You'd better see that Leo is looked after. You know where to find me if there's any news.'

'Yes, of course. Try not to worry, Bertie.'

'If we don't get a ransom note from Ewart I'll go to the school and question anyone who saw what happened.' Wilder laid his hand on Bertie's shoulder. 'Your son will be returned to you safe and sound, no matter what.'

Bertie nodded wordlessly and Wolfe pushed the chair in the direction of the drawing room.

'Come with me, Leo. You need some food inside you before you even think of going out again.' Patricia led the way to the dining room where Jennet had just finished laying the table.

'Jennet, we'll have breakfast now, and I think Sir Bertram would like coffee in the drawing room.'

Jennet's eyes were wide with curiosity. 'Is it true, my lady? Has Master Tommy been kidnapped?'

Patricia sighed. 'Words gets round quickly. Yes, it

389

is true, but that fact stays within these walls. Master Tommy's life may depend upon it.'

'I understand, my lady.' Jennet backed out of the room.

Patricia turned to Wilder with tears in her eyes. 'It's so terrible, Leo. Tommy is just a boy and he had a terrible upbringing until we rescued him from the chimney sweep. The poor child has suffered the horrors of being a climbing boy and he doesn't deserve to suffer now.'

Wilder wrapped his arms around her, holding her close. 'We'll get him back unharmed and as quickly as possible.'

'Ewart is a madman, but he's also clever.' Patricia took a step away from him. It would be too easy to succumb to despair, especially when comfort was so near and so desirable, but Tommy's safety was paramount. 'Did you know that Ewart has taken over the Goat and Compasses?'

'I discovered that yesterday. It seems that he has to possess anything that belonged to someone he wishes to harm.'

'I suppose he knows that you were behind the police raid on the house in Paris.'

'He's worked that out and I am now his worst enemy, which is why you must be very careful.'

She looked up at him, puzzled. 'How does that affect me?'

'Because he knows the best way to hurt me is to harm the one I love most in the world.'

'You love me?' Patricia said dazedly.

Leo smiled. 'One day I'll tell you how much, but not now.'

'Ordinarily I wouldn't allow you to get off so easily,

but these are extraordinary times. I really don't know what to do, Leo.' Patricia sank down in her usual chair at the table and Wilder took a seat beside her.

'Why did you leave London without telling me?'

She shot him a sideways glance. 'After I'd spoken to Ewart and found out that he intended to ruin my family I didn't have much choice. I needed to warn Bertie, but as it happens I was too late.'

'When I get my hands on him, Ewart will make everything good, and that's a promise.'

They were interrupted by the appearance of James, who knocked on the door and entered without waiting for an answer.

'Begging your pardon, my lady, but Mr Jarvis sent me to tell you that a messenger has arrived with a note for Sir Bertram.'

Patricia glanced at Wilder, but he was already on his feet and heading for the door. His booted steps clattered on the polished wooden floorboards as he strode towards the main entrance. Patricia rushed after him, but she held back when she reached the doorway. Wilder had the man by the collar and was questioning him in a way that would have scared anyone, let alone an innocent courier.

'Please sir, I only carry the messages. I dunno who wrote it.' The man cowered in Wilder's firm grasp.

'Tell me how this piece of paper came into your hands and describe the person who gave it to you.'

'I live in Exeter, sir. A man came knocking on my door. He said his master would pay me well to ride here and deliver the note.'

Wilder took the folded and sealed document from him and handed it to Patricia. 'Give this to your brother. I'll hold this fellow until Bertie's read it.

Maybe this chap's memory will be clearer if I hold his head in the horses' drinking trough for a while.'

'No, sir. Please don't. I'm telling you all I know.'

Patricia hurried to the drawing room and handed the paper to Bertie. 'This is from Ewart. Leo has the messenger by the throat. You need to read it quickly so that I can tell Leo to release the poor fellow.'

Bertie tore at the seal and unfolded the letter. He scanned the lines and handed it back to Patricia. 'Read it out loud. My eyes keep blurring.'

Patricia studied the spidery scrawl. 'It says that Ewart has Tommy and he wants the deeds to Rockwood Castle in return for Tommy's life. That's appalling, Bertie. I can't believe that even Ewart would stoop that low.'

Bertie opened his mouth but he seemed at a loss for words. Wolfe cleared his throat. 'Is that all it says? Is there no hint of where it came from?'

'It says he will contact us with the details of where to take the documents. This is outrageous, Bertie. I think we should take this to the police.'

Bertie shook his head. 'No, not the police. If Ewart is as mad as I think he is, that would be Tommy's death sentence.'

'Maybe you're right. I'll take this to Leo. He's holding the messenger so perhaps he can get more information out of him.' Patricia returned to the main entrance at a run. 'Read this, Leo.' She placed the document in his free hand while he held the bearer of bad news in a vice-like grip.

'A child's life depends on this, fellow,' Wilder said through clenched teeth. 'Have you nothing extra to tell us, or do I march you to the police constable's house?'

'I told you all I can, sir.'

'Can you describe the person?' Patricia spoke softly, not wanting to scare the man even more. He was white and trembling and seemed genuinely frightened.

'He was dressed like a servant, ma'am. He might have come from a hotel or a coaching inn.'

'Was he wearing livery of some sort?' Patricia asked eagerly.

'Not exactly, but I think he was in dark green,' the messenger said vaguely. 'With brass buttons.'

'Anything else? Please think hard. The man who sent this is dangerous and he's abducted a young boy.'

The man swallowed convulsively. 'The person wore knee breeches, ma'am. And shoes with brass buckles.'

'That sounds like a hotel porter's uniform,' Leo said thoughtfully. He released the terrified messenger. 'Are you sure that's all you can remember.'

'Yes, sir. On my honour. I'm very sorry about the child. I got kids of my own.'

Leo took a handful of coins from his pocket and gave them to him. 'For your trouble. You may go now.'

The messenger leaped onto his horse's back as if he had springs on his heels and he rode away, urging his mount to go faster as if afraid he might be pursued.

'What do you think?' Patricia demanded anxiously.

'It sounds as if Ewart is staying in a hotel in Exeter or nearby.'

'We have a description of the uniform worn by the hotel staff. It's clumsy of Ewart to overlook the fact but he might have chosen the messenger from somewhere different to give us a false clue.'

'Come inside, Leo. We need to speak to Bertie and Alex. I'll send James to fetch Walter. This is a family matter and we should all be involved.'

'I agree. You speak to James and I'll go and prime Bertie.'

Wilder strode back into the house, leaving Patricia to give the footman a message for her brother. Having done so, she followed Wilder to the drawing room. Alex and Rosalind were there, both of them looking stunned and anxious.

Bertie met Patricia's gaze with a serious look. 'We've decided that the only thing to do is to split up and visit all the hotels and inns in the Exeter area.'

'We don't want to arouse suspicion in any of the places we call at,' Alex said slowly.

'In that case I will come with you.' Rosalind grasped her husband's hand. 'We'll pretend we are travellers looking for accommodation.'

'I'll go with you, Leo,' Patricia said eagerly. 'Rosie's right. It won't look so odd if there are two of us.'

Nancy had been sitting quietly but she jumped to her feet. 'I'll go with Walter. I don't suppose Louise wants to leave her baby.'

'Wolfe can take me.' Bertie glared at each of them in turn as if expecting an argument. 'We will simply be travellers.'

'We will have to be careful to visit hostelries where we aren't known,' Patricia said hastily.

Rosalind released Alex's hand and crossed the floor to open her escritoire. She selected a sheet of paper and a pen. 'Give me the name of the hotels and inns you've visited. Then we can decide where to go.'

They had just finished their list when Walter burst into the room. 'Is it true what James said? As Tommy been kidnapped?'

Hester followed him at a slower pace. 'Why didn't you call me earlier?'

394

Patricia hurried to her side. 'We need you to stay here, Hester. It's important that there is someone in charge while we all go in search of Tommy.'

'Yes, indeed.' Rosalind rose from the chair, holding the list in her hand. 'I'm going to put this on the table in the middle of the room and I want you all to write your names by any hotel or inn that you've visited in the last year or so. We mustn't risk being recognised. Ewart is very sharp and if he gets wind of the fact that we're looking for him and Tommy that would be a disaster.'

'Why am I not included?' Hester demanded.

'Because I say so.' Bertie glared at her. 'Patsy just told you that we need someone to take charge here. Should Ewart send another message you would be the one to deal with it. No one must know what we're doing. Fletcher will keep the servants from gossiping and you will take my place as head of the house, albeit temporarily.'

'I am Lady Carey,' Hester said smugly. 'Sometimes people forget that. You're right, Bertie. I am the one who will keep things going at home. You may trust me.'

'I knew I could.' Bertie turned to Wolfe. 'Hand me the list. I'm known in many of these places so I need to be very careful.'

Patricia and Rosalind exchanged meaningful glances. Bertie always knew best how to handle Hester.

★   ★   ★

An hour later Patricia and Leo called at the first inn on their list. Leo made enquiries of the landlord

395

while Patricia studied the uniforms worn by the staff, but there was nothing to suggest that the person who delivered the ransom note was an employee. It was the first of many places they visited that day, all of them proving unhelpful. Dispirited and exhausted they returned to Rockwood Castle.

Hester was waiting for them. 'You're the first to return. This came by messenger while you were all out looking for Tommy.' She waved a piece of paper in Patricia's face.

Patricia snatched it from her and studied the scrawl. 'It's addressed to Bertie but I'm going to open it. He should be here soon, anyway.'

'Come into the drawing room,' Hester said anxiously. 'You never know who's watching.'

'Did you get a chance to speak to the messenger?' Leo asked.

'No, I didn't. He wanted to give it to Bertie, but I told him that the master was feeling unwell and was not to be disturbed.'

'That was quick thinking.' Patricia broke the now familiar seal and opened the document.

'The fellow left too quickly for me to ask him anything.' Hester moved closer. 'What does it say?'

Patricia's hand trembled as she handed the piece of paper to Leo. 'I'm even more worried now.'

'What does it say?' Hester demanded.

'It says I am to go on my own to the sawmill at midnight and I'm to take the deeds with me, if we want to get Tommy back unharmed.' Patricia turned to Leo. 'Of course I will go.'

'You're going nowhere alone. That's final.'

'You saw what he put. Ewart knows you won't allow me to go on my own. He wants you or Alex to

396

go with me so that he can do his worst. We have to put Tommy first.'

'I'd like to get my hands on that villain,' Hester said angrily. 'If Ewart's harmed that boy he will have me to deal with.'

'Why would Ewart choose the sawmill?' Patricia frowned. 'How would he know that it's not being used at the moment?'

Wilder shrugged. 'Perhaps he's had a hand in making the business fail. He seems to know everything that's going on here.'

'We've got a few hours to talk this over,' Patricia said, sighing. 'Let's wait for Bertie and the other to return. We need to work out a plan to rescue Tommy and to make sure that Ewart doesn't escape this time.'

'He'll have thought of that.' Wilder walked towards the doorway, and Patricia followed him out of the room. 'I'm going to visit Constable Burton.'

'Leo, you can't do that. What if Ewart gets wind of the police being involved?'

'I'll make sure that Burton understands the situation. I want him to let his superiors know. We are going to catch Ewart tonight and put him away for good. He's kidnapped the son and heir to Rockwood Castle — that is a hanging offence.'

Patricia clutched his sleeve. 'Wait a minute. I've had an idea.'

'Can't it wait?'

'No, Leo. I think I know where Ewart might have placed Tommy.' Patricia took a deep breath. 'Ezra Trimble!'

Wilder shook his head. 'Who on earth is Ezra Trimble.'

'He's the brute who claimed to be Tommy's father.'

'But Tommy is Bertie's son.'

'Bertie fell in love with a servant girl and they married in secret. She gave birth to Tommy but she died and her sister, Emmie, took care of him. Then Emmie married a brute called Ezra Trimble, and as soon as Tommy was old enough, Ezra sold him to Hodges, the chimney sweep.'

'Poor boy,' Wilder said, frowning. 'But how did the boy return to his rightful family?'

'One day Rosie was in Exeter, visiting her dressmaker. Tommy ran away from the sweep and he almost sent Rosie flying as she left the dressmaker's house. She could see what a state the poor child was in and she refused to let Hodges take him back. She brought Tommy home and the rest of his story came out, but Trimble bears us a grudge. I suspect that Ewart discovered Tommy's history and that's where we'll find him.'

'Do you know where this fellow lives?'

'He lives somewhere near the prison. I remember hearing Rosie talk about the time when he accosted her outside the prison gates, but I think anyone would know where he lives.'

'I'll go there now.'

'I'm coming with you. You'll never find his place on your own and it will be dark soon.'

'All right, but you must promise to do as I say. I don't want you to get hurt.'

'I'd better tell Hester what we're doing.'

'I wouldn't, if I were you. If she tells Bertie he'll want to join in and that could be fatal. It's best if we do this on our own.'

'I agree, but Bertie will still go to the sawmill at midnight. He'll take the deeds to the castle there unless we've rescued Tommy.'

'All right. Leave a message to say that we'll be there too, unless we can find the boy beforehand.'

'I'll go and tell Hester now. You get the horses saddled. I don't need to ride in the carriage.'

★　★　★

It was dark in the back streets of Exeter where the silvery rays of the moon could not penetrate between the narrow streets and tall warehouses. The only light that spilled out onto the cobblestones came from the various public houses as drunks fell through the doors to sprawl on the ground or stagger crab-wise on their way home. Patricia had only seen the area in daylight and she found the darkness confusing, but Wilder was in no mood to hesitate and he grabbed the first man he came across lying in a daze on the ground. He dragged the fellow to his feet and demanded to know where Trimble lived.

The drunken man stared up at him stupidly. 'You're not one of the bailiffs, are you?'

'Just tell me where I might find Trimble.'

'Over there, guvnor,' the man said, pointing. 'You didn't have to manhandle a poor chap like me.'

Wilder released him and tossed a couple of pennies on the ground at the man's feet, stepping over him as he grovelled to pick up the coins from the slippery cobblestones.

'Stay behind me, Patsy,' Wilder ordered as he hammered on the door with his fist. It opened just wide enough for the woman inside to peer out and Wilder pushed past her.

'Are you Mrs Trimble?'

Patricia slipped in before he closed the door. It was some years since she had seen Emmie Trimble. The poor woman looked even thinner and more ragged than Patricia remembered, and now Emmie looked terrified as well.

'Mrs Trimble, do you remember me? I'm Patricia Carey. You knew my sister, Rosalind. We're trying to find Tommy. Do you know where he is?'

A baby lying in a drawer lined with a tattered blanket began to cry and Emmie snatched it up in her arms. 'I had nothing to do with it, your honour,' she said, eyeing Wilder fearfully. 'When that man came and offered Ezra so much money I knew he wasn't going to refuse.'

Patricia laid her hand on Emmie's shoulder. 'Please sit down, ma'am. No one is going to harm you or your children. Just tell us where Tommy is.'

Emmie smiled dreamily. 'He's grown up to be such a fine boy. My poor sister would be overjoyed if she could see him now.'

'Yes, Emmie, but where is he now?' Patricia raised her hand to stop Wilder from interrupting.

'Thank God your sister saved him from Hodges. Tommy wouldn't be like he is now — a proper gentleman with book learning and manners.'

'Where is he, ma'am?' Wilder demanded angrily. 'Where has your husband hidden the boy?'

'What will happen to Trimble if they catch him?' Emmie asked tremulously.

'He'll go to the gallows, ma'am. Unless, of course, he decides to cooperate with us. Where is he?'

Emmie's pale eyes filled with tears. 'I'm afraid, sir. That gentleman what came here, he was a bad 'un and no mistake. He bribed Ezra to do his dirty work for him.'

'What was this person's name, Mrs Trimble?' Patricia said gently.

'I dunno, miss. That's the honest truth, but he had a carriage and pair and he took Ezra and the boy to the sawmill at Rockwood. I overheard that much.'

'You are sure they took Tommy with them?'

Wilder fixed her with a hard look that made Emmie tremble even more.

'Y-yes, sir.'

Wilder took a watch from his pocket and studied it in the light of a single candle. 'We can make it back by midnight if we ride hard, Patsy. You must go home and I'll take care of the rest.' He was out of the door before she had a chance to reply, but she hurried after him.

'I'm coming with you. Bertie knows that he should be at the mill. He'll be there with the deeds to the castle, if I know my brother. He loves that boy and he'd do anything to keep him safe.'

'All right.' Wilder untethered their horses and before she knew what was happening, Patricia found herself tossed up onto the saddle. Wilder mounted his horse and urged it to a trot as they left the dark quarter of the town. As soon as they reached the main road the horses broke into a steady canter and Patricia allowed Wilder to take the lead, even though she knew the road well. Besides which, he had the faster horse and speed was of the utmost importance if they were to get to the sawmill before Bertie handed over the deeds. It was a good hour's ride but the horses were strong, well fed and used to travelling on rough roads. The countryside flashed past, illuminated by a full moon, and the deep purple sky was studded with a myriad stars. The summer night was cool and as they neared the sea the air was fresher and spiked with a briny tang. It was a mad ride and by the time the lights of Rockwood came into view Patricia's hair was flying loose around her shoulders and her bonnet lay somewhere behind on the road to Exeter. They were so near now that they were passing the high walls that surrounded Greystone Park. How odd that she had once been mistress of that estate and had lived in the great house. Her return there had been brief and she realised now that the property meant little to her. The present was all Patricia cared about now, and finding Tommy was uppermost in her mind.

Wilder reined in his horse some distance from the sawmill and she did the same. She slid from the saddle, tethered her horse to the fence and dismounted, her heart beating furiously.

26

Wilder held his finger to his lips. 'Follow me,' he said in a low voice. 'But if there's trouble I want you to leave immediately and fetch Constable Burton, although he should be on his way by now.'

Patricia nodded. 'I understand. I just hope that they haven't harmed Tommy.'

'Your brothers and Wolfe should be here soon. If there's a scuffle I'd put my money on Wolfe. Now, I'm going in. Keep well behind me.' Wilder approached the entrance cautiously but he came to a sudden halt. 'That sounds as if the standing engine has been fired up.'

'No one has been working there for days,' Patricia said worriedly. 'Alex said the mill wasn't paying its way and they'd closed it down. Ben Causley has gone back to work for his father in the pub.'

'It sounds to me as if they weren't operating it properly.'

Patricia eyed him curiously. 'How would you know?'

'Working in a sawmill was one of the many jobs I tried my hand at when I left the sea. It's hard work but very satisfying.'

Patricia stiffened. 'I thought I heard Tommy cry out.'

'You're right. I can't wait for Bertie to arrive. I'm going in, but I want you to stay here.'

Patricia followed him anyway. She had no intention of lurking outside when Tommy was in danger. The sight that met her eyes as she entered the building made her utter a cry of horror. A single lantern hung over the saw bench where Tommy lay bound and gagged. Ewart was standing by his side while Trimble stood by the steam engine, which was rumbling and belching smoke like a terrifying giant. Deep shadows closed in upon them, as if night was attempting to smother the occupants, and a feeling of menace lingered in the dusty air.

'Let him go,' Patricia cried in desperation. 'Don't harm the boy.'

Ewart stepped forward, his eyes glittering with malice. 'I could slice the kid in two if I chose, but that depends on your brother handing over the deeds. I told him to be here at midnight and I'm not a patient man.'

'Stop the engine, Trimble.' Wilder moved closer to him, fisting his hands at his sides.

'You ain't the boss here.' Trimble obeyed reluctantly, keeping a weather eye on Ewart as he did so.

'That's better.' Wilder turned to Ewart. 'Let the boy come with us. You can't profit from this.'

'It has nothing to do with you,' Ewart snapped. 'My business is with Sir Bertram. Where is he?'

The sound of wheels churning up the gravel outside had Patricia spinning round with a sigh of relief as Wolfe wheeled Bertie into the mill. They were followed by Walter and Fletcher, whose jaw was set in an uncompromising line.

'Have you brought what I asked for?' Ewart demanded.

Bertie held up a scroll of vellum tied with red tape. 'I have the deeds to Rockwood Castle, and I want my son. Get him off that bench this instant.'

Ewart's lip curled. 'You aren't in the army now,

404

Sir Bertram. You can't give me orders, and when you hand over the deeds you won't even be the owner of Rockwood Castle.'

'Don't give them to him,' Wilder said firmly. 'Ewart is going to prison for a very long time.'

'Shut up, Wilder. You have no authority here.' Ewart turned to Trimble. 'Start the saw. Let's see how brave these people are then.'

Trimble hesitated. 'Threats is one thing, mister. I ain't a murderer.'

'Do as I say, man. It's the only way to get through to these people.'

Tommy wriggled and moaned in fear, his eyes glazed with terror. Patricia tried to get near to him but Wilder held her back.

'Leave this to me, Patsy. We're dealing with a maniac who would happily stand by and see a child murdered for the sake of his own twisted sense of importance.'

'Turn it on,' Ewart shouted. 'Or do I have to do everything myself?'

He made a move towards Trimble, but Wilder and Wolfe, acting as one, charged at him. Ewart was overpowered in a few seconds. Fletcher flew across the sawdust-covered floor and before Trimble had a change to dodge, she felled him with a right upper cut to the jaw. He went down like a tree in a gale and lay there stunned, gazing up at her as she leaned over him, flexing her fingers.

'Frighten a poor child to death, would you?' Fletcher screamed. 'I'll show you what it's like to be scared out of your wits.' She pummelled his flabby stomach until he cried out for mercy.

'Get her off me.'

Walter turned off the engine and the great saw

wheel stopped spinning with a rusty groan. Patricia was about to help Tommy but she stood back in amazement as Bertie rose from his wheeled chair and staggered a couple of paces to the saw bench. He lifted the sobbing child to a sitting position and held him, murmuring soothing words into the terrified boy's ear. Patricia had tears coursing down her cheeks as she removed the gag from Tommy's mouth. Outside, the sound of booted feet crunching on the gravel announced the arrival of Constable Burton, who marched into the mill accompanied by two younger police officers.

'You were almost too late, Constable,' Bertie said shakily. 'I wasn't going to allow that villain to terrorise my family a moment longer. I want you to arrest Blease Ewart on a charge of kidnap and attempted murder, and the same for Trimble.'

'Blease Ewart, you are under arrest.' Constable Burton and his colleague stepped forward to grab Ewart, who struggled and fought, protesting his innocence and his rightful ownership of Rockwood Castle.

'All right, Constable,' Trimble said wearily. 'I know when I'm beaten.' He allowed the constable to lead him outside to the waiting police wagon.

'You have enough evidence to convict Ewart ten times over.' Bertie slipped his arm around his son's shoulder. 'My boy had a narrow escape.'

Constable Burton nodded. 'Don't worry, Sir Bertram. I know all about Blease Ewart, or Ewart Blaise, as he used to call himself. He will go in front of the magistrate tomorrow and he'll be up for trial at Exeter assizes. The same goes for Trimble. We know him of old.' He followed the other outside, shouting orders.

Wolfe helped Bertie back to his chair and eased

him onto the seat.

'Are you all right, Tommy?' Wilder cut Tommy's bonds and lifted him to the ground.

Tommy nodded tearfully. 'They were going to slice me up.'

'We would never have let that happen.' Patricia gave him a hug. 'You're safe now and we'll take you home.'

Tommy managed a wobbly smile. 'Did you see my papa stand up and walk? He came to my rescue.'

'Yes, it was a miracle, Tommy. That's what love can do. Your papa loves you better than anyone in the whole world.'

Tommy dashed his hand across his face. 'I'm not crying. I have dust in my eyes.'

'Of course you do.' Patricia planted a kiss on his cheek. 'Come on, let's go back to the castle. I'm sure Hester has asked Cook to make something very special for a very late supper. I'm hungry. I don't know about you.'

'I'm starving,' Tommy said, grinning. 'Those people don't have any proper food in their house, although Emmie did give me some bread and dripping. She was kind to me.' Tommy watched the police sergeant leading Trimble outside to where a police carriage was waiting.

Fletcher wiped her hands on her black linsey-woolsey skirt. 'I gave him a sore head. He deserves to hang for doing what he done to the poor child.'

'I am all right, thank you, Fletcher,' Tommy said politely. 'But you gave him a good walloping. Will you teach me how to fight like that?'

'Come on, Tommy.' Bertie reached out his hand. 'We're going home. No more talk about unpleasant things tonight. You are safe and that's all that matters to me.'

'You were so brave, Papa,' Tommy said admiringly. 'You must have been a very gallant soldier.'

Wilde pushed the wheeled chair out into the night with Tommy walking by his father's side, clutching his hand as if he would never let it go. The sight of them safe and together brought fresh tears to Patricia's eyes.

'Are you all right, Patsy?' Wilder put his arms around her. 'It's been a hard time for all of you.'

She turned to look up at him with an attempt at a smile. 'You were wonderful, Leo. I doubt if the police would have caught Ewart, but for you.'

He brushed her cheek with a whisper of a kiss. 'I helped, but we all played our parts. The main thing is that Tommy is safe and Ewart is in custody, as well as Trimble. It's time to go home.' He released her reluctantly and blew out the lantern before leaving the building. He locked the door, hesitating for a moment outside. 'You know this should be a profitable business. It's a pity that Bertie and Alex intend to sell it.'

Patricia went to untether her horse, and Wilder came over to lift her onto the saddle.

'Perhaps you ought to take over the sawmill,' Patricia said cautiously. 'It would mean you could stay here in Rockwood instead of returning to London.'

'I haven't got that sort of money, Patsy. I couldn't afford to buy it from your brother.'

'I'm sure that Bertie would be only too pleased for you to manage it for him.'

Wilder climbed agilely onto his saddle. 'I don't work for others, Patsy. After I left the navy I vowed I'd never put myself in that position again.'

'You are a stubborn man,' Patricia said crossly. She dug her heels into the horse's flanks. 'Walk on.'

Rockwood was safe from Blease Ewart at last. Constable Burton called two days later to say that Ewart had been up before the magistrate, and was now in prison awaiting trial at the assizes. He was likely to be hanged or sent to the penal colony, which seemed like poetic justice after Piers' long sentence.

After much discussion, Wilder had agreed to run the sawmill for a month to see if its fortunes could be turned round, although he refused Bertie's offer of taking it on permanently as manager. He moved into the house attached to the mill, having also refused the Careys' invitation to stay on in the castle. Patricia could understand Wilder's ambition to be his own boss, but she knew that as each day passed she was falling deeper and deeper in love with him. The prospect of life without him was unbearable, and yet she could hardly go against tradition and propose marriage. She knew that he still thought of her as Lady Greystone, and as far as he was concerned the gulf between them was too wide. Even so, he encouraged her to be true to herself and to think seriously about a career in the theatre. He acknowledged her undoubted talent when her own family treated it as a passing phase. Leo understood her so well, and yet not at all.

One hot day at the end of July they went for a walk by the backwater. The sun beat down from an azure sky and fluffy white clouds danced freely in the light airs. The water reflected the intense blue and ducks dabbled happily in the shallows. Overhead a skylark trilled its sweet song and the grassy banks were studded with buttercups, dandelions and daisies. Patricia wore a straw sun bonnet and she carried a parasol, but she furled it and raised her face to the warm rays of the sun.

'It's so peaceful here. You do love it as much as I do, don't you, Leo?'

'You know I do, but I'm only managing the sawmill until Bertie finds someone more capable, and then I must return to London. I can probably rent another pub.'

'But you enjoy running the mill, Leo. You said so yourself.' Patricia sat down on the warm grass, arranging sprigged muslin skirts in a circle. 'Stay in Rockwood and make a life here with me.'

'You know that's not going to work, Patsy. I love you with all my heart, but marriage isn't for the likes of me. I'll only make you unhappy.'

'Then I'll come to London with you. Maybe John Wilton will give me another chance.'

He sat down beside her. 'And I suppose we'll both take rooms at Bridie Salmon's lodging house? I want better for you than that, Patsy. You are Lady Greystone, whether you choose to admit it or not.'

Patricia plucked a daisy and twirled it between her fingers. 'I can change my name. You could call this daisy a carrot, but it would still be a lovely flower.'

Wilder laughed and tickled her cheek with a piece of grass. 'You wouldn't want to be called a carrot, and you would soon get tired of singing to drunken Londoners every evening. It's not glamorous like your mother's circuits of the grand opera houses. I couldn't take you to a life like that.'

'You don't understand,' Patricia said crossly. 'You say you love me and when you hold me and kiss me I know it's true. I wish you'd stop trying to be a gentleman, Leo Wilder. It doesn't suit you.'

He recoiled as if she had slapped his face. 'That says it all, Patsy. If we married and had to live a hand-to-mouth existence in London, you would grow to hate me and everything I stand for. I can't take you away from all this and watch you grow old before your time or bitter because the reality isn't like your dream.'

'So there's no future for us. Is that what you're saying? You don't love me, Leo. You just think you do. If you had real feelings for me you couldn't bear to be parted from me.'

He stood up, looking down at her with a perplexed frown. 'You're making this very difficult, Patsy.'

'Go away then. Leave Rockwood and go back to London. I don't believe you ever cared for me, not deeply, anyway.'

'You have no idea how I feel, Patricia. If you did you wouldn't question my love for you, which is why it's best if I return to London. I've stayed on for four weeks and I've made a good start with the mill. Bertie can find someone else to take it over. I'll leave tomorrow.' He walked away, quickening his steps until he was out of sight. Patricia thumped her hand down on a patch of daisies and was immediately sorry for damaging the frail flowers. She scrambled to her feet and walked on to where the backwater flowed into the sea.

Leo Wilder was a proud and stubborn man. He would come round to her way of thinking in the end. She walked slowly back to the castle.

* * *

Two weeks later, on a hot summer morning, Patricia was late going down to breakfast after a sleepless

411

night. She found that she was the last one to eat, and after a quick meal, she went to find Rosalind, who was in the nursery with the children, even though Jennet was a perfectly good nanny and eminently capable to taking care of them. After a brief conversation, punctuated by shrieks and squeals from the little ones, Patricia went to look for Nancy and Tommy, who were playing croquet on the lawn beyond the rose garden. They invited her to join the game but she was not in a mood to play. Bertie was in his study, going over the accounts with Hester, and Patricia found herself with nothing to do. She sent for her horse to be saddled and rode over the Greystone Park.

Sylvia was lying on a day bed in the shade of one of the ancient oaks. A table at her side was set out with her medicine and a jug of lemonade. She looked thin and pale but her smile was genuine when she saw Patricia.

'It's so good to see you. I didn't have a chance to thank you for looking after me. I know Christina was short with you and I'm sorry.'

'She threatened me with Martha Collins and Miss Moon,' Patricia said, smiling ruefully. 'They would scare anyone.'

'I know, but Martha has organised the servants and Miss Moon just follows her round all day like a lap dog. They really don't bother me much. I leave everything to them.'

'You are looking better, Sylvie. I'm glad.'

'Dr Bulmer is quite pleased with my progress. I might even get well.'

'Of course you will. You just have to rest and do what he says.'

'I heard about Blease Ewart and poor little Tommy.

You must have had a terrible time.'

'It's all over now. Tommy is safe and Ewart was up before the judge in Exeter yesterday. We have yet to learn the outcome but hopefully he will be put in prison for a very long time.'

'What will you do now, Patsy? It's all round the village that you are going to marry that man from London. Leo Wilder?'

'It's just gossip,' Patricia said hastily. 'I admit that I like Leo, but he doesn't want me. He made that perfectly clear when he returned to London. He was doing so well with the sawmill, but he refused to stay on as manager.'

'Are you going to let him get away?' Sylvia laughed. 'That's not like you, Patsy. You always get what you want.'

'Not this time.' Patricia shook her head sadly. 'He still thinks of me as Lady Greystone, even though I've earned my own living by singing on the stage and in the market place. I can't convince him that I don't care about wealth and titles.'

'Then you're not the Patricia Carey I knew, or the woman who married my father when we were so much against it.'

'You know, you're right, Sylvie. I've allowed the man I love to walk away without putting up a fight.'

Sylvia smiled. 'That's more like it. You know what you must do next. Come back and let me know when he's declared himself. If he doesn't, just send him to me. I'll put him straight.'

Patricia leaned over the bed and kissed Sylvia on the cheek. 'I will, I promise.' She glanced over her shoulder and saw a large woman advancing on her across the lawn like a ship in full sail.

'I'm going now, but I promise I'll come back and tell you everything.' Patricia walked away, nodding to Miss Collins as they passed. 'Good day, Miss Martha. I'm just leaving.' She did not wait to find out what Miss Collins thought of her brief visit. Her conversation with Sylvia had made her see her future with a different eye. Grandpapa had fought Napoleon's navy at sea. If he could do that then she, Patricia Carey, could fight her own battles.

When she reached the stables at Rockwood, Patricia left the horse in Hudson's capable hands and headed for the main entrance where a messenger was just leaving.

'What news, Jarvis?' Patricia asked anxiously as the man rode off in a cloud of dust.

'I'm not at liberty to say, my lady.'

'But you know something.'

'Sir Bertram and the rest of the family are in the music room, my lady. I suggest you ask them.'

Patricia hurried into the castle and went straight to the drawing room that overlooked the rose garden. The double doors were open and the scent of roses filled the air. Sunlight filtered in through the tall windows, creating a tracery of patterns on the richly coloured carpet. It was a peaceful scene and yet the atmosphere was buzzing with anticipation.

'What's happened?' Patricia demanded when there was a sudden silence.

Bertie cleared his throat. 'Good news, Patsy. Ewart has been found guilty.'

'Is he going to the gallows?'

'No, better still, he's being transported to Australia.'

'It's more than that,' Rosie added, smiling. 'He escaped the gallows because he admitted his part in the crimes that Piers committed. We can now hope that Piers will be pardoned and allowed to go home to Trevenor. Lady Pentelow needs him and so does Aurelia.'

'I'm glad,' Patricia said quietly.

Bertie reached out to clasp her hand. 'And there's more.'

'Really?' Patricia sank down on a dainty gilt chair. 'What else?'

'Ewart admitted his part in the Paris robbery. He told the police where to find the rest of the French woman's jewels. There's a substantial reward, which will go to Leo because he led the police to Ewart and Lord Eldon.'

'How much is the reward?' Patricia asked eagerly.

Bertie smiled. 'Enough to buy a major share in the sawmill, which will help us all, if Leo is willing to agree.'

Patricia jumped to her feet. 'He will. I know he will. I need money, Bertie. I'm going to London to find him.'

Rosalind was seated on one of the sofas with Alex. She clutched his hand, smiling. 'No need, Patsy. I sent a servant to the shop with instructions to send a telegram to Bridie Salmon's house in Wellclose Square. Leo told me that he could be contacted there if necessary.'

Patricia stared at her open-mouthed. 'Leo told you and he didn't tell me?'

'You must take that up with him when he arrives.' Rosalind's lips twitched and her eyes twinkle. 'Unless I'm mistaken, he'll be here later today.'

'You're very sure, darling,' Alex said, smiling.

'I had several conversations with Leo when he was

here. I'll eat my best bonnet if he doesn't come as quickly as possible. If ever there was a man in love, it's Leo Wilder.'

Patricia stared at her sister in disbelief. 'He told you that?'

'Patsy, he didn't need to put it into words. You have that man's heart in your pocket, only you were too stubborn to see it.'

Hester rose to her feet. 'I think the news about Ewart deserves a proper celebration. What do you think, Rosie?'

'I agree entirely. Tell Cook to forget about economy. Tonight we'll dine like royalty, and I've no doubt we'll be having a double celebration.'

Patricia clasped her hands tightly in her lap. 'What if he doesn't come?'

'That's the first time I've ever heard you doubt yourself in an affair of the heart, Patricia Carey,' Rosalind said, smiling.

★ ★ ★

The rest of the day passed in a flurry of activity. Rosalind seemed determined to keep her sister busy and Patricia was given the task of picking and arranging flowers for the dining room, and even more for the drawing room. Walter brought Louise and baby Charlotte to the castle and Jennet was given the baby to look after, which pleased her, as Phoebe was getting on for eighteen months old and no longer a tiny baby, and Jennet adored tiny babies.

Patricia tried not to run to the window every few minutes, although common sense told her that even if Leo did catch the earliest train he would not arrive

416

until late afternoon. She rehearsed what she would say to him in front of her mirror, changing her mind more often than not. In the end she went for a long walk by the backwater, where they had parted just a couple of weeks ago, although it felt like a lifetime.

At seven o'clock the family were assembled in the drawing room, sipping glasses of sherry, although Bertie and Alex preferred a tot of rum. The children were all in bed and baby Charlotte was to spend the night in the nursery so that Louise and Walter could relax without worrying about their daughter.

Hester was in high spirits, having taken control of the kitchen from Fletcher for the occasion, and apparently Cook agreed with her: Fletcher would have made a good sergeant-major in the army, but the servants were all terrified of her.

There was, however, no sign of Wilder, and Patricia was beginning to think that he had either not received the message, or he had decided to remain a free man. Maybe he had found himself a suitable pub close to his old haunts and that's where he would be happiest. She tried to picture herself as landlady, but she knew that she did not possess the skills or experience to deal with the motley crowd who frequented such places. Perhaps Leo had come to the same conclusion.

She took a seat by the window and accepted a glass of sherry from Walter, although she had little taste for it. Bertie and Alex were talking enthusiastically about the way that Leo Wilder had gone about reviving the flagging fortunes of the sawmill, while Rosalind and Louise chatted about the children. Nancy and Tommy sat at a table playing a noisy game of backgammon. Despite the difference in their ages they had been inseparable since Tommy's terrible experience at the

417

hands of Ewart, although Tommy seemed to have recovered completely, with Nancy's help.

Hester looked on benignly, sipping a glass of port wine, her favourite drink. She was happy now that she was back in charge of the household, and Fletcher spent most of her time in the sawmill, where she had been left in charge until a new manager was employed. Wilder had found her work to do there and the men they employed behaved better when Fletcher was put in charge than they ever had under Alexander's management. Fletcher knew nothing about business, but she did know how to handle men and Patricia thought secretly that they were all slightly scared of her. Fletcher's ability to knock a man for six had been the talk of the village ever since Trimble's arrest, adding to her already formidable reputation.

Patricia sat back in her chair. It was getting late, dinner would soon be served with no sign of Leo, and it was her own fault. She had sent him away when she should have begged him to stay. She was suffering from her own pride as well as his reluctance to take a chance on their relationship. She was so deep in thought that she did not hear approaching footsteps and when the door opened and Leo walked into the drawing room unannounced, she stared at him in stunned silence.

Rosalind was the first to react and she stood up, holding out her hand. 'Leo, you came. Welcome home.' Patricia rose slowly to her feet. 'Leo.' Her voice was barely a whisper but he saw her and embraced her with a smile.

Bertie leaned forward in his chair. 'It's good to see you, Leo. Won't you take a seat?'

Wilder made his way to Patricia's side and pulled

418

up a chair. 'Do you know what this is all about?'

She shook her head. 'Bertie, Walter and Rosie have had their heads together. They haven't told me what they're planning.'

With difficulty, Bertie rose to his feet to a muffled gasp from the onlookers, followed by a burst of applause.

'As you all know we've received a considerable reward for the return of Lady Oakley's jewels. But we all agree that it belongs to you, Leo,' Bertie said, smiling. 'I can't stand up for long, but I can keep to my feet long enough to offer Leo the majority share in the sawmill.' He sat down heavily, holding up his hand as Rosie was about to reprimand him. 'I'm fine, don't worry.' He took a deep breath. 'The reward money is yours. You earned it, Leo. But if you care to accept our offer and you are prepared to stay and take over the mill, you will soon make enough profit to purchase the whole of it.'

Patricia grasped his hand. 'Accept the offer, Leo. Please say you will. I don't want you to go back to London.'

Leo drew her to her feet. 'If you will all excuse us, I have something I want to say to Patsy.'

'Of course,' Rosalind said, nudging Alex, who grinned smugly.

'You have my blessing,' Bertie added as they left the room.

'The rose garden.' Wilder led Patricia towards the music room and he opened the door to the fragrance of flowers with the setting sun adding a Midas touch to the garden. Even the deepest red roses were turned to gold in its dying rays. He stopped by the arbour, where scented jasmine added its own delicate perfume to the air. 'You didn't know what your brothers and sister intended?'

Patricia stepped onto a bed of fallen rose petals. She shook her head. 'They didn't consult me, but I agree wholeheartedly. I shouldn't have let you go in the first place, Leo.'

'I know I can make the sawmill profitable, but could you live in the small house that goes with the business?'

She slid her arms around his neck. 'Leo, after everything we've been through I could live with you in a mud hut. I really don't want all the trappings of wealth.' She hesitated. 'I mean, of course, I love luxury, but that could come later. All I want is you.'

He held her in a close embrace and kissed her until she was clinging to him like a drowning woman. 'I love you, Patsy. I've always loved you from the first moment you walked in the Goat and Compasses, but I didn't think I stood a chance with someone like you.'

'I can't say I fell for you in the beginning,' Patricia said candidly. 'But you've grown on me, Leo. I can't imagine my life without you now. I've changed my mind about so many things.' She pulled his head down until their lips met in a kiss that melted her heart. 'I do love you now and for ever.'

'Will you marry me, Patricia Carey?'

She gave him a dreamy smile. 'Need you ask, Leo Wilder?'

We do hope that you have enjoyed
reading this large print book.

Did you know that all of our titles
are available for purchase?

We publish a wide range of high
quality large print books including:
Romances, Mysteries, Classics
General Fiction
Non Fiction and Westerns

Special interest titles available in
large print are:
The Little Oxford Dictionary
Music Book, Song Book
Hymn Book, Service Book

Also available from us courtesy of
Oxford University Press:
Young Readers' Dictionary
(large print edition)
Young Readers' Thesaurus
(large print edition)

For further information or a free
brochure, please contact us at:
Ulverscroft Large Print Books Ltd.,
The Green, Bradgate Road, Anstey,
Leicester, LE7 7FU, England.
Tel: (00 44) 0116 236 4325
Fax: (00 44) 0116 234 0205

Other titles published by Ulverscroft:

WINTER WEDDING

Dilly Court

Christmas is coming. But the happiest time of the year is marred by a cruel twist of fate. Rosalind Blanchard's husband Piers is gravely wounded in a shipwreck, and she finds herself head of crumbling Rockwood Castle once more. Pregnant with his child and alone, she turns to the only man who has ever made her heart sing — Piers' brother Alex.

However, though Alex was her old love, Piers must be her future. Until shocking news changes everything. As the first snowflakes begin to appear, so too does another chance of happiness for Rosalind. One that might just include her beloved home and true love Alex by her side . . .